Jane—Our Stranger
A Novel

by

Mary Borden

Jane–Our Stranger
A Novel
by Mary Borden

ISBN: 978-93-62201-17-1

Published by

DOUBLE 9 BOOKS

2/13-B, Ansari Road
Daryaganj, New Delhi – 110002
info@double9books.com
www.double9books.com
Tel. 011-40042856

ABOUT THE AUTHOR

Mary Borden was an American-British novelist and poet whose work was inspired by her experiences as a military nurse. She was the second of three children born to William Borden, who built a fortune in Colorado silver mining in the late 1870s. Mary Borden, also known as May by her friends and family, was born into an affluent Chicago family. Her brother, William Whiting Borden, became well-known in conservative Christian circles for his evangelical zeal and early death while training to be a missionary. Mary attended Vassar College and graduated with a BA in 1907. When the First World War broke out in 1914, she used her own considerable funds to equip and staff a field hospital for French soldiers near the Western Front, where she worked as a nurse from 1914 until the war's end (see Voluntary Aid Detachment). There, she met Brigadier General Edward Louis Spears, with whom she had a romance at the Front. Her husband had separated from her and taken custody of their children. Following her divorce, she married Spears in 1918.

CONTENTS

PART II

PART I

I

It is a pity we do not die when our lives are finished. Jane may live another twenty years — a long time to wait, alone between two worlds. Jane is forty-three, I am five years older, Philibert is fifty-six, my mother nearly eighty, we are all alive, and strangely enough *Maman* is the only one whose life is not yet ended. Hers will not end till the moment of her death. She has been a wise artist. She is still embroidering delicately the pattern of her days; she still holds the many threads in her fingers. Quietly, exquisitely she will put in the last stitches. They will be the most beautiful of all; they will be her signature, the signature of a lady. Then she will close her eyes and commend her soul to God and the perfect work of her worldly wisdom will be finished.

As for me, I see no reason why I should not live on indefinitely just as I have done, and on the whole I am more comfortable here than in Purgatory, a place that I imagine to be like the suburbs of London. I see myself there, tapping with my crutch, along endless tramway lines between interminable rows of dingy perky villas. This little street in the Faubourg Saint Germain is much nicer. It is old and proud and secretive; a good street for a cripple to live in; it shelters and protects him. Once he has entered it he has no distance to go to get home. It is usually deserted and the great pale houses show discreet shuttered windows with no one behind the shutters to stare at him. I am Philibert's crippled brother. Something went wrong with me before I was born. Nothing else of importance has ever happened to me, except Jane's marrying my brother.

Jane loved this little street. She said that it told her the story of France and conveyed to her all the charm of the Paris she loved best, the proud gentle mysterious Paris of the 18th century that with all its fine reserved grandeur assumes modestly the look of a small provincial town.

I came to live here when Philibert sold our house in the Rue de Varenne that is just round the corner, and my mother went to her new apartment near the Étoile. That was twenty years ago, and very little has changed in the street since I came to these rooms at the bottom of this little courtyard between Constantine's big white house and the Embassy. The little man who peddled bird-seed has vanished long ago, his voice is no more to be heard chanting, but other street vendors still come by with their sing-song calls. What indeed was there that could change, save perhaps old Madame Barbier's grocery shop at the corner, tucked up against Constantine's stable wall? But even Madame Barbier has remained the same. Her hair is as smooth and glossy black, her tight corsage as neat, and her trim window with its glass jars of honey and the nice bright boxes of groceries is as it always has been. A thrifty respectable woman is Madame Barbier, with a pleasant word for her neighbours. For the rest, on the opposite side of the street there is the convent, with its pointed roof and the chapel belfry showing above the wall, and there are the five big houses with their great gates that make up the whole length of the street. Not a long street—often when I turn into it at one end, I recognize a familiar figure going out of it at the other, the good Abbé perhaps going home after confessing the sisters in the convent, or old Madame d'Avrécourt in her shabby black jacket, her fine little withered face under her bonnet, wearing its habitual enigmatic smile. Monsieur l'Abbé says that her voluminous petticoats are heavy with the sacred charms he has sewn into the hems, and that may well be; I know that her devotion is very great and her interest in the outside world very small, and the sight of her is comforting to me.

It is so quiet here, and so confined. It is like a cloister—or a prison—I am glad of that.

Tonight, Good Friday night, I can hear the good sisters in the chapel singing. The mysticism of their haunting chant penetrates the walls of this old house, and tonight because of their lamenting, because of their dread disciplined agony of supplication, the street is immensely deep and high, whereas yesterday it was just small and dim and worldly, with its houses blinking over its walls, a proud battered deceiving old street, hiding the rare beauty of its dwellings, guarding the secrets of its families behind mute shutters, till the day it should crumble to pieces or an insolent government should turn it upside down like an ash-bin.

It never, of course, could get used to Jane. Who of us did get used to Jane? Did I myself? Wasn't she a big troubling problem to us all till the very end? How could we not be afraid of her? Poor magnificent Jane—fine timid innocent child—dangerous nature woman—dreadful crying message from a new bellowing land—what was she? What was she not? How could she fit in here? She was as strange here as a leopard beautifully moving down the grey narrow pavement. How she used to frighten the good Abbé. I have seen him scuttle into a neighbouring doorway to let her pass, as if there were no room for him along the stones she walked so grandly. It was true. There was no room for any one but Jane when she came, and now that she is gone never to come back again, the place is as dreary and empty as an abandoned cemetery and the light is as insipidly pale as the half shadow in a sick room. She has left a sickness in this place, because she came here sometimes to see me—and won't come any more.

And yet I stay on here. I shall stay here always. I have no reason to go anywhere now that I have been to America to see Jane, and have come back with the accurate awful knowledge of the great distance between us. Ah, that wide sea, that New York, a high cold gate into a strange over-powering country, those immense prairies, and those tiny farm houses, with tiny women watching the train; Jane, a tiny woman, Jane a speck, in a town that is a dot on the map. I will write down Jane's story. I will remember it all, everything that she told me and everything that I saw, and will put it all down exactly with perfect precision and accuracy, and then, perhaps I shall understand her. Poor Jane—she wanted to understand life. She believed always that there was a reason for things, an ultimate reason and a purpose. She was no philosopher, she was a woman of faith. She should have been the wife of a pioneer, the wife of such a man as Isak, who went into the wilderness with a sack over his shoulder. Jane was made for such a man. I can see them together going out under the sky, he, grave, deep-chested, long-limbed, "a barge of a man," and beside him a woman like a ship, moving proudly. And she married Philibert. Could any one who has ever seen her with Philibert miss the meaning of their extraordinary contrast? Philibert with his clever jaunty little body, his exaggerated elegance, his cold blue eyes and his impudent charm. She made him look like a toy man. She could have broken him in two with her hands. Why didn't she? It is a long story. People say that American women are very adaptable, very imitative. Jane wasn't. She never became the least like us, except in looks and that meant nothing. Paquin and Chéruit and Philibert did that for her almost at once, but her looks, even without their aid, were always a disguise, never a revelation of her self. Some women are all of a piece with their charming exteriors, Jane was a child cased in armour. As she grew older she learned to use it, she made it answer, but she used it to become something she was not. I call up her image as I write. I evoke Jane as she was that last year in Paris, the most elegant woman in Europe, the most stared at, and the most indifferent. I remember the cold hard nonchalance that so frightened people she did not like, and the brilliant metallic grace that rippled over her like gleaming light when she was pleased. I remember her excessive hauteur in public, the disdainful carriage of her strange head that was like a coin fashioned by some morose craftsman of Benvenuto Cellini's time. I recall the sidelong glitter of her little green eyes. I remember her in public places, towering above other women like an idol, mute, glittering, enigmatic, her curious profile with its protruding lower lip, the tight close bands of jewels round her forehead. What a figure of splendour she was in those days, when Philibert had done breaking her heart; and when at the age of forty she had ceased to care and had reached the perfection of her physical type.

I think of her as she was when her mother brought her to Paris and married her to Philibert; a great strapping girl with a beautiful body and an ugly sullen face that deceived us all. How could one see behind it? Can one blame them? I alone caught a glimpse. And she developed slowly in our artificial soil. It took twenty years for her to become a woman of the world, une grande dame. That was what they made of her. I say they, but I suppose I mean primarily Philibert. It is horrible to think of how much Philibert had to do with making her what she finally was. And Bianca had a hand in it too. That is even worse.

We had realized the moment of Jane's apotheosis. We had seen her beautifully and gravely spread her wings. We held our breath, waited entranced, and then, just then, she disappeared. Suddenly we lost her.

I refer, now, to our group, the little Bohemian group of kindred spirits who loved Jane; Ludovic, Felix, Clémentine and the others. Extraordinary that these friends of mine should have been the ones to love Jane best. They were a gay lot of sinners, quite impossible judged by any standard but their own. My mother only knew of their existence, through Clémentine. She has always been in the habit of discussing artists and writers as if they were dead. It was distressing to her that Clémentine who was related to her by blood and had married a Bourbon, should have held herself and her name so cheap as to consort with men and women of obscure origin and problematical genius. As for me, a man could do as he liked within measure, if he did not forget to keep up appearances. She regarded my friendship for my wonderful Ludovic and all the rest of them as a substitute for the more usual and less troublesome clandestine affairs of the ordinary bachelor. As I could never "*faire la noce*" like other men I was allowed these dissipations of the mind, but *maman* never forgave me for introducing Ludovic to Jane. Dearest mother—it was no use telling her that Ludovic was the greatest scholar of his day. I didn't try to explain. After all Ludovic needed no championing from me. I had wanted to do something for Jane; I had wanted to relieve in some way the awful pressure of her big bleak dazzling situation. Hemmed in by the complications of my relationship to her, how many times had I not groaned over the fact that she had been married by that awful mother of hers to the head of our house and not to some one else's devilish elder brother, instead of to mine, I had pondered and tormented myself over a way of helping her that would not give Philibert the chance of coming down on me and shutting the big strong door of his house in my face, and at length my opportunity had come. It had seemed to me that for her at last the battle was over, and that she had achieved the desolate freedom which we could turn into enjoyment. Fan Ivanoff was dead. Bianca had disappeared. As for Philibert, he had grown tired of bothering her. Her sufferings no longer amused him. Her loneliness was complete. Although still to my eyes a figure of drama while we were essentially merry prosy people, she appeared to me to have acquired that spiritual mastery of events which made her one of us. I had reckoned without her child, Geneviève.

How could I have understood then the fear with which she contemplated her daughter's future? And even supposing that I had understood everything, and had the gift of seeing into that future and had beheld the shadow of that lovely monster Bianca swooping down on Jane again to drive her to extremity, even supposing I had known what was going to happen and how that would take her away from us forever, I still could have done nothing more than I did do. It had seemed to me that we could provide her with a refuge, and so we did for a time. If Paris were to offer her any reward, any consolation, any comfort, then such a reward and such comfort was, I felt sure, to be found in the sympathy of these people who had gravitated to one another, out of the heavy mass of humanity that populated the earth, like sparks flying upwards to meet above the smoke and heat of the crowd in a clear lighted space of mental freedom. I gave her the best I had; I gave her my friends; and if they thought she had come to them to stay, well then so did I. Our mistake lay in thinking that because we were sufficient to each other we must be sufficient to Jane as well. I do not believe it occurred to any one of us how little we really counted for her; I, at least never knew it until the other day. Actually I had never realized that her soul was always craving something more, something like a heavenly certitude or a divine revelation.

Conceited? I suppose we were; but then you see the world did knock at our door for admittance. We had all literary and artistic Europe to choose from, and we did realize the things we talked of. I mean that we translated our thoughts into things people could see, ballets, pictures, bits of music. We worked out our ideas for the mob to gape at, and our success could be measured by the bitter hostility of such people as Philibert, who fancied himself as a patron of the arts—a kind of François I—and found us difficult to patronize.

Jane realized our worth of course. She had a touching reverence for our ability. She saw clearly the distinct worlds represented by my mother, and Ludovic; the one exquisite and sterile, beautifully still as a sealed room with panelled walls inhabited by wax figures; the other disordered and merry, convulsed by riotous fancies, where daring people indulged their caprices, scoffed at facts and respected intellect.

What Jane did not realize was the humanity underlying this life of ours. She thought us uncanny, but she could have trusted us in her trouble. And we on our side did not know that we did not satisfy her. After all, for the rest of us our deep feeling of well-being in one another's company was like a divine assurance, an absolute ultimate promise. It was all the heavenly revelation we needed. When we gathered round Clémentine's dinner-table with the long windows opening out of the high shabby room into the shadowy garden where we could hear during the momentary hush of our voices the note of its flutey tinkling fountain, or when we settled deep in those large worn friendly chairs before Ludovic's fire on a winter's night, in the cosy gloom of his overcharged bookshelves, it would come to us over and over again, like the repeated sense of a divine conviction, that this exquisite essence of human intercourse was nothing less than what we had been born for.

Jane could never have had that feeling, but we thought she shared it with us. We did not know about that deep relentless urge in Jane that was as inevitable as the rising tide. We never took seriously enough her fear of God.

And so when she went away they thought—Ludovic and Clémentine and the rest of them—"She will be here tomorrow, she will come back just as she was, and she will find us just where she left us." And they continued to talk about her as if she had left them but an hour before to go and show herself as she was often obliged to do in some great bright hideous salon. Her chair was always there by Ludovic's fireside, and they took account in their discussions of her probable point of view, as if she'd been there with them. There was something touching in their expectancy. There was that in their manner to remind one of the simple fidelity of peasants who lay the place of the absent one every night at table. The truth did not occur to them, and I who wanted to be deceived let their confidence communicate itself to me. I told myself that they were right, that she was bound to come back, that they had formed in her the habit of living humourously as they did, that they had given her a taste for things she would not find elsewhere, and that she would never be content to live now in that big blank new continent across the Atlantic. The word Atlantic made me shiver. I must have had a premonition; I must have known that I was going to cross it, urged out upon that cold turbulent waste of horrid water by a forlorn hope and an anguished desire to see her once more.

I hugged to myself during those days of suspense my feeling of the irresistible appeal of my city. Had Jane not told me, one day on returning from Como, that in spite of the problems her life held for her here, she experienced nevertheless each time she went away such a poignant home-sickness for Paris, its streets, its sounds, its river-banks and its buildings, that she invariably came back in a tremor of fear, positively "jumpy" at the thought that perhaps during her absence it had changed or disappeared off the map altogether? If she felt like this after a month's sojourn in Italy, what had I now to fear I asked myself? Had we not initiated her into the very secret heart of Paris? Was there a remnant of an old and lovely building that we had not shown her, or a fragment of sculpture or a picture worth looking at to which we had not introduced her? Had she not come to feel with us the difference of the temperature and tone of the streets, the excitement of the jangling boulevards, the bland oblivion of the Place de la Concorde, the ghostliness of the Place des Vosges, the intimate provincial secretiveness of our own old peaceable quarter? Had not Ludovic called into being for her out of the embers of his fire the historic scenes that had been enacted in all these and a hundred other places? Had he not made the whole rich fantastic past of our city unroll itself before her eyes? Was it a little thing to be allowed to drink at the source of so much humanized knowledge? Where in that new country of hers would she find so fanciful and patient and tender a friend as this great scholar?

So I piled up the evidence, and then when her letter came I knew that I had foreseen the truth, and when I took them the news and they all cried out to me — "Go and bring her back, and don't come back without her" — I knew while their high commanding voices were still sounding in my ears that already I had made up my mind to go, and I knew too, lastly and finally, that I would not be able to bring her back.

She had enclosed in her letter to me a note for them which I gave to Clémentine, who read it and passed it on. One after another they scanned its meagre lines in silence. I saw that Ludovic's hand was shaking. When he had finished he closed his eyes for a moment and his head jerked forward. I noticed in the light of the lamp how white he had grown in the last year, and how the yellow tint of his pallor had deepened. Clémentine said looking at me — "It is not intelligible. Perhaps you can explain." And I was given the sheet of paper covered with Jane's large careless scrawl:

> "Dear Friends," I read, "I am not coming back. I am here alone with the ghost of my Aunt Patty in the house where I lived as a child. It is a wooden house with a verandah at the back. There are snow-drifts on the verandah. I am trying to find out what it has all been about — my life, I mean. If I

believed that I would understand over there on the other side of death, then perhaps I would not be bound to stay here now, but I know that Ludovic is right, and that the hope of eternal punishment like that of immortal bliss and satisfied knowledge is just the fiction of our vanity. My punishment is on me now, since among other things I have to give you up.

"Jane."

They had cried out at me when I told them, but after reading the letter they were silent. It was as if they had been brushed by the wings of some strange fearful messenger from another world, as if some departed spirit were present. We might all have been sitting in the dark with invisible clammy hands touching our hair, so nervous had we become. The fall of a charred log in the fireplace made us jump.

Felix forced a laugh. "The ghost of her Aunt Patty," he mocked dismally. "Now what does she mean by that?"

"Her Aunt Patty was the person who took care of her as a child. Miss Patience Forbes her name was. She seems to have been a remarkable character. Jane often spoke of her."

My words only added to their mystification. An old maid in America, dead now, a remarkable character. What had she to do with them? What power had she over their brilliant courageous Jane? Were they nothing that they could be replaced by the wraith of an old puritan spinster?

The room seemed to grow chilly. Some one put a fresh log on the fire. A little fitful wind was whimpering at the windows. Now and then a gust of rain pattered against the glass with a light rapid sound like finger-tips tapping. Felix had wandered away down the long dim room, his hands in his pockets, his shoulders hunched as he stood with his back to us, and his nose close to the packed shelves of books against the farther wall. The tiny gilt letterings on the old bindings glimmered faintly in the lamplight. He seemed to be searching among all those little dim signs for an explanation. Far away beyond the network of gardens and old muffling houses one heard from some distant street the hoot of a motor. From the translucent depths of gleaming glass cabinets the small mute mysterious figures of jewelled heathen gods and little bronze Buddhas and curious carved jade monsters looked out at us as if through sheets of water.

Under the aged shadowy eaves of that room, full of strange old symbols and rare books and still rarer manuscripts, where so many ideas and faiths and records had been sifted, examined and relegated to dusty recesses, its occupants remained silent, staring at the new disturbing object of their mystification. Clémentine, tucked into a corner of the sofa, her boyish head that she dyed such a bad colour, on her hand, scrutinized the tip of her foot that she held high as if for better observation, in one of her characteristic angular attitudes. Her slipper dangled loose from her toe; now and then she gave it a jerk of annoyance.

They tried to take in the meaning of what they had read. The emotional content of that scrawled page was so strange to them as to appear almost shocking. They were rather frightened. Here indeed their philosophy of laughter broke down, for they loved Jane and could not make fun of her superstitions.

"We were never hard on her. We treated her gently."

"Even when her seriousness bored us we were patient."

"She can't have loved us. We have never really known her then, after all."

Clémentine jerked about. "I was always wanting her to take lovers. She wanted me to give up mine. Poor child—we were friends all the same."

Felix's falsetto came down to us in a shrill wail of exasperation.

"But we never attacked her religion. We left her alone. We were good to her."

Clémentine nodded. "Yes, we were good."

I remembered the day I had first brought Jane to them, clothed in her silks and sables, glittering with the garish light of her millions and her high cold social activities. I had brought her straight from the preposterous palace she had let Philibert build her to this deep dim nook where we laughed and scoffed at the world she lived in. I had been nervous then. I had been afraid they would find her impossible. But they had seen through the barbarous trappings, intelligent souls that they were. Hadn't she realized how they had honoured her? Hadn't she known what dependable people they were?

I heard Clémentine say it again. "We were good, but she thought we were wicked because we broke the ten commandments. She thought a lot of the ten commandments."

"It was the puritan spinster looking at us over her shoulder all the time."

And still they pondered and puzzled, bewildered, depressed, at a loss, annoyed by their incapacity to picture to themselves even so much as the place where she was, alone at that moment. "St. Mary's Plains, Mohican County, Michigan" was the address she gave. What an address to expect any one to take seriously. If it had been a joke the mixture of images would perhaps have conveyed something to them, but as a serious geographic sign they could do nothing with it. It had the character of a new glazed billboard, of a big glaring advertisement for some parvenu's patent. To think of Jane sitting down away off there in the middle of a desert under it was too much for them. But the very outrageousness of the enigma helped them.

"She couldn't do it from inclination," some one of them said at last. "There must have been something terrible."

Then it was that Ludovic startled us. He spoke slowly as if to himself.

"She was only beginning to learn how little conduct has to do with life. For others she had come to understand that what one does has little or no relation to what one is. I am convinced that she, poor child, is persuaded that she has committed some dreadful crime."

But it was Clémentine who said the last word that I carried away with me.

"If she hadn't married into your family," she said, glaring out at me from the door of her taxi, "she would have been all right. Why, she should have chosen Philibert—"

"But, *chérie amie,* she didn't. It was her mother who did it all."

"Rubbish! She loved him. She loves him still."

II

My mother was a Mirecourt. The family was of a prouder nobility than my father's. Her people were of the *Grand Chevaux de Lorraine*. They fought with the English against the kings of France in the fourteenth century. One reads about them as fighters during several hundreds of years beginning with the Crusades. Sometimes they were on the right side, sometimes on the wrong. Later generations were not proud of the part they played in the siege of Orleans. But they were proud people and acted on caprice or in self-interest with a sublime belief in themselves. They did not like kings and were loth to give allegiance to any one. When Louis XI took away their lands, they went over to the king, but it is to be gathered from the letters of the time that they considered no king their equal. Richelieu was too much for them. He reduced them to poverty. To repair the damage the head of the family made a bourgeois marriage. They were sure of themselves in those days. Marrying money caused them no uneasiness nor fear of ridicule. My mother said one day when talking of Philibert and Jane—"We have done this sort of thing before but always with people of our own race who had a proper attitude. With foreigners one never knows."

My father was a Breton. Anne of Brittany was the liege lady of his people. His *aieux* were worthy gentlemen who played an obscure but on the whole respectable part in history. An occasional spendthrift appeared now and then among them to add gaiety to their monotonous lives. The spendthrifts being few and the tenacity of the others very great, they amassed a considerable fortune and were ennobled by Louis XIV: a fact of which my aunt Clothilde used occasionally to remind us. Aunt Clothilde was my father's sister. She had made a great match in marrying the first Duke of France, but she seemed to think nothing of that nor to have any consciousness of the obligations of her class. She made fun of the legitimists, scoffed at the idea of a restoration and despised the Duc d'Orleans for the way he behaved in England. She and my mother did not get on. My mother thought her vulgar. She was, but it didn't detract from her being a very great lady. She was always enormously fat, a greedy, wicked old thing, with a ribald mind, but with a tremendous *chic*. Philibert called her *La Gargantua*. She was Rabelaisian somehow. I liked her. She never seemed conscious of my being different from other men, and she was kinder to Jane than the others.

There were a great many others. We made a large clan. It seemed strange to Jane that half the people in Paris were our cousins or uncles or aunts. But of course it is like that. One is related to everybody.

As a family we had the reputation of having very nice manners. It was thought that we knew very well how to make ourselves agreeable and what was more characteristic, how to be disagreeable without giving offense. My mother was reputed to be the only woman in Paris who could refuse an invitation to dinner in the same house six times running without making an enemy of its mistress. My mother was perpetually penning little plaintive notes of regret. She was greatly sought after and stayed very much at home. After my father's death it became more and more difficult to get her to go anywhere, but she liked being asked so that she could refuse. The result was that she became something precious, inapproachable, a legend of good form and grace and she remained this always. I have on my table a miniature of her painted when she was married, at the age of eighteen. She was never a beauty. A slip of a thing, gentle and pale, with dark ringlets and very bright intelligent eyes. Her power of seduction was a thing that emanated from her like a perfume, indefinable and elusive. Claire, my sister, has the same quality.

One of my mother's special pleasures as she grew older consisted in having her dinner in bed on some grand gala evening, and telling herself that she was the only lady of any importance in Paris who had refused to be present. Sometimes on such evenings she would send for me to come and sit with her for an hour. I would find her propped up on her pillows, her eyes glowing with animation under the soft old-fashioned frill of her voluminous boudoir cap, and presently I would become aware that she was submitting me to all the play of her wit and her charm, and I would know that out of a pure spirit of contradiction she was giving me, her poor ugly duckling, the treat that she had withheld from that brilliant gathering, whether to amuse me most or herself it would be difficult to tell. We understand each other. Her manner to me was always perfect. It was a beautiful and elaborate denial of the fact that my deformity was unpleasant to her. She went to a lot of trouble to pretend that she liked having me about. If she wanted a cab called in the rain and there wasn't a servant handy—we didn't have too many—it was a part of her delicacy to ask me to do it rather than have me think that she had my infirmity constantly on her mind. If she required an escort to some public place she would choose me rather than Philibert, but she would not always choose me, lest I should come to feel that she forced herself to do so. She had the humblest way of asking my advice, and then when she did not take it, went to the most childlike manœuvres to deceive me and make me think she had. When I came back from school in England,

I remember wondering what she would do about me and her friends. She had an evening a week and received on these occasions a number of stiff old gentlemen and gossipy dowagers, a handful of priests and all the aunts and uncles and cousins. The question for her was whether she should inflict on me the penance of talking to these people in order to show me that she liked to have me about, or whether she would let me off attendance and trust to my superior understanding to assume that I was in her eyes presentable. I believe she would have decided on the latter bolder plan, had I not taken the matter out of her hands by asking her to excuse me. Her answer was characteristic.

"But naturally, *mon enfant*. You don't suppose that I think these old people fit company for you. Only if it's not indiscreet, tell me sometimes about your doings. I, at least, am not too old nor yet too young to be told."

Dear mother. She would have gone to the length of imputing to me a dozen mistresses if she had thought that would help me. And yet in spite of it all, perhaps just because of it all, I knew that the sight of me was intolerable to her. But this I feel sure was a thing that she never knew that I knew. It was a part of my business in life never to let her find it out.

My being sent to England to school had been to me a proof. Though my father had taken the decision I knew it was to get me out of my mother's way. It was not the habit of our family to send its sons abroad for their education. Philibert had had tutors at home. None of my cousins had gone away. We were as a clan not at all given to travelling. In the extreme sensitiveness that engulfed me like an illness during a certain period of my youth, I had told myself bitterly that I was banished because they could not abide the sight of me, but my bitterness did not last, thank God; and when after my father's death I came home to live, I set myself to matching my mother's delicacy with my own. I arranged to convey to her the impression of being always at hand and yet I managed to be actually in her presence a minimum of time. I did things for her that I could do without being aggravatingly near her; such things as running errands and visiting her lawyer and looking after her meagre investments, accumulating these duties while at the same time I withdrew more and more from sharing in her social activities.

I had kept, for reasons of economy and in order to be near her, my apartment in a wing of her house over the porter's lodge, in that part of the building that screened the house from the street. My windows looked on the one side across the street into some gardens and on the other side into our court yard. From my dressing-room I had a view of my mother's graceful front door with the wide shallow steps before it and the gravel expanse of the inner carriage drive. Sometimes when I came home in the evening,

Madame Oui, the *concierge's* wife, would tap on the glass in her door that was just opposite my own little entrance behind the great double portals that barred us into our stronghold, and would tell me that my mother had come in and would like to see me. Or I would find a note bidding me come to her lying on my table. She wrote me a great number of notes, sprightly amusing missives that reminded one of the fact that Frenchwomen have been for centuries mistresses in the art of letter-writing. They gave me the news, recounted the latest family gossip, contained tips as to how to behave if I came across an aunt who owed her money, or an uncle who had lent her some, warned me against this or that person whom she did not want to see any more, asked me to pay a call on one of her ancient followers who was in bed with a cold, enclosed a tiresome bill that she hadn't the money to pay immediately, or implored me in witty phrases of complaint to use my influence with Philibert and try to get him away from some woman: in all of which matters I did my best to meet her wishes save as regarded my brother. "My influence with Philibert" was one of my mother's least successful fictions. I wonder even now that she kept it up. I suppose it would have seemed to her shocking to admit even tacitly that her two sons never spoke to each other if they could help it. Yet she must have known that although he lived nominally in my mother's house up to the time of his marriage I scarcely ever saw him unless at a distance in some crowded salon. The few mutual friends we possessed never asked us to dinner or lunch together, and strangely enough in the one place where we might often have happened to come across one another, that is in my mother's own boudoir, we never did meet. My mother must have managed this. She must have manœuvred to prevent such encounters. She arranged to see us always separately and yet continued to talk to us, each to the other, as if she supposed that beyond her door we were amusing ourselves together, thick as thieves.

She would say—"I hear this latest friend of Philibert's whom he has so made the mode this year, is really quite pretty. Tell me what she looks like,"— assuming me to be perfectly aware of this affair. Or—"Your brother's new tailor is not successful at all. He gives him the most exaggerated shoulders. Fifi is not tall enough to stand it. I wish you would get him to go back to the old one." Or even—"Tell me what your brother is up to. I never see him." As if I knew what Philibert was up to.

My rare meetings with him took place at my sister's. She used sometimes to have us at her house together. Her husband would bring him home to lunch unexpectedly, or I would drop in unbidden and find him there. Poor Claire had married the biggest automobile works in the country, and had been taken to Neuilly and shut up there in a gigantic villa. She was finding that it tasked her philosophical docility to the utmost to meet the demands of the uxorious individual who paid all her bills from his own cheque book and was generous only in the way of supplying her with babies. She had had four in six years, and her health was a source of anxiety to my mother, who was frankly exasperated by the turn her daughter's affairs had taken.

"My dear," she said to me one night on her return from Neuilly, "I supposed that that man had married Claire to get into society, and now that I've given her to him he has taken her off to the wilderness. I don't know what to make of it. The poor child is wasting away. He simply never leaves her alone. They go to bed together every night at ten o'clock. It is horrible."

Claire may have bemoaned her lot to my mother in those long tête-à-têtes of theirs, but she never complained to me, nor did she, I believe, to Philibert, who was in the habit of borrowing money from her large, oily, sleek-headed husband. She had some of my mother's mannerisms, her little way of quickly moving her head backwards with the slightest toss; the same light flexible utterance; the same sigh and sudden droop of irrepressible languor. I believe her to be the only person of whom Philibert was ever unselfishly fond. She pleased him. Her physical frailty, appealed to his taste which was in reality so fastidious, however vulgar some of his amusements might be, and her mocking spirit was congenial to him. When one thought of Claire one thought of her dark shadowed eyes with the deep circles under them marking the tender cheeks, and her truly beautiful smile. She was a collection of odd beauties combined in a way to make one's heart ache, but there was something sharp in her—something hurting. Lovely Claire, cynical siren, how caressingly she spoke to me, how she drew out of my heart its tenderness, and how often she disappointed me. Not brave enough to be happy, far too intelligent not to know what she was missing, she took refuge in self-mockery and when faced with a crisis subsided into complete passivity.

One evening in the early summer, more than twenty years ago now, I found a note from my mother tucked in the crack of my door asking me to come to her at once as she had news for me of the utmost importance. I found my sister with her, and something in the attitude of the two women, who were so closely akin as to reproduce each one the same physical pose under the stress of a deep preoccupation, conveyed to me a suspicion that Philibert had that moment skipped out through the long open window. They sat, each in a high brocaded chair, their heads thrown back against their respective cushions, their hands limp in their laps and their eyes half-closed. I thought for an instant that both had fainted. My mother was the first to make a sign. She lifted an arm and in silence pointed a finger at a chair for me.

"Your brother," she said, when once I was seated, "has sold this house over my head. He is going to be married."

"To a little American girl," breathed Claire.

"The fortune is immense," added my mother.

"The daughter of that awful smart Mrs. Carpenter," said Claire, opening wide her eyes the better to take in the horror.

"She asked me three times to luncheon," said my mother. "I have never seen her."

I looked from one to the other—"But if the fortune is immense—" I ventured.

"It is all tied up," wailed my mother. "Her trustees insist on his debts being paid beforehand. I understand nothing—but nothing." Her head dropped forward. She pressed her thumb and forefinger against her worn eyelids. She began to cry.

Claire, with a strange sidelong look at her expressive of compassion and exasperation and wonder, got up and walked to the window and stood with her back to us looking out into the garden.

"I should have thought my son-in-law would have saved me this humiliation," said my mother, fumbling with her left hand for her handkerchief. "But Claire says he has already lent Philibert very considerable sums." I saw my sister's slender figure stiffen. "What curious people Americans are. It seems that the father made such a will as passes belief. The child comes into the entire fortune but can only dispose of the income. The mother has an annuity, Claire says it must be a big one as she entertains a great deal. Why did you not tell me your brother was getting so dreadfully into debt? The girl is just eighteen. It appears that in America girls reach their majority at eighteen. Her name is Jane. A most unpleasant name. Philibert says she is not pretty. These *mésalliances* are so tiresome. If only he could have married that exquisite little Bianca. I shall be obliged to receive the mother. I am sure she has a very strong accent."

My poor mother stretched out her hand to me. "What is to become of us?" she wailed gently. I felt very sorry for her. I understood that she was afraid of the invasion of a horde of big noisy strangers. I tried to comfort her. She seemed to me for the first time pitiful, and I saw that her youthfulness was after all, just one of the illusions she cast by the exercise of her will. It fell from her that evening as if it had been some gossamer veil destroyed by her tears.

Claire remained silent. Only once during all my mother's broken lament did she speak, and then she said without turning—"I should have thought one such marriage in a family was enough."

It transpired that Philibert needed five hundred thousand francs to put him straight, that the house was being sold for a million and that the remaining half was my mother's, since they owned the property between them. He had brought her the deed of sale to sign that afternoon, and had gone away with the signature in his pocket. She said—"Naturally I could not refuse. It is not as if he could have sold half the building."

I felt humiliated for my mother. It seemed to me that my brother had injured her in a most offensive way. There was a kind of indecency about the proceeding that made me ashamed. It was the kind of thing I had hoped we were none of us capable of doing. He was taking away from her not only her shelter and security, but a part of her own personality. It was as outrageous as if he had forced her to cut off her hair and had taken it round to a wigmaker to turn into a handful of gold. I saw that without that fine old house, so like her own self expressed in architecture, with its bland and graceful exterior and delicate ornamented rooms, she would lose a vital part of her entity. She was not one of those people whose public and private selves are distinct. The proud little bright-eyed lady who drove out of those stately doors in her brougham to dispense finely gradated smiles to the meticulously selected people of her acquaintance, and the passionate intriguing mother so given to subterfuges of kindness and ineffable make-believe of disinterested affection, were one and the same person. She had no special manner for the world. There was no homely naturalness for her to subside into, no loose woolly dressing-gown of conduct and no rough carpet slippers of laziness to don in the presence of her family or by her lonely self. What she was when in attendance on the Bourbons that she was in her own silent bedroom. Even about her weeping there was a certain style. Her tears were pitiful but not ugly. They had destroyed the illusion of her youthfulness, but they had not marred her elegance. There was measure and appropriateness and dramatic worth in her weeping. Her son had not broken her heart or her spirit; he had merely dragged off some of her clothing. She stood denuded, impoverished, a little shrunken in stature, that was all. It was that that enraged me. I said—"What a brute." My mother pulled me up sharply.

"My son," she said to me, with more of haughtiness than I had ever seen in her manner to any one of us. "I have consented to do what your brother has asked. I have approved of his conduct. That is sufficient."

I felt then the finality, the hopelessness. I believe I smiled. The change was sudden. It had always been like that with mother. She might complain of Philibert but no one could criticize him to her.

"Ah, well," I said, "if you have made up your mind to accept her—"

Mother lifted her head quickly. "Whom?"

"Your new daughter-in-law."

I am almost sure that she turned pale. I cannot have imagined it. Her words too, gave me the same painful impression.

"I have accepted it, not her, as yet."

And suddenly I thought of the girl, Jane Carpenter, whom I had not yet laid eyes on, with an immense pity.

"Yes," said Claire, coming back to us, and looking at us with her least charming, most bitterly mocking air. "We prepare a nice welcome for her. I wonder how she will like us."

But my mother had the last word.

"We shall, I presume, know how to make ourselves agreeable," she said, putting away her handkerchief into her little silk bag. I saw that she would shed no more tears over the girl, Jane Carpenter.

III

Mrs. Carpenter was an American who apologized for her own country. She had found it incapable of providing a sufficient field of activity for her social talents and called it crude. The phrase on her lips was funny. There was much about her that was funny, since one could not in the face of her bright brisk self-satisfaction call her pathetic.

The flattery of such migrations as hers is mystifying to Parisians like myself, who know that our city is the most delightful place in the world, but do not quite understand why so many foreigners like Mrs. Carpenter should find it so. She seemed to derive an immense satisfaction from the fact that she lived in Paris. But why? Where lay the magic difference between her Paris and her New York? She had established herself in a large bright apartment in the Avenue du Bois de Bologne. Her rent was high, her furniture expensive, her table lavish, her motor had pale grey cushions and silver trimmings. All these things she could have had in New York. She might have paid a little more for them over there, but that would only have added to her pleasure. She liked to pay high prices for things. It may be that I am doing her an injustice. There were moments when her indefatigable pursuit of us all filled me with scornful pity and made me think that she did hide under her breezy successful manner a wistful and romantic admiration for things that were foreign and old, and a touching respect for things she did not understand. She once told me that she had wanted to take an old hotel in our quarter, something with atmosphere and a history and old-world charm. But somehow she had not found what she wanted. The houses she saw were dark and gloomy and insanitary. They were wonderfully romantic but they had no bathrooms. She had wanted one in particular, had wanted it awfully, but the owner had insisted on staying on in little rooms under the roof, which meant his using her front stairs, so at last she had given up the idea. Her apartment was certainly not gloomy. It glittered with gold — golden walls, gold plate, gilt chairs. She ended by liking it immensely, but was sometimes a little ashamed of being so pleased with it. Perhaps, at odd moments, she called it crude.

I used to go there sometimes, long before Jane came to Paris. I am sorry now that I did. Had I known Mrs. Carpenter was going to be, for me, Jane's mother, I would not have gone. It is not nice to remember that I used to make fun of Jane's mother, and accept her hospitality with amused contempt. We all did. She was to us an object of good-humoured derision. Poor old Izzy. She fed us so well; she begged us so continually to come. She seemed to derive such pleasure from hearing the butler announce our names. I am sure she believed that awful flat of hers to be the social centre of a very distinguished society. The more of a mixture the better to her mind:—Austrians, Hungarians, Poles,—she liked having princes about, and their dark furtive eyes and beautifully manicured hands filled her with joy. It was only after Philibert got hold of her that she began to understand that perhaps, after all, too cosmopolitan a salon was not quite the thing. Philibert took her in hand. He had learned somehow about Jane. He already had his idea.

And now I come upon a curious problem. I find that two distinct Mrs. Carpenters exist in my mind, and I cannot reconcile them. One was a beautiful romantic creature whom Jane—far away in the Grey House in St. Mary's Plains—called mother and wrote to once a week and loved with a pure flame of loyalty; the other was Izzy Carpenter, whose loud voice and tall elastic fashionable figure was so well-known in Paris: Busy Izzy, who was run by Philibert, and a group of young ne'er-do-weels. I find it very difficult to realize that this jolly slangy woman, with curly grey hair and a blue eye that could give a broad wink on occasion, was identical with the figure of poetry Jane dreamed about night after night in her little restless cot at the foot of her Aunt Patty's four-poster bed. It is disturbing to think that even about this decided hard-edged vivacious woman there should have been such a difference of opinion, such a contrast of received impressions as to make one wonder whether she had any corporeal existence at all. I think of that stern humorous spinster Patience Forbes comforting the child who was always asking questions about her mother; I think of her taking the aching young thing on her gaunt knees in the old rocking chair with its knitted worsted cushion, and lulling that troubled eager mind to rest with stories of her mother's childhood.

I can see the grim face of Patience Forbes while she searches her memory for pleasant things about her heartless prodigal sister. She sits in a bay window looking out into the back garden where there is a sleepy twittering of birds. The trams thunder past up Desmoine's Avenue. The milkman comes up the path; the white muslin curtains billow into the peaceful room that smells of lavender and mint. There is sunlight on the old mahogany. Jane's great-grandmother, in an oval frame, looks down insipidly, her eyes mildly shining between the low bands of her parted hair. And Jane has her arms round her Aunt Patty, and her face, so unlike the gentle portrait, is troubled and brooding, a sullen ugly little face with something strange, half wild, that recalls her father and frightens the good woman who holds her close and goes on answering questions about her sister Isabel. And then I think of Mrs. Carpenter not as Jane's mother, but as the daughter of old Mrs. Forbes of the Grey House, and I am again bewildered. Those people in St. Mary's Plains, Jane's grandmother, her aunts and her uncle, were people of sense and character and taste. Who that knew Izzy Carpenter would have thought it? Who that knew Jane could deny it? I suspect Mrs. Carpenter of having been ashamed of them. Jane's loyalty saved her from any such stupidity.

When I went to St. Mary's Plains the other day, Jane showed me, on the wall of her uncle's study, an old print representing the first log cabin of the French settler who had come there across the Canadian border in 1780. In the picture a Red Indian carrying a tomahawk and capped with feathers skulks behind the trees at the edge of the clearing, and in the foreground a group of Noah's Ark cattle are guarded by a man with a gun. Under the print is written—"St. Marie les Plaines," and the signature "Gilbert de Chevigné." It was a Monsieur de Chevigné from Quebec, Jane told me, who built the Grey House. The name had been corrupted to Cheney; the Cheneys were her grandmother's people. Many of the families in St. Mary's Plains traced a similar history. The town in growing had cherished the story of its French foundation and its social element had grown to believe that it had a special sympathy with our country. Its well-to-do people were constantly coming from and going to France. With an indifference bordering on contempt, and an ease that suggested the consciousness of special claims and opportunities, they would cross the really tremendous expanse of territory that lay between their thresholds and the Atlantic sea-board, ignoring the existence of Chicago, Buffalo, Boston, Philadelphia and New York, and set sail for Cherbourg. It was considered a perfectly natural occurrence and one scarcely worthy of self-congratulation for a girl from St. Mary's Plains to marry a foreigner of real or supposed distinction, but those who neither married abroad nor at home, but were led astray by the vulgar attraction of some rich man from the far west or east were the subject of pitying criticism. Such had been the case with Jane's mother. Silas Carpenter had come bearing down on St. Mary's Plains, a wild man from the great west; like a bison or a moose breaking into a mild and pleasant paddock. Isabel Forbes, headstrong, discontented, covetous, had fallen to his savage charm, his millions and the peculiar oppressive magnetism of his silence, that seemed filled with the memories of unspeakable experiences. The first rush to the goldfields of California loomed in the background of his untutored childhood. Later he had gone to the Klondike. Gold—he had dug it out of the earth with his own great hands. Then he had taught himself oddly from books. A speculator, a gambler, he had a passion for music, and played the flute. A strange mixture. To please Isabel's family he gave up poker, went to church, was married in a frock-coat. People said he had Indian blood in his veins. It seems possible. He had the long head and slanting profile and the mild voice characteristic of the race. Society in St. Mary's Plains was genuinely sorry for Isabel's family when she married him. But she went away to New York to live and was forgotten until on Silas' sensational death her departure for Paris revived interest in her doings.

"The Grey House" as it was known in St. Mary's Plains, had the benevolent patriarchal air of a small provincial manor. Built sometime in the seventies it had not had too many coats of paint during its lifetime, and its calm exterior with the double row of comfortable windows each flanked by a pair of shutters was weather-stained and worn like the visage of some bland unconcerned person of distinction who is not ashamed to look in his old age a little like a weather-beaten peasant. It stood well back from the street in the centre of a wide plot of ground not large enough to be called a park, though containing a few nice trees. The lawn indeed merged in the most sociable way into the grounds of other neighbouring houses and ran smoothly down in front to the edge of the public side-walk where there was no wall or railing of any kind. A scarcely noticeable sign beside the path that led from the street to the front porch with its two wooden pillars said "Keep off the grass."

There were only two storeys to the Grey House and a garret with dormer windows in the grey shingled roof, the rooms of the ground floor being raised only a foot or two from the level of the street, so that Jane's grandmother, sitting in her armchair by the living-room window could look up over the tops of her spectacles and see and recognize her acquaintances who often even at that comfortable distance would bow or lift their hats to the little old lady as they passed.

Every one in St. Mary's Plains knew the Grey House. When one of the Misses Forbes went shopping, she would say "Send it to the Grey House, please," and the young man in the dry goods' store would answer— "Certainly, Miss Forbes, it'll be right along. Mrs. Forbes is keeping well, I hope? Let me see, it's ten years since I was in her Sunday-school class." And Miss Minnie—it was usually Minnie who did the shopping—would smile kindly at the chatty young man who certainly did not mean any harm.

The occupants of that house were people content to stay at home, who did not always know what day of the month it was, and who found a deep source of well-being in the realization that tomorrow would be like today. I imagine those gentlewomen doing the same thing in the same way year after year, wearing the same clothes made by the same family dressmaker, and opposing to the disturbing menace of events the quiet obstinacy of their contentment. I watch them at night go up the stairs together at ten o'clock, kiss one another at the door of their mother's room and go down the dim corridor, Patty staying behind like a sentinel under the gas-jet, her bony arm lifted, waiting to turn the light still lower once they were safe behind their own closed doors. Jane in her bed used to hear their voices saying, "Good-night, mother dear, pleasant dreams. Good-night, Minnie. Good-night." And if the man of the house, Jane's Uncle Bradford, were at his club playing whist, Beth, from the rosy interior of her cretonne chamber would be sure to call out—"I left the front door on the latch for Brad. I suppose it's all right." And Patience would say—"Who would burgle this house?" And Minnie would add—"I put his glass of milk in his room." And then there would be silence disturbed only by the sound of footsteps moving to and fro behind closed doors. And Jane would wait drowsily for Aunt Patty to come in and say "Good gracious, child, not asleep yet? It's past ten o'clock."

To the Forbes family the doings of the outer world were a pleasant distant spectacle that interested and amused but made them feel all the happier to be where they were. When a letter arrived from Izzy bearing its Paris postmark, they would read it together, become pleasantly animated over the news and then settle down with relief at the thought that they didn't have to go over there and do all those things. The letter would then be added to a package bound with an elastic band and put away in the secretary until some one came to call and asked how Isabel was getting on.

I seem to see them all, on these occasions, sitting there in their habitual attitudes. I imagine the little grandmother, with the letter open in her black silk lap, adjusting her spectacles on the slender bridge of her arched nose, and Jane on a footstool beside her, waiting to listen once more with absorbing interest to the extracts from her mother's letter that she already knew by heart, and the two or three friends sitting round rather primly on the old mahogany chairs, and Aunt Beth with her embroidery on the horsehair sofa, and Aunt Minnie making the tea, and Aunt Patty teaching one of her birds to eat from her lips at the window, and perhaps Uncle Bradford, who has come home from his office, visible across the hall through the door in his study with some weighty volume on his knees, and a good cigar between his lips. I seem to hear the purring song of the tea kettle and the pleasant sound of voices calling one another intimate names. I see the faded carpet with its dimmed white pattern and the stiff green brocaded curtains in their high gilt cornices, and the pleasant mixture of heterogeneous objects selected for use and comfort. I have in my nostrils the perfume of roses opening out in the warmth of the room, and of the newly baked cakes made for tea by Aunt

Minnie, and still another finer perfume, the faint fresh fragrance of the spirit of that little old lady who ruled the house in gentleness and was beloved in the town. A humourous little old lady who was not afraid of death, and believed in the clemency of a Divine Father. She liked Jane to read aloud to her while she knitted,—Trollope, Charles Lamb, Robert Burns, were her favourites, and she enjoyed a good tune on the piano, and would beat time with her knitting needles when Beth played a waltz. But on Sundays Beth played hymns and the servants came in after supper to sing with the family "Rock of Ages," "Jesus Lover of my Soul," "Abide with Me." Jane liked those Sunday evenings. They made her feel so safe, was the way she put it.

All the inmates of the Grey House were God-fearing but Minnie was the most religious. She had a talent for cooking and a craving for emotional religious experience. The kitchen of the Grey House was a very pleasant place with a window that gave onto the back verandah, and often on summer mornings Aunt Beth who was young and pretty, would take her sewing out onto this back porch while Aunt Minnie in the kitchen was making cakes, and they would talk through the open window with Jane curled up in the hammock beside Beth's work-table. Beth, would call out in her very high small voice that expressed her plaintive dependence and blissful confidence in the protected life she so utterly loved—"Minnie, Minnie!" and the sound of the egg-beater in the kitchen would cease, and Aunt Minnie would call through the open window in her lower, deeper tone—

"Yes, what do you say?"

"I forgot to tell you that Mrs. Blatchford asked me if I'd ask you to make six cakes for the Woman's Exchange Fourth of July Sale."

And Aunt Minnie would exclaim—

"Good gracious. Six angel cakes, that makes thirty-six eggs." While beating up the whites of eggs for her famous cakes Minnie would ponder on the power of mind over matter, the healing of physical pain by faith, and the ultimate purifying grace of the Divine Spirit. One day she announced that she had joined the Christian Science Church. The family took the news seriously. Jane's grandmother turned very white. She leaned back in her chair and closed her eyes and whispered—"Oh, Minnie dear, I'm so sorry." Uncle Bradford brought his fist down on a table with a crash and shouted— "Don't you do it, Minnie. These newfangled religions are no good." Beth wept. Patience said "Hmph."

Jane didn't like the new look on her Aunt Minnie's face, but the religious mystery behind it had a worrying fascination. She listened to the talk of her elders hoping to learn about this new faith, but it was characteristic of them not to argue or discuss things that affected them deeply, so she learned little, and she was afraid to ask her Aunt Patience who seemed somehow not at all patient with Minnie just now. So she was reduced to talking it all over with Fan, her friend, who lived next door. They would sit astride the fence that divided the two back gardens and talk about God and their elders.

"Aunt Minnie has got a new religion," Jane announced. "Religions are funny things. I don't think I like them but they do do things to you."

"Pooh! I know. It's not half so queer as Mormons and Theosophites and Dowyites."

"What's all that?"

"The Mormons have lots of wives. They live in Salt Lake City and practice bigamy. The Dowyites are in Chicago. There's a big church there full of crutches of all the lame people Dowy has cured by miracle."

"Well, Aunt Minnie says there's no such thing as being lame or sick, and everything is a miracle."

"He-he! I'm not a miracle"

"Yes, you are."

"No, I'm not."

"Who made you?"

"My mother."

"How?"

"I dunno."

"Well, that's a miracle."

"Oh, Jane, you are a silly."

"I'm not silly. I know you've got to have a religion or you can't be good, but I don't like it all the same."

"Who wants to be good?"

"I do."

"Why?"

"Because I'd be afraid to die."

Fan had a complete worldly wisdom that could cover most things, but she was obliged to admit, though with her nose in the air, that she, too, would be afraid to die if she went on being very bad up to the last minute.

Fan Hazeltine was an orphan. She lived with a stepfather who hated her and sometimes didn't speak to her for a week. She and Jane had met on the back fence the day after Jane's arrival in St. Mary's Plains. Jane was six years old then, Fan eight, but I imagine that Fan was very much the same at that time, as when I met her twenty years later. She was always a wisp of a thing no bigger than an elf with a wizened face. Life gave her no leisure for expansion. She was one of those people who never had a chance to blossom out, but could just achieve the phenomenal business of continuing to exist by grit and the determination not to be downed. What she was in her stepfather's inimical house that she remained in the larger inimical world, a small under-nourished undaunted creature, consumed with a thirst for happiness, hiding her hurts under an obstinate gaiety, a minute lonely thing steering her bark cleverly through stormy waters, keeping afloat somehow, sinking and struggling, her grim little heart hardening, her laughter growing shriller and louder as the years went by. There is no difficulty about understanding Fan. I can see her astride that fence, screwing up her face while she told Jane what she was going to do in the world, and I can see her set about doing it.

"I'm going to have a good time. You wait. You just wait. I tell you I'm going to have a good time—fun, fun, fun. That's what I want."

But Jane did not say what she wanted from life.

IV

Patience Forbes was a woman of science, an ornithologist. When she died years ago she was recognized in America as one of the foremost authorities on birds. I remember her death. Jane got the news in Paris. It was at the time of the final struggle over Geneviève's marriage. She showed me her Aunt Patience's will. It read:—"To my beloved niece Jane Carpenter now known by the name of the Marquise de Joigny, I leave the Grey House and everything in it except my collections and manuscripts. These I leave to the Museum of St. Mary's Plains. But the house and all the furniture I leave to Jane in case she may some day want some place to go."

Jane looked at me with strange eyes that day.

"Isn't it queer," she said. "How could she have known?"

But I understand now that Patience Forbes was the only one who did know. She must have been a shrewd woman. She must have followed Jane in her mind all those years, with extraordinary accuracy considering the little she had to go on. But she never betrayed her misgivings. There is only that sentence in her will to indicate what she thought.

She was an imposing woman, plain of face, careless of her appearance and masculine in build. Her nose was crooked, her neck scrawny and her hands large and bony. But she had an air of grandeur. When she tramped through the woods or across the open country that surrounded St. Mary's Plains, her field glasses and her camera slung across her shoulder, she had in spite of her quaint bonnet and long black clothes the look of a grizzled amazon. She would walk twenty miles in a day and frequently did so. Many of the farmers round about knew her. They called her "the bird lady" and asked her in to their kitchens for a glass of milk and a slice of apple-pie, and often while sitting there with her bonnet strings untied and her dusty skirt turned up on her knees, she would receive gifts from sun-burned urchins who, knowing the object of her pilgrimages would bring to her in the battered straw crowns of their hats, rare birds' eggs that they had discovered in the high branches of trees or the secret fastnesses of tangled thickets.

She was the dominating personality in her own home. Her mother and sisters were a little afraid of her. When her brother Bradford married and she announced that she was going to hold classes in the parlour of the Grey House and charge for them, they dared not object, although they would have preferred going without the comforts that Bradford's shared income had provided rather than have a lot of strange people invading the house.

It was characteristic of the family that they never spoke to Jane of money and never gave her any idea that she was or ever would be an heiress. She made her own bed in the morning, and sometimes if she were not in too much of a hurry to get off to school she helped Aunt Minnie with the others. On Saturday mornings she darned her own stockings, or tried to, sitting on a low chair beside her grandmother, but this was by way of a lesson in keeping quiet. I am afraid she took it as a matter of course that Aunt Beth and her grandmother should mend her clothes for her.

She gave a great deal of trouble. Not only was she always getting into scrapes, but she was subject as well to storms of passion that sometimes, as she realized later, seriously frightened her grandmother. Her accidents— she had a great many little ones and one at least that was serious—were episodes marked in her memory as rather pleasant occasions that procured for her an extra amount of petting. There was a high bookcase at the top of the stairs in a dark corner of the upper hall, full of old and faded volumes. Here she spent hours together on Sunday afternoons, sitting on the top of a step-ladder that she dragged out of the housemaids' cupboard. One day, finding among those dusty little books a copy of Dante's "Vita Nuova," she became so absorbed in the lovely poem, though it was only a lame translation in English verse, that she began chanting the lines to herself, unconsciously swaying backwards and forwards on her perch, until all at once the ladder gave way beneath her, and she fell to the floor, breaking her arm. The days that followed were among the happiest of her life. She was installed in her Uncle Bradford's room that gave out onto the sunny back garden where a pear tree was in bloom. There, propped up in the middle of the great white bed, her arm in a sling and not hurting too much to spoil her voluptuous sense of her own importance, she seemed to herself a romantic figure, and received Fan with benevolent superiority, while deeply and deliciously she drank in with every feverish throb of her passionate little heart the tender devotion of the patient women who loved her. Her Aunt Patty slept on a cot beside her at night; her Aunt Minnie brought her meals to her on the daintiest of trays; her grandmother and her Aunt Beth came with their sewing to sit with her in the afternoon. Often when she felt herself dropping into a doze after lunch, before finally closing her eyes to give herself up to the sleep that was creeping over her so softly, she would for the pleasure of it open them again to look through her heavy eyelids at her grandmother's head that she could see above the foot of the great bed outlined against the sunny light of the window; and she would see the little old lady lift a finger to her pursed lips and nod mysteriously smiling at Beth and glance towards the bed as much as to say—"The child is dropping off, we mustn't make a sound." And the child, with such a sense of security and peace as to convey to her in after years the memory of a heavenly instant, would let herself float blissfully out into the still waters of oblivion, knowing that she would surely find them there when she awoke.

She was given the book, "La Vita Nuova" for her own, and lay in bed dreaming of a poet who would one day love her as Dante had loved his Beatrice.

It was about this time that Mrs. Carpenter began working out her schemes with Philibert.

Jane was according to her own testimony subject to fits of such violent temper that she scarcely knew what she was doing. At such moments she frightened every one round her and herself as well. One evening stands out in her memory as peculiarly dreadful. The family were gathered in the drawing room before supper waiting for her, when she burst in on them, her face as white as a sheet, and flung herself on her Aunt Patty with the words—"I've killed a boy. Come quick. He was torturing a beast. He's out in the garden lying quite still." And shuddering from head to foot she dragged her aunt out after her. The boy was not dead, but lay as a matter-of-fact unconscious on the path near the back gate. Jane had knocked him down and half throttled him. There had been three boys shooting with sling shots at a lame cat to whose leg they had tied a tin can so that the wretched beast could not get out of range. Jane had seen them from the window and had rushed to the rescue. The affair made something of a stir in the town. It got into the papers. The boy had to be taken to a hospital. Jane's Uncle Bradford needed all his influence to avert a public scandal. Unfortunately it was not the first case of Jane's violence that had come to the knowledge of the neighbours. People talked of her as "that savage girl of Izzy's" and told their children they were not to play with her any more. She was taken out of school for a time.

It is difficult to get at the exact meaning of this story. All that I know is what Jane has told me herself, and she may have exaggerated its social importance. At any rate, to her own mind it was an immense and horrible disgrace. She felt herself a monstrosity, and for weeks could not bear to go into the street. Her Aunt Patience too, had taken a very serious view of the affair. She sent for Jane to come to her in her study the next morning; the child was, I suppose, too nervous and shaken that night to listen to anything in the way of reprimand, and Aunt Patience showed her a riding whip on a peg in the corner against the wall. It was a cowboy quirt, a braided leather thing with a long lash.

"Jane," said her Aunt Patty, "that quirt belonged to your father. He left it here once long ago. It is yours. I have put it there on that peg for you. I am giving it to you for a special purpose. When a dreadful act is committed against a human being, some one has to suffer, to make things equal. Usually the one who does the evil deed is punished, but I can't, Jane, punish you like that." And here Aunt Patty's stern voice quavered. "I can't because I can't bear to. You are my child. I love you too much. I have lain awake all night thinking about it. When God is angry he punishes people he loves. He has the right. He is wise and perfect. But I am not in the place of God to you, and I can't do it. I am going to do something quite different. I am going to do it because something has got to be done, some one has got to suffer for what you have done. You are to take that whip down now from that peg and give me three lashes with it across my shoulders. I am going to take your punishment on me because I think that will make you understand. Do as I say."

The child was terrified. In a kind of trance she took the leather weapon in her shaking hands. Her aunt stood straight and still in the middle of the room. "Do what I say, Jane," she commanded again. Her voice was awful. Jane advanced a step towards her as if hypnotized, looked a long moment at the stern face, then suddenly collapsed in a heap at those large plain feet in their worn flat slippers.

"I can't, Aunt Patty," she whispered. "I can't! It's enough. It's enough."

After this Jane spent more and more time in her aunt's company. The dreadful experience drew them even closer together. Jane would almost always accompany her aunt on her long tramps into the country, and although as Patience so often said she never took any real interest in the science of birds, she nevertheless became an adept at climbing trees and going through thickets, and learned to imitate the songs of birds in an astonishing way. This accomplishment indeed, she never lost; even when she had long since forgotten all she learned about Baltimore Orioles and Brown Thrushes and Scarlet Tanagers and the migrations of birds in the spring time, and their marvellous intricate manner of fabricating their nests, she could throw back her head and fill the room wherever she might be with the most bewildering joyous riot of warblings and twitterings and liquid trills. She became so expert at this that sometimes she would play pranks on her aunt, and climbing into the tree outside the study window, she would imitate the song of some little feathered creature so perfectly that her Aunt Patty would leave her work and tip-toe softly to the window only to be greeted with a squeal of triumphant laughter.

The classes in bird lore that were held in the parlour were for Jane little more than a chance of giggling with Fan in a corner. The lectures indoors went on during the winter, but in the spring and early summer Miss Forbes took her followers by train to a village on the edge of the forest, and there, in the leafy fastnesses of those sunny enclosed spaces would give her pupils demonstrated lectures. Jane has told me that when following the sound of a bird's note heard overhead at a distance, her aunt's face would become transfigured; a little mystic smile would come over her plain features; she would sign to her throng to make not the slightest noise, and silently her head bent sideways and upwards, she would lead the way, stopping now and then, her finger on her lips, to listen for the clear note that guided her, until at last she would catch sight of her beauty, high up on a swaying leafy bough, and all her being would strain upward towards that tiny creature, and her face would light up with even a brighter joy, and she would point a gaunt finger mutely at the object of her worship as if calling attention to some lovely little celestial being. Then if some one, as was always the case, made a sound and the bird flew away, a shadow would fall on her face, her pose would relax and she would turn to the heavy human beings about her, a dull disappointed glance, looking at them all for a moment in deep reproach before she recollected what she was there for, and began to tell them of the habits and customs of the songster who had just disappeared over the treetops.

On one occasion Fan went so far as to say these rambles were ridiculous, and Jane flared up at once.

"My Aunt Patty ridiculous?" she cried out. "How dare you? She's the greatest ornithologist in the world, and I love her, I love her more than all the outside world together and everything in it."

When Jane was fifteen her grandmother died, and a year later her Aunt Beth was married, and Jane, who was sixteen, had a white organdie bridesmaid's dress and carried a bouquet of pink roses, and after that Aunt Minnie went away to be a Christian Science healer in New York, and Jane was left alone in the Grey House with her Aunt Patty.

Her grandmother's death left her with no impression of horror. The little old lady had gone to sleep one day quietly in her accustomed place by the window and had not wakened again, that was all. Aunt Patty at the funeral in a long black veil, looked like some grand and austere monument of grief, reminding her vaguely of a statue she had seen somewhere of emblematic and national importance, but she made no fuss over her sorrow, and told the child that night of her own mother's imminent arrival from Paris.

This was a piece of news sufficiently wonderful to offset completely the effect of death in the house. Jane said to herself, "She is coming to take me away to be with her at last." And she went up and hid in her room so that her Aunt Patty should not see how excited she was.

But Jane was mistaken. Such was not Mrs. Carpenter's intention. She had come to America on receiving her sister's telegram partly out of deference to her mother's memory, partly to consult her lawyers, and partly for the purpose of putting Jane in a fashionable American boarding school. The sadness in Jane's memory long connected with those days has little to do with her grandmother's funeral, but is the lasting indelible impression of the discovery she made then, that her mother did not like her.

Mrs. Carpenter came out with her ideas for her daughter abruptly on the evening of her arrival. She had no idea that her daughter adored her. Jane's letters beginning "My darling Mummy" and ending "Your loving daughter" had conveyed to her nothing of the writer's emotion. No doubt they bored her, and no doubt she supposed that they bored the child who was obliged to write them. It would probably have seemed to her incredible that a little girl who scarcely ever saw her should go on wanting her for ten years from a distance of a couple of thousand miles. If she justified herself to herself at all, I suppose she made use of this argument: "Well, if I don't care for her because she is so dreadfully her father's daughter, then that proves that I am too different for her ever to care for me. The best thing for us both is to leave her with people who won't let her get on their nerves as she would on mine."

Mrs. Carpenter was not subtle, and she hated wasting time, so she opened the subject at once sitting with Patience in the back parlour, her slim silk-stockinged legs crossed easily, one smart foot dangling, her modish head tilted back above the trim cravat of black crêpe and white tulle that her French maid had fabricated for her during the crossing, and a jewelled hand playing with Jane's long pigtail. Her sister Patience sat opposite her at her table, her head in her hands, her bony fingers poked up among her meagre locks, and Jane took in that evening with a kind of anguish of loyalty the contrast between the two women. It seemed to her somehow very pitiful that her Aunt Patty should be so ugly when her mother was so beautiful. With a childish absence of any vestige of a sense of humour, she felt at one moment ashamed for her aunt and almost angry with her mother, and then ashamed for her mother and angry with her aunt.

"I wanted to tell you, Patty, that I think it would be a good thing now for this big gawk of a girl to go to a finishing school in New York. You'll probably be giving up this house soon, and I don't want her with me yet awhile."

Jane in talking to me of this moment said that she felt as if her mother's hand that was playing affectionately with her hair an instant before had suddenly picked up a hammer and hit her on the head. For an interval everything was blurred and dark in the room, with sparks that seemed to be shooting out of her brain. It was her Aunt Patty's face that brought her back to her senses. It was a suffering, angry face, and presently she heard Patience say—"I am not going to give up this house, but I think you ought to take Jane to live with you. She wants to go, and she's right. You are her mother."

But Izzy paid no attention to her older sister.

"That's nonsense! Paris is no place for a girl of her age. What in the world should I do with her? She'd be dreadfully in the way. Besides she must learn how to walk and manage her hands before I show her to people."

The thing was done. Jane knew. She knew that her mother did not like her and never had liked her, and she knew somehow that her mother did not like her because she was ugly and reminded her of her father Silas Carpenter. She knew too that her Aunt Patty had always known this, and that her aunt loved her as her mother never would love her, and that the mottled flush on her grim face was due in part to anger and in part to the fear of losing her. She understood that her aunt had determined to help her to attain her heart's desire, even at the price of losing herself the one thing more precious to her than anything in the world. She dared not look at her mother and she could not speak, and still she waited though incapable now of taking in the meaning of their voices. She heard vaguely her aunt saying something about making enough money by her lectures and publications to keep the house going, but paid no attention. A question addressed directly to herself by her mother at last roused her.

"Well, Jane, what do you say? Would you rather stay here alone with your Aunt Patty than go to boarding school with a lot of jolly girls of your own age?"

She did not hesitate then for an answer.

"Oh yes, if you can't have me let me stay here," and turning she cried, "Keep me, Aunt Patty, keep me," and flung herself into those long trembling arms.

Mrs. Carpenter seems to have been mildly amused by this display of affection. With her face buried in the black woollen stuff of her aunt's blouse, Jane heard her say —

"Well then, I leave it to you two. You can carry on as you like for the next two or three years. When you are eighteen, Jane, you will make your début in Paris society. You'll want to bring Patty with you, I suppose, when the time comes."

Mrs. Carpenter left three days later. The subject of Jane's future was not broached again in her presence, but she heard the two women talking about professors of French and Italian and dancing classes, and the advantages of a saddle-horse and a pony cart. Her mother's last words to her were —

"Now make the most of your time and don't run about all over the country in the sun. Your complexion is the best thing about you." And yet she didn't hate her mother. Her idea of her mother had not even undergone for her any fundamental change. It was all the other way round. It was her opinion of herself that had suffered. With the dogged loyalty that seemed at times positively a sign of stupidity and was to influence every important decision of her life, she defended her mother to her own heart. If her mother did not like her it was because she was not likeable, because her father had been a dreadful man and had handed down to her some secret dangerous element of his own nature that made her antagonistic and unpleasant to brilliant happy people. Her Aunt Patty loved her because she was sorry for her. Her Aunt Patty was different from her mother. She, too, was ugly and a little queer; that was the bond between them. Poor Patience Forbes! Jane was to do her justice later, but for the moment she almost hated the sympathy between them, while her mother's image like some magic adamant statue possessing a supernatural inviolability remained for her persistently and brilliantly the same. And when she was gone the question Jane put her aunt represented the result of hours of heart-broken weeping in which no whisper of a reproach had mingled.

"Aunt Patty," she said, "how can I make my mother love me?" and her Aunt Patty had replied rather grimly—

"By trying to be what she wants you to be, I suppose."

It was after this that Jane began sleeping at night with a strip of adhesive plaster across her mouth from her chin to her upper lip. Her aunt must have known but she did not interfere. I can imagine her standing over her niece's bed when she came up from her protracted studies in the library, with a lamp in her hand, a tall grizzled figure in long ungainly black clothes, looking down at that sleeping face with the court-plaster pasted across the mouth, and I can see her weather-beaten face twist and tears well up in those shrewd intelligent eyes, and I seem to hear her utter—"Poor Jane, my poor lamb. If you could only take some interest in science. I don't know what is to become of you."

V

I begin to feel uncertain in telling this story. I am not at all sure that I have a just feeling for that American life of Jane's. I have put down the facts as she told them to me and have described the people there as they came into being for me, from her talk, but how am I to know that they were really like that? Perhaps had I seen them with my own eyes I should have found them quite different: narrow, dull people with shrill twanging voices and queer American mannerisms. It may be that they would have bored me as they bored Mrs. Carpenter. St. Mary's Plains I have seen for myself, but what did I see? A railway station, a few streets, a deep wide muddy river flowing by full of ships and barges. The town expressed nothing to me. It remained enigmatic. Of the hidden life going on in all those houses I knew nothing. I did not even understand what I saw. There were billboards all about the railway station advertising American products. Enormous nigger babies three times life-size stared from wooden fences. The Gold Dust Twins? Why gold dust, why twins, why nigger babies? How should I know? There were other garish things: I seem to remember flags and red, white and blue streamers festooning telegraph poles, in celebration I suppose of some national holiday. It was all too foreign. I could not translate it to myself. It made me feel very tired, and now this effort to recreate the atmosphere makes me weary. It is such a strain for the imagination. I know that my picture is incomplete and therefore false. I have touched on the gentleness and good breeding of Jane's people, on the quiet of their God-fearing lives, but that word God-fearing: it is strange; it suggests something stern and uncompromising that is very different from anything we know in Paris. It suggests a great seriousness, a bare nakedness before the mystery of the unknown, a challenge of fate and an exaltation, of virtue. It affects me like a bleak wind. I turn away from it with relief. I look out of my window with a sigh. There is the good Abbé coming out of the convent gate. He has been hearing confessions; he has been taking away the sins from burdened hearts and tying them up into neat little bundles to be dropped into the Seine. God bless him, and thank God for our wise old priesthood and our wonderful beautiful old compromises, and thank God again for the jaunty swing of that black cassock. Ugh! I feel better. The little street is dim this morning. It has been raining. Dear, weary little old street—

There is no room here for American Puritanism. Paris is too old, too wise to harbour such things. Was it that that haunted Jane? Did she always see herself measured up to a fixed fine standard like a flagpole, the flagpole of American idealism, with a banner floating over her head, casting a shadow, purity, honesty, fear of God, written on it in shining letters? Payment, atonement, the wages of sin is death—old Mrs. Forbes reading out the words, believing but not worrying, but Jane making them terribly personal, questioning, puzzling, burying them in her mind. Heaven and hell; realities! Our actions leading us toward one or the other. Patience Forbes saying one had to suffer for a bad deed. The mystery about Jane's father—something curious about his death. He was an unhappy man, his silence, she remembered it, she remembered him. She knew she was like him in some inexplicable way that frightened her. A world of stern simple values, all smoothed over for her by the gentleness and kindness of those people, the Forbes. Of course they were gentle and kind. They loved her. It was all right as long as she had them, but it was a curious preparation for life with Izzy in Paris.

Izzy sent for Philibert on her return from America. She must have talked to him about Jane. They must have had a curious conversation. I am certain that it was then that they elaborated their plan. The scheme was one of grand proportions. They became partners in a great enterprise. Mrs. Carpenter was to supply her daughter, who had enough money to realize even Philibert's dreams, and he was to supply the required knowledge, as well as the *billet d'entrée* into the social arena of Europe. These two suited each other perfectly. They knew what they wanted and each saw in the other the means of getting it. Broadly speaking they wanted the same thing, and if Philibert's conception of their common destiny was utterly beyond her that was just what made her faith in him perfect. Audacious in her way, his audacity far outdid hers: whatever her idea his was always much grander; he made her feel beautifully humble by brushing away some of her most cherished hopes as unworthy of their attention.

"A palace in Venice?" I seem to hear him say, perched on one of her little straight gilt chairs, nursing his foot that was tucked under his knee. "But every one has palaces in Venice. Why not a Venetian palace in Paris, the Doge's Palace itself, reproduced stone for stone, if that takes your fancy?"

And she would catch her breath with the beauty of the idea. Not that Philibert ever intended to do anything so silly as spoil a site in Paris by such a freak of humour. He was a *farceur* if you like, but he had too much taste for that. He intended having his palace, and it was to be of such supreme beauty as to draw pilgrims from all over the world, but it was to be in harmony with its surroundings. The allusion to the House of the Doges was just his little happy joke. He was very cheerful in those days. People used to say—"Fifi does have luck. Look at him. Who is it now that adores him? Was ever a man so blatantly successful in his love affairs?" I must say he did have the look of being happily in love. His smooth cheeks were pink, his eyes, usually as expressionless as bits of blue enamel, were suffused with light, and the soft flaxen fuzz that grew round the bald spot on his head like the down on a little yellow gosling, seemed to send off electricity. Never in all his immaculate dandyism had he been so immaculate, his linen was superlative and the shine on his little pointed boots was visible halfway down the street. There was a giddy swing to his hurrying coat-tails, and he carried his shoulders superbly. Almost, but not quite, he achieved the look of being taller. And his contempt for the rest of us was of course greater than ever. Born with a gnawing consciousness of his own genius, he had for years been as exasperated as a Michael Angelo or a Paul Veronese forced by lack of space and a sufficiency of paints to spend his time doing little water-colour sketches: but he now saw himself on the way to realizing his inspirations in all their splendid amplitude, and of displaying before the eyes of men the finished gigantic masterpiece of his art. For Philibert was an artist: even Ludovic and Felix and Clémentine recognized that. He was an artist in life on a grand scale. He dealt with men and women and clothes and string orchestras and food and polished floors and marble staircases as a painter deals with the colours on his palette, or perhaps more exactly as the theatrical producer deals with stage properties. His stage was the world itself; he produced his plays and his pageants and his *tableaux vivants* in the midst of the activities of society, and his actors, reversing the method of our modern stage where the players come down across the footlights to mingle with the audience, were selected by him from the general public without their knowing it, and found themselves playing a part in a scene he had created round them and for them as if by magic. Audacious? Ah, but who could be more so? Who but Fifi would have had the impertinence to take a real live king and make him, all unconscious, play the principal part in a pantomime before a handful of spectators? Mrs. Carpenter had dreamed of entertaining kings. Philibert entertained them, but he did something much more extraordinary; he put them into his play and made them entertain him.

Who in Paris will ever forget the night he threw open his door for the Czar of all the Russias? Who does not remember how he stage-managed the crowd outside, how troops of singers from the Opera mingled with the mob far down the street and sang hymns of acclamation as the royal guest approached his fairy palace, so illumined as to shine like a single rosy jewel? And the golden carpet thrown down on the marble stairs, and Jane standing alone at the top of that fantastic staircase, like an emerald column, her train arranged by Philibert's own clever hands sweeping down the steps beneath her to add supernaturally to her height, her strange face under its diadem of jewels looking as small in the distance as the carved image cut out of a coin. Do people not talk even now of that night, and allude to Philibert as the last of the benevolent despots? "He was unique," you can still hear them say it, "there will never be any one like him. No one can amuse the world as he did." And no one ever will. The War has changed all that. François I. was his father; the Medici were his forerunners; he was the last of his kind.

But he refined on this sensational achievement. He went farther. Only a few realized quite how far he did go. In his most brilliant days, I was on the point of saying during the most brilliant period of his reign, he played plays at which he himself was the sole spectator. I remember the occasion when a certain popular Prince, heir at that time to one of the most solid thrones in Europe, expressed a desire to come and shoot at the Château de Ste. Clothilde. Mrs. Carpenter had been all of a tremble with pleasure. It was the first royal visitor to sleep under his roof. Philibert had restored our old place in the country, and had in five years managed by a miracle to have there the best partridge shooting in France. "You will have a large party for His Royal Highness, I suppose?" Mrs. Carpenter had ventured timidly. How humble and self-effacing she had grown by that time, poor thing. "Not at all," replied Philibert. "There will be no women and not more than six guns." And he added then with a sublime simplicity unequalled, I believe, by any monarch or any court jester in history, "When royalty comes to Ste. Clothilde for the shooting, there is another place laid at table, that is all."

Poor Izzy, she was completely at a loss. No longer could she attempt to follow him. It was Jane who understood. She looked at him curiously through her gleaming half-closed eyes; I remember the look, while she breathed in a whisper—"Take care, you will have nothing left to live for." I remember the tone of that remark.

But I am anticipating too much. I meant to speak here merely of his matrimonial expectations. These hopes gave his person an added lustre and his fine family nose an accentuated sneer. Nevertheless he kept them secret: no one knew that Mrs. Carpenter even had a daughter. She never mentioned her to any of us. On the other hand she never mentioned Philibert in her letters to Jane. It was part of the scheme. They had worked it out completely between them to its smallest details. Jane would be dangerously independent. She would be in no way answerable to her mother for all that immense lot of money. It was best then that she should suspect nothing. She would arrive, the Marquis de Joigny would be presented to her and would fall in love with her at first sight. Her mother would leave her free to choose for herself. Philibert made himself responsible for the rest.

And, in the meantime, while these two master minds were at work, Jane still waited in the Grey House for her mother to come and fetch her, waited as the appointed time drew near with little of the old exultant expectancy, but instead with nervous misgiving. She was afraid of not pleasing her mother, she was in an agony at the thought of leaving her Aunt Patience.

And I find myself now, as I sit here, painfully counting with suspended breath the last days of Jane's girlhood in St. Mary's Plains. I see them silently slipping by over her unconscious head as she sat in the back garden among her Aunt Patty's hollyhocks, or walked with her French governess along the homely streets, swinging her school books by a strap, humming a tune under her breath, her neat modest clothes swinging to the rhythm of her beautiful young body, her strange little ugly ardent face lifted to the sweet air in frank animal enjoyment. Patience Forbes stands on the front stoop between the two wooden pillars waiting for her to come running up the path, waiting for the generous clasp of those strong young arms, waiting to feel once more the contact of all that pure vital youthfulness, and I hear as they sit down to supper opposite each other, with the tall candles lighted on the old mahogany table and the hot muffins steaming under the folded white napkin, the sound of the grandfather clock in the hall, ticking out the last precious fleeting moments of their time together.

This is very painful, I will not linger over it. I bring myself back, I falter, what then am I to think of? Where turn my attention? So much is ugly. Ah, but Jane, why go any further? Is it not enough? Is it not clear to you as it is to me? Is there any need to say more? Was it not all just as I say? Now that you are back there at last alone, now that we have lost you for ever, now that you have gone, irresistibly drawn out of your splendour to the little shabby place you loved, what is there to torment you? Philibert, Bianca? What have they to do with you now? They hated you. How can you be beholden to people who did you nothing but harm? But Jane, there were some of us who adored you, and if you had told us everything, as you at last told me, we would have loved you only the more.

I sometimes wonder whether Mrs. Carpenter ever suspected what a narrow shave she had towards the end, and how all her plans very nearly came to nothing at the moment of their fruition because of Bianca. It is probable that she had little more idea of the danger than a vague uneasy suspicion that Philibert for a time was distraught by some influence whose source she ignored. She had met Bianca but did not connect her with Philibert; knowing almost nothing in those days of what she would have called Philibert's family life. There was no one to tell her that Philibert had once wanted to marry Bianca and that old François had refused him as a suitor for his daughter's hand because of his lack of fortune. Izzy knew nothing about the strange intimacy of these two. How should she? Philibert was not likely to tell her and certainly none of the rest of us were in the habit of discussing with her the private affairs of our families. My mother knew of course; she doted on Bianca, and Claire, and all the family. They had all desired the match. Bianca was a pearl that they collectively coveted, and when things went wrong they had all been annoyed with the old rake her father. Aunt Clothilde had gone so far as to rap him over the knuckles with her fan one day when he took her out to dinner, and to say in her best rude manner—"You've done a pretty thing, spoiling the lives of those two children. And what's Bianca got from her mother? Five hundred thousand francs a year. Just so, and you will leave her the same when you die, which will be before long at the pace you are going. And Philibert has nothing but his debts, but then, who knows, I might have given him something. I'm not so in love with him as some, but still he's my nephew, and the two of them were made for each other. Now you'll see, they'll both turn out badly." But François only laughed as if he were enjoying a wicked joke that he was not going to share with her. He was always like that, chuckling to himself in a sly sort of way that made you creep and roused the curiosity of women. Sometimes he would stare at me with his pale, red-rimmed, half-closed eyes and that smile on his face as if my deformity was very amusing. I hated him. I could have told them what kind of a father he was to Bianca.

In any case she was married a year later to her well-to-do nonentity, and we all went to the wedding, and Aunt Clo, being a near relative, walked in the *cortège* with François and made faces behind her prayer book. But Philibert was white as a sheet and kicked a wretched dog out of the way as he came down the church steps with such violence that he broke its paw. Bianca was, I remember, as lovely and serene as a lily. She didn't speak to Philibert at all the day she was married. She just kept him standing there near her, not too near, during the reception, as if he belonged to her, as if he were a flunkey of some sort, and never once so much as looked at him. But she spoke to me. She asked me why I had not proposed for her hand. "I might have accepted you, you know" she said in that small reedy penetratingly sweet voice of hers—"just to spite them all,"—and there wasn't a trace of a smile on her clear curving lips. Devil—she meant it for Philibert, of course, and of course he heard.

My mother used to say that Bianca reminded her of a very young Sir Galahad. Claire suggested half-mockingly St. Sebastian. I thought she was like a fox, quick and cruel with a poisonous bite. As a matter of fact, in those days she looked a harmless little thing. Her small snow-white square face was sweetly modelled and framed as it was by a cap of short black hair that was cut *à la Jeanne d'Arc*, it had the look of a mediaeval Italian angel. Only her enormous eyes very blue and deep and her voice gave her away. If one watched closely one caught glimpses in those eyes of the invisible monster locked up in that light smooth body; if one listened to her voice one heard it. She seemed to know this, and much of the time she kept her eyes lowered. Cool and aloof and monosyllabic she hid herself, her real self, calculating her power and economical of it, deceptive, waiting till it should be worth her while to disengage the magic that lurked in the smooth complexity of her little person. Her voice was not a pure single note, but a double reedy sound that had a penetrating harmony. One remembered it with a haunting exasperation. It was rather high in pitch, and the words it carried did not punctuate the sound of it, but seemed to be strung like beads on a sustained vibrating chord as if on some double coppery wire. Each word was distinct and beautifully enunciated by her lips without interfering with the sound that flowed through them. There was nothing guttural or emotional about Bianca's voice, but it was disturbing; it irritated and seemed to correspond to some secret nerve-centre of pleasure in the listener's brain.

I have watched her sometimes using her voice for special purposes of her own, but for the most part in company she tried to subdue it, and would often stop herself in the middle of one of her rapid speeches with a little annoyed laugh. She would then look down and move away, but even her floating stiffly off like a rigid little broomstick with a pair of wings or wheels on the end of it had a strange charm.

Her gestures were very restrained. She had a way of holding attention so closely when apparently doing nothing, that when she did make the slightest movement it conveyed exactly what she intended it to convey.

Philibert was a connoisseur fit to appreciate her, and she knew it. They had in their precocious youth recognized each in the other a rare complementary quality, but even in the days when Bianca with abbreviated skirts had let me make love to her, the affinity between Philibert and herself had made her hate him. It was a curious attraction I thought that made them constantly want to hurt each other. I knew well enough that Bianca was only sweet to me in order to make Philibert angry. Sometimes in the garden of our house, where we played while François paid his respects of my mother, she would kiss me, looking sideways at Philibert all the time, and he would pirouette on one toe and pretend not to care, and would yell with laughter at me and call out—"Don't think she loves you. You're crooked. You will never be any better. You can't do this. Look at me. She loves me." And Bianca would turn away from us and look at him as he told her to, and say to him—"I don't like you at all," and then stalk away into the drawing room where she would wheedle from her father a succession of lumps of sugar soaked in cognac, and if we followed we would find her rubbing her smooth little cheek up and down against François' whiskers and making little gurgling noises of pleasure. François was certainly a queer kind of father. Philibert and I could have told tales about that.—If it had only been lumps of sugar dipped in brandy—. We took note with a kind of shocked envy. Once she took us down to the pantry and showed us a bottle of "Triple Sec." "That's the nicest," she said, "it's like honey fire."

When she was ten he turned her loose in his library, or at any rate finding her there with some dreadful book in her lap, only laughed. Every one knows what that library contained. Rare editions, old bindings, a priceless collection; bibliophiles came from far to finger those volumes. François was a discriminating collector. But for Bianca—no one discriminated for her. One can see her like a little greedy white lamb browsing in the poisonous herbage of that field of knowledge. She began with the memoirs of Casanova. She had picked it out because it was by an Italian. She was always dreaming about Italy, her mother's country. Her mother had died while she was a baby, but Bianca seemed to remember her. She often spoke about her, and every Friday went with her governess to light a candle in St. Sulpice for the repose of her spirit. As for her literary discoveries, Philibert alone was aware of what she was up to, and even he didn't know much about it. Occasionally she would drop a hint, or lend a book. She would never have admitted even to him that she read all the books she did read. She understood Philibert perfectly. As she grew older she allowed him to suspect that she was wise, but not too wise. She was willing to be for him an object of mystification, but never of vulgar curiosity. Gradually she grew conscious of a purpose in regard to Philibert, and I believe that this purpose had something to do with her refusing to marry him. For, after all, she could have brought her father round had she tried to. No, it was not her idea to marry the man she liked. Her idea was far more amusing than that.

What happened just before Jane's arrival in Paris was simple enough. Bianca had been married two years. She had been to Italy and had come back to find Philibert thick as thieves with a great grey-headed American, and she had asked herself what this meant. It didn't take her long to find out. She had a way of knowing what he was up to. Probably he told her outright, and she was not pleased. For the moment she did not like the idea of Philibert's marrying any one, least of all a colossal American fortune. She was far too clever to make a scene. She had other means of getting her own way, and now out of caprice she exerted them. I imagine her opening her monstrous eyes just a little wider than usual and allowing Philibert to look into them. I can see her move ever so slightly with a small jerk of the hips and upward undulation of her slim body, and I watch her lean forward to allow the faint suggestion of that magic essence of hers to disengage itself from her person, through her lifted eyelids, through her sweet parted lips, through the tips of her long delicate fingers, and I see Philibert falter in his talk about the American girl, and silently watch her, and get to his feet like a man in a dream and come close but not too close. For a fortnight she kept him like that, in a trance; everywhere he followed her.

Mrs. Carpenter lost him. It was during the month of May. Bianca went about a good deal that Spring and was very much admired. It was at a big afternoon affair that I saw her, standing with Philibert looking out at the crowded gardens. She was very young still; she was nothing more than a very thin slip of a thing with pretty little sticks of legs and a pair of long delicate arms hanging close to her sides, the fingers pressed against the folds of her slinky muslin frock. She stood very still and rather stiff, her heels together and her lovely head just tilted very slightly away from Philibert as if she had drawn it back quickly and gently at the sound of a disturbing murmur, or as if perhaps she were enticing that murmur, as yet unuttered, from his lips. I watched them. They did not look at each other. Their eyes traced parallel lines of vision before them over the heads of the crowd. Nothing betrayed their deep communion save this common stillness. I did not hear them speak or see their lips move, but I know that Philibert was speaking; I learnt afterwards what it was he was saying.

He was asking her to bolt with him.

It was the moment of supreme danger for Izzy Carpenter. The marvellous edifice she had so carefully fashioned with Philibert hung suspended by a thread. Like some great gorgeous glittering chandelier with a thousand candles hoisted into the air by Bianca's little finger, it hung there swaying in space, held up to the ceiling of heaven by the thread of her hesitation. Philibert, his hands behind him holding his top hat and gloves against the neat back of his morning coat, watched it. Through closed teeth he had spoken without looking at his companion and now he waited in silence. If she assented the whole thing would be dashed to the ground in a million pieces. He took in all that it meant for him. Like one of those drunkards whose faculties are most keen when they are under the influence of liquor, he saw with excruciating clearness, through the superlative excitation of Bianca's fascination that was working upon him, the beauty and magnitude of the thing he was sacrificing. And yet if she had said it, the word he awaited, he would have turned away from all that débris with a sneer, so perfectly had Bianca made him feel that she was worth it, worth anything, worth more than even he, with his formidable imagination could conceive of.

She didn't say it. She didn't say anything. She merely lowered her head after an instant's utter stillness and floated away from him. I wonder if there was the slightest of smiles on her lovely averted lips. Perhaps not. Her smile was deep down in the well of her abysmal being. She had had an inspiration. She had thought of something much more amusing than what he proposed. She would reveal it to him later; there was plenty of time. Or perhaps she would never reveal it to him at all, but just make him do as she wished without letting him know that she had thought of it long before. In any case she would leave him alone now.

And so Mrs. Carpenter was saved and went to America to fetch Jane.

VI

Philibert had given himself a month in which to win Jane's hand, and it took him five. I don't know why I find any comfort in this fact, but I do. I am glad she kept him waiting. I am glad the two conspirators were uncomfortable, even for so short a time, and there is no doubt that they were uncomfortable. Jane paid no attention to her mother's funny little friend, who wore corsets and high heels and used scent. She sized him up in a long grave glance that covered him from tip to toe and then seemed to forget about him. The truth was that she was absorbed in her mother. To her great delight she had found in that quarter an unexpected cordiality. It almost seemed as if her mother had decided to like her. She had never been half so nice.

And she fell in love with Paris.

Wonderful enchantress city, queen woman of cities! It had assumed to greet her its most charming and gentle aspect. She arrived one evening in June. She held her breath as she drove across the Place de la Concorde, where the light was silver and blue, and up the Champs Elysées towards the Arc de Triomphe that stood out against the sunset glow like a great and lovely gate into Heaven. She thought, so she told me afterwards, of the magic city under the sea in the poem by Edgar Allen Poe. The following morning she was up with the milkman and had slipped out of the house alone before any one was awake, and had walked from the Avenue du Bois down to the Tuileries Gardens and back again as the newsvenders were taking down the shutters of their kiosks. They smiled at her and nodded. A little morning breeze laughed in the trees. A woman came by wheeling a cart full of flowers. She filled her arms and arrived at her mother's doorway breathless with pleasure. Mrs. Carpenter had the sense not to scold her, but she was obliged during the days that followed to engage a special duenna who could walk far enough and fast enough to keep up with her daughter. It appeared that Jane had read a good deal of French history. She visited churches, monuments and museums and made excursions to Versailles, la Malmaison, Fontainebleau. The Rue de la Paix amused her, she liked the clothes her mother bought her; but after a long morning at the dressmaker's, standing to let little kneeling women drape silks on her young body, she would gulp down her lunch and start out again to explore, on foot, refusing to take the motor.

One day she turned into this little street. I saw her. I thought at first that she was a Russian, some young Cossack princess perhaps. Her dog, a Great Dane, walked beside her, his head close to her splendidly moving limbs. I had never seen any one walk like that. She came on, her head up, her arms down along her sides, and the wind, or was it the force of her own swift movement, made her garments flow back from her. It was the *Victoire de Samothrace* walking through the sunlit streets of Paris. I watched her approach with a strange excitement. Behind her trotted her valiant duenna, a hurrying little woman in black. And as the radiant white figure came nearer I saw that she was very young, scarcely more than a great glorious child, and her strange ugly face under her close white hat shaped like a helmet seemed to me, all glowing though it was with health, to be half asleep. When she was gone I turned back to my rooms and sat with my head in my hands thinking of how curious it was, the regal carriage of that fine free controlled body, and that face that did not know itself. I felt oppressed and exhilarated and somehow full of pity. It was dangerous to be like that, so young, so brave, so unknowing. Yes, an ugly face, but her walk was the most beautiful I had ever seen.

Through July Philibert made no progress with his suit. It was a puzzling problem for him and for Izzy. Mrs. Carpenter found herself the all too successful rival of the man she had selected for her daughter. Jane's attitude was simple enough. She enjoyed everything immensely and felt that this was just what she had hoped to find. Her wonderful mother who had appeared at one time not to care for her was now giving her daily proofs of affection. And so she was happy. Mrs. Carpenter must have been nonplussed. The connection was obvious, for the more contented Jane was the less sign did she make of wanting anything else. She was delighted at being with her mother: how could it occur to her to want to get married?

And Philibert's artfulness with women was of no use to him here. His professional tricks were wasted. He could only hold her attention by telling her about the things she looked at; histories, anecdotes, dissertations on art and architecture she would listen to with profound interest. She kept him for hours in the galleries of the Louvre discoursing on the great masters, and occasionally she would say with a sigh while he mopped his exhausted head—"How much you know." It was the only tribute he got from her.

For August they went to Trouville. Monsieur Cornuché had not yet invented Deauville. The trip was very nearly Philibert's undoing. He was very hard put to it, was our Philibert, during that month of August. And how he must have hated it. Nothing but sheer grit kept him going, nothing less than the most enormous prize would have induced him to put up with so much misery.

She rode, she swam, she played tennis, she hired a yacht and sailed it. He was most of the time quite literally out of breath with running after tennis balls, carrying golf clubs, galloping down the sands after her vanishing figure; and to add to his discomfiture some of his friends, those whom he could not be seen with under the circumstances, saw him all too often and laughed behind the screen of the little red and white bathing tents. I enjoy in retrospect his discomfiture. Such as it was it constituted for Jane an unconscious revenge. For a month she kept her mother and Philibert on pins and needles, and I believe that if her mother had not been constantly at hand to dress him up again and again in all the trappings of romance, that Jane would have found him finally and irretrievably ridiculous, just a poor exasperated absurd little man who was no good at games and got blue with cold in the water. For of course what saved Philibert in the end was Jane's desire to please her mother.

Mrs. Carpenter was obliged to take a definite line. It had not been her intention to do so, but she found that she must if the plan were to come off at all. I don't truly believe the woman was more double-faced than most. She would if one hauled her out of the grave to make her defence, put up, I suppose, a respectable argument. She would say that she had done what thousands of mothers do every day, and what all of them should do. She had picked out a husband whom she considered a brilliant match for her daughter and had married her to him. The only reason that obliged her to resort to subterfuge, and hers, she would say, was of the vaguest and slightest, was the girl's complete financial independence. Her own extraordinary husband had given her no hold over her daughter, but had put everything into the hands of a trio of bumptious bigoted American citizens. What she really was doing when she had made her plans for Jane and then got her to fulfil them without knowing it, was not bamboozling the child, but getting the best of those horrid trustees. If it had not been for them and the grotesque will they kept waving in her face, she would have said to Jane simply, "Here, my darling, is the man I have chosen for you. You will be married in a month's time." But she couldn't do that. She was forced to make her daughter take him of her own free choice, and so she would go on, briskly explaining that she had done it all for the best. Was it not a creditable desire on her part to see her child the leader of French society? And had not Jane subsequently become even more than that? Was there a town in America that did not read with envy the newspaper accounts of her triumphs? Did it not all come out quite as she had foreseen? If the two were not happy what did that prove? Just nothing at all beyond the tiresome truism that marriages always ended in making people hate each other.

Mrs. Carpenter had adopted a jocular easy manner with her daughter on bringing the girl to Europe that seemed to express her happy sense of their being comrades and equals. The rôle she assumed was that of an elder sister who was ready to give any amount of good-natured advice when asked for, but would in no way interfere with the freedom of the fortunate youngster. This was Izzy's way of being careful and of making it impossible for Jane ever to turn round and say—"It was my mother who urged me to do it." Fortunately for her peace of mind Jane hid nothing from her and was constantly asking for guidance.

It was Mrs. Carpenter's habit to have her morning coffee in bed at nine o'clock after an hour's massage, and to let Jane come and talk to her while she sipped it and ran through her letters. The girl would come in from an early ride, plunge into a cold bath, and all aglow and smelling of soap and youth would run to her mother's wonderful scented bedroom where, draped in her dressing-gown, she would stretch herself out on a chaise-longue; and Izzy, under her lace coverlet, enjoying the sensation of her willowy figure rubbed down once more to smooth well-being, would encourage Jane to talk. It was her hour for getting together the data that she would hand on later in the day to Philibert.

Jane would say—"Our little Marquis was riding this morning. He joined me. His eyes looked puffy. They had funny little pouches under them." And Mrs. Carpenter, who, with a languid finger turning the page of a letter, had pricked up her ears, would sigh inwardly and say aloud—

"The poor man must be tired. He has so many demands on him." And then secretly irritated but maintaining a bland countenance, she would listen to the girl telling how she had given her would-be suitor a lesson in riding.

"You know, Mummy, he was really hurting that horse's mouth dreadfully, and he didn't seem to be sorry when I showed him. Do you think he is just a tiny bit cruel?"

And again Izzy would reply mildly, in defense of the absent one—"My darling, I know him to be the kindest man in the world."

But Jane did not always by any means show interest in the Marquis de Joigny, and much as it annoyed Mrs. Carpenter to hear him criticized, it disturbed her even more when he was not mentioned at all for days together. Jane would bring with her a letter from her Aunt Patty and read aloud long extracts about St. Mary's Plains and its tiresome doings, about

Patience's rheumatism and Patience's bird lectures, and Uncle Bradford's last new case, and the Mohican bank's new building on Pawamak Street, and Aunt Beth's housekeeping adventures in Seattle, until poor Izzy was bored to tears; or she would be full of the problems of Fan's life with her Polish husband. She saw Fan much more often than her mother could have wished. One day she said—"I don't think Fan is happy. I suppose it's because she has married a Roman Catholic. It doesn't seem to work very well, changing your religion." And Izzy in alarm scribbled a note of warning and sent it to Philibert by a special messenger. She usually wrote to him on the days she couldn't manage to see him. Somehow or other he must be kept every day, *au courant*. I can imagine these messages.

"The child's head is full of Fan and her wretched Pole, and the effect of religion on marriage. Don't for anything touch on the subject in talk. You had better keep away from churches when you take her out. She is disturbed by Fan's money troubles and Ivanoff's gambling. Don't for heaven's sake go near the Casino while we are here."

It would be comic if it were not something else. I see my elder brother perusing these missives with fervour and tossing them away with exasperated petulance.

Go near the Casino? Had he done so? Was he not the perfect nursemaid?

It was Fan who told me about all this afterwards. She had been in Paris three years before Jane, had got herself brought over by some chance acquaintances who had paid her passage across the Atlantic, and had allowed her to benefit by their loose indifferent chaperonage once she got here. It was all she needed. In six months she had married Ivanoff and knew everybody in Paris who from her point of view was worth knowing. Mrs. Carpenter had been civil to her, but not friendly. Nevertheless it was in Izzy's drawing room that she had met Ivanoff.

Ivanoff was one of Izzy's satellites. She was one of the people he lived on. He could expect to win twenty thousand francs from her at Bridge during a winter. Besides that she gave him many meals and introduced him to other people who could be fleeced for more substantial sums. We all knew Ivanoff. His title was supposed not to bear too much looking into, and his estates in Poland were not, I believe, to be found on the map of that country, but he was very presentable and was renowned for his success with women. Fan fell in love with him promptly. He was big, he was dark, his brown face with its mongolian cast of feature, slanting eyes and thick sleek black hair seemed to her beautiful, and she believed that he had a deep romantic soul. Moreover he was a prince and he was like wax in her hands. She could not and did not resist him. Her stepfather made her an allowance of twenty-five thousand francs a year and showed no interest in what she did with it. There was no one to enquire into Ivanoff's affairs or habits on Fan's behalf. She was alone in the world and must make her own way. Life with Ivanoff would be a continual stream of parties; Monte Carlo, Paris, Biarritz, Deauville. The prospect glittered before her. Where could she have a good time if not in these gay haunts of pleasure? The thought of going back to St. Mary's Plains made her feel sick.

She had been married a year or so when Jane joined her mother. Ivanoff was her slave. She could do anything with him except keep him from the gaming table. Her one worry was money, but she did not allow this to worry her much. Jane exasperated her that first summer. Fan felt herself much the wiser and years the older. Jane's lamblike devotion to her mother "gave her fits." And Jane seemed utterly indifferent to the enormous power of her money, she was too stupid, the way she let her mother and Philibert manage her. But Fan thought Philibert a great catch. She knew her Paris well enough to know that if Jane became Philibert's wife her position would be immense. So she didn't interfere, merely watched and laughed and thought Jane a fool not to see what Philibert was after.

October saw them all in Paris and Philibert not appreciably nearer his goal. Jane no longer ignored him, she now took him for granted, which was almost worse. He determined to be personal. It was not easy with Jane, but he must risk being thought impudent. One day he asked her what kind of a man she wanted to marry. She hesitated, thinking a moment. "A hero or a friend," she answered. But when he said that he hoped he was her friend she smiled, refusing to take him seriously. The word hero however, gave him his cue. He had too much sense to try and pose as one himself, but the thought occurred to him that perhaps by telling her of other heroes who had belonged to his family and his country, some of the glamour of the past would touch him with a reflected brilliance for those candid romantic eyes. And the task was not uncongenial to him. He had a gift for story-telling and could gossip endlessly about historic personages. Where history was meagre he could rely upon his imagination. He began with the lovely story of Bayard and Du Guesclin and she listened with glowing eyes as he talked of those chivalrous knights. He had found the key. It was easy now to hold her attention. There followed hours and days filled with legend and anecdote, tales of brave chivalry and quaint custom. *Philippe le Beau* and *Jeanne la Folle*, *Saint Louis*, *Henri IV*, *Clothilde de Joigny*, the saintly lady whose name was still honoured in the family, *Monseigneur de B— —* who had had his tongue cut out during the *Massacres de Septembre*; it was a rich field, and one where he knew his way about, and to supplement his talk he gave her little books of folklore and poetry, and songs of the Troubadours, the poems of

Ronsard, and found for her an old parchment copy in script of that charming anonymous ballad that begins "Gentils Galants de France."

And Jane, delighted, treated him with a new attentive kindness. He had gained her confidence and had touched her imagination, but there again his success seemed to end. He could get no further. It did not occur to her to ask why he took such pains to supply her eager mind with lovely legends. And so he fretted and fumed once more. I can imagine him wracking his brains for a solution. The problem would have presented itself to him with simple brutality. How rouse the girl's emotions without frightening her? He hit on a plan. Mrs. Carpenter took a box at the Opera. There under cover of the music Philibert whispered adroitly to romantic youth, told her on every note of the scale that she was young and wonderful, that life was full of magic mystery, that the throbbing of her heart was its response to the summons of love, and that some day a man would come to her and beg her to allow him to carry her up and out on the surging torrent of that inspiration into a heaven of pure delight.

It worked. Under the hypnotic influence of the orchestra with its disturbing rhythm and moving harmonies, ravished by the seeming beauty of those sentimental voices, soaring, floating, dropping deep to caress and moan and shiver, all unconscious of the mediocrity, the coarseness, the bold sensuality, her little being stirred, and her senses, waking slowly in their chaste prison responded to the appeal of the man behind her in the shadow, who took on a little the romantic look of the hero on the stage. She did not know what was happening to her. She would come out of the theatre in a daze and walk silently between her mother and Philibert to the carriage and sink back into her corner, her head throbbing, and through half-closed eyelids would gaze with confusion and fear and vague painful pleasure at the tall hat and white shirt-bosom of the man facing her in the intimate gloom, and as though the smoothly moving carriage were just another box for the continuation of the performance she would hear the same voice speaking to her that had mingled with all that music, and she would find it impossible to distinguish between her companion's reality and the magic charm of the glorious fiction.

One night when he left them at their door after an evening of this kind, she heard him say to her mother who had lingered behind—"C'était très réussi ce soir," and give a little dry laugh. She did not ask herself what he meant, but his tone struck her ear as discordant and she remembered it afterwards. It was one of the things that flashed up out of her memory when Philibert, some years later, wanting once and for all to answer her questions as to why he had married her, told her with his incomparable lucidity all about the way he and her mother had used her. He put it to her completely then, explaining to her the details of their method and summing it all up with the words—"At least half the credit was your Mamma's. Though she did not seem to be doing much she was working all the same like a galley-slave. Of course it was not her duty to make love to you, but it was she who prepared your mind for the seed I sowed in it, and it was she who kept me informed of your mental progress. I say mental; you know what I mean. Call it anything you like, but give full credit to your charming mother for what she did for you. She showed signs of positive genius."

Thus it was that they put their heads together, and after the successful experiment of the Opera evenings had run its course for a month, Jane's manner began to change. She no longer came rollicking into the room of a morning like a great roystering puppy. She no longer talked so much or so freely, and sometimes, heavy-eyed and pale, as if she had not slept well, she would lie silently on her back staring at the ceiling, and blush crimson when asked what her thoughts were. These facts were reported faithfully to Philibert of course, also the incidents of the morning, when Jane got up with a bound and placed herself abruptly before her mother's long mirror and cried with the accent of despair—"Am I always to be so ugly?"

But I imagine Mrs. Carpenter in telling Philibert did not finish the story. She had said to Jane—"No, my child, you can be considered a beauty if you want to. With that body your face doesn't matter. Men will admire you, never fear; in fact I know one that does already."

Jane at that had turned away from the glass and had come to the foot of her mother's bed and had said earnestly, with a flood of crimson mantling her face and throat—"But it's not a man's admiration I'm thinking of, mother dear, it's yours." The child had then become speechless and had gulped strangely with the effort not to break down and had given it up and gone quickly out of the room.

If Mrs. Carpenter was touched she did not say so, and she never referred to the incident in her subsequent talks with Jane, limiting her remarks on the girl's appearance to a voluble flow of worldly advice.

"Never go in for curls or ribbons or fluffiness. That's not your style. If you must look like a Chinese mummy then look it even more than you do. Make the most of your queerness. People won't know whether you are ugly or handsome, but they'll be bound to look at you. That's all that's necessary. Anything is better than being unnoticed. That you never will be. Nonsense, you must get used to being stared at. Most girls like it. Wear your hair straight back and close to your head. Never mind your lower lip. Don't make faces trying to draw it in. Stick it out rather. Carry your head high. Look as if you were proud of your profile. Your dresses should always be straight and stiff like an oblong box. That one you've got on is too soft, and there's too much trimming. You will be able to wear any amount of jewellery later, but never let yourself be tempted by lace. You walk well, and your back, thank God, is as flat as a board. You'll never need to wear corsets if you're careful, but you must learn what to do with your hands. You're always clenching your fists as if you were going to hit somebody. And I don't like those boys' pumps you wear; they're too round at the toe." And so on and so on. And Jane, rather bewildered, would try to make out from all this whether her mother herself liked the person she was giving advice to or not.

But in the end, in spite of all her cautiousness, Izzy was obliged to commit herself. Jane didn't let her off. On the contrary she went straight to her one evening with the proposal Philibert had made her. It was late and Mrs. Carpenter was sitting in front of her fire, wondering whether she had been right in leaving the two alone together for so long in the drawing room. She had never left them alone before. It had been Philibert's suggestion and she had agreed with some slight misgiving. It had occurred to her of a sudden that perhaps he would not have dared to make such a proposal to one of his own people, and she felt a flush of annoyance. Strange inconsistency on the part of a woman who had so thrown to the winds the spiritual decencies, but there you are; she was worried and mortified, and when Jane entered, turned to her with a warmer gesture than was her habit. The girl responded by kneeling at her side and winding her arms round the slim waist and saying—

"Do you really want me to do it, Mother dear?"

The question put in that way, suggesting as it did a keener insight on Jane's part into her mother's heart than had even been imagined by the latter, must have been startling. Mrs. Carpenter hesitated, hedged, was at a loss.

"What do you mean, child?"

But Jane was not to be put off.

"You know what I mean, Mummy darling. The question is, do you really want it? I told him that I would do what you said, and I mean it." And then rather quaintly she added—"I don't suppose Aunt Patty would approve of me. She likes independence. But I have made up my mind to do as you wish."

There it was. Mrs. Carpenter was forced into it. Jane, all unknowingly, had her. It was no use asking the girl if she liked him: she only said she felt she undoubtedly would if she made up her mind to, and so at last after some more hesitating Izzy was obliged to say—

"Well, darling, since you will have it so, I must tell you that your acceptance of this distinguished man would make me very happy." And Jane, still uncommunicative and by some marvellous instinct of profound youth hiding at last the tumultuous feelings of her heart, accepted her mother's decision sweetly and calmly and went away to her room.

If she saw there in her mirror, as we are told girls do on such occasions, a new strange creature, the difference was in her case less fictitious than most. A very rapid transformation does seem to have come over her after this. It was as if in accepting Philibert she had walked bravely up to him and had given him the secret key to her soul, and as if in turn he had thrown a handful of dust in her eyes. The effect of the interchange was instantaneous. Philibert had seemed to her in the beginning, an old man, excessively foreign and occasionally ridiculous; he was now a hero. I cannot explain the change. I only know that it was so. The mystery of her girlhood remains to me a mystery. Who am I to understand her love for my detestable brother? Who am I to understand the love of any innocent girl for any man? I only know that Jane's passion was derived from her own romantic nature and not from him. I have a feeling that had she once made up her mind to love an iron poker, she would have loved it with the same fire and the same ecstasy. At that period of her life the object of her affection was scarcely more real than a symbol. Philibert represented for her not himself but her dreams. It may be so with most young people. I do not know. But what Jane meant when she said to her mother that she was sure she would come to like him if she made up her mind to, was really that she knew she would adore him if with her mother's approval, she let herself go, i. e., let her imagination control her feelings. What she wanted from her mother was not only an indication but a guarantee. Her mother's consent to her marriage she took as a sign that she could gloriously give her heart its freedom.

And Jane's heart now that he had won it was a surprise to Philibert. He had gone a-hunting for a dove or some timid sparrow, and he found himself with an eagle on his hands. He was expected to soar with this young companion that he had captured. There was no hesitation about Jane. Spreading wide the wings of her beautiful belief, she flew, she was making for heaven.

Poor, wonderful, ignorant Jane. It was to her of a simplicity. Since she knew now, because her mother had said so, that he was worth marrying, then he was worthy of all her confidence. Shyly but bravely she told him so. She spoke to him of God, of life with him after death, of sharing with him all her thoughts. She unbared to him her ideals, confessed her dreams, faltered out her fear of her own wild impulses, recounting to him simply the affair of the boy in St. Mary's Plains she had almost killed. She told him all about the Grey House and her Aunt Patty and her grandmother's death and her Aunt Minnie's religious fanaticism. It is dreadful to think of. He has said that he was never so bored in his life. I have heard him say so, and of course he would have been. After a rubber or two at the Jockey, he would turn up at Izzy's flat for tea and find Jane waiting for him, her face charged with grave confident sweetness. She would put a hand on each of his shoulders and kiss his lips, and then drawing him to a sofa beside her would hold his hand in both of hers and pour out to him the secrets of her heart, and he, beside himself with boredom, would listen and make his responses to the clear chant of her young voice singing its joy.

"We will be everything to each other, Philibert."

"Yes, dear."

"We will share each other's thoughts."

"Of course."

"You will teach me how to love you."

"I will."

"And be worthy of you."

"My darling."

"Love is very wonderful, Philibert."

"Yes, dear."

"I feel one should be very much alone to understand. You and I alone. We must keep ourselves free to be alone together."

"Yes."

"Sometimes I am sorry that we have so much money."

"Why, my darling?"

"It will create obligations. We shall be expected to see so many people and do so many things. But I am glad to have it if you like it. I am proud to bring you something. I would give you everything in the world if I could. I am yours, and what I have is yours, to do with as you like. But you must never feel indebted to me, for there is no indebtedness. I can't quite explain what I mean, but it humiliates me even to think of giving between you and me. The money is ours, that is all, and therefore yours. You will control it and give me an allowance for dresses. I say this now because I don't want to speak of it again. You understand, don't you, Philibert? Let's not talk of it any more, ever."

Such was her attitude, such was her idea, and all he had to do was to let himself be loved.

But I don't like to think about Philibert in his relation to Jane. I wish I could leave him out of the story altogether.

In the meantime Mrs. Carpenter, while highly gratified that her plans had worked out so well, was nevertheless a little taken aback at the extravagant turn they were taking. She may well have been more then a little worried at Jane's going ahead at such a pace. There was no comfort for Izzy now in conferring with Philibert. The shape of the triangle had changed. The coveted man had drawn away from her and was as close now to her daughter as he had once been to her. She found herself no longer the strong base that held them together. They could exist now without her. And Philibert began very delicately to make her feel this. His manner conveyed—"You have done your part, and very well on the whole, but still you know it's finished. You're really no use to me now. I shan't of course go back on my bargain. You shall have your share of the fun. Only don't bother me by continually making mysterious signs. You will only succeed in awakening her suspicions and wearing out my patience."

Poor Jane, it would have taken more than her mother's irritable gaiety to rouse her suspicions. If any one in those days had come to her with a full recital of the truth, she would not have believed a word of it. And when her Uncle Bradford did come in his capacity of trustee to have a look at the fiancé, she flew into a rage with the good man at the first sign of his disapproval. I did not see Bradford Forbes. I never saw him. Jane tells me that he was a large heavy man with a strong American accent, a rosy face and a pince-nez. I should like to have seen him. I should like to have seen the image of Philibert reflected in those eyeglasses. The sight would have been edifying.

Mr. Forbes had said to Jane—"Well, I don't think much of your little Dude. I'd rather you had taken some one more your own size. I guess he can't come much higher than your shoulder." And Jane had flown at him like a wild cat and had told him that he had no business to make fun of her lover, who was the most important man in Paris and a million times cleverer than anybody from their home town. If her Uncle Bradford had had any hope of dissuading her from the step she was about to take he seems to have abandoned it then and there. He could find out nothing positively wrong with the head of the house of Joigny. The little Marquis proved satisfactorily that though his income was pitiful he had no debts. And when Mr. Forbes pointed out to him that there could be nothing in the way of a marriage settlement, Silas Carpenter's will making such an alienation of property impossible, Philibert had taken his breath away by the graceful ease with which he accepted the situation. How was the kind shrewd American citizen to know that Philibert already had the will by heart, and long ago had accepted the inconvenience and risk of hanging on to his wife's property by hanging on to her? He made a better impression in their hour's talk than Jane's uncle wanted to admit to himself. The good man was obliged to fade away as he had come, and float off like some wistful porpoise across the Atlantic leaving behind him only light ephemeral bubbles of amused disapproval. All the same he had done enough to make Jane very angry and obstinate and produce from her hand a long letter to her Aunt Patty in which she inveighed against the obtuse narrow-mindedness of the entire American nation. Patience Forbes seems not to have answered this letter. She had sent Jane a note by her uncle of terse affection and grim good wishes, but her correspondence with her niece during the months preceding and following the marriage almost entirely ceased. I imagine that after listening to her brother's account of the man in Paris who was to claim her Jane, she was filled with foreboding, and being powerless chose to remain silent. And Jane was too happy to wonder why her aunt did not write to her. She did not often think of the Grey House during those days.

VII

My family, as I think I have already mentioned, had a way of doing disagreeable things gracefully. They could even when necessary carry off affairs disagreeable to themselves with every appearance of special pleasure. When Philibert asked my mother to gather together the clan, all the uncles and aunts and cousins on my mother's side and my father's, so that he might present to them his fiancée, my mother apparently felt obliged to meet his wishes, not quite understanding the need for so much fuss, suspecting perhaps the truth that the ceremony was a concession to that tiresome Mrs. Carpenter, yet determining once she had decided to do it, to do it nicely. Our relations in their turn recognized with the best possible grace the obligation she gently laid upon them in a series of little plaintive invitations to tea, and turned up smiling. Their smiles were various, there was plenty of variety in the family: we went in for cultivating our personalities; but there was nevertheless in the light of their expressive countenances a pleasant family resemblance, the stamp of a kinship that was cherished and valued. They all conveyed that it was for them at any time and without ulterior purpose an honour and a pleasure to be received by my mother, and that, however important the present occasion might be, the agreeable importance lay for them much more in finding her well than in meeting a stranger, her prospective daughter-in-law.

My mother, in marrying my father, had married a second cousin, so that the two sides of the family were representative of but one after all, and if within our own circle we admitted that the Joignys had in the last half century shown a more progressive spirit, had taken a more active interest in the affairs of the Republic, and had rubbed shoulders more freely with industrials and politicians than had the Mirecourts, the resulting difference felt was so slight, the nuance of manner and bearing so delicate, as to pass unperceived by the outer circle of society. We did not criticize each other. Some of the Joignys had made money, and one or two had married it. My father had been a royalist deputy, my Uncle Bertrand had been a Senator; on the other hand the Mirecourts had had an occasional relapse into the army and numbered even now a couple of cavalry officers. If there was among us a tacit understanding that the only thing worthy of us was to do nothing for the government we detested, we never said so, and never blamed any one of our members for succumbing to the temptation of seeking an occupation. We were privileged people who could afford to amuse ourselves with modern affairs if it so pleased us, and at the expense of society if this took our fancy. Our philosophy was vaguely speaking to live as we had always lived under the Kings of France, and yet to keep intellectually very much abreast of the times. We had an abundance of ideas about everything. Modernism in art did not displease the younger members. On the contrary it was one of our characteristics to keep our old customs and discover at the same time new movements in music, painting and literature. We considered ourselves not in the least musty or moth-eaten. On the afternoon that I speak of we produced an effect the reverse of dingy or dreary, an effect of subdued brightness, of sprightly gentleness of unmodish elegance. We looked and were sure of ourselves. Republican France beyond our doors did not disturb us. We knew that we were clever enough to get the best of it for another generation or two anyway. We had clung to our lands, our forests and our meadows. We would cling to them still. We trusted to our wits to preserve us from the clumsy clutch of democracy. In the pleasant sanctuary of our family mansion we made fun of the outside world.

My mother, looking very nice with a black lace scarf round her shoulders and her dark hair arranged in an elaborate pattern of close little waves and puffs, received the homage of my aunts, uncles and cousins with wistful vivacity, asking them all with little gusts of enthusiasm about their affairs, and then tenderly sighing as if to convey to them how sympathetic was her appreciation of all their rich activities, in which she asked their indulgence for playing so passive a part. It was the last occasion in which she was to receive in the house that had been already sold to allow Philibert to marry the girl who was to be on view that day, but my mother gave no sign of appreciating any irony or any sadness in the situation. If the little gathering represented for her a trial of some cruelty, she kept her sense of this perfectly disguised. With her boxes actually packed and her new modest apartment already cleansed and garnished preparatory to her arrival, she sat calmly and sweetly by the little wood fire at the end of the long suite of drearily august salons where she had known so many seasons of secluded temperate grandeur, holding a small embroidered screen between her face and the modest blaze of crackling birch logs. It was a cold November day. The rooms that had been thrown open were chilly. Not magnificent in size or in richness, but sparsely furnished, they were sufficiently vast to seem with their fifty odd occupants comparatively empty, and presented to the eye polished vistas of waxed parquet, bland expanses of delicate panelling and high, dimly gilded cornices that were multiplied in numerous long mirrors. The rooms, as I say, were cold, and they looked cold. The dull day was darkening rapidly beyond the long windows. The lighted candles on the chimney-pieces left about them wide vague pools of shadow and made pockets of gloom behind important pieces of furniture.

I remember feeling, while we waited for Jane, how beautifully all my relatives were behaving. There was in their modulated gaiety an absolute denial of discomfort or curiosity or suspense. Their gestures, their chatter, their light laughter, expressed a perfect oblivion of the lowness of the temperature round them, or the imminence of an ordeal for my mother, or the general consciousness that Philibert had done something unusual and was about to ask for their approval. They had put on frock-coats, some of them, and others had put on silk dresses, but their way of greeting each other signified that any little extra effort of toilet was made simply out of courtesy to the family. I remember thinking, as I observed them, that there was perhaps no other family in France that took so much pains to be pleasant within its own circle, and that really on the whole we succeeded very well. It came to me too, looking at *Tante* Clothilde, *Tante* Belle and *Tante* Alice, and *Oncle* Louis and old Stanislas and Jean and Paul and Sigismond, that it was comparatively easy for us because we were gifted. Yes, I admitted, we were certainly gifted. We understood music and some of us were very passable musicians ourselves; and then there was *Tante* Suze who had translated Keats into French, and saintly *Tante* Alice who restored Cathedrals and Jean who wrote plays and Sigismond who did bacteriological research. Our gifts and our occupations, quite apart from our amusements, gave us plenty to talk about. Actually it was not a charming make-believe; we did enjoy meeting. And of all this give and take of affectionate recognition, Claire my sister was the centre. The aunts and uncles and cousins adored Claire. She was the perfect product of their blood, and they understood her, and loving her they appreciated themselves and were conscious of the solidarity of their indestructible social unity. She meant even more to them than my mother because she was young, and since her unfortunate marriage she had for them the added charm of a martyr. If they had ever been willing to criticize my mother they would have blamed her for giving her daughter to such a man as my brother-in-law. There was not a man in the room who did not dislike him and who would not have taken up the cudgels for Claire at the slightest sign of her finger. The unpopular outsider was not there. He had perhaps understood that he was expected to stay away. Even an automobile merchant can be made to feel when he is not wanted. The poor brute's skin was perhaps not as thick as they thought. No one, however, remarked on his absence. No one asked after him or mentioned his name. Had he behaved as he had been expected to behave, and had Claire wished it, they would have been kind to him, but he had made one or two mistakes, and Claire had shown no signs of wanting them to take him into their circle.

He had taken her away to Neuilly, had almost literally locked her up there, and had offered to lend several of them money, at a high rate of interest. Also he had asked Bianca's father, (who was there by the way that day, though Bianca was not), to get him into the Jockey Club. It had been impossible not to snub him. They all felt very sorry for Claire.

Philibert's affairs were different. A man need never be the slave of his *ménage*. Philibert they knew could quite well look after himself. They had heard that the fortune of the young American was gigantic. Philibert would know beautifully how to spend millions, they said to themselves. That was one of the things that we, as a family, had always known how to do. They admitted willingly that Philibert was in his way eminently worthy of themselves. His faults were in keeping with their traditions; he had never made any of them blush. They trusted he was not about to do so now. They hoped the young American girl would not be too impossible. Some Americans whom they knew were charming, but it was not always the richest who were the nicest. Alas, one could not have everything. They would be kind to the child, however awful she might be. It was always worth while being kind, and besides did one really know how to be anything else to a woman? Had one, as a matter of fact, any bad manners tucked away anywhere to bring out on any occasion?

But of course, none of this appeared in their conversation, and as I say, no one could have detected in their manner any sign of curiosity or nervousness. And when at last the butler announced at the far end of the *Grand Salon* "Madame Carpenter et Mademoiselle Carpenter," it was with a scarcely perceptible shifting of positions and straightening of attention that they made a kind of circle extending out on either side of my mother, who rose from her chair by the fire in the inner apartment and advanced two steps towards the distant figures that appeared in the far doorway of the outer room.

I recognized Jane at once as the girl who has walked down my street, my cossack princess, my wild crowned creature of the steppes. She had a long way to go and she came on slowly and smoothly, with a lightness in her gait that had about it a certain grandeur and a dignity that seemed at the same time somehow rather shy and timid. She reminded me of some nervous creature who was accustomed to traversing vast tracks of open country and who might be frightened away by the stir of a twig. I saw in another moment that she was not frightened. She gave my mother the slightest and most correct of courtseys, and then stood quite still while her own mother talked to the lady who had so persistently and gently snubbed her. It was, however, to strike me very soon as one of the interesting things about Jane that, although she was not frightened when she first came in, she was beginning to feel so ten minutes later. I put this down as the first proof she gave me of being intelligent.

Mrs. Carpenter may have drained from that hour in our paternal mansion some deep draught of pleasure; I do not know. It is possible that she regarded her entry into our chilly drawing room as a social triumph; if so she betrayed no such feeling. She, too, as well as my mother, was capable of elegant dissimulation. Her rich black figure, marvellously moulded into its lustrous garment, was of a dignity that surpassed everything that quite put my gentle mother in the shade. I can imagine her full, bright consciousness of this. There was something in the poise of her high modish grey head that expressed astonishment as she shook hands with her little hostess. It was as if she marvelled that so unimpressive a woman, with really no pretensions at all to a figure, should hold such sway in the world. A good many of the others she knew. Some had eaten from her golden plates, others had left cards but not eaten, a few had invited her to "evenings." She greeted them with an easy security of manner that was quite sufficiently a match for their own shriller effusiveness. If they were not inordinately pleased, well they seemed so, and if she was, then she did not show it. The comedy was well played by both sides.

She had dressed her daughter rather cleverly for the occasion. Jane had on a straight close-fitting costume of some mouse-grey material that had the texture of a suede glove. As I remember it, it was cut like a Russian jacket, trimmed with bands of grey fur, and topped by a close grey fur hat with a green cockade that matched her eyes. That was all; the dress was warm and plain, well adapted to the weather and to the girl's age, and gave her no look of wealth. The most it did was to set off with severe modesty the splendid proportions of her strong young body.

What I think we all felt when Jane entered was the warmth and vitality of her youth. She was so very much more alive than all the rest of us that we could not help noticing it. We felt cold and dry beside her, and rather small. We were literally, almost all of us, smaller than she was. This was disconcerting: I caught actually on my mother's face after the first presentation had taken place an almost comic expression, and could not make out what she was after as she looked quickly from one to the other, until I discovered that she was simply looking for some one to put next the girl who was tall enough to look well beside her. My mother had an eye for *tableaux vivants*; she did not like to see a woman towering above men. Not finding any one she was reduced to sitting down herself, and motioning the great long child to a stool at her knee. It was then that I realized Jane was growing frightened, and was struck by the keenness of her perceptions. There was nothing obvious to frighten her, and yet there was something in the air for a fine sensitive nostril to sniff at in alarm if it were fine enough; just the faintest whiff of antagonism, an antagonism tempered and mingled with curiosity, surprise and humour.

My family saw possibilities in Jane. Of that I became growingly conscious. It was evident in the way they eyed her with rapid sidelong glances, appraising tilts of the head, steps to the side to get a closer or different view, and in their murmured undertones. They did not discuss her then and there, they did not whisper, they were not rude, God forbid, but they showed that they were struck. She engaged their attention and was more of a person than they had bargained for. They looked from her to her mother and back again with lifted eyebrows. They were surprised to find that Mrs. Carpenter had such a daughter. It was clear to them that something could be made out of Jane.

The girl sat on her low seat quite still, one hand in her lap, the other hanging down by her side, and while she answered my mother's questions, shot an occasional clear glance from under her eyebrows at the people around her. I saw that she was nervous, but not too nervous to take in a great deal. I was impressed by the amount she did seem to take in.

Philibert all this time hung off in a corner and watched her. She never once looked at him. She seemed determined not to do so. If he were putting her to some sort of a test she was obviously going to go through the ordeal without an appeal for aid. It was a fine performance; unfortunately no one but myself appeared to appreciate it.

Her nervousness evidently had something to do with her deep desire to please, and her increasing realization that these relations of Philibert's were not people easily pleased with anything or any one. She felt that she was the object of a finer scrutiny than she had ever before undergone. Her eyes searched rapidly one face then another, and veiled themselves again under lowered lids. The one thing that might have consoled her in her sense of their superlative fastidiousness was, however, just the thing that she could not divine. She didn't know that they none of them cared a fig for pretty doll faces and found her ugly strangeness a very good substitute. It had not yet dawned on her, in spite of her mother's preaching, that her countenance was just the sort of thing that would have worth for sophisticated people.

I don't remember just how long this part of the show lasted, or just how Philibert suddenly changed its character and made the whole thing seem like a circus performance with himself as ringmaster and his fiancée as the high-stepper whom he was showing off to the spectators, but that is nevertheless what happened.

I had taken a long look at my brother that day. It had come to me, watching the attention and respect with which my august uncles treated him, that perhaps I had never done him justice. It was obvious that they liked him and that he not only amused them vastly, but imposed himself on them. He had talked to them with even more than his usual brilliance, and all Paris knows what that means, and I had listened to his talk marvelling at the power of words. Paris can never resist words; France succumbs inevitably to talk. No one, I was forced to admit, was such a talker as Philibert. Like a consummate juggler keeping half a dozen ivory balls in the air, he played with ideas and phrases. Gaily he tossed up epigrams and paradoxes, let fly a challenge, caught it with a counter-challenge, argued two sides of a question, flung wide a generality, chopped it into bits in a second, was serious for two minutes, mimicked a public character, gave a sketch of the political situation, recounted a recent scandal. The faces of his auditors were a study. They were the faces of delighted spectators at a play. Positively I expected them now and then to applaud. My Aunt Suze was wiping her eyes, weeping with laughter. Uncle Louis was waving his handkerchief excitedly and ejaculating *"Parfaitement, parfaitement. Je vois cela d'ici."* Bianca's father, his rubicund face wrinkled into a masque of comedy, was watching out of the corner of his sporting eye and muttering affectionately—*"Ah, le coquin, ah quel comédien."* And my dear little mother from her place by the fire was smiling shyly over her fire screen, her eyes filled with gentle adoration.

I have heard women rave about the fineness of Philibert's features, the nobility of his nose, which was certainly a good and generous example of our high type, signs of the race in the drawing of his head. I suppose it is true that he had something special about his head. It was the same head after all that had hung on our walls for generations, capped by Cardinals' bonnets and courtiers' wigs. Nevertheless, when he called to Jane he looked suddenly like a ringmaster in a circus. With his little waxed moustache and his little perky coat-tails and his lightly gesturing hand positively creating in space the image and sound of a delicate long-lashed whip, he put Jane through her paces. He had her beautifully trained. He had done it all in a month. She was perfectly in hand.

At the sound of his voice she had sprung to her feet. Yes, it was a spring, quite sufficiently quick to startle my mother. Ha, but that was a mistake at the very beginning. She was made to turn and mutely apologize. Whist! she obeyed the sign and crossed to the venerable and monstrous Aunt Clothilde who sat like a large brown Buddha by the window. "A lower curtsey this time and kiss the plump old hand. Step backward now and smile at these gentlemen. Hold up your head. Right about turn, straight across the ring.

Not too fast—proudly do it—show them how you can walk. Aha, what made you do that? No stumbling, mind you. High-steppers don't look at their feet. Flip—just a flick of the lash to put more life into you."

I watched fascinated. I watched till I could bear it no longer. I said to Claire—"Lead the way into the dining-room. Tea's been ready this hour." And Claire went forward gracefully and put an arm through the trembling creature's and led her away from her master; but I saw the girl's eyes ask for leave, and I saw him condescendingly grant it. By the tea-table I joined her, and heard the rattle of the cup in her hand against the saucer. She greeted me with a smile of extreme youthfulness that tried to conceal nothing. Looking down at me timidly from her splendid height, her pale countenance made me the frankest fullest confession and asked wistfully for help, and seemed presently to find relief.

"Philibert did not tell me there were so many of you," she said quaintly in French.

"We are all here, every one of us," I rejoined. "We rushed to welcome you."

She accepted this in silence, and I saw her gaze travel across to my sister who stood in the window, and rest there with vivid interest.

"You admire my sister?" I asked in English.

"Immensely. I hope she will like me. If only she did I wouldn't mind."

"The others? But they all will."

"Do you think so?"

"I am sure of it."

She sighed and looked at me gravely. She seemed to be thinking deeply, and she seemed very very young.

"There are so many differences," she said after a moment's hesitation.

"Not so many as you imagine," I protested.

"I don't always understand what they mean," and then with a quick lighting up of her expression—"You will interpret."

"But you speak very excellent French," I again objected.

"Ah, it wasn't the language I meant," was the reply that came from those grave parted lips.

Philibert at that moment approached and laid a finger on my shoulder. His words, however, were not addressed to me.

"Don't you think," he said lightly, "that such an absorbing tête-à-tête might be postponed to another day? It's not very polite to your elders."

I saw the poor girl quiver. I saw the slow flood of crimson mantle her face and forehead and flush to the tips of her ears. I saw her stare at my brother humbly, and then I watched her slink off at his side, like a great dog that he led by a chain and to whom he had given a whipping. The sight filled me with disgusting pain. I turned on my heel and joined Claire in her window.

"A pretty sight, isn't it?" I spluttered.

"But, *mon cher*, she adores him."

"Just so."

My sister eyed me a little strangely.

"You don't like that?" she asked.

"Do you?" I retorted.

She shrugged her shoulders and gave a little laugh. "Of course it would be still nicer," she mocked lightly, "if he adored her as well. But what will you? Such is life?"

I felt how hopeless it was. I had a foretaste of how my sympathy for Jane was to isolate me.

"She admires you any way extravagantly," I persisted with petulance. Claire only laughed.

"I should think she would do everything extravagantly," was her reply as she floated away.

"Do be a little kind to the child," I cried out after her, and she just nodded at me over her shoulder. How charming her face was seen thus, framed in her dark drooping hat and black furs, the slender glowing olive oval, the sombre eyes, the lovely teeth, how charming, how teasing, how elusive; and her slim figure with its trailing draperies, how easily it slipped away from all effort, all responsibility.

Jane was gone when I re-entered the drawing room. I gathered that she had made a favourable impression. Aunts and uncles and cousins were taking leave of my mother with phrases of congratulation.

"*Elle est charmante.*"

"*Une taille superbe.*"

"Philibert will dress her beautifully."

"So young, so healthy."

"Such nice manners."

"And how she adores him, it's quite touching."

"Fifi always was lucky."

The masculine element was almost vociferous.

"*Sapristi*, an enormous fortune, and a fine young creature like that."

One by one they bowed over my mother's hand, and went away. My mother looked very tired. She motioned me to remain. Claire hung over her tenderly.

"*Pauvre petite mère*," she said, kissing the top of her head. "You must go straight to bed. All these emotions have been too much for you. I will come in the morning to see to the packing of the last things. Don't stir. Just stay quiet. All the same, it's too bad, her turning you out of your own house."

I said nothing. Something warned me not to take up Jane's defence just then, and I, too, felt sorry for my mother. When we were alone, she laid her head against the back of the chair and closed her eyes. Presently, however, without opening them she spoke with surprising energy.

"I have had to promise to dine with that woman," was what she said.

VIII

Jane had made no impression on my mother. Mrs. Carpenter had made too much of one. She had deflected my mother's attention from Jane to herself and this, with unfortunate consequences. Mrs. Carpenter affected my mother like a loud and unpleasant noise, and my mother hated noises more than anything in the world. I am not trying to be witty. I mean this literally. I have seen my mother grow pale with a sort of nervous nausea and close her eyes in a desperate effort to control the faintness that came over her at the sound of a harsh ugly voice raised in anger. There was something about Mrs. Carpenter that set her nerves on edge in the same way. Her metallic jingling clothes, her loose easy swagger, her wiry grey curls, her humorous rolling eye, made up an *ensemble* that though to most people not seemingly at all "loud" gave my mother sensations of clashing and clanging. When she was about it was impossible for *Maman* to think of or listen to any one else. All the effort of her hypersensitive nervous organism was concentrated on just simply bearing her, and she was obliged now to bear her often and for hours at a time. Mrs. Carpenter didn't let her off. She had wanted to know my mother; she knew her now and she made the most of her.

During the weeks that preceded the wedding, Izzy was incessantly with my mother. She was in the highest of gay good humours. A big fashionable wedding to prepare for, she was in her element. Having achieved her ambition she professed to take it all as a joke. She treated the approaching marriage of her daughter as a great lark and wanted my mother to have her share of the fun. She consulted her about everything, submitted lists and samples of engraved invitations, dragged her to dressmakers who were preparing the trousseau and made her come and help open presents. I have a picture of my mother in a corner of Mrs. Carpenter's drawing room, limp and pale in her black clothes, submerged in cardboard and tissue paper, while the indefatigable Izzy on her knees in the middle of the floor held up one object after another and gave vent to shouts of indiscriminate rapture or groans of unenlightened contempt. Poor, dreadful Izzy. She had such definite ideas about things. Her ignorance was confident and documented. She had priced every marble and bronze in Paris. No jeweller's shop held any secrets for her. She was a connoisseur in lace. But the little tarnished faded treasures sent by some of our relatives to Philibert's bride belonged to no such category, and were viewed with bewildered disdain. Antique furniture had never been seen in her own apartment, but she knew that cracked lacquer and tarnished gilding was respectable in tables and chairs. Beyond that she could not go. Her instinct had stood in the way of her desire to learn. She clung irresistibly to baubles and coveted with passion the massive silver tea service sent by Aunt Clo. I know that Aunt Clo hesitated between this and an exquisite Ingres drawing. I remember Izzy weighing the monstrous kettle in her hands, her face a study of shrewd gloating apprisal and her knee planted firmly on the face of a poor little Louis XV doll that had come from Aunt Marianne's cabinet of XVIII century toys.

It was unfortunate that my mother was forced to assist at these séances, and that Jane herself was so often absent trying on clothes. The absence of the one and the ignorance of the other were proofs to my mother that neither knew how to behave. She judged Izzy as if she were a Frenchwoman and supposed that because the noisy creature did not know a treasure of art when she saw it that she most probably put her knife in her mouth. And so during those days that would have exhausted a much more robust woman than my mother, Izzy did, I believe, at the very beginning of Jane's life with us, use up all the vitality that *Maman* could dispose of on behalf of Philibert's American family.

The dinner she was obliged to attend for which Mrs. Carpenter had collected two ambassadors and a slangy Duchess was the last straw. My mother had never been to such a dinner in her life, and I confess to a complete sympathy with her when she gasped out afterwards that it was incredible that she should have been preserved from such ordeals throughout her youth when she had enough energy to bear them, only to be subjected to them in her old age when she hadn't. That dinner, with its ten courses, was the funeral feast of a relationship not yet born, but that might truly have come into being and flowered to full sweetness between the grave awkward girl in the straight white frock, and the little quivering lady whose twitching eyebrows and frightened hurried glances alone testified to her acute agony of soul. Poor *Maman*, poor Jane, poor Izzy. I was there. I saw, and I did not realize the full meaning. I did not realize how lasting the effect would be. I was on the contrary absurdly reassured because of Jane herself. I saw in her silence, her gravity, her perfect timid deference to my mother, a promise of future felicity. I gathered that she would never be guilty of publicly blushing for her own parent, but that she would and did appreciate mine. I was right in this, but I was wrong in believing that my mother would appreciate in her turn the tender tribute. I reckoned without her nerves, her weariness, her discouraged sense of being victimized and exposed, all the accumulations of her years of abhorrence of the thing that was now thrust upon her. She had complained so little that I had failed to understand how deeply humiliating to her were the circumstances of her son's marriage. She considered it indisputably a *mésalliance,* and yet she was forced to appear to rejoice in it with indecent exhibitions of familiarity. Mrs. Carpenter not only had disregarded her request for a little family gathering but had evidently succumbed to the desire to show her to just those people who, not having yet seen her, would especially relish the sight. "Just as if, *mon cher,*" my mother wailed afterwards, "I were anything to look at. Fancy wanting to show me, a skimpy bundle of black clothes." She had done violence to herself in going to that dreadful apartment in the Avenue du Bois, and the effort was too much for her. The place was too much for her. She never forgot it and, I believe she never looked at Jane without remembering those golden plates, those loud nasal voices, those large glasses full of crushed ice and green peppermint, those horrid scraping fiddles. To my mother such an evening was a souvenir to last her the rest of her days. The most she could do after that was not actively to dislike her daughter-in-law, and she seemed to achieve this by cultivating in all that concerned that young person a consistent vagueness. When people talked of Jane she only half listened and answered irrelevantly. Her phrase was always the same—"*Mais oui, elle est si gentille.*" When Jane herself was there she would look absent-mindedly beyond her and put her phrase in another form and murmur—"*Comme vous êtes gentille.*" Jane could never get any further than that. It constituted a barrier, graceful and light as gossamer, impenetrable as steel armour. All the girl's longing to be loved and to please, all her naïve attentions, all her thoughtful plans for the older woman's comfort, were met with the same sweet gentle vagueness. When she brought flowers, when she asked advice, when she put her motor at the other's disposal, when she asked her to come to her, it was always—"*Comme vous êtes gentille,*" followed by a little plaintive sigh that the girl gradually came to understand. Even when she worked out and carried through all on her own, a scheme for adding considerably to my mother's material ease, the formula was merely changed to "*Vous êtes vraiment trop gentille*" and finally when Jane's baby was born, and she believed that at last her mother-in-law would show some warmth of feeling, the words that greeted her when she opened her eyes and saw the latter leaning over the bassinet, were—"Comme elle est gentille," this time addressed to the slumbering infant.

I know that my mother tried to be kind to Jane, and I believe that she was never positively unkind, never at least during those first years of her marriage, but aside from the unpleasant pressure Mrs. Carpenter had brought upon her and that had given her a kind of chronic nervous depression in all that concerned Jane, there was also the fact that Jane was not the sort of person who would ever have appealed to her. My mother liked Bianca and had wanted her for a daughter-in-law; how then could she love Jane who was the antithesis of Bianca, and who by usurping Bianca's place, so my mother put it to herself, brought the contrast constantly to her mind? I have heard my mother say that she liked people to be more interesting than they looked, and found it amusing to be with people whom she was led on by some subtle provocative charm to discover. She recognized this charm in Bianca without ever discovering the sinister meaning of it, and she felt that Jane showed too much and therefore promised too little. Jane was too big and too striking to please her. She made, to my mother's eyes, too much of a display. My mother liked above everything "*mesure.*" Her favourite form of condemnation was to call a thing "*exagéré.*" What at bottom she cared most for in a person was their being "*comme il faut.*" I don't believe that she ever went so far as to consider her daughter-in-law vulgar, but there were things about her that she would have called "*outré.*" If she had ever allowed herself to depart from the vague affectionate affability that she preserved so consistently and so bafflingly, she would have said, (perhaps she did say something of the kind to Claire, I know they discussed Jane between them) that there was something almost shocking in a young woman with such an ugly face having such a beautiful figure. They, Claire and *Maman*, would have liked the ugliness of the face better if it had not been held so high on such splendid shoulders. They would have forgiven Jane her profile if it had not been for her really marvellous hands and feet. In the same way they would have known better how to deal with the whole striking physical being if it had not gone with such shyness and such humility. What they could not make out, and found it hard to put up with, were her incongruities. Such looks should aesthetically have been combined with audacity and hardness. Instead they found on their hands a poor quaking creature of a pathetic docility who seemed to present to them on her lovely palms an exposed and visibly pulsating heart, that they didn't know what to do with, didn't want to touch, were positively afraid of. It seems strange, but it was nevertheless true that Jane frightened them. Her need of them exposed there quite simply to their gaze, her simple, inarticulate but all too visible desire to love them and be loved, made them turn away in a kind of flurry that was partly delicacy and partly fear. There was an intensity about her that opened dangerous and wearying vistas of emotion which they wished at all costs to avoid. Claire said to me one day—

"Mother is afraid Jane will crush her, throw herself on her, I mean, literally, and hug and squeeze her, and she doesn't like physical contact of that sort, you know that."

Of course I knew. We all knew. From our earliest years we had always approached *Maman* as it were on tiptoe, delicately, as if she were made of some precious perishable stuff that would be broken at a rude touch. Our sense of this had been for us one of her subtlest charms. When she allowed us to kiss her we did so lightly and quietly. The touch of our lips on her hair or her soft worn cheek, was the fleeting pleasure of a winged instant, yet it was a pleasure; she had a way of conveying to it a quality, a fine quick elusive meaning. We never felt that we had been cheated, on the contrary, her kisses were rare and might have been deemed meagre, but they were beautiful. There was a grace in the way she laid her hand on one's arm and drew one down that was more than artistry; it conveyed a sense of something precious that had never been vulgarized by handling and mauling. I do not remember her ever folding any of us in her arms, and if my memory of her demonstrations is particularly acute because they were more often for Claire or for Philibert than for me, that only proves that I know what I mean and in no way diminished the beauty of what I was so often able to observe from my distance. The act of opening wide her arms would have been extraordinary in my mother. I never saw it. With Claire who was the person in the world to whom she was closest, I often noticed how delicate and restrained was her manner, and yet somehow with scarce any demonstrations of affection, they conveyed to each other an infinite tenderness. They were constantly together, they talked everything over. Claire had, I believe, no secrets from *Maman*. They depended on each other. Together they tasted the ineffable sweetness of almost perfect communion. And yet I never saw them cling together, I never surprised them in each other's arms. So strangely alike, so perfectly in harmony, they reminded me sometimes of characters on the stage, two figures in some graceful pantomime who had been drilled to make the same gestures in time to the same music and who moved always through the close articulate measure of their parts in perfect unison, tracing parallel patterns in the space round them, mysteriously united yet never touching and scarcely ever looking at each other.

Such an impression I sometimes had in the old days when I still lived in the bosom of the family, and now, as a kind of moral outcast, looking back I find even more in it than I did then. I see them not so much as actors who had learned a part, but almost as hypnotized beings who, whether they wished it or not, were bound to move and act and speak in a certain way. What it all comes to, I suppose, is that they were the fine perfect products of a system that held their individualities chained. So perfectly representative of their class, of their race, of the discriminative intolerant idea of their forebears, as to have been born with a complete set of gestures and prejudices and preferences and vocal intonations all ready for them, existing in them regardless of their own volition. I see them as the slaves of a hyper-sensitive, super-subtle inheritance, and I understand that with them many things were more truly impossible than with most people. It was impossible for them to make an ugly abrupt movement. The strong occult force of their breeding controlled their limbs and gave them a kind of grace that if one watched carefully was reminiscent of heavy powdered wigs and unwieldy panniers. It was impossible for them to mingle in crowds or walk along the street or take an interest in public affairs. It was impossible for them to look at the public without scorn or subject themselves to the physical contact of poor people in crowded trains. Instinctively they manœuvred to hide themselves from the eyes of the public. It was really as if they had lived under another régime and could not quite realize this one.

How could I not understand what Claire meant when she said that *Maman* was afraid that Jane would crush her? Jane was no reincarnation of some spoiled beauty of another century. If she represented any one but her glorious healthy self, it was more likely a Red Indian princess or a blond Norse amazon. Jane had not learned in a previous existence how to conceal one set of feelings and delicately convey another. She did not even know that such feats were expected of her. She would learn, but it would take time. For the moment she was just obviously what she seemed, a brave ardent young thing, capable of all sorts of mistakes. She would come in with her long beautiful stride and tower over my mother and sweep down to her; to Claire it seemed like swooping not sweeping, and my mother would huddle in her chair and struggle against the inclination to shut her eyes, and then the confused, intimidated, glowing creature in the marvellous clothes of Philibert's designing, would sit dumbly, wistfully, waiting and wanting something, anything in the way of a crumb of comfort; would watch for any sign of unstudied natural joy at her presence and would accept in its place the pleasant flow of my mother's vague affability, and would go away humbly, to come back the next day with an offering, flowers or a book or some precious little gift, and always my mother would say—"*Comme vous êtes gentille.*"

And besides all this the things that Jane and Philibert did were not calculated to amuse my mother in the least. She had never cared about public shows, and had always considered the fine art of entertaining to exist in the number of people one eliminated. Philibert's enormous parties, his balls, his dinners of a hundred couples, his fantastic "*Fêtes Champêtres,*" dismayed her. She thought they were Jane's parties. It was Jane whom she held responsible for all that was spectacular in the brilliant existence of her son; it was Jane she blamed for the phenomenal marble Paris mansion. It would have been impossible to have explained to her that Jane had scarcely glanced at the plans of the house when Philibert presented them to her.

She refused to go to any of their parties. Her dislike of magnificence was a part of her deep absolute view of what was *"comme il faut."* Magnificence was suitable to crowned heads, and though she would not have admitted that anything was too good for her son, she did not like to see him playing at being a king, and perhaps because all her life she had cherished a loyal personal sentiment for the destitute Orleans family, taking their political mourning for her own, it filled her with horror to find her son surrounded by all the trappings of an actor monarch and scattering largesse to the rabble, in a way her impoverished, unrecognized, exiled sovereign could not do. His enormous house, which she persisted in believing to be Jane's, depressed her. The really phenomenal harmony of its richness escaped her. The regal vistas of its apartments, all warmed and glowing and made by her son's consummate artistry habitable left her cold. The fine tapestries, the riot of blended colour, the audacious effects of light and shadow, the profusion of precious lustrous silks and gleaming brocades, wearied her gaze. Knowing well enough, who better, good things when she saw them, there were here too many to look at. I have pathetic memories of her shrunken black figure tripping through those immense chambers on Philibert's arm. I see her pass with little pattering steps across the endless expanse of polished floor, her lorgnon to her eyes, her head turning this way and that with quick bird-like movements, pretending to look at everything while refusing to see anything at all. The size of the place oppressed her and made her suspicious. She could not believe that such enormous rooms could be full of fine little treasures. Her experience told her that fine pieces were rare and were kept under glass, and were not to be bought, save at a price. Even Jane's fortune, which she had been so often made to feel was too much for good taste, could not in her opinion have filled that house with genuine things. Her son had been led astray. He was guilty of imitation. If he took her straight up to a gem of a cabinet and made her scrutinize it, well, she admitted its existence, but what was one cabinet in a room where there were twenty? She was in her way incorrigible. She did not believe in miracles, and while the rest of Paris was gaping it only made her feel dreadfully tired to be so put upon. That was her real feeling about the gigantic mansion. It made her feel tired. She was obliged to take the grand staircase slowly and stop on each landing. With her hand on the polished marble balustrade she toiled up it panting, gently catching her breath in the presence of mocking marble fauns and disdainful goddesses. Dear little fragile figure, growing smaller and more bent with time in her unmodish garments and simple black bonnet, fine proud gentle lady, I believe in the bottom of her heart she was sometimes afraid one of the army of constantly changing footmen would mistake her identity and show her to the housekeeper's room. It was the sort of thing she would have taken as a horrid joke with a dreadful moral.

I find that I am taking a vast deal of trouble and time in explaining my own family, and seem to be getting absolutely no nearer my goal, that is the heart of Jane's own problem. And yet I am sure it was all a part of it. In going into my mother's feelings in such detail, I do so because of what happened later, and I sometimes wonder whether perhaps my mother foresaw what was going to happen and knowing whichever way it turned out that she was going to take Philibert's part, made up her mind at the outset that it would all be much simpler if she never gave Jane any encouragement to expect anything else. Her attitude of increasing aloofness as time went on becomes more explicable if one interprets it as an anticipation of trouble. Heaven knows trouble was obvious enough to anybody who was interested. Weren't there bets on at the club as to how long Philibert would stand it, that is, his enforced conjugal felicity? And other bets as to how long it would take his wife to find out certain things that every one else knew? It required no special prophetic gift to foresee that some day something was bound to happen, and I am sure my mother foresaw it. But I am a little puzzled as to why Philibert himself chose to make matters worse by keeping his wife and mother estranged, for I am perfectly sure that if Philibert had wanted my mother to love Jane, she would have done it, simply because she always did what he asked her. And again, if *Maman* had brought herself to care for Jane, she would have influenced her and guided her; she might even have prevented her from precipitating a crisis. One would have thought Philibert would have availed himself of such aid. But no, that was not his idea. His idea was quite other. He wanted his mother to dislike his wife for reasons of his own, or, at any rate, he did not want any understanding intimacy to exist between the two. On the other hand he asked Claire to make friends with her and help him with her education. And he seemed content that Jane and Bianca should be friends. Was this because he knew Claire would never care for Jane, however much she saw of her, and was afraid my mother might? I don't know, I am not sure. There are aspects of the case that grow more obscure the more I think of them.

As for Bianca—and Jane—that I learned about afterwards.

IX

Claire was a person who attracted people to her in spite of herself, even those people whom she did not like. It had been so in the case of Jane. My sister charmed more often than not without wanting to do so. People in general were to her uninteresting and indiscriminate admiration annoyed her. She was constantly worried by having to snub would-be admirers who bored her. It was generally accepted in the family that she was the victim of her own charm, and we often half-laughingly commiserated with her. My mother once quite seriously said, "*Cette pauvre* Claire, with whom every one is in love and who cares for no one, it is really very tiring for her."

Jane's devotion was to her from the first unwelcome, though for a year or two she put up with it kindly enough. When Philibert asked her to help him with Jane's education, she replied that she already had four children of her own to bring up, but she nevertheless let Jane go about with her, gave her advice about people and clothes, let her do errands for her; and in a mild way returned the girl's demonstrations of affection, but it all bored and worried her. There was for her no pleasure in being adored by a young woman whom she found to be stupid. She did not on the whole care much for women, and often said she did not believe in their friendship. Her need of affection was abundantly supplied to her in her own family. Between her mother and her children she found all the tenderness she required; in society she asked merely to be amused. At bottom she was a confirmed cynic. Human nature appeared to her unsympathetic and pitiable. Her family represented for her a refuge from a world that disgusted her more than it interested. There was for her something ultimate and absolute in the ties of blood that gave to the members of a family, all of them mere ordinary human beings, a special precious significance for each other. If she had ever analyzed it she would have said—"But of course I know that *Maman* and Philibert and Blaise and *Tante* Marianne are no different from other people, but that does not matter, they are different for me. It's not that I believe in my brothers as men, it's that I believe in their relationship to me, and that, is the only thing I do believe in. Philibert may be the most selfish man in Paris; nevertheless he would not be selfish to me. That's all, and that is enough. I don't believe in men. I don't believe in women. I don't believe in myself or in love or happiness, but I believe in my family." But of course she never did so express herself. She was not given to talking about herself.

Philibert realized from the first that Claire was necessary to his scheme, and somehow or other he prevailed upon her to exert herself on his behalf. She was constantly at his house and became its chief ornament, and one of its most potent attractions. Jane had her place, usually at the top of the staircase, but Claire's corner was the corner people looked for. Always more quietly dressed than any one else, (and I believe that Philibert planned the contrast of Jane's gorgeous brocades with an eye to the dramatic effect of the two women) my sister created about her an atmosphere, a hush, a kind of breathless attention. I have seen her often appear in one of those great doorways, a slim, shadowy figure, in trailing grey draperies, and stand there silently while gradually her presence made itself felt, drew all eyes to her and created a feeling among the assembled people that a new charm, a finer quality, had been conveyed to the atmosphere by her being there. Wonderful Claire, clever Philibert; they played beautifully into each other's hands. I do not mean that they were coldly calculating in regard to each other. On the contrary, their mutual admiration gave them, each one, the warmest affectionate glow. They rejoiced each in the rare qualities of the other, and Claire, knowing that in Philibert's house she would find men worthy of appreciating her, knowing too, that no artist could so set off her full value as her brother, seemed unlike my mother to derive a certain amount of half-cynical amusement from what went on in that mansion. It is, of course, possible that at bottom she was no more averse to lunching "*dans l'intimité*" with royalties than was Mrs. Carpenter. In any event, princes of royal blood paid court to her in Philibert's salons. And Philibert was right when he placed her beside him in that house. She made it *comme il faut*. Her presence was to it a benediction.

It had taken three years to build Philibert's palace, and by the time it was finished, Claire had prevailed upon her husband to move into Paris and buy there a very nice house of his own. On the whole, things had turned out for her better than any of us had expected. Six years of what he would have called I suppose conjugal bliss had tempered the ardour of my brother-in-law, who had to his wife's immense relief begun to look elsewhere than in his home for his pleasures. Though she had never complained of her slavery and now never spoke of her freedom, we all knew what had happened and were relieved. My mother was delighted. "*Enfin*, he hasn't killed her," was her way of expressing it to me. "The poor child is prettier than ever, and she manages so as not to be talked about." What it was that she managed I had no reason for asking. If Claire was happy, if at last she had selected some one from among her numerous admirers whom she could love and who was beautifying her life for her, then all was well. I had no fault to find with her there. My mother's reading of the case seemed to me the true one. My mother had suffered over her daughter's marriage, and was glad to have some one make up to her child some part of the joy of life she deserved.

All this was quite satisfactory. It never occurred to any one of us to disapprove of Claire. How could we? Why should we? Had she done anything preposterous like running away with a footman we should still have stood by her. As it was she remained one of the most admired women in Paris, and the least talked about, and her sentimental life was for us a vague rather romantic secret realm which we took for granted and respected. We never pryed into her affairs, and when one day Philibert, in my mother's drawing room, twitted Claire with the fact that her beauty increased in proportion to her husband's infidelities, she merely laughed shyly and said nothing, knowing well enough that we expected no explanation. The episode would certainly have passed unnoticed, if Jane's face had not shown it to be for her a moment of quite terrible revelation. It was, I remember, on a Sunday afternoon. We had all been lunching with my mother, Philibert, Jane, Claire and I, and were sitting by the fire with our coffee cups. Philibert, with his coat-tails over his arms, standing on the hearthrug, had been quizzing me. He was in excellent spirits, having just brought off some one of his social coups—I think it was the Prince of Wales that week who had dined with him, and Philibert was particularly pleased with Claire. His little sally had been meant and received as a token of affection. Unfortunately he had forgotten Jane; or it may be that he had not forgotten her and had spoken deliberately. It is possible that he thought the time had come to carry her education a step further. He probably felt it tiresome to be always on his guard as to what he said in her presence for all the world as if she were a *jeune fille*. She had heard and continued to hear in the houses she frequented, enough talk of all kinds, heaven knows, to enlighten her as to the habits of our world, but for all that we had instinctively all of us in her presence been careful of what we said to each other. It was, I suppose, our tribute to her innocence, or perhaps even to our fear of her judgments. More than once I, for one, had stammered under the gaze of her candid eyes and had swallowed the words that were on the tip of my tongue. On this occasion the phrase spoken would not have struck me as dangerous. I did not look at Jane to see how she took it. I merely happened to be facing her on the sofa and couldn't help seeing the pallor that mantled her face like a coating of wax. It was like that, not as if she had grown pale because of the ebbing of blood from her face, but as if a kind of coating of misery and fear had visibly enveloped her in whiteness. For a moment I did not understand, and failed to connect Philibert's words with her aspect. "But, Jane," I exclaimed, "what is it? Are you ill?" Fiercely she motioned me to be silent, gripping my arm with her strong hand so as to hurt me, and conveying somehow without speaking, for she could not speak, that she wanted me not to attract the attention of the others. Unfortunately Philibert had taken it all in. He may have been watching for the effect of his speech. His next words and his general behaviour give colour to such a theory. He literally jumped forward toward her across the carpet.

"But, my poor child," he cried out derisively, "don't make up a face like that. It's most unpleasant. *Voyons*, what a way to behave in your mother-in-law's drawing-room. If I had known you were so stupid, I should have left you at home."

Those were his words. They were uttered with animation, with an almost ferocious gaiety, and to accompany them he tweaked her playfully but not gently by the ear. I got up from my place beside her, feeling myself flush to my hair. I turned my back to get away from the sight of that cowering creature huddling back from the hand that held her.

Exaggerated? Certainly she was exaggerated. Idiotic? Perhaps so. Understand her? Of course I didn't. It was not until long after that I began to understand her. It was enough for me at that moment to understand Philibert and perceive that never, even if she lived with him for twenty years and maintained intact the dignity of her honesty, would he respect her.

Claire had been a passive spectator of this little passage between husband and wife. A slight flush had mounted to her cheek, a flush I took to be of annoyance, for she rose a moment later with more than usual abruptness and kissed my mother good-bye, ignoring completely the other two, not so much as looking at them as she made for the door. Jane, however, was too quick for her, and wrenching herself free from Philibert, was upon her before she turned the door knob.

"Don't go like that," she cried, "don't be annoyed. I know he was joking. I know he did not mean it." She seemed to be trying to grasp Claire in her arms, to get hold of her, to cling to her. I had a confused impression of something almost like a scuffle taking place between the two women, and of Claire actually throwing her off. I may be wrong. It may have been merely the expression on Claire's face and the tone of her voice that sent Jane backwards. I don't know, but it was quite pitifully horrid, and again I turned away my eyes, and with my back to them heard Claire say in her coldest tone, and God knows how cold her lovely voice can be—

"Ne soyez pas grotesque, je vous en prie. Laissez-moi partir."

I do not mean to suggest that I sympathized with Jane that afternoon, for I did not. It was all too absurdly out of proportion. She had created out of nothing, out of the blue, a scene in my mother's drawing-room, and one had only to look at the little delicate crowded place to know that scenes were abhorrent there. I believe actually that a small table full of trinkets had been overturned in Jane's rush for the door, and I know that a coffee-cup was broken. It was the sort of thing one simply never had conceived of. My mother's nerves were very much upset, and when Jane turned to her after Claire had shut the door in her face, wanting to beg her pardon, *Maman* could only wave her hands before a twitching face and say, "No, no, my child. Don't say any more, it is enough for today."

After that I did not see Jane for some weeks. Neither she nor Philibert came to lunch with my mother the following Sunday, nor the Sunday after. On the third Sunday Philibert came alone and explained briefly that Jane was indisposed. He seemed preoccupied. He talked little, ate nothing, and drank a number of glasses of wine as if he were very thirsty. His lips twitched constantly, forming themselves into a kind of snarl, and he was continually jerking the ends of his moustaches. I remember thinking that he looked for all the world as if he wanted to bite some one. He had never appeared more cruel. I began to have a sickening foreboding. Claire eyed him strangely. I wondered if she had something of my feeling. How I wished she had!

It all came out after luncheon. He could not contain himself. He was beside himself with exasperation. Jane's stupidity was too colossal. He could not put up with being loved like that any longer. She had made him a scene after the absurd affair of the other day and had asked him to swear that he would never be unfaithful to her. Here he raised his eyebrows, hunched his shoulders and threw out his hands. It was incredible how she had gone on. She had said that she had been thinking over his remark to Claire and was frightened by it, that when he had spoken so lightly of his brother-in-law's infidelities it had come to her as a tremendous shock that such a thing was possible. An abyss had opened before her—that was her word. How could Claire go on living with a man who was unfaithful? She could not understand. What did he mean by her sister's growing more beautiful in proportion to her husband's infidelities? Had he meant anything, or was it only a joke? Did Claire know her husband made love to other women? She loved Claire, she thought her wonderful, but she didn't understand. And so on and so on.

Philibert recited it all to us. His voice grew shriller and shriller. He piled up phrase after phrase in a crescendo of exasperation until he burst into a loud laugh with the words—"She talks, she talks of our marriage being made in Heaven." He grasped his head in his hands.

Claire's face wore a sneer.

"She professes not to know then, how it was her mother made it?" she asked.

Philibert came as it were to a halt. He looked at us all one after another. His face was of a sudden impudent, cool, smooth. He began to explain lucidly.

"Imagine to yourself, she really did not know it. She believed it was a love match. She believed it till yesterday, I mean last night, or it may be it was this morning, I don't remember looking at the time. Anyhow, as she wouldn't let me sleep I told her. I told her all about it."

"I don't believe she didn't know," said Claire.

He took her up quickly. "There, my dear, you are wrong, and you miss the whole meaning of her boring character." He was enjoying himself now, was my brother, dissecting a human being was one of his favourite pastimes. In the pleasure it now afforded him to analyze Jane, he forgot for the moment his personal annoyance.

"One must remember," he mused, "that she is a savage, with the mentality of a Huguenot minister. If you could hear her talk of the sacrament of marriage! She is of a solemnity, and her ideals, *Mon Dieu!* what ideals! She once said to me that her grandfather loved her grandmother at the day of his death just in the same way that he loved her on the day of her wedding. When I replied 'How very disgusting' she merely stared and left the room. She is always quoting her grandmother and her Aunt Patty. What a background—I ask you? St. Mary's Plains! It would appear that in St. Mary's Plains they always marry for love and live together in endless monotony. Faithfulness—she is in love with faithfulness; purity too, she thinks a great deal of purity. In fact she has a most unpleasant set of theories. They fill up her brain. There is no room for reality. What goes on before her eyes means nothing to her. No, Claire, you are wrong. She knew nothing of her mother's bargaining with me for her little life. Believe it or not, it is true. She married me for myself and believed the good God sent me to her, and my revelations were a shock. Impossible she should have simulated the emotion they caused her. The finest actress in the world could not have done it. I admit that as a piece of acting it would have been a fine performance. On the stage I would have enjoyed it, but in one's own bedroom, the conjugal bedroom—ugh! no."

"What did she do?" asked Claire.

"She leaned up against the wall, face to the wall, I mean, flattened against it, her hands high above her head, palms on the wall, too, as if she were reaching up to the ceiling."

"I don't see anything wonderful in that."

"It was a fine picture," said Philibert. "But she stayed there too long. She stayed like that some minutes. In fact I went on talking for a long time to that image, that long back and those outstretched arms. It reminded one of a crucifixion, modern interpretation. I was not sure that she was not dying and expected her to fall backwards."

My mother had been fussing nervously with her shawl, her sleeves, her hair, giving herself little pats and tugs and looking this way and that. Her face was drawn and working. She kept moistening her lips and saying—"Is it possible? Is it possible?" She now broke in and cried plaintively—

"But, my son, all this is terrible. I do not understand. What was it you told her?"

"I told her quite simply, mother dear, that I had married her for her money, that I had managed it all with Mrs. Carpenter before I had ever seen her; (Old Izzy is done for with Jane now, I am afraid, but that can't be helped) that I was tired of making love to her and would be grateful if she would become less exacting."

"*Mon Dieu, Mon Dieu!*" wailed my mother. "Was it necessary to do anything so definite? Couldn't you have gradually—*enfin*, does one say such things?"

"No, one does not, not in a civilized world, but Jane isn't civilized. You've no idea what it is with her."

Claire had risen and wandered away to the window with her usual drifting nonchalance.

"*Et après?*" she asked over her shoulder. "What did she say afterwards, when you had finished?"

"She said nothing, she fell down in a swoon."

"Backwards?"

"No, she had turned and was standing with her back to the wall and her hands against it, leaning forward and glaring, rather like a tiger, ready to spring when I had finished. But she didn't spring. When I mentioned a certain evening before our marriage on which I had taken her to the Opera, the queer light went out of her eyes. It was like snuffing out a candle. Then she fainted. I had to call her maid. It was two hours before she came round. She faints as she does everything else, too much, too much. *Quel tempérament, tout de même.* You have no idea what it is to live with her—and at the same time so fastidious. Certain things she won't put up with. Professes a horror of—of the refinements of sentiment. A prude and a *passionnée*. Ah, it is all too difficult. Anyhow, it is finished, thank God for that."

At this *Maman* wailed out—"Finished? What do you mean, finished?"

Philibert laughed. "I only mean that she won't bother me any more; not that she'll leave me. Ah, no, she won't leave me." He ruminated; after a moment he sighed. "And I may be wrong, she may bother me after all, in a new way, in a new way. She is very obstinate. She may try to make me love her, now that she knows I don't. It all depends on whether she hates me or not. One never can tell. And, of course, she knows nothing but what I have told you. It never occurs to her that I could be like other men. Even now she doesn't suppose that her husband is unfaithful, and even now I imagine that fact will be of some importance to her. It is all very curious. I have told you in order to warn you. It is quite possible that she will come to you for help."

He pulled down his cuffs, twisted his moustaches into place, looked at himself in the glass over the chimney piece, and bent over my mother, kissing the top of her head.

"*Au revoir, Maman chérie.* Don't let her worry you. Just quiet her down a little. But if it tires you to see her, of course you needn't. I only suggest it for her sake, and for us all. She will settle down. Au revoir."

He went to Claire and spoke to her in an undertone. I saw her shake her head. "*Non,*" I heard her say. "*Je ne peux pas. Tout cela mécœure. Elle est vraiment trop bête.*" He shrugged his shoulders. For me he had no word of instruction, nor any of good-bye. From the window I watched him cross the pavement to his limousine. For a moment he stood, one patent leather foot on the step of the car, talking to his footman and arranging as he did so the white camelia in his buttonhole. His face was bland. His top-hat had a wonderful sheen. We all knew where he was going. Bianca had returned to Paris after a six months sojourn in Italy and had refused to go back to her husband. The connection for us was obvious. We had been aware for some time of the renewed intimacy of these two.

Philibert waved his gloves at me through the window of his limousine and grinned. A new light dawned on me. It had all been a comedy. He had done it on purpose. Bianca had put him up to it. If it had not been for Bianca, he would never have precipitated a crisis with Jane. All that about her affection being insufferable was nonsense. It was in his interest that his wife should adore him, and no one when left to himself could look after his own interests so well as Philibert. In quarrelling with Jane he had done something from his own point of view incredibly foolish. Had Bianca not interfered he would never have done it. But what was she up to? That was the question. How should I know? Who on earth could ever tell what Bianca had hidden away in that intriguing Italian mind of hers? That she meant no good to any one, of that I was certain.

When I turned away from the window, Claire was stroking my mother's hand. She looked at me inimically. Something in my face must have betrayed me, though I said nothing. "Don't ask me to sympathize with Jane," she brought out, "for I can't. I wash my hands of the whole affair."

My mother's look was kinder than Claire's. Her eyes held that proud plaintive sweetness that denied all passion, either of anger, reproach, or pity. Her face was very white and her eyelids reddened, but her remark was characteristic.

"She has her own mother to go to, and her own mother to thank if she is unhappy."

And with that she drew me down to her with one of her beautiful gestures, and kissed me. I must have been in a highly excited and unnatural state of mind by this time, for the rare caress, so often awaited in vain, aroused in me at that moment a vague suspicion. Was she too, I remember asking myself, afraid I would try to get her to help poor Jane? If so her fears were unnecessary. Jane did not go to them. Philibert had been mistaken in thinking that she would rush to them for help. The time was to come when they would go to her, but of that later. She spoke to no one of her trouble, and neither Claire nor my mother laid eyes on her for months. We heard later that she had gone to Joigny with Geneviève, her little girl. She stayed at the Château de *Sainte Clothilde* all summer alone. Long afterwards I found out that she had not even so much as spoken to her own mother. Jane never reproached Mrs. Carpenter, never opened her lips on the subject to any one, until the other day when she told me everything. Poor old Izzy died the following winter, in ignorance of what her daughter thought about it all.

X

I am no fatalist. I do not believe that the good God has ordered to be written down in a book what all the millions of little souls on the earth are to be doing this day a year hence. He, no doubt, in his wisdom has a general idea of such coming events as famines, earthquakes, wars and pestilences, but man must remain full of surprises for his Maker; his activities are incalculable, and tiny circumstances, the effect of his minute will, have a way of spoiling the fine large trend of the great cumulative power of the past that we call fate. It is true that such characters as Bianca and Philibert have about them the quality of the inevitable. Certainly, as compared to Jane, they were not free people. They were the children of an old and elaborate civilization, and impelled by obscure impulses that they themselves never recognized and that had their source in some dim dark poisonous pocket of the past.

Bianca, more than any women I have ever known, seemed fated to be what she was and to do as she did. She appears to me now as I remember her as the little white slave of the powers of darkness. But she liked her darkness. She dipped into it deeper and deeper. She sank of her own will and because of her own morbid and insatiable curiosity.

But Jane was free. One had only to be in her presence to feel it. No morbid complexes in her, one would have said. Compared to her we were like so many pigmies in chains, and Bianca beside Jane was like a ghost or a woman walking in her sleep. Of course Bianca hated Jane. I don't believe in their friendship. As it was, I found it disgusting of Philibert to let Jane go about with Bianca. And Bianca must have been pretending to care for Jane out of perversity. Their natures were as antipathetic as their looks were opposed. Bianca with her little snow-white vicious face, so white that it showed pale bluish lights and shadows, her eccentric emaciated elegance of body, her enormous blue eyes fringed by their thick eyelashes that were like bushes and that she plastered with black till they stuck together: Jane, magnificent young animal, strong child amazon, towering shyly above us, looking down on us with her serious wistful gaze, holding out her marvellous hands to Bianca, suspicious of nothing, wanting to be friends—Jane insists that they cared for each other—I can't admit it. Of course Bianca hated her, and the fact that until she saw Jane's hands she had seen no others so beautiful as her own made it no easier for Jane, for Bianca may have been a priestess of the occult powers of darkness, she was as well a vain and envious young woman. A cat, Fan Ivanoff called her simply.

On the other hand I believe that if Paris had not mixed itself up in the long duel between these two women it might have ended less tragically, at any rate less tragically for Jane. Had they lived in London or Moscow or New York it would have been different. They would not have been so conspicuous. The vast and impersonal life of a great community would have absorbed them. But Paris held them close and watched them. It held them for twenty years. If they went away for a time they always came back and met face to face and could not get away from each other, for Paris is small and Paris is more personal than any city in the world. It is a spoiled beauty, excessively interested in personalities. I speak now of Paris, the lovely capricious creature that has existed for centuries, that has kept the special quality of its bland sparkling beauty through invasions, revolutions and massacres, and is still elegant under the dominion of the most bourgeois of governments. I speak of the Paris that seems to me to possess a soul, the soul of an immortal yet mortal woman, seductive pliable, submissive and indestructible. Do I sound fantastic? I have communed with my city for years, at night and in the morning and at mid-day. I have been a lonely man wandering through its streets and it has confided to me its secrets. Most often at night, when all the little people that inhabit its houses are asleep, I have listened, and like a sigh breathing up from its silvery bosom, I have heard its voice and understood its whispered confidences that carry a lament for days that are gone and are full of the tales of its many amours. Ah, my worldly-wise beauty, mistress of a hemisphere, what you do not know of men is indeed not worth knowing. And still they come, covetous, lustful, enamoured. What crimes have they not committed, what birthrights not denied, what fortunes not wasted, what fatherlands not repudiated, to win your favour?

It was this Paris that took part in the affair of Jane and Bianca. Why not? How could it have done otherwise? It has always been attracted by intrigue. It has a taste for drama. I repeat it dotes on personality; any personality that is striking, that catches its attention. The type matters little. Having long ago substituted taste for morals it has no ethical prejudices. It does not dislike a bandit; it adores a *farceur* such as Philibert. It delights in demagogues and artists and men of intelligence whether they are criminals or saints. Once in a hundred years, like a woman surfeited with pleasure and sensation, it will respect a person of character.

Bianca and Philibert were true children of Paris. They were its spoiled and petted darlings and they knew this and laid store by it. At bottom it was Paris that Philibert was continually making love to. He had a quite inordinate liking for his city, a jealous proprietory affection. I believe that had he been exiled from it, he would have died, and I believe that his desire to curry favour with it was the motive of most of his actions. It was for Paris that he gave his wonderful parties and concocted his fanciful amusements. He treated it literally as if it were his mistress. He cajoled, he flattered, he bullied, he caressed, and he spent on it millions, Jane's millions. It was not merely an ordinary vanity that impelled him. He saw himself as the benevolent despot of Paris, its favourite lover and its protector. To add to its brilliance he enticed to it princes and celebrities from every country of Europe. Europe was to him nothing more than a field to be exploited for the amusement of Paris. He would have beheld every city in Germany, Austria, Russia or Italy razed to the ground without a twinge of regret or horror, but when in 1914 the Germans were marching on Paris, then he was like a man possessed. I can remember him, white to the lips, rushing in from Army Headquarters to see the Archbishop. He had had long before any one else the idea of piling sandbags round Notre Dame to protect the stained glass windows. He was like a maniac.

As for Bianca, she was unique and Paris wore her like a jewel. The fact that she was half Italian seemed strangely enough not to mitigate against her, though her mother, the wonderful bacchante who had become in memory a legendary figure, had found it at first none too easy to please, according to Aunt Clothilde. The Venetian had been a woman of quick passions and child-like humours. She was remembered for her many love affairs, the garlands of bright flowers she wore in her hair, and the habit she had of sticking pins into little wax effigies of people she wished would die. An impulsive, playful, improvident creature, with the beauty of a peasant and the naïveté of a child. She had died when Bianca was a child of six, died of home-sickness so they said, for her beloved Italy. I don't know, I imagine that François her husband had something to answer for there. It was said that he had found a wax effigy of himself in her room, containing no less than three hundred pins, and had laughed delightedly. He was a cynical devil. Aunt Clo says that he used to lock up his wife in their dismal château in Provence and keep her on bread and water for days at a time. In any case he did not lock up Bianca, nor did Bianca seem to have inherited any of her mother's aptitude for getting into scrapes. One could not easily detect in her the Italian strain, one only noticed that she was a little different from French women, with a different timbre of voice and an occasional mannerism evocative of something foreign, something lazy and sly and mysterious, and if she had inherited secret affinities with that warm romantic southern country of intrigue and superstition, she kept them hidden, together with all manner of other things, strange things, violent obsessions, curious tastes, dark obscure desires, and knowledge of a dangerous kind. She chose to appear at this time, I allude to the period covering the first years of Jane's marriage to Philibert, as merely the supreme expression of the elegant world of Paris.

It is curious to watch the rise and fall of women in society. Women loom on the horizon; suddenly for no apparent reason. A gold mine, a rubber plantation, a motor-industry, suddenly looms into prominence. It takes the fancy, it is advertised, it becomes popular, people buy shares in it, the shares go higher and higher, the rush to buy becomes a scramble, and then perhaps a fraud is discovered, there is a collapse, and a large number of people find they have been expensively fooled. So it is in society. Women loom on the horizon; suddenly for no apparent reason they take the popular fancy. Comparatively plain women or women we have all known for years and have considered insignificant, become all at once conspicuous and important. Some one calls her, the plain woman, a beauty. Some one else repeats it. People become curious. They look at her with a new interest. A number of men who were before indifferent to her charms begin to pay her marked attention. The boom begins. Every one agrees that they have heretofore been mistaken. Her nose is not a snub nose. She is a beauty. It is whispered that so-and-so is *très emballé*. She is the success of the season. And after, when her day is over, she still retains something, once having been acclaimed a beauty she remains a beauty. Only the men who dubbed her nose Grecian look at it now with the same indifference that it inspired when they called it "snub." They have been engaged in a little flurry in the social stock market. They do not admit having been fooled, but being inveterate gamblers they turn their attention elsewhere. The boom of the gold-mine is over, they go in for rubber. The men, i. e. the gamblers, are always the same in these affairs; it is the women who come and go.

Bianca was not one of these. She was no shooting star in the social heaven, she was a fixture, the little central shining constellation in a firmament of lesser planets. As a child she had been an institution. Strangers were taken to the Bois to look at the beautiful little girl, who, all in white, white fur coat and white gaiters, and followed by a white pom, walked there with her governess. She never sought the favour of Paris. She laid her will upon it and it submitted. As she grew older she made few women friends and tolerated no rivals. She was nice to old men and old ladies, people like my mother adored her, but most young women were afraid of her. Jane was an exception. Jane loved her. The two as I say used to go about together. The intimacy was shocking to me—I loathed Philibert for allowing it.

Jane had no suspicions. Her confidence in Philibert was such as to make us as a family quite nervous. What would she do, we asked ourselves, when she found out? Paris took little account of Jane. After the first flurry of excitement over her wedding, it lost sight of her. She disappeared behind Philibert. Curious how such a little man could hide from view a woman so much bigger than himself. It was a case of perspective. He stood in the foreground. To the more distant public she was invisible; to those who came nearer she appeared as nothing more interesting than a large fine piece of furniture. Philibert sometimes in moments of good humour alluded to her as his Byzantine Madonna.

I should defeat my own object in telling this story if I did not do Philibert justice. Yet how do him justice? If he were a centipede or a rare species of bird my task would be easier. But he lived on the earth in the guise of a human being, and he was not quite a human being. And it is difficult to be just to a brother such as Philibert. He always loathed the sight of me. I don't blame him for that. I loathe the sight of myself. I am an ugly object. But Philibert found it amusing to hate me and to make me constantly aware of my deformity. My twisted frame seemed to produce in him a kind of itching frenzy, to tickle him to dreadful laughter, to irritate him to nervous cruelty. And I was unfortunately never able to grow a thick enough skin to protect me from him.

I suppose that I have always been jealous of Philibert. I loved life, but it pushed me aside. I wanted it, I wanted it in all its fulness, but it was Philibert who had it. And my incapacity to taste so many of its pleasures has only made me regard it with a closer, more wistful attention. I was like a ragamuffin in the street with his nose plastered against the pastry-cook's window, a ragamuffin who dreamed that his pockets were full of gold, but who always found that the bright coins he jingled so lovingly in his fingers were not accepted over the counter. After repeated rebuffs, I gave up trying to get anything, but I could not take my eyes from the feast and so, even in my childhood, I resorted to the fiction of considering myself an invisible spectator of other people's doings, and I helped along this little game by sitting as much as possible in dark corners or behind the kindly screen of some large piece of furniture such as the schoolroom piano. All that I asked of the world that so prodigiously attracted my interest was that it should not notice me, and thus leave me free to notice it, and I came at last to feel when some one out of kindness or cruelty dragged me out of my corner, a sense of outrage. So it was when Philibert, taking me by my collar, exposed me to kicks and to laughter. So it was years later when Jane, taking me by the hand, exposed me to the responsibilities of a friendship that demanded action. I used to dodge Philibert when I could. I would have avoided Jane's confidence had I been able. Philibert's tormenting in no way involved me. I could just let him kick and was when he finished as free as before to subside into my corner; with Jane it was different. Jane involved me in everything.

And now that I am obliged to think of my own personal relation to Jane, I have as I do so, a feeling of pain that is like the throbbing of some old hurt or the recurrence of an illness. Jane was magnificent and healthy and whole. She was half a head taller than I. I am cursed with a visualizing mind. As I set myself to the business of remembering her life, I see her constantly moving before my eyes, visibly acting out her drama, and I see myself, a wizened little man looking up at her from a distance. I have an acute sense of an opportunity lost for ever, of precious time wasted. For years I refused to sympathize with her as her friend. For years I would not talk to her because I was afraid she would complain to me of my family. How little I knew her!

Slowly she imposed herself. Like a woman coming towards me in a fog, I saw her grow more clear and more definite, until at last I recognized her for what she was.

Was I merely in love with her? Was it that? Was that all? If so she never suspected it. If so I did not recognize the feeling. It is, of course, the accusation my brother brought against me. He spoke of my criminal passion for his wife. It is very curious. The cleverest men are sometimes very obtuse. Philibert's intelligence was of the kind that made it impossible for him to understand simple things.

In love with Jane? I find that I have no idea what the phrase means and cannot apply it. It is as if I were trying to fit a little paper pattern to a cloud floating off there in the heaven. My tenderness for Jane does remind me a little of a cloud. It has changed so often in shape and hue. At times it has seemed to me a little white floating thing of celestial brightness, at others it has enveloped me in darkness and always it has been intangible, vague, unlinked to the earth.

And yet, even to me, she did seem at first very queer. It seemed to me that she was really too different to be innocent of all desire to make trouble. She often annoyed me by remaining so silent when any one else would have burst out with a flood of protest, and by going pale as death when a moderate flush ought to have expressed a sufficient sense of disturbance. The excessive emotional restraint evidenced by those sudden mute pallors of hers used to worry me with their exaggeration. I understood how this sort of thing, displeased my mother. I can remember moments when I expected to see her bound across the room and go crushing through the mirror, so tense was her physical stillness. Claire used to look at her then with lifted eyebrows and turn away with a nervous shrug of impatient disdain. I felt with Claire. I understood this sort of thing little better than she did. We were accustomed to people whose gestures were used to enhance the fine finished meaning of spoken phrases, not to dumb creatures whose eyes and quivering nostrils and long strong contracted fingers betrayed them in drawing rooms. I, caught up in the fine web of my family's prejudices, had found myself from the midst of those delicate meshes seeing her as they saw her, as some gorgeous dangerous animal who was tearing the very fabric of their system to pieces with its many gyrations. As I say, I doubted her innocence. I suppose like every one else in the family I was affected by the glare Mrs. Carpenter's obvious ambition threw over her. It didn't seem to me possible that Jane had married Philibert simply and solely because he fascinated her. Not that I didn't know Philibert to be capable of fascinating any one he wanted to, but because such fascinations had never seemed to me to contain in themselves any basis for marriage. The truth involved too great a stretch for my imagination. I had to find it out gradually. It necessitated too, the admission on my part that for Jane the name of Joigny counted for absolutely nothing. I couldn't be supposed to know that Jane didn't care a straw about marrying our family, when her mother so obviously laid great store by her doing so.

But I started to explain Philibert, and suddenly it comes to me; I believe that at the bottom of everything he did was the controlling impulse of his hatred of life. Undeniably he despised humanity. It exasperated him to tears. Its stupidity put him in a nervous frenzy. He was animated by a kind of rage of mockery. Everything that humanity cherished was to him anathema. He had been born with a distaste for all that men as a rule called goodness, and was nervously impelled towards that which they called evil. And yet the evil he courted didn't do him any harm. I mean that it didn't wear him out or spoil his digestion or stupefy his intelligence. On the contrary it agreed with him. He had begun to taste of life with the palate of a worn out old man. The good bread and butter and milk of the sweetness of life was repulsive to him and disagreed with him. He could live to be a hundred on a moral diet that would have killed in a week a child of nature. Sophistication can go no further. His equipment was complete, and he had, I suppose, no choice. His nature was imposed on him at birth. His punishment was that he lived alone in a world that bored him to extinction.

Seriously, he appears to me now, as I think of him, as a man living under a curse. I believe him to have been haunted by a sense of unreality. To get in contact with something and feel it up against him, that was one of the objects that obscurely impelled him. His extravagances of conduct were efforts to arrive at the primitive sensation of being alive. He did not know this. He only knew that he hated everything sooner or later. He was conscious merely of an irritating desire for sensation and amusement. His fear was that he would run through all pleasure before he died and find nothing left for him to do. It may have occurred to him at times that the world minus human interest did not provide endless sources of amusement. The things one could do to distract oneself were not after all so very many. Even vice alas, its limitations, and it was not as if he were really in himself vicious. He had an absolute incapacity for forming habits good or bad. Could he have saddled himself with one or two the problem would have been simpler. Could he have become a drunkard how many hours would have been accounted for! If women had only had an indisputable power over him, what a relief to let himself go. But no. He was the victim of no malady and no craving. Drink as he might, his head remained excruciatingly clear, debauch himself as much as he would, he remained master of his passions, and day after day, year after year, he was obliged to plan what he would do with himself.

He found in the world only one kindred spirit. Bianca was the one creature on earth who was a match for him. She was more, and he knew it; she was in his own line his superior. Many people have been astonished at Philibert's *liaison* with Bianca. They have considered the intimacy of these two people strange. I believe that Philibert's feeling for Bianca was as simple as the feeling of a good man for a good woman, and as inevitable as if he and she were the only two white people in a world of black men. I believe that Philibert turned to Bianca in despair and clung to her out of loneliness. He and she were alone on the earth, as alone as if they had been gods condemned to live among men. She was his mate, moulded in the marvellous infernal mould that suited him. *Voilà tout.*

But she was a more refined instrument than he was. She filtered experience through a finer sieve. She had a steadier hand. Hers was the great advantage of being able to wait for her amusement and her effects. She was economical of her material. Philibert was afraid of running through the whole of experience and exhausting too soon the resources of life. Bianca was not afraid of anything, not even of being bored. She meted out pleasure with deliberation. She calculated her capital with fine precision, she measured the future with a centimetre rule, and poured out sensation into a spoon, sipping it slowly.

Philibert was a spendthrift. Bianca was as close as a peasant woman. And on the whole Philibert was honest. He did not try to deceive the world. He was too impatient and despised it too much. When he fooled it he did so openly and if people found him out he laughed. But Bianca was deep as a well and as secretive as death. What Philibert was so he appeared, but no one knew what Bianca was.

During the summer that Jane spent alone at Joigny with her child, Philibert and Bianca saw a great deal of each other. Bianca had musical evenings that summer, in her garden, and little midnight suppers that were quite another variety of gathering. Philibert never drank too much at these suppers, neither did Bianca; as much cannot be said of some of the others, if Philibert's own account of these graceful orgies was true. It was at one of them that poor Fan Ivanoff's husband threw a glass of champagne in her face, cutting her cheek. Neither Fan nor her wretched Russian were asked again. Bianca did not like that sort of thing.

Jane has told me that she did not go to America that summer because she hoped that Philibert would come to her at Joigny. She had found it impossible after the first shock of his revelations to believe that they were true. She told herself that he had been carried away by one of his fine frenzies of talk and had said things he had not meant. It was incredible to her that he should really mean that he cared nothing for her. He had, to her mind, given her during those years of marriage too many proofs to the contrary. Thinking it over alone she came to the conclusion that there was some mystery here that only time would make clear to her, and she therefore determined to wait. For a month, for two months, for three, she believed he would come and if not explain, at least put things on some decent footing, but he did not come for the simple reason that Bianca wouldn't let him.

One has only to stop a moment and remember what he had at stake to realize the extent of Bianca's power over him. He was entirely dependent on Jane for money. There was no settlement of any kind and he had none of his own. With her enormous income pouring through his hands, he had not a penny to show if she left him, and when people accused him later, as some did, of having put aside a portion of that revenue for himself they were wrong. His code of ethics, morals, what you will, his idea anyway, of what was permitted and what was not, allowed him to spend all her income and even run into debt; but not keep any of it for the future. It did not shock him in the least to spend Jane's dollars on his various mistresses but it would have disgusted him to find any of these coins sticking to his palms. As long as he poured them out he was satisfied with himself; had he hoarded it he would have been ashamed.

In any case he knew the risk he ran, for he understood Jane, and knew that the fear of scandal would not keep her if she once decided to break with him. Nor could he have diminished the magnitude of the catastrophe that this would mean. His sensational reign had only begun, but it had already become vital to his happiness—I use the word happiness, for lack of another. He had done great things, but nothing as yet to compare with what he intended to do. The fame of his entertainments had already reached the different capitals of Europe, he had seen to that, but this was mere advertisement, preparatory work necessary to the realization of his ultimate purpose. He was in the position of a company promoter who had sent out his circulars and gathered in a certain amount of capital, but had not yet founded his business, and was still far from holding the monopoly he aimed at. He was certain of success but he must have time. If his plans miscarried now he would be his own swindler.

Jane, he realized perfectly, felt little interest in his schemes. It was one of the grudges he had against her. Her attitude from the first had been galling in its simplicity. When on the eve of their marriage he had proposed to her building a house, she had suggested that perhaps one of the beautiful old ones already existing in Paris might do, but on his insisting that none could compare with the image he had in his mind, she had given in with a sweetness and promptness that had taken his breath away. It is characteristic of him, in this connection, that though he wanted his own way and intended to get it, his pleasure in doing so would have been very much greater had she made it more difficult. Her pliability seemed to him stupid and when she merely said, looking over the plans he proudly spread out before her, some weeks later, "It's dreadfully big, but if you like it I shall," he came near to gnashing his teeth. It was equally galling to him neither to impress her nor to anger her, but he was obliged to contain himself, for after all, as he put it to Claire, he couldn't go and tear the thing up just to spite himself. She would calmly have put the bits in the waste-paper basket.

When it came to arranging the house she had said—"I want one room at the top for my own. No one is to go there. I shall arrange it myself," and the rest she left to him. I believe he never entered that room and never knew what she had done to it. If he thought about it at all, he doubtless thought she had arranged it as a chapel. He probably imagined an altar and candles and photographs of the dead. Jane never told him about it. Some obscure instinct of mistrust must have been at the bottom of her shyness. She had furnished it quite simply like a room in the Grey House in St. Mary's Plains. Her Aunt Patty had sent her a rocking chair, an old mahogany dresser, the window curtains from her old room, and some of her special belongings that she had left behind when she came away. It was the strangest room at the top of that mansion. I remember well the day Jane took me to it. She had come in from some function and was looking more worldly than usual. I remember gazing beyond her outstretched silken arm with its jade bracelets into what seemed to me the most pathetic of sanctuaries. The window curtains were of faded cretonne. The worn rocking chair had a knitted antimacassar. Two battered rag dolls sat on an old spindle-legged dresser against the wall. A spirit dwelt there that I did not know.

But I am wandering away from my subject. What I started to say was that Philibert's life hung by the thread of Jane's belief in him and he knew it. If he thought that thread was an iron cable then that fatuous belief alone might explain his putting such a strain upon it, but I don't believe it was so. However far he thought he could try Jane, there was no sense in doing so, and he wouldn't have done so had he followed the dictates of his own wisdom. It would have been so easy to have gone for a week to Joigny. Two days would have sufficed. A three hours' journey in the train, two days away from Bianca, and Jane would have been reassured and his own future secure. So he would have reasoned it out had he been left alone, but Bianca did not leave him alone.

Her motive was quite simply to make mischief. She wanted Jane to suffer. She loved Philibert but she wanted him to suffer as well. There was nothing more in it than that. The most subtle people have sometimes the simplest purposes. Bianca's subtlety often consisted in doing very ordinary things in a way that made them appear extraordinary. Her cleverness in this instance lay in the fact that Philibert did not suspect her motive. It is even doubtful whether he knew that it was she who prevented his going. Certainly she never did anything so stupid as to tell him not to go. It was rather the other way round. If they discussed it at all it was Bianca who urged upon him the advisability of his doing his duty as a husband. I can imagine her lying back on her divan with her lovely little spindly arms over her head and saying with a yawn, that really he was too negligent of his wife. His wife adored him. She was ready to fall into his arms. She was probably very sulky now, but once he appeared she would welcome him with all the ardour she was saving up during her *villégiature*. I can see Bianca looking at Philibert through half-closed eyes, while she touched up for him a portrait of Jane calculated to make him shudder.

Bianca herself was going yachting in the Mediterranean. She wanted to be hot, to soak in enough sunlight to keep her warm for next winter. They were to laze about the Grecian islands. G— — the historian was to be one of the party. While she was giving her body a prolonged Turkish Bath and taking a course in Greek history, he would be free to bring in the cows with Jane. No, he couldn't come with her, it would be too compromising for him. American women began divorce proceedings on the least provocation.

And Philibert, of course, did go on that yacht to the Grecian isles, but to judge from his humour when he returned, he did not get out of the trip what he had expected. Bianca having lured him out there seemed to forget that he had come at her invitation. She left the party at the first opportunity and went off inland on a donkey, and didn't come back, merely sent a message for her maid and her boxes to meet her at Athens.

Nor did Philibert find Jane waiting for him in Paris as he had expected, nor any message from her. It was the butler who informed him that Madame had gone to Biarritz with the Prince and Princess Ivanoff, and it was to Biarritz that Philibert was obliged to go to fetch her home.

XI

Things had been going very badly with the Ivanoffs. Their combined resources left them poorer than either had been before. Ivanoff's resources consisted in debts, but debts that he never was obliged to pay, because he couldn't. His creditors, those I mean who were in the business of money-lending, became more hopeful when he married and approached Fan without delay believing of course, that being an American she was rich. Poor Fan with her few meagre thousands a year meted them out bravely enough at first, paying here and there, the minimum that was nevertheless her maximum. Ivanoff had a small rather shabby flat on the Isle St. Louis, with one big room. It could be said of it that the place had atmosphere and would attract their friends if they made the most of its Bohemian charm. So they decided to live there, thinking thus to keep down their expenses. But Fan needed many things that had been unnecessary to the existence of Ivanoff. She required cleanliness, a bathroom with a hot-water installation, cupboards to hold her clothes, a lace coverlet for her bed, and enough wood and coal to keep the place warm. Ivanoff had never realized the damp and cold; when he was cold he drank vodka or brandy. He had not been over fond of washing; he took his baths at the club or in a public bath house. Fan's maid was a complication. There was no proper room for her. She was constantly grumbling about Fan's discomfort and served her little mistress with grim disapproval, making continual scenes with the Prince for the way he failed to look after the Princess, and going out herself on the sly to buy things for the house that she felt were wanted. The one department in the *ménage* that ran well was the kitchen. Ivanoff had a gift for cooking. He could train any youngster and turn him in three months into an excellent cook. When they gave parties he would go into the kitchen, put on an apron, roll up his sleeves and cook the dinner. He did his own marketing, going out with a basket on his arm. One ate better at his table than anywhere else in Paris. He used to make a bit now and then by passing one of his cooks on to a friend. He bought his wines in out of the way corners of France, and got them cheap, and these too, he sometimes sold at a profit. Nevertheless their expenses during the first year of their marriage were more than double their income. They had many friends; a great number of Russians, French, Italians, and Spanish and a few Americans came to their suppers, that were served in the big living room. People ate reclining or squatting on cushions with little tables before them. When the tables were carried out, some as yet undiscovered artist from a distant country turned up with a violin under his arm, or Ivanoff himself with his guitar on his knees would sing the folksongs of his country, with the long window open to the moonlit river and the dimly-looming towers of Notre Dame. All this was very gay and pleasant, but they could not keep it up unless they did something to make money. For a year Fan tried to find a respectable employment for her husband, but she was met everywhere with polite, but to her, mystifying refusals. Even the antique dealers refused to employ him to buy for them. Yes, they admitted, he had an exceptional "flair," but he had no idea of money, and if he fell in love with a piece was as likely as not, in a burst of enthusiasm, to pay the owner more than he asked. And Ivanoff himself said that he had no capacity for steady work of any kind. She would send him to interview some financier or banker; he would go and talk charmingly about all manner of things save the business in hand, and then say "You know the Princess my wife wants you to do something for me. I have come to please her, but of course you and I understand that it is no use. It wouldn't last a month, and I might make some mistake that would anger you." And he would come away happily, to report to Fan that there was nothing he could do in that line. She was obliged to admit him to be incorrigible. The only thing he could do to make money was play cards. He played Bridge superlatively well. If he played enough he could count on making a hundred thousand francs a year.

I believe, because Jane has insisted that it was so, that Fan was for a long time unaware of the fact that Ivanoff made a living at cards, and I know that when she discovered that his stories about rents from properties in Russia were fairy tales and that the sums he turned over to her were really his winnings at little green baize tables, that she took it very hard for a time, and made him stop playing, but how could they then pay their bills? For six months she held out and he obediently stayed away from his clubs, spent his time wandering along the quays, twanging his guitar on his sofa, and cooking the dinner, while Fan's little wizened face grew sharper and her laugh shriller and her cough more troublesome.

The inevitable happened. She caught cold. There was no coal to heat the flat. The maid, Margot, flew at Ivanoff, in a paroxysm. Ivanoff wept and tore his hair, fell at the foot of Fan's bed, implored her forgiveness and rushed off to the Club. One is obliged to accept the inevitable. Fan asked no questions after that. I thought that I detected a furtive look in her eyes and a note of high bravado in her gaiety, when she staggered out of bed to go about again amusing herself. I imagined that she was ashamed. I may be wrong. In any case though every one knew their circumstances, she remained enormously popular.

The strange thing was that Ivanoff could always find people to play with him. The certain knowledge that they stood to lose heavily, irresistibly attracted men to his table, rich men, of course, he only played with rich men. He couldn't afford Bridge as a pastime. And I know for certain that he derived from it no amusement. If his victims approached that square of green baize with pleasurable shivers of excitement, it was not so with him. Winning money at cards was no more interesting to him than is the breaking of stones to an Italian labourer. He played with what seemed to most people an exaggerated pretence of boredom, but his boredom was no pretence. Ivanoff never pretended in his life. He was a child of nature, a great dark abysmal child of the Slavic race. People liked him, they couldn't help it. He was considered rather mad and utterly undependable. He had a way of disappearing mysteriously, and of reappearing again suddenly, and he never attempted to account for these absences. "Where have you been this time Ivanoff," some one at the club would ask him, and he would smile his wide mongolian smile that narrowed his eyes to slits making him look like a chinaman, and then a worried wistful look would come over his sallow face and he would smooth carefully his heavy black hair—"I don't know," he would say, "I really can't remember," and somehow one believed him. He drank heavily, and when he was drunk he would talk about God, and the soul of the Russian people that was a deep pure soul besotted with despair, and would say that God in His wisdom must put an end to human misery very soon. He had an extraordinary gift for languages. Indeed he had many gifts and no capacity and no ambition. It never seemed to occur to him that he ought to provide for his wife, or look after her. For the most part, between his disappearances he followed her about like a great tame bear. He had an immense respect for her. "What a head she has," he would say. "What a head for figures, and what a will. She can make me do anything, anything, except the things for which I am incurably incapacitated. I am like wax in her hands."

Poor Fan! If he had had a little more respect for himself and a little less for her, it would have been easier for her. He drank more and more heavily as time went on. Night after night he would come home to her drunk and lie in a stupor wherever he happened to fall. Again and again he would beg her forgiveness, throw himself at her feet, kissing them and weeping like a heart-broken child. And because she found him beautiful, and because she believed he loved her, she did, over and over again forgive him, but she was worried half out of her mind. It began to dawn on her that his card-playing wasn't enough; that he borrowed money of everybody. She foresaw that the day would soon dawn when every one of his men friends was a creditor. It didn't occur to her at this time that he borrowed money from women as well. Nor did it occur to her as a possible solution to cut down her expenses by changing her mode of life. She and Ivanoff, and a lot of their friends for that matter, lived on the principle that, as Montesquieu said, it was bad enough not to have money, but, if in addition one had to deprive oneself of the things one wanted, then life would be intolerable. She had married Ivanoff to be a princess and to have a good time. She was still pleased with being a princess and more determined than ever to enjoy herself. Pleasure, noisy, distracting absorbing pleasure was becoming more and more necessary to her. As her troubles thickened, her craving for excitement grew. The more she was worried the more she needed to laugh. Her life became a staccato tune of laughter and hurting throbs and petulant crescendoes of gaiety. It was a tinkling dance with a drumming accompaniment of worry, the rhythm of it moving faster and faster as her problem deepened.

And people as I say liked her. Even Claire continued to see much of her. She was considered original and very plucky. Her parties were amusing, and she herself could be trusted to make any dinner a success. Her very shrill yell of laughter came to have a definite social value. She talked with a hard gay abandon that affected people like a spray of hot salt water. Fagged and blasé spirits turned to her for refreshment. She would enter a drawing-room on the run, and call out some extravagant yet neat phrase, and every one would become perky and animated. Always she had had some amusing and extraordinary adventure five minutes before her arrival. Her taxi had dumped her into the street, or a man had tried to abduct her or she had found a bill of a thousand francs lying on the doorstep. One never questioned her veracity. Nobody cared whether these things really happened or whether she made them up for the general amusement. It was all the more to her credit if she took the trouble to invent them. And enough things did happen to her, heaven knows, dreadful things. She was always in trouble. Her health was execrable. People mentioned phthisis. She had a way of fainting in the street and waking up in strange houses from which she had miraculous escapes. Decorated by her amusing gift of description, made entertaining by her contagious laughter, her miseries and her unfortunate adventures came to be an endless source of amusement in society. Her misfortune was her social capital; she turned it all to account.

Jane alone was not amused. Jane alone took Fan's troubles seriously as if they had been her own, and watched her with concern and tried to reason with her. But Fan didn't want any one to reason with her and was annoyed by Jane's anxiety. At bottom I believe, during this period of their existence, that Jane bored her. She loved her, of course, in a way, because of their childhood, she knew that she could count on her in any crisis, but she preferred talking to Philibert. When she lunched in Jane's house, she and Philibert would sit together after lunch and scream with laughter, and then, when she was about to leave, her little face would suddenly turn grey with fatigue, and she would say to Jane's anxious enquiry—"Yes, my dear, I'm as sick as a dog. I haven't slept for a month. I'm living on *piqûres*," and then, tearing herself out of Jane's embrace she would go away coughing, coughing terribly all the way down the stairs. Jane gave her a good many clothes. Fan told me so herself. "My dear," she said, "I'm not going with Jane any more to her dressmaker's. She insists on my taking too many things, and if I don't she's hurt. I escaped from Chéruit's this morning with nothing more than a chinchilla coat. What do you think of that? I shall send it back when it comes, and there'll be a scene." And she did send it back, and there was I suppose, what she would call a scene. Jane spoke of it too, for she had overheard. She said—"Of course I'd rather give Fan blankets and coals, but as I can't do anything sensible for her, why shouldn't she let me do something foolish?"

I will say for Fan that she did not sponge, neither on Jane nor on any one else. She left that part of it to Ivanoff. And again Jane insisted that she didn't know about Ivanoff. In any case it was Ivanoff who gave Jane her opportunity, as she believed, to help Fan. He came to see her one afternoon in a high state of excitement, made her swear she would never tell Fan a word of what had passed between them, and then asked her for fifty thousand francs. He said that they would be turned out into the street if he couldn't get the money in two days, and that every stick of their furniture would be sold. It was unnecessary for him to explain to Jane why Fan should not be told. Jane knew, at least she thought she knew, that Fan would refuse the money. So she gave Ivanoff a cheque payable to herself and endorsed it and felt happy to have been able to help them. Ivanoff had pointed out that it would be best for her not to make out a cheque in his name. This was the thin end of the wedge.

Ivanoff having been well received, came back six months later and again after that. He had from Jane all told about two hundred thousand francs during a period of two or three years, not a large sum to Jane certainly. She easily enough hid the payments from Philibert by paying the amounts out of her personal account for clothes, travelling, flowers, trinkets, and so on. Occasionally she would countermand an order for a fur coat and feel that she was making a personal sacrifice for Fan, and this added a very real element of joy to her pleasure. And there was no doubt in her mind that this money did go to help Fan. Ivanoff always had some tale of Fan's illnesses, her doctors' bills, her need to go to some watering place for a cure, her last unfortunate venture in the stock market. Nevertheless Jane was worried. She was worried, God help her, because she was deceiving Philibert. The subject was heavy on her mind. At times she felt she must tell Philibert all about it, but Philibert did not like Ivanoff. She was afraid to tell him for fear he should put a stop to her doing anything more in that quarter. Philibert tolerated Fan because she was amusing and helped to occupy Jane, but he would not tolerate Ivanoff, and refused to have the Russian in his house. He was unaware of the latter's quarterly afternoon visits. This, too, Jane had been obliged to keep from him. If she told Philibert that Ivanoff had been to call and had been received, she would have to explain why. Philibert seldom showed any interest in the people she received on her day in the afternoon, but he did occasionally ask her who had been there, and suggest that one or another was really too stupid or too ugly to be welcomed under his roof. He did not wish his house to be invaded by touring Americans or by the halt, the lame and the blind, so he exercised a sort of censorship over his wife's calling list. Ivanoff was one of the people who to Philibert were beyond the pale. Up to the night of Bianca's supper party he had forced himself to greet the big Russian with civility when he met him in other people's houses, but after the beastly exhibition the latter had made of himself there, he had let it be known that he did not wish to find himself again anywhere in the same room with him.

It was therefore extremely unpleasant to Philibert to learn from his butler that Jane had gone to Biarritz with the Ivanoffs. Nothing, indeed, that Jane could have done could have been so disagreeable to him. Had she planned it on purpose as a revenge, she could not have calculated better, and he believed she had done so. He had come to his senses. He had perceived during the train journey north that he had been very foolish to take such risks. It occurred to him that he had not heard from Jane for two months, and that he did not know where she was. She might have gone to America, she might be there with the intention of not coming back. She was capable of anything. The news he received on arrival was a relief that left him free to enjoy his exasperation. He was not in a desperate fix after all, it was Jane who was in a fix. She had at last given him a definite cause of complaint and had incurred his displeasure in a way that made it easy for him to act against her. If this were her way of taking a line of her own and paying him back, she had played beautifully into his hands. He took the train for Biarritz, smiling and revolving pleasantly in his heart the things he would say.

But Jane had had no ulterior motive in what she had done. She had come back to Paris at the end of September and had found Fan lying exhausted by haemorrhage in an untidy bed with a bowl of blood beside her, and Ivanoff on the floor, his head in his hands, sobbing, while Margot stormed at him for his uselessness. Jane had simply picked Fan up in her arms, and had carried her away, and Ivanoff like an unhappy dog had followed, his tail between his legs. The haemorrhage had thoroughly frightened him. It was a fortnight later that Philibert, one brilliant afternoon announced himself at the Palace Hotel Biarritz. Fan was better and Ivanoff had recovered from his terror. Philibert found the two women in an upstairs sitting-room overlooking the sea. Fan was on a couch, her little wizened face screwed into a smile of bravado under her lace bonnet, and a cigarette between her rouged lips. Jane looked the more ill of the two. Her usual glowing pallor had turned to the whitish-grey of ashes, there were purple circles under her eyes. She was looking out of the window, her hands clasped behind her head, and when Philibert entered she wheeled at the sound of his voice, and then stood silently trembling.

Fan cried out at him, gaily impertinent. "Hullo, Fifi, you didn't come too soon, did you?"

He didn't answer her. "Come with me," he said to Jane briefly, and she followed him out of the room. He had passed Ivanoff below in the bar. The sight had added nothing pleasant to his humour.

What he said to her was what he had intended to say. Her wasted face made no impression in her favour, on the contrary. He read in her agitation signs of guilt and seemed to have forgotten that he had abandoned her during six months on the pretext that she loved him too much.

As for Jane, she listened to him in a silence that she tried to make natural and easy.

Telling me about it afterwards she said, "I had determined this time to give him no opportunity of laughing at me. I made scarcely a movement. Though I was trembling, I managed to sit down in a comfortable chair and cross my legs and lean back, as if he had come to tell me something pleasant."

He expressed without preamble his displeasure at finding her in the company of the Ivanoffs. He was surprised to find that she cared for such people. She knew, that he loathed Ivanoff and considered him an unfit companion for any respectable woman. He saw no reason why his wife should make his name a by-word in the glaring publicity of such a place as Biarritz. Here she was in the centre of a dissolute set of cosmopolitan adventurers, behaving like a common woman of light character, or at least giving the impression to the world of so behaving. He presumed that the Ivanoffs were her guests and were costing her a pretty penny. That was a side issue. The Russian was a dissolute ruffian who lived not alone on his winning at cards but on women. He was a man kept by women. As for Ivanoff's wife, she knew what her husband was up to and profitted by his earnings. Jane, with white lips interrupted him here.

"I don't believe you," she said quietly. And then more sharply, "You forget that Fan is my best friend."

He sneered. "I do not forget. I am merely unable to congratulate you on your taste. As for Ivanoff's habits I can give you precise details. There is a woman in this hotel—" Something in Jane's face stopped him. She did not speak at once, but leaning slightly forward, one arm on the table before her, looked at him calmly and smiled. She had done a good deal of thinking during those lonely months at Joigny. Alone and unobserved she had passed through her crisis. She was no longer the same person. Day after day, tramping the country, she had passed in review the years of her marriage and had scrutinized their every content, discovering slowly their meaning. She had learned a great many things. She was beginning to understand more than she had ever dreamed existed, of complication and danger in her surroundings, and she had determined if Philibert came back to her to put up a fight for her life, she meant her life with him: for the one thing she had not yet learned was to despise him. She still blamed herself for not having made him love her. She still cared for him. But she had learned a great deal, and among other things she had found out that she was alone. There was no one for her to turn to. His family, with one possible exception, myself, she realized now disliked her.

So she met him calmly. His attack had actually been a relief to her. Her agitation had been due just simply to the marvellous fact of his having come back to her, and she read in his annoyance a proof of his not being after all as indifferent to herself as he tried to make her believe. She voiced this.

"I was not aware," she said quietly, "that you in the least cared what I did." Her words and her tone startled him. He looked at her quickly. It was clear to him that she was older and wiser and would be more difficult to deal with than he had supposed. A gleam shot out at her from his eyes. It met an answering gleam. In silence their wills clashed. They were both aware that a struggle had begun. It was she who, after a moment, continued—

"I do not believe what you say about Fan and Ivanoff. I know that your worst accusation is untrue. Fan is incapable of accepting such money." She paused as if to calculate her effect and added deliberately. "As for Ivanoff, if he lives on women then I am one of them. I have lent him money myself."

He had turned away from her, but at this he whirled round like a top, his face contorted.

"What? What do you say? You? You have given him—?"

"Yes, I have given him money on several occasions."

Her immobility had its effect. He hung over her speechless, his lips twitching, and she continued to look at him. At last she spoke.

"What do you think I gave him money for, Philibert?"

He saw instantly his danger. Her tone conveyed it to him. If he voiced a suspicion of anything so horrible he destroyed himself for ever in her eyes. His brain worked quickly enough to save him. Marvellously and lucidly he knew she would never forgive him for suspecting her, and suddenly he knew that she could not be accused. Her virtue that had so bored him was unassailable and her pride frightened him. Whether he liked it or not there it was before him, and as if he couldn't bear the sight of it he whirled away from her and stalked to the window, muttering peevishly something about his not knowing why or what she had been up to. But she didn't let him off. Her voice followed him across the room.

"I gave Ivanoff money for Fan. You understand that, don't you, Philibert. You don't suggest for a moment anything else, do you?"

He remained with his back to her, and she remained where she was, waiting, watching his nervous hands that twisted his coat-tails, and his foot kicking the window-sill, watching her image of him shrinking, wavering, changing. At last she rose. She was afraid now, afraid of despising him, afraid to watch him any longer. She moved to the door and from her further distance spoke again.

"I have given Ivanoff in all two hundred and fifty thousand francs. If you have anything to say about my doing so, please speak now. I am waiting."

And he, at last, found the words with which to meet her.

"I don't believe Fan ever got a penny of it."

At that she faltered a moment, but only a moment. Her tone when she spoke was smooth and light.

"Well, if she didn't it's lost." She could take it as high as that. She gave a little shrug, just the slightest shrug. It may be that she really did strike him as almost coming up to his own standard at that moment. In any case he chose the instant for his own recovery. He had seemed not to know what to do. He had made a very painful impression. His indecision had humiliated her more than his violence. She felt ashamed for him now, and all the pent-up passion in her surged uncomfortably, hurtingly, against the shock her opinion of him had received, sending hot waves of blood pounding through her veins, that gave her a feeling of sickness. He divined something of this. It was time that he recovered himself, and his recovery was beautiful. It shows him, I maintain, an artist. He went up to her deliberately and took her hand, and looking into her eyes said—"You are astounding," then watching his effect he added, "You are superb. I do not understand, but I admire." And then deliberately with consummate gallantry he kissed her hand.

And poor Jane was pleased. On top of all her deep misery she was conscious of a little silvery ripple of pleasure. Though it would never be the same with her again she thought that she had won a battle, and made an impression, and with a kind of anguish of renunciation she accepted his offering. She knew now that he would never give her what she wanted, but she believed that he was prepared at last to give her something, and she was bound to allow him to do so.

They left Biarritz the next day, having agreed between them on a number of things. Jane was to inform the Ivanoffs that their rooms were retained for a fortnight longer. Philibert promised that he would never allow Ivanoff to know that he knew Jane had given him money. Jane in return agreed not to repeat the experiment and to have no further dealings with Ivanoff of any kind. She refused, however, to give up seeing Fan as she had always done.

XII

One day toward the middle of the winter of that year, Claire said to me; "What has happened to Philibert? He acts as if he were in love with his wife." It was true. We had all noticed it. I mean Claire and my mother and myself, but gradually we came to notice something else as well, namely that Philibert's increased attentions did not seem to be making Jane happy. She was strangely preoccupied and for her, strangely languid. Her old buoyancy was gone, and with it the impression she had so often conveyed of an over-powering awkward energy. *Maman* need never fear now that Jane would fall on her and crush her. Claire need not worry about being pushed into corners. When Jane did join our family parties, and she came much less frequently than in the early days, she was almost always so absent-minded as to seem scarcely to realize where she was. She would come in with Philibert and the child Geneviève, kiss my mother gently on the forehead and then sink into a chair and forget us. We might now have said anything preposterous that came into our heads. She would not have noticed us. She did not listen to our talk, and when we addressed her directly would give a little start and say—"*Je vous demande pardon, je n'ai pas compris.*" Sometimes I caught Philibert watching her as if he too were mystified and troubled. He would drag her into the conversation. "*Mais, mon amie, écoutes donc, quand on vous parle,*" he would exclaim in affectionate remonstrance, and she would flush a little and make a very obvious effort to pay attention. My mother felt there was something wrong. It may have seemed to her that she was herself responsible. She may have felt a certain contrition about Jane, or she may merely have found it intolerable that any one should derive from her drawing room circle so little apparent interest. In any case she made on her part an effort and talked to Jane much more, and in a different more intimate way than she had ever done before. And, of course, when actually talking directly to *Maman* Jane was perfectly attentive and perfectly courteously sweet-tempered. But when my mother turned her head toward some one else, Jane, as if released from the end of some invisible string that had held her erect in her chair, would slip back and lean her cheek on her hand, and the light in her eyes would be veiled by that invisible glaze that means an inward gazing. Such are the eyes of the blind. One could at such moment have waved one's fingers an inch from Jane's face, and she would not have blinked, at least that was my impression.

And she was incredibly thin. Many people thought this becoming to her, but to me it was painful. I had no wish to find Jane beautiful if I felt that she was going to die, and there were days when I did feel she was, as one says, going into a decline. She had been so harmoniously big that one would never have supposed she carried much superfluous flesh, until one saw it wasting away and found her still alive, and not a hideous skeleton. Her marvellous hands and feet were now, I suppose, even more marvellous, but to me their beautiful exposed structure of lovely bones was a source of pain. Her wrists and ankles were so slim that one felt if she made a wrong movement they would snap, and her rich lustrous clothes seemed to find round her waist and bust nothing to cling to. Only her broad shoulders and narrow hips seemed to support them. One could not tell where her waist was. Sometimes under the silken fabric of her skirt one saw the shape of a sharp knee bone. Her face seemed to have grown much smaller. The cheeks hollowed in under prominent cheek-bones, and her small green eyes were sunk into her head—that was more than ever like some carved antique coin and had taken on a quite terrifying beauty; I mean that the charm of her ugliness had received its special ordained stamp, the mark that the god or imp who made it had meant it to have. She reddened her lips a little now; otherwise her face was untouched by powder or rouge. The skin was of the palest ivory colour, a close smooth dull surface, without a blemish, soft and pure and dead. There was about the texture of her skin something curious. It made one dream of a contact so cold that if a butterfly brushed against it the little living thing would fall lifeless to the ground.

And a new charm disengaged itself from her person. She seemed possessed of a hitherto-unused and undiscovered magnetism, and she dwelt with it silently, wrapped in a kind of gentle gloom that she tried now and then to throw off as one throws off a wet clinging garment. I do not want to give the impression that she was moody, for that would be untrue. She was, on the contrary, of an uncanny equanimity, and when she smiled her smile crept slowly and softly over her face and as softly faded away. There was no jerk of nerves about it. Nervous was the last word one could apply to her. She was superlatively quiet, unnaturally calm, and yet at times she looked at me like a haunted woman, a woman haunted not by a ghost but by an idea, perhaps by some profoundly disturbing knowledge.

We were increasingly troubled. We wondered if at last she had found out things about Philibert, particularly about Philibert and Bianca, and somehow the fact that we knew he was devoting himself more to Jane and less to Bianca did not console us. What indeed was it but just the most disturbing thing of all that Philibert's new devotion to Jane produced in her no flush of responsive joy? My mother was very worried indeed, and we were affected by her anxiety. Even Claire began to watch Jane with a questioning puzzled attention. Often I found Claire's dark eyes travelling from Jane to Philibert, from Philibert to my mother, from my mother back to Jane. And simultaneously my mother's eyes moved from one to the other, and so did Philibert's and so did mine. We were all looking from one to the other, watching, referring, puzzling, comparing. Jane alone looked at no one.

I should have felt this to be humorous had it not humiliated and annoyed. It seemed to me that we were slightly ridiculous at times, and at other times lacking in delicacy. The last impression irked me exceedingly. For my mother and sister to be guilty of indelicacy was strangely unpleasant, I knew they were not impelled in their new interest by affection. They did not even now care for Jane. She had become to them an enigma; that of course was something more than she had been; there was a shade of admiration now in their wondering, but no genuine feeling for her and no sympathy. Their sympathy was for Philibert, and perhaps, a little for themselves. In any case they were afraid for Philibert. They saw his great social edifice swaying. They were holding their breath. And Jane gave them no sign. Had she calculated her effect with consummate art her manner could not have been more perfectly tuned to the high fine note of suspense. And they dared not to ask her anything.

But as the weeks passed, they gave way to asking each other. In her absence they constantly talked of her. It was curious how much of their attention she took up by staying so much away. Claire and my mother could now often be heard to say—"Have you seen Jane? What is the child doing with herself? I find her looking very unwell. Has she complained to you of feeling ill?" and now and again with a sigh of reproach either my mother or Claire would say to the other—"What a pity you never won her confidence. She tells us nothing, but absolutely nothing. It's as if she didn't trust us."

And Philibert seemed as much at a loss as they. He could enlighten them very little. Gradually as their nervousness made them less discreet they took to questioning him. "But what is the matter with her?" they would ask, and he would shrug his shoulders. He didn't know. Did he think she was ill? No, she wasn't ill, she had never been so active. Was she then unhappy? Ah, who could say? She was now and then very gay, much gayer at moments than he had ever known her. She went out constantly. She had ideas of her own about receiving. She was arranging a series of musical evenings for the audition of unpublished works of young French composers. She was multiplying her activities. Sometimes he did not see her alone for days together. And here my mother gently and timidly interrupted him. "*Mais mon enfant*, when she is alone with you, is she amiable, is she kind? *Enfin*, is she gracious?" And Philibert again, but this time with a more exaggerated movement, shrugged his shoulders—"*Comme cela.* I have no right to complain."

And then quickly I saw them all look at each other and saw the same thought flit from one mind to the other and dodge away out of sight, and the spectacle of those intelligent evasive glances exasperated me.

"Yes, it's a different story now, isn't it?" I didn't care for their combined shocked stare, now centred on myself, and continued to Philibert—"After all, you've got what you wanted, haven't you? You remember you told her not to love you so much."

"Blaise!" My mother's exclamation was a check. I had a sensation of shaking myself free. "Well, isn't it so? Weren't you all awfully bored with her caring too much for you, and now that she doesn't, now that she has withdrawn, is leading a life of her own, you are troubled, you wonder. How can you wonder? Isn't it all quite simple?" But I knew that it was not so simple after all, so I stopped.

"You think then," put in my sister gravely, "that she no longer cares for us?" Her tone made me stare in my turn. It was earnest and enquiring, and I heard Philibert to my astonishment echoing her words. "Ah, you believe she no longer cares?" And most wonderful of all my mother's phrase. "Tell us, Blaise, what she does feel. I believe that you understand her better than we do."

It was quite extraordinary. I had the strangest feeling for a moment of pride and power. They had all turned to me. They had all recognized simultaneously that I possessed something valuable. And for a moment I enjoyed the novel sensation. They wanted something from me, that was pleasant, but what they wanted was Jane's secret. They believed she had confided in me, and they believed I would tell them. I felt again weary and impatient and humiliated, and I brought out the truth abruptly. "I know no more than you do what is going on in Jane's mind, she has told me nothing." But I saw that they did not believe me.

The room, my mother's room, seemed to shrink visibly. It appeared very small and trivial. Its innumerable bibelots and souvenirs winked and glinted, mischievous and precious, minute tokens of delicate prejudice, obstinate and conventional and colourless. It all looked small and meaningless and pale. I could have laughed. I was important there at last. But it was a tiny place to me now. I pitied it. I felt suddenly free and alone. I thought—"Jane has told me nothing, it is true, nevertheless she trusts me," and I felt them reading my mind and it didn't matter. They might know for all I cared that I knew nothing, they would feel all the same that I knew Jane as they would never know her. But what they would never know was, that knowing Jane as I did, I knew many other things, wonderful things. I felt a lift, a lightening, a widening of space, a fresh rush of wind as if I was being blown upon by the breath of those wide American forests. Somewhere in my mind vistas opened. I heard the murmuring of a free wind in high branches. And all the time I saw my frail little mother in her damask chair, in her little crowded silken room, and I loved her with tenderness and compassion. An impulse seized me. I went over to her. I took her hand.

"If only you would love her," I said, "everything would be all right." Then I saw that I had blundered. How could I have been so stupid as to have imagined that they had been with me for that moment in those wide high spaces where I knew Jane lived? My words sounded grotesque and fatuous. I saw a shade come over my mother's face. I heard Claire's swish of impatient drapery. Philibert snorted. I felt myself blushing. My face tingled. I had made myself ridiculous. My mother's hand kept me off. Its nervous clasp pushed me from her while she murmured plaintively—"*Mais je l'aime bien, mais je l'aime bien.*"

Claire followed me out of the room. In the little dark hall we stood close together. She had closed the door of the drawing room after her. Beyond it we heard Philibert's high nasal voice arguing. "What do you really think, Blaise?" My sister's voice was low and confidential. I felt her mind pressing upon me with gentle insistence.

"I don't know."

"But you see a great deal of her, she talks to you."

"Yes, but not about herself."

"Come, Blaise."

"Not about the present, only of the past, her home over there."

She made an impatient gesture.

"Does she never mention Philibert?"

"Never in any way that matters. How can you think—? Do you imagine then that she is vulgar?"

But Claire's eyes, tranquil and dark with their usual mournful depths of mystery, looked at me deeply as if she had not heard.

"I am afraid," she said, "of Bianca."

I was startled. The idea that Claire was afraid, so afraid as to voice her fear to me in that low tone of secret confidence, seemed to make everything worse, much more miserable.

"Why?" I asked, searching her face that so often evaded me with its mockery and now was so grave and deliberate.

"She may do something."

"What?"

"I don't know, but she's jealous."

"Jealous of Jane?"

"Yes, hadn't you noticed? She follows her about?"

"Bianca follows Jane about?"

"Just that."

I thought how strange women are, seeing things that we none of us notice. I followed Bianca, Jane and Claire in imagination, moving about Paris in smooth rapid motors, slipping in and out of crowded streets, shops, drawing-rooms, theatres, watching each other. But how could Claire see one pursuing the other with all those people round them, all the music, the waiters, the footmen, the lights scattered along dinner-tables, the obstructing tables and chairs, the endless engagements? My mind wavered, I felt dizzy. I saw each one of the three women stepping out of her car, going into her house, the door closing upon her, hiding her from the world.

I came back to Claire's delicate face and brooding eyes.

"But why should Bianca be jealous?"

"But why not?"

"You mean she thinks Philibert is escaping her?"

"And isn't he?"

"I don't know." Suddenly I felt at the end of my strength, as if I had been undergoing a great nervous strain. "How should I know anything about Philibert? You all seem to think I know what Philibert is up to." I felt strangely exasperated. "And what, *mon dieu*, is there exactly between Bianca and Philibert?"

"Ah," my sister smiled faintly, "that I cannot tell you, but whatever it is, it is enough."

"Enough to make trouble, you mean?"

"Yes, enough to make trouble."

"Well, if you really want my opinion, it is that Jane does not bother at all about Bianca." And I began irritably to get into my coat. But Claire, helping me on with it, still pressed me and said over my shoulder—

"So you don't think Jane in her turn is jealous?"

"I don't think anything about it. What I think is that it is none of my business." And I grabbed my hat and left her, but looking back as I went down the few steps to the outer door, I saw her looking after me with an inscrutable smile, as if she had learned something from me that she had wanted to know, and I determined to keep away from such family talks in future.

I had my theory about Jane during those days, of course, but according to Clémentine I was wrong. Clémentine thinks that Jane loves Philibert even now, even now over there in that dreary little house. I can't believe it. But what does Clémentine mean by love, anyway? Clémentine is a Latin, the smooth willing exponent and devotee of her senses. She has known love—"*elle a rencontré l'amour plusieurs fois.*" If she means anything, if there's anything in what she says about Jane, it is that Philibert still has the power to affect Jane, to make her pulse beat quicker, even now. I wonder, but I don't want to think about it.

I believed that winter that Jane had ceased to care for Philibert, and that that was the explanation of her strangeness, that made her appear so often like a sleep-walker. I argued that to a person like Jane it would be more terrible to no longer love than to be no longer loved. There were moments when alone in my room with her image before me, I was certain that she was beginning to despise him. How could she help it I would ask myself, and be filled with an exulting bitterness. I see now what it was. I wanted her to despise him, and so believed it. But it was not so much that I fiendishly wanted Philibert to suffer, for I did not believe he would suffer. I wanted Jane to right herself. That was it. I wanted her to get loose from her bonds that seemed to me to expose her in an attitude humiliating and pitiful. I couldn't bear to contemplate her as Philibert's slave. It was this thought that sent me out at night to walk the streets in a fever. Ridiculous? Perhaps. But haven't I a phrase of Jane's sounding in my brain even now that justifies all my sickening suspicions of the past, one phrase, the only one that she ever let fall that threw any light on her relations with her husband.

It was only the other day in St. Mary's Plains. Time had made it possible for her to speak as she did. Ten years, fifteen, had passed, but she spoke with an icy distinctness as if controlling a shudder.

"Bianca," she said, "was jealous of that process of corruption that she called my happiness." But this is all too painful. I must stick to the facts of my story.

Claire's fear was all too well founded. Bianca was jealous and Bianca was going to intervene. Philibert was slipping away from her and falling in love with his stupid wife. That could not be tolerated. She stirred uneasily. Moreover Paris was beginning to take account of Jane. People were talking about her wherever one went. They argued about whether she was ugly or just the most beautiful woman in Europe. Sides were equally divided. But what did it matter whether one called it beauty or ugliness, once her appearance had made its impression upon the receptive mind of Paris? The Byzantine Madonna or the Egyptian mummy or whatever it was that she had been said to resemble had come to life. Paris recognized her as singular, and that was all that was necessary. Soon she would be the rage. Some one would set the ball rolling. Bianca saw it all quite clearly. Like a little witch bending over a boiling pot she made her preparations. It would be funny to think of if it had not come off just as she intended. The sorceress was again on the move astride her broomstick. She was chanting her incantations that were meant to bring a woman to the dust and a man to her side. But first she sent for Fan and told her all about Ivanoff and Jane and about Philibert's interference in Biarritz. She had got the whole story from Philibert and used it now with just the effect she wished. She began lamenting the fact that she saw so little of Jane, Jane was dropping her old friends. Hadn't Fan noticed a difference? No, Fan hadn't. But Ivanoff—surely Jane didn't see anything much of Ivanoff these days, not at any rate as she used to? Fan laughed. If Bianca thought Jane capable of flirting—. But Bianca meant nothing so silly. Bianca meant simply that Jane had been very foolish and that Philibert was angry with Ivanoff and wouldn't have anything to do with him because of Jane's foolishness. Fan at this, had grown suddenly serious. The rest was easy. It all came out. Ivanoff had had large sums of money from Jane. Philibert had found out, and Jane had made him swear to do nothing about it so that Fan should never know. This, of course had been most unfair to Ivanoff as the latter had been given no chance to clear himself with Philibert. Ivanoff might have been able to explain many things that remained obscure.

The result of this conversation was all that Bianca would wish for. Poor Fan rushed home to her dilapidated attic on the Isle St. Louis and flung it all at Ivanoff's great sleek meek head. He had been taking money from Jane. How much money? When? Why? Where was it? How could he? How had he come to think of such a thing? Didn't he have any sense of honour? Didn't he have any shame? Ivanoff bowed his head. Meekly and humbly he let her rave at him until exhausted, she flung herself on the bed in a torrent of tears, and all that night he sat on the floor beside her bed, extravagantly ashamed, thinking vague dark hopeless thoughts, and now and then heaving a sigh.

It didn't occur to him, the next day or the next or any day after that to explain anything. Probably he was unaware that Fan's second thoughts were more poisoning and disturbing to her than the first. Ivanoff was no psychologist. If he noticed that Fan was strained and looked at him queerly, he remained passive and mute, and no light of curiosity seemed to strike down into his abysmal calm. When suddenly Fan flashed out the question—"Did you make love to her?" he merely shook his head, and when at last after a week of fidgetting she announced that she had written to Jane to tell her that they couldn't pay the money back and that she would understand the wisdom of their not seeing each other any more, he stared vacantly, then frowned and sat down in a heap on the divan for the rest of the day. Judging by his fantastic subsequent behaviour, he must have been pondering upon the question. He probably thought—"Women are worthless cattle. Jane has told. She has given away the secret. She has hurt Fan. I am getting tired of Fan. Some day I will go away, but Jane hurt her and made her tiresome and she must be hurt too, before I go. But how? But how?" That was the difficulty. He must think of some way. And all the time he was sitting there thinking, he could hear Fan coughing and tossing in her room, and he could see her little tame chaffinches jumping about in their cage in the window. Fan was often like that, like a neat little bird flitting and hopping about, but now she was sick and ruffled and not gay and chirpy at all.

XIII

I come now to the night of old François's ball that he gave for his daughter Bianca, that dreadful night of climax and exposure when the fabric of appearance was torn to shreds and we were left there, betrayed by ourselves to the eye of God, stark naked in all our senseless passion and trivial brutality. The experience of that night stands up for me out of the past bald and glaring in all its garish savagery like a totem pole in a glittering desert. I circle round it. The habits and tastes of civilization appear there like a mirage. I see the actors of the drama behaving like primitive creatures possessed by demons. Civilization skin deep? The banality is apt here. I have called Philibert and Bianca the spoiled darlings and perfect exponents of an ultra-refined social system, and so they were, but that didn't prevent their behaving like a cave man and woman. The only difference was that they knew what they were doing. They were calculating and deliberate and amused. They turned loose the reckless savagery with the little dry laugh of knowledge.

I did not go to the ball myself. I had been away, had come back unexpectedly, and had found myself by some extraordinary mischance, some curious combination of circumstances, locked out of my rooms and without a key. It was late. I remember being unwilling to rouse my mother at that time of night, and standing in the street wondering which one of my friends I would ask for a bed, I don't know why I suddenly decided to go to Philibert's. I had never spent a night in his house in my life, but now, as if Paris were suddenly an unknown city of strangers and his roof the only prospect of shelter, I found my way in a fiacre to his bleak and imposing door.

I remember the emptiness of the house as I entered, the great silent entrance hall with its sleepy porter, and the coldness of the wide marble stairway and my unwillingness in spite of the solicitations of a couple of men servants to go to bed anywhere in any one of the blank luxurious rooms offered to me, until Philibert or Jane came home to authorize me to do so. "*Monsieur et Madame* would undoubtedly be very late," the footman told me, "they were '*chez Monsieur le duc*,' where there was a ball." I listened vaguely, accepted a tray of refreshments and sent the men to bed, saying that I would wait up for the master. But the wine and biscuits placed in the library did not tempt me to ease or somnolence. I felt restless and oppressed. How big the place was to house a man and a woman and a child. What a distance to little Geneviève's nursery. I picked up a book, put it down. A long mirror opposite me reflected a portion of the great high shadowy room and my own small wizened figure seated like a gnome in a circle of light. The sight of myself, always unpleasant, set me wandering. I turned on lights here and there. All was still and smooth with the vast ordered beauty of a cold enchanted palace. The thought of Philibert's success as a house decorator passed through my mind without engaging my attention, that seemed somehow to be fixed on something else, something deep and elusive that had a meaning could I but find it. What did they stand for, those high polished walls with their lovely panellings? What did they enclose beyond so many treasures of art? The rare still air in those gleaming spaces seemed to have a quality, a presence, cold, enigmatic, and final. I tiptoed round the immense deserted salons like a thief. I waited and waited with a growing sense of the ominous, and then at last I heard the whirr of a motor coming into the porte cochère, and going out along the gallery to the great wide shadowy stairhead, I looked down and saw the light flash out, filling the vast white lower hall, and saw Jane come in alone, trailing her long gleaming draperies behind her, and advance across that expanse of marble like a woman in a trance, holding up and out in her hand before her, well away from her as if she were afraid of it, a small object that I identified when she had almost reached the top of those interminable stairs as a small dead bird with a jewelled pin run through its body.

She spoke in a queer tired voice that grated slightly.

"I found it in the car, on the cushion. Ivanoff must have put it there. It is one of Fan's birds. A chaffinch—you see—He meant it as a symbol."

It was as if her teeth were almost chattering, and she were controlling that shaking of jaws with an effort. And as she spoke, I saw Ivanoff distinctly, taking that tiny feathered thing out of its cage and wringing its neck with his strong brown fingers, and smiling through his slits of eyes. Jane continued to hold it out before her and stared at it. Presently she said again in that queer rasping voice—

"Look, it's quite dead. It has been speared through the heart. The pin is one I gave Fan years ago. The bird is her pet chaffinch. My Aunt Patience used to tame chaffinches. There was one that used to perch on her head while she worked. That was in St. Mary's Plains."

She stopped and looked at me a moment in silence enquiringly. We were standing at the head of the stairs. Something in my face must have arrested her attention. "Come," she said in a sudden tone of command.

"Come into the drawing room. We will wait together for Philibert." She said the last three words much more loudly than the others. They seemed to go rolling down the long gallery like rattling stones. I remember thinking that she must be very ill and that I ought to persuade her to go to bed. We moved in the direction of the drawing rooms. She was dressed in some shining glittering sheathlike thing of a silvery tone and wore emeralds in her ears and on her hands. Her eyes were as green as her earrings, and her face the colour of yellowish white wax. She dragged a chinchilla cloak after her as if it were terribly heavy. It had slipped off her shoulders and I noticed that her skin was covered with little beads of moisture. I thought—"The Lady of the Seas." She looked as if she had been in an accident—been wounded somewhere. I half expected to see a red spot spreading over her side as she let fall her cloak in the great drawing room and turned on, one after another, a blazing circle of lights. The effect was startling. There was no stain of blood on her gown, but the livid pallor of her face and arms in that glare of light suggested that she was all the same in the state of one who had all but bled to death. Under the glittering lustre of many crystals, her face was a gaunt mask of yellowish bone and pale greenish shadow, and her lips were drawn tight across gleaming teeth. Her expression was famished, thirsty, breathless.

I was frightened, and at the same time strangely excited. Where was Philibert? What was the meaning of Jane's feverish icy glitter? Why were we there, she and I, at three o'clock in the morning, transfixed in a blaze of artificial light in a room that was as inimical as a palace in Hell? As she turned away and moved to the mantelpiece, where she stood with her back to me, leaning her elbows on the black carved marble, I had a moment's respite. What did she want me for? Wouldn't Philibert think it queer our waiting up for him in such ridiculous solemnity. I addressed her long shining back.

"Do you often wait up for him?" She turned half way round.

"No, but tonight we must wait, we must wait until we know."

Her words gave me a feeling of weakness. I was obliged to sit down. All that light, all that gleaming parquet, all those precious cabinets, full of rare glimmering treasures, and the night outside, wheeling towards day, and Philibert coming from somewhere in a motor, and all the people of Paris sleeping, quite still, in their beds but being whirled through space on a turning globe, made me dizzy. I heard her say from a great distance—

"Fan is not dead. She was at the ball. She avoided me. She looked very ill. Ivanoff wanted to frighten me. I would have been, if I hadn't been more frightened by something else. Fan was my friend, so was Bianca. I have no friends now. It is very strange to be quite alone when things are going to happen."

"What is going to happen?" I tried to speak naturally.

"I don't know. We must wait. We will find out."

She came across to me and then looked at me shyly. It was suddenly as if she had come to herself again, and whereas she had seemed terribly old, as old as a deathless woman of some strange legend, she was now for a moment merely young and helpless and unhappy.

"You will be a friend to me, won't you?" she asked dropping into a chair before me. I nodded, unable to speak.

And so we sat on in the centre of that immense room in two gilt fauteuils under the full glare of the chandelier. Occasionally she said something, then would sink into silence and seem to forget that I was there. But each time that the clock on the mantelpiece struck the quarter or the half hour she would start convulsively.

At a quarter to four she said—"Ivanoff meant me to feel that I had broken Fan's heart, but Fan is all right. I saw her. She looked quite happy tonight and she danced continually. What does that mean—a broken heart? What makes one feel pain in one's left side when one is unhappy? Just the power of suggestion? Perhaps if that power were strong enough it would affect the actual heart in one's body, make it burst in one's side." Then without transition, "I would have sent for my Aunt Patience, but I did not want her to know. I was safe in her house. Sometimes I think of the Grey House as the only safe place in the world. If I went back there now, I wonder if I would feel the same, or whether it would seem very small and stuffy and shabby. My people there were very simple people. They loved me. They were all very religious except my Aunt Patty who believed in science. One ought to believe in something—I don't. I can't. I joined the Catholic Church to please Philibert but I don't believe. If my Aunt Beth knew she would worry about my eternal life. I wonder if I would find that a nuisance or just the most touching thing in the world. I wonder if they would all look like funny old frumps or seem quite beautiful. One can't tell."

Her voice stopped. We sat in a silence that grew steadily more tense and unbearable. The clock struck four and she started to her feet, and a spasm twisted her features and she began to talk very rapidly while at the same time she seemed to be panting for breath.

"I have found out tonight. I found out at the ball. It was like a revelation from heaven. I saw it all in a blinding burst. The noise of the music, the crowd, pale faces wheeling round me, bobbing ducking, they couldn't hide it from me. Bianca was there, at the centre, cold, sharp, like a silver needle, watching Philibert, drawing him to her like a magnet. Every one was there. I was alone. I saw Fan in the distance. She avoided me, but I heard her coughing and her high little voice crying out through her hacking cough to some one—'Yes, my dear, I'm dying. Why not? 39 of fever, but I simply had to come. What's a woman's life worth if she can't dance.' And then that cough again. Every one danced interminably. I saw Aunt Clothilde sitting like a bronze fountain with a watershed of grey silk spreading all round her, in a corner of the library; she was saying witty things in her squeaky voice to solemn old men in wigs. I stood alone in a window, watching Bianca watch Philibert. I must have spoken to a number of people, I don't remember. Hands reached for mine, voices murmured, voices addressed me by name. Other voices laughed and whispered and cried out round me. The music throbbed. Faces whirled past. Some women shrieked and giggled out in the garden. Waiters and footmen moved about. Motors hooted in the street. The waves of darkness welled up behind me to meet the waves of light rolling out of the hot rooms. I was cold, cold as ice, my face burning. Some one going past shouted at me, 'I say, you look ghastly. Have something?' I didn't answer. I was watching Bianca. Bianca was my friend—I loved her. I watched men and women approach her, touch her fingers, move away. I watched other men circle round her, keep coming back, hang forward humbly, shoulders hunched, heads bowed, waiting for a word from her, fascinated men who desired and pleased her. Philibert was among them, but he didn't hang forward bowing. He stood near her, twirling his moustaches, talking to one and then another, making gestures, laughing, frowning, snubbing people, being impertinent, being amusing, flattering old dowagers, glaring at presumptuous youths, criticizing women with his cold eyes, and every now and then exchanging a look with Bianca. They scarcely spoke to each other, but I could see their communion was uninterrupted. I saw and understood—He has always loved her. They have always been together like that, always. That is what I have found out, and more, more. It was so before I came, before he met me, while we were engaged, when we were married, always Bianca, she was always there.

"Tonight I saw them together, perfectly. I watched them. I wanted to fathom them, to know what it was they possessed between them. I knew it was evil. I longed to know their evil. The sight of Bianca roused in me a horrible envy. I stood like a stone watching her. She used to be my friend—I loved her. Evil appeared to me upon her face beautiful, shining out like a sickly light, potent, alluring. Suddenly I heard a squeaky voice say—'Come here, child. You shouldn't show yourself with a face like that. If it's so bad lock yourself up. Men are all brutes. Some day you won't care.' I looked at your Aunt Clothilde, blind with rage, you know, blind, and turned and went out through the window into the garden. At the far end in the dark I walked up and down alone. The music and the light streamed out of the long windows. I saw innumerable heads bobbing. It looked like a madhouse. Philibert and Bianca were in there together, cool, sane, infinitely wise. I was the insane person. At one o'clock I went in again and crossed to where Philibert stood beside Bianca and asked him if he were ready to come home. Bianca was in white. She was almost naked. She had a cloud of white round her and her body was as visible through it as a silver lily through water. She looked fresh and cool as dew. Philibert answered but did not look at me. 'You need not wait,' was what he said, but I was watching Bianca's face and I saw there something else. Her eyes were wide open. They poured their meaning into mine. Her face was like a still white flower holding two drops of deadly poison. She did not move. She did not smile. It was all in her eyes. I looked down into them for an instant, one instant. It was enough. I had a feeling as I turned away of coming up out of a great depth, of breaking a spell. The Duke took me through the rooms to the top of the stairs. I walked beside him, my hand on his arm. I didn't look back. I left them together.

"I found Ivanoff's dead bird in the car. It didn't frighten me. But I was frightened. I felt as I drove away like some one who has had a narrow escape, a very close shave. Why? What was it? Nothing had happened, nothing visible, nothing to disturb the still immensity of the spell-bound avenue. I drove on alone, up the Champs Elysées. The sky was studded like a shield with hard pointed stars. The double row of roundheaded lamps lining the black gleaming surface of the pavement stood like sentinels put there to conduct me out through the Arc de Triomphe into desolate uncharted space. I held Ivanoff's dead bird in my hand, and I felt as if I were driving away from that crowded ball room straight over the rim of the earth. The sight of you here, at the top of the stairs brought me to my senses. I remembered. I understood on the instant of seeing you that I had wanted to kill Bianca, tonight. That was what had frightened me. That was my close shave. You stood there, worried and tired and kind. I recognized you."

Her voice stopped suddenly. She covered her face with her hands. I rose to my feet and took a step towards her, and just then the clock struck five and its little gilt angel stepped out with his tiny jewelled trumpet. She whirled towards it, lifting her face that was drawn like an old woman's.

"Philibert will not come ... I know now," she whispered. "He has gone away with Bianca." She swayed, looked this way and that around the wide gleaming room, them at me, holding out her hands. "Help me, Blaise."

In a moment she had given way to sobbing. Ah, then, then I, who had never touched so much as her hair or her cheek or the fold of her dress, then indeed, I would have taken her in my arms to comfort her, as one takes a child. But she was the great strong creature, I was the weakling. I could only kneel by her chair and try to steady her convulsed frame and heaving shoulders with my own arm round them in futile incompetent anguish, while I heard her heart breaking as if it were so much strong stuff being splintered there in her side.

It was six o'clock when she went to her room. The servants were not yet about. The house was still, impenetrably calm, the curtains still drawn, the formality of its beautiful equanimity unchanged.

Six o'clock; Bianca and Philibert were well on their way by that time, travelling south, rolling smoothly along over long white roads between mysterious poplars in a misty dawn. They had provisions with them in the car. I can see them now as I think back, opening a bottle of champagne, eating sandwiches, and I can hear their laughter. They were very gay, very pleased with the way they had done it. They had walked straight out of François' house together at three thirty in the morning, had stepped into the motor in the presence of a crowd of departing guests, and had disappeared. The audacity of the thing was of a kind to tickle them immoderately. They must have laughed a good deal. I wonder that Jane and I, spellbound under that glaring chandelier, didn't hear them. Strange that the echoes of their light laughter didn't travel back to us across that widening distance, while we waited and listened. Strange to think of that old *roué* François wandering back through his emptied rooms, among the débris of that night's festival, all unsuspecting. Very curious to think of Philibert and Bianca murmuring to each other, their laughter giving way to the bitter and exultant growling of their excited senses, while I led Jane back to her room. No one saw her go tottering down the hall leaning against me. No one saw her swollen face looking through the door and trying to smile at me before she closed herself in alone.

PART II

I

That was long ago. We were young then. What a haunting annoying phrase. One meets it everywhere, in books, on people's lips, or unspoken in their eyes. The other day in the Grey House, sitting opposite Jane in the shabby little parlour, there it was again. She spoke it, but not wistfully, more with relief than regret. I stayed ten days in St. Mary's Plains and during those days she told me the rest of the story, bit by bit, till she came to the end—I put it down now as she told it—what follows are her own words as I remember them.

That was the end of my youth and the beginning of life. Until then I had been made use of, but after that I acted and I became responsible for myself.

Fifteen years ago, we sat till morning waiting for Philibert. I no longer remember what I felt. Have you tried to recall sensations of pain, and by thinking very closely about all the little circumstances surrounding them, to experience again the stab or the ache? One can't. I can't feel again that agony. I suppose it was agony. You remember it better than I do, for you saw it. One remembers things one has seen and things one did, but not what went on inside one's own dark, impenetrable body and soul, invisibly. I remember what I did at that time and what I said and what other people said and looked. I remember your face, and Jinny's fear of me, and her fretting for her father, and Fan's coming and saying that I looked like a mad woman, and from these facts I deduce the other fact that I was suffering, but I have forgotten the feeling. That is very strange when you come to think of it, for how, then, can I know that it was so? I don't know. It is all merely conjecture. One would have thought, from the way I behaved and the way it changed everything that my emotion of that time was tremendous; was immensely important. But it wasn't. It had no substance. It didn't stand the test of time. It has vanished completely. Other things have lasted.

What are these feelings, emotions, passions that we make such a fuss about? Nothing but sparks struck from an impact, a collision of some kind. They seem to burn us up, to consume us for a moment, then they vanish.

They have no body, no staying power, no reality, but we mould our lives by them.

I am a woman. My life has always centred about people. In tracing the course of events, I find that their causes were invariably personal—My life is a long strong twisted rope made up of a number of human relationships, nothing more. There was first my mother, and my Aunt Patience, then Philibert, Bianca and Geneviève. Philibert went away. I did without him. One can do without anything,—everything. I am proving it now. But Bianca kept coming back; I never got rid of her.

My life is a failure. It is finished. It is there in its dreadful, unchangeable completeness spread out before me. I look at it, as I would look at a map, and when I think that it is I who made it, this thing called a human life, I am bewildered and ashamed. How did it come about that I made so many mistakes, and did so much that was harmful to others? There was no desire in my heart to hurt, no will to do wrong. On the contrary I wanted to make people happy, I wanted to do right. It is very strange. It is almost as if the intensity of my will to do right forced me to do the wrong thing. Is there some explanation? Is there a key to the problem of living that I never found? Or was it all simply due to Bianca? My Aunt Beth used to say that the only way to live rightly was to do the will of God. But what does that mean? How is one to know what the will of God is? Often I wonder whether my failure is due to my never having found out about God. Most of my people here in America would not hesitate to say yes—but I am not sure. It seems to me that I was even more eager to do His will than I would have been if I had been certain of His existence. It would have been an immense relief to me to have known that God was in His Heaven and that I did not have to bother about my own soul. "Put your troubles on the Lord," our parson used to say in St. Mary's Plains. Well—I don't know. That is a solution for many. If they do that—just shelve everything and go by texts in the Bible for their order of daily conduct, living must be very much simplified—but I couldn't do that. Something stiff and hard and honest in me wouldn't allow it. I couldn't believe that I could talk to God and ask His opinion. I used to try— when I was a child and when I was a woman. Praying was like whispering into a chasm, a void, an echoing emptiness. My questions came back to me, unanswered, mocking echoes of my own tormented soul.

So I floundered along.

I do not excuse myself. I am to blame. I am responsible. I know that. I lived among charming people. I had, as people say, almost everything heart can desire. My husband did not love me, but beyond that what had I to complain of? I had money, health, power, friends. I was one of the fortunate. Hundreds of women, no doubt, envied me.

I hadn't the gift of living. Your mother has it, so has your sister. It is common among French people, they are artists in life, but I was for ever looking beyond life for its purpose, and thus missing its savour and its meaning. The people I loved were too important to me and the people I hated—but I can see now that Bianca wasn't as interesting or as important as she seemed. She was only a vain and selfish woman after all. But she was for twenty years my obsession.

I must talk about Bianca. It was really in order to talk about Bianca that I asked you to come, for I am not yet rid of her. She haunts me here in this innocent old house. Enigmatic in death as she was in life, her personality persists, exquisite and depraved and relentless. She comes to accuse me. Having ruined my life, she accuses me of her death.

I did not kill her. Some of you thought that I did. You didn't mind. You didn't blame me, but you thought so. Ludovic, I am sure, is convinced of it, and if he does not precisely approve, he at least accepts the fact as the inevitable outcome of our long exhausting duel. More than once he told me that until I could rid myself of the obsession of Bianca, I should be unable to understand the first little thing about life. He was the one person who understood my feeling for her and hers for me. In his uncanny wisdom, so devoid of all prejudice, he knew that our hatred was based upon an intense mutual attraction, and that we hounded each other to death because under other circumstances we would have loved each other. The long and dreary spectacle of two women hating each other for years with intense sympathy, or if you like, loving each other with an exasperating antagonism and hatred, was to him pitiful and contemptible. He would have had me put an end to it somehow, anyhow, at any cost. Taking another's life is to him no crime compared to ruining one's own. Well, it is at an end now. Bianca is dead, and I am buried alive. We did each other in, but it took twenty years, and I never touched her with my hands, or did anything to bring about her death, save will her to die.

And her death came too late to do me or mine any good. Philibert was finished. My life was in pieces. There was nothing left to patch up. She had come between me and my husband and child, while living, but her death cut me off from them, more absolutely than anything she could have done alive. And, fiendishly, as if with consummate cunning, she died mysteriously leaving with me the unanswerable question, as to whether or not, I had made her kill herself. I go over and over it all, day after day, week in, week out. I remember my last view of her alive, in that hotel corridor, the look she gave me over her drooping shoulder, leaning against the half open door, her hand on the door knob, her long languid weight on it, one pointed foot trailing, and on her grey face, a desperate vindictive longing, a wistful cruelty, a question, a threat, a prayer. Was she at last imploring me? Did she in that moment remember everything? Was she mutely and bitterly asking me to come and hear her confession? Would it all have been put right by some miracle had I gone to her before it was too late? I don't know—I shall never know. I only know that our wills clashed again for the last time, that for the last time I resisted her, and let her drag the incredible weight of her diseased and disappointed spirit out of my sight, for ever.

And how am I to know that her death wasn't an accident, and that her look of desperate appeal wasn't just such a piece of acting as she had treated me to, at intervals for twenty years? Over and over again, she had done the same trick. Invariably, after one of her pieces of devilry, she would approach me with that wistful penitent masque, and stir me to forgiveness and compassion. Repeatedly, she fooled me. I could save her—I could influence her for good. I was strong and balanced and sane. If only I would give her what she needed, what she lacked, some relief from herself in some external thing, some faith, some definite obstinate purpose, beyond the gratification of her own vanity.

And each time I believed, each time I forgave, each time looking into her wonderful face, I thought I saw there, a spiritual meaning. It is enough to make one scream with laughter. It was all acting. It must have been. It was all done for the purpose of tormenting me more exquisitely afterwards. For years she fooled me—for years I wouldn't believe she was what she was, a woman of immense personality and no character, but I am at last certain that this was so. Ludovic says that it takes as strong a character to be really wicked as really good. He used to rave over Bianca, to anger me, I suppose, call her perversely—"*une femme admirable—la plus courageuse damnée qu'il avait jamais vue.*" I don't agree with him. I do not mean that Bianca had a weak character. I mean literally that she had no character at all. Where one feels in the average human being, the strong resisting kernel, the stern spiritual centre that contains identity there in Bianca there was nothing. At the middle centre of her being there was emptiness. She had, morally, no core. She was as formless as one of those genii in the Arabian Nights who came out of Ali Baba's earthenware pots.

I ought to know, for I loved her. She was my friend during the happiest years of my life, when I believed in Philibert, and was confident. I say it again, we were friends. I believe even now, in our early friendship, in those days, Bianca was actually, and much to her own surprise, fond of me. That she began being nice to me out of a spirit of mischief is no doubt true. The idea of making Philibert's wife, her intimate, was the sort of thing likely to appeal to her but having made the advances out of perversity, she found herself interested and attracted. Why did she like me? It is difficult to say. Perhaps because I was a new type and one that wouldn't in the ordinary course of events come her way. I puzzled her. To her I was something primitive, savage, and dangerous. She used to call me her *"Peau Rouge."* She said I made her think of Buffaloes and Bison and prehistoric animals, of black men round camp fires in jungles, of snake dancers and deserts and the infantile magic of savage races. She wove stories about me and hunted up old prints of queer outlandish people who she insisted had my type of head. I was, she asserted, only half-tame, and being with me gave her the same kind of pleasure as having a leopard about. She was physically afraid of me. Not only at the beginning, but always to the very end, but in those days, my losing my temper, she found, *"un très beau spectacle."* Her blue eyes would shine, her lips part in amazement, and timidly she would stroke my shoulder, murmuring—"How wonderful you are. What a volcano."

She used to ask me endless questions about my childhood and appeared greatly intrigued by my obstinate attachment to what she affectionately termed, my ridiculous impossible background. She would make me tell her about life in the Grey House, the baking of cakes in the kitchen, the hymn singing on Sunday evenings, and the summer trips to the wilderness, to the woods of Canada, or across the prairies of Omaha, Dakota, and Arizona. She would lie on her couch in her boudoir making patterns in the air with her lovely fingers and purring like a pleased little cat while I described the plains, stretching endlessly under the sky to the white horizon, the lonely wooden shacks blistered in the sun, and infested with flies, the lazy cowboys on indefatigable loping broncos—and she would murmur—"*Ah, je comprends cela—c'est grand, c'est monstrueux, c'est beau.*"

As for me, need I explain why I loved her? Who has not felt the quality of her beauty? What man or woman that ever saw Bianca, failed to respond to the peculiar penetrating charm of her personality? I see her in memory, a vivid creature, perfect, compact, clear in the midst of a crowd of blurred and colourless shadows. Her beauty was incisive, keen. It cut into one's consciousness sharp as a stab. It stamped itself on one's brain, indelible and certain. I see her face as clearly today as I saw it the day I first laid eyes on her when she came up to me in your mother's salon and said—"You must like me, I insist." It is there close to me, rising out of the grave as pure, as firm, as precisely drawn as if I held the perfect indestructible masque in my hand.

I see her eyes open lazily, wider and wider, and shine out suddenly, bluest blue, so blue that they seem to send out a blue light through their black lashes. Ah, how lovely she was! How could I not believe in that loveliness? Blue, brilliant fire-blue eyes set far apart under a fringe of black hair and pointed curving thin red lips. I could model her now exactly — the cup of her small chin, her long round white throat, flat bosom and shoulders flowing down thin arms to her narrow beautiful hands. Her body was a fragile thing, strong as steel.

And women of Bianca's breeding never give themselves away in ordinary life. They are closed and secret books, open only to those who have the key. No one can read them who is not of the initiated. I did not know the language. There was nothing about her to convey to me that she was anything more than she seemed, a remarkable and gifted woman of great distinction, a creature so refined as to seem to me to belong to another planet from the one on which I had been born. It seemed to me extraordinary that such a person should notice me at all. I was filled with gratitude. I was humble, devoted, flattered, and Philibert gave no sign. If not actually enthusiastic about our friendship, he still seemed content enough, and I was happy in the thought, that this wonderful woman who had been his comrade from childhood was now, my friend too.

And she was careful, as we grew more intimate, to show me, only those aspects of herself that she knew would flatter and delight me. Never did she mention subjects likely to frighten me. Her talk was all of art shows and music and books and the ridiculous absurdities of *"le monde"* and those things in her life that I couldn't help noticing with concern, she explained in a way to enlist my sympathy. She was desperately unhappy, she told me, in her marriage, her husband's immorality was a great grief to her; the sorrow of her life was, that she could have no children and so on, and so on. Once she even confided to me that there was insanity in her family, and that she was constantly haunted by the fear of going insane. I was, at this, in a tumult of sympathy. I was prepared to forgive her a far greater number of eccentricities than she ever showed me.

She was, she told me, of a mixed strain of southern blood, a Venetian on her mother's side, on her father's a *Provençale*. From her I learnt that the old Duke, her father, was descended from the *Comtes de Provence* of a line that had numbered kings in the middle ages. For many generations they had been *Seigneurs* of a wild and mountainous region north of Avignon. Their fortress, the *"Château des Trois Maries"* stands high against the sky on a spur of rock that reaches out from the ragged hills, above the wide valley of the Rhône. This was Bianca's home. There in that sad and wonderful country of brown sunlight, she was as nearly happy as she could ever be on earth. I went to Provence with her one summer. And now that she is dead, I think of her, not as she was in Paris, languid, perverse, and irritable, but as she was in her own country. I see her against the swarthy background of those ruined hills scarred by the hordes of invading Saracens. Her little person seems to ride above that sunbaked land of blistered roads and dry river beds, on the wings of legend through a burning and sanguinary past of repeated invasions; of Barbary pirates from across the sea to the south, and Visigoths from the north, of wandering Bohemians, of steady marching Roman armies, of Popes flying from Italy for refuge, of gentle saints stranded in tiny boats on the desolate marshy shores of the *Camargue* and I see her as she ought to have been and as she was sometimes, down there, her face brown, her blue eyes flashing, and her thin body, lean and hard, mounted on one of the small fleet horses of the country, galloping at the head of the thundering fighting bulls towards the arenas of Nimes or Arles. This was her proper setting. It was here at the *Château des Trois Maries* that she showed herself to me, as she would have been had she not been accursed.

I remember one day in her room in the west tower of the Castle, her talking of herself, as she never talked to me before or since, honestly, as honestly as she could, and with light laughter breaking into her short light biting phrases. From the high window we could see the white dust of the road whirling down the valley before the hot scurrying wind, groves of poplars bending their plumed heads, little brown houses surrounded by close vineyards huddled behind screens of cypress trees.

"I was born here," she said, "of a woman who loathed her husband and hated this country—but I wasn't really born—I was made by witches one hot windy midsummer day. They made me out of the burning sun and the shrieking mistral and the hot white dust, in the black shade of cypresses, and they added to the hot mixture, ice water from that mountain stream; then they each laid on me a curse. One said, the oldest and wickedest—'She will covet the earth, but only love herself.' The second said 'She will be haunted by the evil spirits of dead men.' The third said—'Since the people of this country are fond of wild jokes and pranks,—they are you know, *très blagueurs, les Provençaux*, she will be much given to playing mischievous jokes that will do others harm.' Then they left me in the dark cypress grove, where my mother who was wandering about and longing for the laughter and music of her Italy, found me. She, poor darling, invoked the three Marys for my protection, *les Saintes Maries de la Mer* who are carved in the stone over the great door, *Marie Salomé, Marie Jacobé* and *Marie Madeleine*; their shrine is in the grotto behind the house—but they had been shipwrecked themselves and were too inefficient to cope with my witches—and so that you see is what I am—burning hot and icy cold, and with a dry wind, shrieking in my heart, and three times accursed. I feel it. I know it. I have known it since I was a child—At first I struggled, then gave in, took my curses in my arms and made them mine, made them, I tell you—my religion—" She gave her dry laugh. Her voice was high and sweet and careless. She spoke, without passion, in her dry conversational tone. "If I could never love any one but myself, never forget myself, try as I might in excesses of every kind, then I would love myself utterly. If I was to be haunted by the unfulfilled ideas of men and women long dead, then I would give myself up to those ideas, and if my pranks were fated to do people harm, well—what business was it of mine? I would enjoy doing people harm—idiots that they are, why should I care for their thin silly feelings?

"You think I am talking nonsense. If you believed me, you would be horrified—*eh, bien*—be horrified—but you will never understand. You will never believe that I am as bad as I am. That is the reason I like you—that is the reason I talk to you. You are obstinate and faithful and strong—and beside that you have demons too—I see them in your awful sullen face that I like.

"I tell you—that I am used by ideas that are not my own—that do not come out of my own head, that come to me from I know not where. They come persistently—out of the sky, circling back again and again like black birds coming out of the sky to this tower. For instance; an idea comes to me that I must go to Nimes and see a certain matador and send for him and make him love me—I know he will be stupid and coarse and disgusting, and I refuse. Then things happen. Every day lines appear in the papers—his name is everywhere, in every village on every stable wall—I laugh—and give in—and it is all stale and horrid before it begins, but the idea had to be carried out. That you will say is just the stupid giving into caprice of any idle woman—but it is not always so ordinary. Suppose that some day the idea comes to me that I must entice my husband into the oubliette. I laugh at the idea and chase it away. Six months later it comes back more insistent, a thing with a voice. It says 'Get him into the north tower. He is a mean creature. He will fall down the oubliette'—and I say peevishly—'But I don't mind his being alive—he doesn't bother me, I am not interested in killing him' and again I drive away the idea—but it will come back, it will keep coming back till it is satisfied. There have been many ideas like that demanding of me to be satisfied. Sooner or later I carry them out—do their bidding. Often in hours of lucidity I see how dangerous they are. I fight against them, distract myself with some idiocy or run away—take the train, go in the opposite direction—but almost always I give in, in the end." She stopped. I see her now against the stone coping of the window, leaning out—her head in the sun—looking down—the wall fell sheer—a hundred feet of masonry and rock. "Sometimes I think I will throw myself down to get rid of them, these ideas of men and women whose restless bones are the hot dust of these mountains—but why should I—why give myself as a sacrifice? It would be silly—the people I will hurt if I live aren't worth it—"

She jerked back into the room and came to my side, laying a hand on my shoulder, and standing so that I could not see her, a little behind me, her lips close to my ear. "There are other things," she whispered, "worse things—ideas—that I couldn't tell—" Her fingers clutched my shoulder, tightening until they hurt me—"You help me, but sometimes I am angry with you for being what you are and want to hurt you. Some day, who knows, the idea may come to me to do you harm. You are safe now because I don't understand you, and feel you are stronger than I—but if I ever detected a weakness in you—or if you ever bored me, then I should hate you, then I would certainly do you a hurt. It's a warning—" she broke off with a laugh, kissed lightly the tip of my ear and left me.

I was not afraid of her then—what she said did not disturb me. I laughed at it; I was happy and confident. I had everything in the world I wanted, and I lived in a daze of joy and excitement—Europe, Paris, the miracles produced by my wealth, still dazzled and amazed me; going to bull-fights with Bianca, or hunting wild boar, with the old Duke, or attending the Courts of Rome, Vienna, Berlin or St. James's with Philibert, everything was marvellous. I had no time to worry, and no reason to do so that I knew of.

But I remembered what Bianca had said, and in the light of what happened, I understood that she had been speaking the truth. It was simply her way of admitting that she was a supreme egotist. Put simply, it meant that the one motive power in her, was her vanity. It was her vanity that held her together and gave her an outline. And as she grew older she developed it as other women develop a gift for music. She worshipped herself, and she made of her egotism an elaborate religion. Her adoration of herself grew into a passion and burned with the ardour of a saint's miraculously revealed inspiration. She would have gone to the stake for it. It incased her in complete armour. No one and nothing could touch her through it. She was the only woman I have ever known who lived consistently and exclusively for herself, and she did so with the sustained passion of a religious maniac. One can only compare her to a Savanorola.

Her vanity was her power and her curse. It was an ogre. It had to be fed. Human beings were thrown to it as to the devouring dragons in fairy tales. We were all victims. I was, and you were, and Philibert and Jinny, and Micky and Fan and all the others. Insatiable vanity, that was all there was to Bianca in the last analysis. That was all the meaning of her, but its manifestations, its results, its devious ways of arriving at its own ends, these were infinite, would fill volumes.

You can see how the curse would operate. It operated through her intelligence. Had she been stupid, all would have been well, but concentrated on the study and care of herself, elaborating year after year her attentions to herself, nursing her body, her face, her senses, supplying to herself stimulants and soothing preparations, searching for curious new sensations, she was aware of her own limited power to please herself. Distinctly she perceived something beyond her reach, a quality of experience outside her range, a beauty she could not attain. She would have liked best to have been a queen of love, whom all men adored, like the radiant Simonetta—fairy queen of Florence, beautifully worshipped by an entire population, and she only succeeded in being *la femme fatale*. With no gladness in her soul, she could not inspire gladness—always in the faces of her victims she saw a reflection of her own darkness. If occasionally, in the lurid light of the excitement she could so easily evoke, she saw in a man's face a flash that resembled joy, ecstacy, delight, she as often saw it fade to a dismal stupidity, or rage or disgust. Impossible for her to create anything more than an imitation of bliss. Her egoism spoiled its own gratification. It contained poison. Her touch was magical and deadly. This, in the end, bored her. She used to complain exasperatedly of people being afraid of her. The care with which they succumbed disgusted her. Men grovelling at her feet, men writing sentimental verses, men touching her with clumsy hands; she came to loathe them. There was nothing in it; she wanted something else, something out of the ordinary, something continually surprising, unexpected, dramatic. Alas! Humanity goes its stolid way comfortably enough in spite of the Biancas of the world. Men will "play up" to a certain point. They will pretend to be dying of love to please a beautiful lady's caprice, but they won't really die. One of the things Bianca longed for was to have a crop of suicides laid to her account. She would have been pleased had some of her victims blown their brains out, but somehow they didn't. They only threatened to do so. Once out of her sight, they recovered the normal and sallied forth from her boudoir to enjoy fat beefsteaks.

Her tragedy lay in understanding what she missed. She observed that inferior people experienced a range of feeling of which she was incapable. Insignificant women inspired the passions she longed to inspire. She envied and despised them. She envied every happy woman her happiness, every lover his love; her eyes watched them all, with curiosity, disdain and exasperation.

What in me began, after our three years of harmony, to get on her nerves, was my monotonous and exclusive feeling for Philibert. That such a sentiment should continue to absorb me and satisfy me, after five years of marriage was too much for her. She became irritable and teasing. She began to make fun of my love for my husband. She called it stupid, vulgar, grotesque, indecent. I lost my temper, she grovelled, enjoying that, but when next we met she began again, professing an extraordinary merriment at the sight of my mawkish sentimentality. With a sudden flash of insight I accused her of envy. She grew livid. In a choking whisper, she told me that Philibert for his part was no such idiot and that all I had to do was to look about me to find out the truth. I left her in a rage and stayed away. I did not see her again until the night of her ball, some months later, to which I went, knowing that she had determined to take Philibert away from me. It was the fact that Philibert as she believed had begun to care for me, that made her finally act. She simply couldn't bear to think that Philibert and I should come to understand and truly care equally for each other.

I went to her ball to make a scene, to frighten her into giving him back to me, but I did nothing. I didn't speak to her. I didn't go near her. I simply stood and watched her. The sight of her paralysed me. I realized that no man who had ever known and loved Bianca, could care for me. And I came away, knowing that between me and Philibert, everything was ended, and I came away terrified. As I left the house, I remember muttering to myself "I must escape"—"I must escape." Escape from what? I don't know. From them both, from what they had done, from what they stood for, from the world of treachery and deadly pleasure to which they belonged.

But I did not get away. I never got away. I never escaped from Bianca. I never got out of range of the sense of her presence and of her infernal charm. I still cared for her. Hating her, I still wondered that she could have hurt me, still wept and called out to her in the dark at night to know why she had done it, still felt her to be the most fascinating woman I had ever known, and it was this that made my jealousy of Philibert unbearable and fiendish. I had been twice betrayed and I knew loving them both, and knowing them both, precisely the quality of the delight they had in each other.

And I knew too, that Bianca was acting as she did because of me— even more than because of Philibert. I was conscious and I was convinced that she was conscious that the real meaning of the whole thing lay in her feeling for me. There was between us, a relationship that had become hateful, but that was still going on, a thing that was going to endure, a mutual sympathy outraged and hideous now, but persisting. If she had only wanted Philibert—well, she had him already. No—what she wanted was to hurt me. And making all allowances for the attraction between them, had it not been for me, he would not have inspired her with a sufficient energy to bolt with him. The situation would have lacked that something peculiar and curious which she wanted, had she not felt as she did about me.

But I may be confused between what I knew then and what I know now. It may be that I did not understand it all so well, then—I forget—I cannot recall my actual state of mind. I give less importance to my preoccupation with Philibert than I should do, and lay too much emphasis on Bianca, because you see, I have got over Philibert, the hurt he did me is long since past and I no longer care about it, but from Bianca—I have never recovered. She never let me go—she never finished with me. It wasn't just one thing— it was a series of things stretching over years, a continual coming back. You see—in the last analysis it was because of me that she ran away with Philibert, broke Fan's heart and laid schemes for corrupting Jinny—and these things took fifteen years to accomplish. There was war between us for fifteen years.

The story of my life is the story of my duel with Bianca. Other people played a part, other feelings absorbed me for long periods, other relationships endured, but my relationship to Bianca was the long strong rope that hanged me. You will see how it was.

Why did she go on with it? I don't know. Unless it was that I never gave in. Had I collapsed after Philibert left me, she might have been satisfied— and satisfied, she would have lost interest in me—and I should have been saved.

II

It is very difficult for me to recall my state of mind during the days that followed Philibert's going off with her.

I've an idea that I was in a kind of stupor, not much noticing anything. I must have given orders that no one was to be admitted, for I learned afterwards that Claire and your mother both called, and a number of other relatives. I think I remained in my room for a day or two lying on the bed with my clothes on and refusing to open the door to my maid. It was Jinny who roused me. The servants were frightened. The nurse brought her down and she pounded on the door with her little fists till I opened it, but when she saw me she gave a shriek and ran away from me and hid in her nurse's petticoats. That brought me to my senses, my child's fear and the servants' faces. I had a bath and something to eat. They brought me my letters obsequiously, and with furtive curiosity. I could hear the servants hanging about whispering. I imagined them talking, talking, endlessly talking it over downstairs. They were strangers to me, Philibert's servants, servants of that great, horrible house that I disliked. I had no reason to stay there now. Nothing kept me—I would go home to St. Mary's Plains.

I started a letter to my Aunt Patience, what was I to say to her? "My husband has run away with another woman. He never loved me. My mother married me to him for her own purposes. Now that she is dead there is no more reason to go on with this horrible farce. I am coming home." Something of that kind? No, I couldn't. I stared at the words I had written— "My dearest Aunt Patty." I seemed to see her sitting off there, at the end of that great distance, adjusting her spectacles, opening my letter with expectant fingers. I saw the shabby room, the sunlight on the worn carpet, the littered writing desk, the piles of books, the stuffed birds in their glass cases. I saw my aunt an old woman, facing old age alone, with equanimity, following year after year the pursuit of knowledge, not afraid of time, not oppressed by solitude, going up to bed night after night in the empty house and kneeling down in her flannel dressing-gown beside her narrow white counterpane to pray to God, and remembering me always, never forgetting me, never leaving me alone.

Once she had said, "When you're in a hole, Jane, and don't know what to do, you can always do the thing you hate doing most and you'll probably not be far wrong."

Looking out of the window I became aware of Paris and I thought of those words. Paris! There it was streaming by, to the races. Was it aware of what had happened to me? I wondered. Did people know that Bianca and Philibert had run away together like a couple of actors, like a pair of quite common people? I imagined society agog with the scandal. I saw them gloating pitying. I heard women saying—"*Cette pauvre femme, elle était vraiment trop bête.*" It seemed to me that every one in the street must be looking up at my windows with curiosity and derision. They were invading my privacy, pulling off from me the last decent covering of my dignity. Well, why sit there and bear it? Why suffer public humiliation? My eyes fell on my engagement book. I observed that Philibert and I were due for dinner that night at your Aunt Clothilde's. I rang for my maid and told her to telephone *Madame la Duchesse* and say that although Monsieur, having been called out of town, would not be able to present himself at her dinner, I would come with pleasure, as had been arranged. My face in the glass seemed much as usual. I had done all my weeping with you, my poor Blaise, three nights before. Having made up my mind to go out I now experienced a certain relief. The coiffeur was summoned and the manicurist. Aunt Clo's dinners were very special affairs, so I chose a nice dress, white, and put on an extra rope of pearls. As you know, my appearance created something of a sensation. I saw that at once. They had thought me already dead and buried, and were gossiping as I suspected, over my remains. My business for the moment was to show them that I was alive.

Ah, but how dreary and trivial it all seems now. Why? Why? What earthly difference did it make what they said or thought? But I am telling you about it, just as it was. I wanted, I needed desperately at that moment, the sense of my own dignity. It was all I had left. So I went out to that dinner party and defended it.

Aunt Clo was nice. She was pleased with me and put me opposite her. It was a vatican dinner, semi-political. I had, I remember, the Italian Ambassador on my right and the Foreign Minister on my left. Your aunt was between the Archbishop and the Duc de B—— recently arrived from Rome. The talk was brilliant, I believe. I heard it in a daze, but managed to keep my end up somehow. Clémentine was there, at her best, in wonderful form. She must have known all about Philibert, for she came up to me after dinner and said—"Blaise de Joigny is my great friend. You must come to see me. We have much in common." Our friendship dates from that night.

But when I reached home I felt more tired than I had thought it possible to be. I went up to the nursery. Jinny was asleep in her cot, hugging a white woolly dog. I knelt beside her and sent out my spirit in search of God, but I did not find Him. I could not pray. I heard my baby's breathing, blissful, trustful breathing. I knelt listening. She was so small and sweet. Above her was an immense blackness. She made now and then happy little sounds in her sleep, and lying there so still I saw her moving on and on, invisibly, into the future to the ticking of the nursery clock, carried along as she lay there on the current of life, life that was an enormous dupery, an ugliness and a lie.

The days passed, separate and distinct, moving in a procession, each one to be watched and endured separately, moving by their own volition, taking no account of me, having nothing to do with me, answerable to some mysterious power that started each one rolling like a bead dropped from the end of a string, and in each one, as in a crystal, I saw the pageant of Paris revolving, but I was outside, drifting in empty space.

The longing to get away from it all was unbearable. I would go—I would go—I must go—Patience Forbes was the only person in the world who could help me—and yet I went on working out my idea that took me about among people, and you, dear Blaise, went with me. Your attitude was of a delicacy rare even in your world of delicate adjustments and sympathies. You understood, you constituted yourself my escort. Do you remember those days, how we went from one place to another, luncheons, dinners, private views, official receptions, and how we tacitly agreed on just the amount we were bound to do for our purpose? I scarcely realized at the time all that it meant for you to do this, and how the family would resent your attitude. I know now that they never quite trusted you after this. As I remember we talked nothing over and did not, I think, mention Philibert save once, when I asked you if you knew where he was. You did know, of course. Every one knew, I suppose, except myself. They had been seen, those two, boarding the Simplon express. They were in Venice, you told me, I had wanted to know for convenience. Having adopted a line, it seemed best to follow it consistently. One was to assume that my husband had gone away for a holiday. I was there to make his excuses to suffering hostesses deprived of his society. The note to be struck was light and commonplace, as if his absence were like any other of his many past absences. The pretence deceived no one, but then the consistent lying made for decency. I was marking time. It was particularly difficult because I was not acting in accord with my nature. Had I been natural at that time I should have been horrible; I should have smashed things. But I was not behaving like myself. I see now what it was; I was behaving like one of you, behaving as Claire, for instance, would have behaved in my place. I was adopting your methods and your standards. Not to give myself away, not to let any one suspect what I was feeling and thinking, not to make a false step, not to make above all a public fuss, that seems to have been my idea. To preserve appearances as beautifully as possible, that was what you and I were working at, as we trailed drearily round from one place to another saying suave things with smooth faces.

And there was another influence working on me, even more subtle and far more pervasive. You will smile, perhaps, when I tell you that my quiet behaviour came from looking every day across the Place de la Concorde to the austere and reserved façade of the Madeleine, or across a silver distance of pale houses to the far alabaster pinnacle of the Sacré Coeur high above the city, but it was so. Paris exercises upon its inhabitants a fine discipline of taste. Those who love it change unconsciously. The long, wide, symmetrical avenues, the formal gardens, with their slim fountains, single waving sprays of crystal water, the calm façades of long rows of narrow, uniform houses, palest yellow in sunlight, pearl white towards evening, these things have an effect upon one's manners that is imperceptible and profound. They spelt to me harmony and restraint and Plato's idea of beauty. My high falsity was at the best only less futile than a good, noisy bout of hysterics. What comforted me in these hours of doubt was that I knew you were no more certain than I. You did not represent your family. You were neither a go-between nor a spy nor a jailor, you were a friend. Positively I believe there were moments when you wanted me to break out, break away, throw caution and carefulness to the winds. Sometimes there was so much compassion in your face that I almost cried out to you not to care so much. I wanted to warn you that it was only for the moment that I was keeping my head up, that I wouldn't be able and didn't intend to go on with it indefinitely and that the thought behind all my smooth social words was; "He has gone for ever. Soon I'll be free to say so."

I did really believe Philibert had left me for good. It never occurred to me that he would ever come back, and that belief was in a way my refuge. I was rid of them both; Bianca, I told myself, would be satisfied now and would leave me alone. She would carry on her mischief elsewhere, not in my life. My life was, I believed, my own, separated for always from hers and from Philibert.

Then one day Fan turned up. She came in jauntily, her head in the air, as if nothing had happened. She looked very smart, her hat set at a rakish angle, her short, pleated skirt flippant above her neat ankles. From across the room she called out "Well,—Jane, we've married a nice pair of men. Here's Philibert's skipped and I've had to send Ivanoff packing. He'd taken to beating me, I'm black and blue all over. Some people like it—I don't." She gave me a peck on the cheek. "Poor old Jane, you're taking it hard, I suppose." She turned back the sleeve of her dress. Her arm had welts on it. "You should see my back." I shuddered, but at sight of my emotion she twitched away from me with a nervous laugh. "Between my Slav and your Frenchman I don't know that there's much to choose. God, if it were only an occasional beating I shouldn't mind." She did a waltz step across the room, twirled round on her tiny feet, lit a cigarette standing on tiptoe, and collapsed into a chair in a spasm of coughing.

"I had it out with Ivanoff, my dear, about you, and I know all about it—just the exact sums you gave him for me, bless your baby heart, and everything. At first I doubted you. I was a fool. I'm sorry. Unfortunately I found out other things. There are other women in the world who don't love me at all, but who pay for my shoes. Do you hear? Do you get what I mean? I find I've been paying my bills with their money. What do you say to that? I ask you simply. And we're on the streets now—at least he's gone—I'm staying with Madeleine de Greux, and the bailiffs have got our furniture." And she went off into a wild scream of laughter. It was incredibly painful. She sat there as neat and smart as a pin. Her small cocked hat on one side of her head, her pretty little legs crossed, one high-heeled patent leather slipper dangling in the air, the other tapping the floor, she puffed smoke through her little tilted nose and looked at me desperately out of her hard, level eyes, while she yelled with laughter just as if some one were tickling her till she screamed with pain.

I went to my desk and got out my cheque book. "Let's pay off the furniture first," I said as prosaically as I could, but she jumped up irritably.

"God! Jane, what a fool you are. Put that cheque book away. Do you think I'd touch another penny of yours? There—don't be hurt. Of course I would if I needed it, but what good will money do? I can't go and hunt out Ivo's mistresses and pay them back, can I? Oh, God! Oh, God! Oh, God!—I did like him. Men are devils. Even now I'm worried about him. I imagine him locked up somewhere or dead drunk in the gutter lying out in the dark—whereas he's probably at Monte having a high old time. By the way, your French family is in a great state about you. Claire says their position as regards you is very delicate. I suppose it is. They don't know whether to come here or to leave you alone. They wonder what you're going to do. They're frightfully cut up about Fifi, and they're afraid you'll do something final like getting a divorce."

"Well, my dear, that's just what I do think of doing."

"I see." She ruminated, chewing her cigarette that had gone out. "They'll never forgive you if you do."

"I suppose not, but I don't see that that matters."

"Oh, but it does. They're so perfectly charming. They'd make Paris impossible for you."

"That sounds charming, I must say."

"Don't be stupid, Jane. You know what I mean. You know how clever they are. They're the most attractive people on earth. But if you set them against you, the whole clan, you'll find life here very different."

"I don't propose to live here."

"Where then?"

"In St. Mary's Plains."

"Heaven help you, my poor misguided lamb."

"I'm homesick," I persisted obstinately.

"Of course, for the moment, because you're unhappy."

"No, not only because I'm unhappy. I like the Grey House. I belong there. It's quiet, it's safe, it's real, it's the place I know best in the world."

"Nonsense. It's a dingy little shanty."

"You can call it names if you like. I don't care what you say. I'm going back there."

"For good?"

"I don't know—perhaps."

"Well, you won't stay, so you'd better not risk it."

"Risk what?"

"Having to eat humble pie and come back to be forgiven."

It was my turn to get up with a fling of exasperation and walk about. She followed me with her bright, piercing gaze.

"Think a little, Jane. Use your brains, if you can. Think of the difference between your life here and your life at home in that Godforsaken hole of St. Mary's Plains. Look at this room. Look out of the window and remember. Don't I remember? Wooden sidewalks with weeds growing between the boards, boys playing marbles in the street, women hanging out their washing in backyards, Sunday clothes, oh, those best Sunday clothes, revival meetings, Moody and Sankey in tents on the lake shore, picnics, bicycle rides, dances at the Country Club, freckled youths kissing you on the verandah, great news—Ethel Barrymore is coming in her new play that's been running a year in New York. Excursions on the lake, fifty cents a round trip and soft drinks, sarsaparilla, ginger ale, buggy rides, shopping down town, talking to old women—cats who gossip about somebody's new red silk petticoat, too flighty, indecent. All going to church and shouting 'Hallaleluja' and eating blueberry pie afterwards till their mouths are all black inside."

"Well," I said. She wriggled about as if sitting on pins.

"You want to give up Paris, this house, your position here, for that? You've got Europe at your feet. You've only got to sit tight and every one in Paris will be on your side. Fifi will come back and be as good as gold. You'll be able to do what you like with him after this."

I stopped her.

"So you think I'd take Philibert back?"

"Yes, I do. We all do."

"And begin again living together, after this?"

"Yep."

"You don't find it appalling even to think of—?"

"No, merely a little uncomfortable to begin with."

"You take my breath away."

She eyed me calmly. "My dear Jane, don't be the high tragedian. All marriages are like that. How many women do we know, do you suppose, whose husbands haven't had little vacations—?"

"If you don't mind we won't talk about it. Other women's marriages are nothing to me."

She shrugged her shoulders and lit another cigarette, and for a time we were silent. I looked at her. She seemed to me terrible, hard as nails and more cynical than any one, and yet she was my friend. Nothing, I knew then as I watched her, nothing that she could say or do would alter that fact. She belonged to me. What she felt would always affect me. In some absurd way I was responsible for her. Our childhood and its meagre austere background, with all that she repudiated, held us together.

Presently she began again. "Now listen to me, Jane. Philibert may be a brute, but he's done a lot for you. He has given you a very great position. You were rich but he knew how to make your money tell. There's not a house in the world like yours. I don't mean only the furniture. Your parties are beyond everything. You're more *recherchée* than any woman in Paris. You can pick and choose from all the great people of the world, the men with brains. Lord! how you could amuse yourself if you wanted to. I only wish I had your chance. Do you think I'd let my husband's infidelity spoil my life? I'd be no such fool. I might not like it, but I'd make up my mind to forget it. Well, here you are and you want to go back and crawl into that little hole in a prairie and stifle there."

"Yes, I do."

"But the people there—" she almost screamed.

"I don't know about the people. They may not be what you call amusing, but they're at any rate natural, common or garden human beings, and anyhow if there weren't another soul there's Aunt Patty; she's the finest woman in the world, and I adore her."

Fan looked at me in amazement.

"I'd die!" she gasped on a long, wailing breath. We were again silent, then, while the image of Aunt Patience took shape before us, gaunt, with her big bones showing under her limp, black clothes, worn, strong, knotted hands, crooked humourous face, weather-beaten like a peasant's, straggling thin, grey hair. And suddenly I saw her as she appeared to Fan, a shabby old maid in frumpy clothes, talking with a nasal twang, saying things like Mark Twain, worshipping Huxley and Daniel Webster and Abraham Lincoln, a child woman of stern moral principles, unaware of the existence of such life as ours, displeased and angry at our doings, hurt deeply by our words and our laughter. I imagined her in Paris, stalking down the Rue de la Paix like a pilgrim from the Caucasus, a figure of grotesque grandeur disturbing the merry frivolous traffic, sublime, terrible spectre of stark simplicity, utterly out of her element in our world. And I was angry with Fan for evoking such an image. I turned away from it in distress, ashamed.

"You've already gone too far," she said impishly. "You can't get back. You're spoiled for your Aunt Patience."

"We'll see," I muttered. My suspicions were suddenly roused by a look in her little squirrel face.

"You've been talking to Claire," I said.

"Well, what if I have?"

"She sent you."

"Yes, she did; but I was coming, anyway."

"I don't believe you. You hate my being unhappy, you were worried, but you'd have avoided coming if you could. The fact that we've always been friends and that you can't help it is a nuisance to you. Well, tell me, what is Claire's point of view?"

"She thinks in some measure that it's your fault. She says Fifi has behaved very badly, but that if you'd been clever he wouldn't have done anything sensational, anything to make a scandal."

"I see."

"She's very unhappy about it all. She says it's making her mother ill. She says that if it were not for her mother it would not matter so much, but that if you divorce Philibert it will kill her."

"Why doesn't Claire come herself and tell me all this?"

"She doesn't dare. She says you don't like her."

"That, my dear, is funny. I've adored her for years and she's consistently snubbed me."

"Well, anyway, you're so different, she feels you wouldn't understand. You see, she puts up with a good deal herself."

"I know. Perhaps I understand more than she thinks I do."

"She's very unhappy in her marriage, too, but she doesn't make a fuss about it. She doesn't expect the impossible."

"Whereas I do?"

"Well, yes. Between you and me and the lamp-post I think you do."

"I only ask to be allowed to save Geneviève from a fate like my own."

"Oh, my dear, if you think they'll let you have Geneviève—"

"What do you mean?"

"A man always has rights over his child in this country, whatever the facts against him."

"You suggest that the law wouldn't give me my own child?"

"It wouldn't, not the French law."

"Well, we'll see about that, too."

"Jane, you're terrible."

"Am I?"

"Yes, you frighten me."

"I'm sorry."

"What shall I say to them?"

"To whom?"

"Claire, Madame de Joigny, your Aunt Clothilde, all of them."

"Say nothing. Why should you serve them? Why should you side with them against me? Weren't you mine years before you ever saw one of them? What's become of our friendship? What's become of your loyalty? You've sold yourself, you're not what you used to be, you'd do anything now for a pleasant life. Because they're attractive and have attractive manners and make pretty speeches you'd do anything for them. What good does it all do you? You're ill, you're worn to a frazzle, your husband has been dragging you down, down, into a darkness, queer, unimaginable, shameful, and you can't get loose. You just dance about in the blackness. Your feet stick in the mud. Having a good time somehow, anything for a good time. Coughing yourself to pieces, raging fever on you, your heart sick with distrust, restless, evasive, evading issues, you go on dancing, laughing, having a good time. Why don't you pull yourself together? Why won't you let me help you? I love you. I love you much better than Claire does. If your husband were put in prison what would Claire do, do you think?"

But Fan had grown deadly pale. I stopped, horrified. She was leaning against the mantelpiece, spitting into her handkerchief: there was blood on it.

That evening when I had taken her back to Madeleine de Greux's—for she refused to stay with me—and we had put her to bed, she clung to me weakly. Her eyes closed. "It's all true, what you said, Jane," she gasped, "but I can't help it, I can't stop. If I stopped amusing myself I'd die."

"But, my darling, let me get you well first, let me take you somewhere."

"Perhaps, later," she whispered, "if you don't go to America. Perhaps we might try Switzerland, but not where there are sick people." She shuddered. "I hate sickness so, and unhappiness. It's so ugly. Being gay is beautiful. It makes things look beautiful. Ivanoff is a devil, but you'll admit he was beautiful. I like attractive brutes better than clumsy saints. So do you, that's why you married Philibert, just because he was so attractive. No one could be so attractive when he tried. Admit it, he gave you wonderful hours, you know he did. Wasn't that something? What's the use of being good if you're deadly dull? Good men aren't our kind, my dear. They'd bore us to death. Philibert made you happy for a time, wonderfully, because he knew how. What more do you want? Don't be a fool. Take it all as it comes. Make an arrangement with him—you owe him something. I'll be all right in a day or so. Let me know what you decide. Americans are hipped on their ideals. All that's no use. French people know what's what. Claire would love you if you gave her a chance. They are all ready to be fond of you, and they're delicious people. Don't be a fool. There, leave me now. We were idiots to quarrel. You have a nasty temper, my poor Jane, and your heart's too big for this world. You'll come an awful cropper if you're not careful."

III

Philibert's family had shown up to this point, a remarkable restraint. As long as I went about as if nothing had happened, they left me alone, but after my scene with Fan I allowed myself a revulsion of feeling. I stopped going out. I shut myself up and sent for my lawyer. Philibert had been gone two months. I saw no reason to put off any longer, the action that I was determined on; I would start divorce proceedings, leave things in professional hands and go home. What else could I do?

July was drawing to a close. The season was ending in a languid dribble of belated garden parties. Fan, with a characteristic spurt of energy, had recovered and gone off to the Austrian Tyrol with the de Greux, leaving me with a last bit of reiterated advice about not being a fool. I observed that I had no place to go, and nothing to do. Biarritz, Trouville, Dinard, would mean carrying on the sickening pretence under an even closer scrutiny than in Paris. The Château de Ste. Clothilde had no charms for me now. I had liked the place, but Philibert had spoiled it with his endless improvements. It was now, his creation stamped with him. Sitting alone in my room at the top of the house with the shabby relics of the Grey House, I thought of him as he had been there in the country, strutting about directing his army of workmen, cutting down trees, pulling up whole lawns to replace them with gravelled terraces, and sinking into the reluctant earth marble basins for the lovely vagrant waters of the park. He had always professed to be the enemy of nature. It was true. What he called—"*Les bêtises de la nature*," filled him with disgust. Spreading trees and green fields dotted with buttercups and bubbling streams tumbling through thickets got on his nerves. "*Regardez donc le laissez-aller de tout cela*," he would cry. "How ugly it is. How stupid. It has no form, no design." Clumps of trees in a meadow he would liken to pimples on hairy faces. He called grass the hair of the earth, and couldn't endure it unless it was close cut. He never saw a stream of water without wanting to use it up in elaborate fountains. Gardens he regarded as "salons" in the open air. One should use the shrubs and trees and flowers as one used silks and brocades in an interior. Everything in a garden must be "*voulu*." Nothing must be left to go its own way, not a vine, not a rosebush, not a tree should be allowed a movement of its own. Nature must be bound and twisted into a work of art. "Ah," he would exclaim, "how it amuses me to torture nature." You know what he did. The result was very fine of its kind, certainly very grandiose. He would lead people out on the terrace and, standing a minute, a shiny dapper little manikin, five foot four in high heels above that great design of gravel walks and fountains and squares of water, with their little parquets of green grass closed in by hedges, like a series of drawing-rooms, he would sparkle with enthusiasm. "You see," he would say, "what I have done, you see how these gardens *s'accrochent au château*, how it is all a part of the house. The château could not exist without the garden, nor the garden without the château. One would have no sense without the other. Before I restored the grounds and elaborated on the old designs of Lenôtre, the house was horrible." He had placed complicated machinery under his fountains that made the waters when they were in play take a dozen varied successive shapes. Nothing amused him more than watching all those waters playing, twisting, turning, tracing strange designs in the sunlight, designs that he himself had imagined. It gave him a peculiar joy to see his own idea produced in crystal drops of water. He had worked in sunlight and limpid flowing water as a painter works in colours, and had in a way produced for himself the illusion of the miraculous.

He couldn't understand why I suffered when he had all those magnificent trees uprooted and when later on I complained that there was no shade anywhere and no place to lie down with a book: "But, my poor child, you've your bed for that, or your '*chaise longue.*' This garden is neither a bedroom nor a boudoir, it is a '*salle de fêtes*.'"

I remembered all this. Certainly for many reasons Ste. Clothilde was out of the question. I would take Jinny home with me to St. Mary's Plains. The moment had come. A strange excitement came over me as I at last wrote out the cablegram to Patience Forbes announcing our sailing on the first of August. On the same day I had a talk with my solicitor. *Maître* Baudoin was a jaded, dry man, I believe honest, and rather dull. He was eager for a holiday and very bored, I could see, at the idea of being kept in town. He gave me little sympathy.

I wished to divorce my husband. That might or might not be possible. It depended, of course, to a certain extent, to a limited extent, on whether I had sufficient grounds, and whether *Monsieur le Marquis* contested the suit. I intimated briefly that I believed I had sufficient grounds. He eyed me gravely through half-shut deferential and sleepy eyes. Did I think my husband would defend the suit, because if he did, no matter what my grounds were, the case might last five years. He told me this as a matter of conscience. Such a case would be lucrative to him, of course, but it might prove fatiguing to the parties more directly concerned. Five years? Yes, or even ten. That was the way in France. A divorce against a man who fought it was very difficult to obtain, and of course the Church did not recognize it.

That was not his affair save in so far as if I had the intention of re-marrying, such a marriage would of necessity be considered bigamous by all good Catholics. I had, I said, no intention of marrying a second time. He seemed at that rather mystified. I desired, then, nothing more than legal separation? That was much simpler. It was all a question of property. Was there a settlement? He supposed I wished *"séparation des biens."* I told him that I had no wish to leave *Monsieur de Joigny* in financial difficulties and that that question might be left until later, but he proved obstinate and kept on talking on the same subject till my head ached. Finally I gathered that he was suggesting as delicately as he could that Philibert might be bribed. "But I can't settle on him a large sum," I objected wearily, "the fortune is tied up for my daughter."

"Ah, a trust?"

"Yes."

"It all goes to your child on your death?"

"Yes, to my children or child, by my father's will."

"I see. She becomes, then, the important factor."

"What do you mean?"

"You would lose her."

"Why?"

"The law courts would not deprive her father of her custody."

"But if he doesn't care for her?"

"Are you sure he doesn't?"

"He has left her."

"For a time, perhaps, but she is his, and if, which would be most unnatural, he did not care for her, he might still care for what she represented."

It was on the tip of my tongue to say that he cared for nothing but his mistress, but I left the vulgar words unspoken. After all, I was not sure that Philibert did not care for Geneviève. His moods of a doting father might be genuine. He might indeed fight for her. My will hardened as I wearily dismissed the tiresome discouraging man of law. It was all more complicated than I had thought.

He had scarcely got out of the house before it was invaded by relatives. With a startling promptitude, they bore down on me. They must have had spies in the house. My secretary must have telephoned the alarm, or the Governess or the Butler, any one, or all of the staff may have been keeping them informed. In any case, there they were, miraculously ushered into my presence without warning one by one, or two by two, or in groups, aunts, uncles, cousins, first, second, third cousins, cousins by marriage once removed, some of them people whom I scarcely knew, strange old women in wigs with withered faces and ragged feather boas, unearthed for the occasion out of their old grand sealed houses; shrivelled old men with stiff knees and watery eyes; it would have seemed funny, had my nerves not been on edge, had their visits not appeared to me so exceedingly misplaced. I soon found that no hinting on my part would make them take this view. They meant business. They were the family. They were acting for the family and as a family. Some of them constituted that sacred thing the "*conseil de famille*" and they were acting in accordance with the rights and duties of a French family in harmony with and under the protection of the law of the French state. With correct and concise politeness they gave me to understand that I was not free to do as I liked, that I was one of them, bound as they were bound, and that if I chose to go against their will, and defy my obligations, then I would do so at my own peril and at the cost of what I held most dear. I saw what they were driving at. They meant to keep Jinny whatever happened. If I declared war, I would lose my child.

I put it brutally. They didn't. They were charming. They beat round the bush. They asked after my health. They drank tea and smoked cigarettes and patted Jinny's head and said charming things to her and gave her bonbons but they made their meaning clear and the more diplomatic they were, the angrier I became.

This kind of thing went on for three days. I remained obdurate. I refused to commit myself, but gradually I was becoming frightened. What frightened me was that I saw that they all, every one of them, even those that I had thought most human, even your Aunt Alice who was a saint and your Uncle Stanislas all sided with Philibert, all stood solid behind him, all would stick to him no matter what he did, before the world and against the foreigner who threatened the close fabric of their community; and I took it as a sinister portent that those of the immediate family, whom I knew best, your mother and Claire and Aunt Clothilde, stayed away. In despair I went to Aunt Clothilde. What, I asked her, did it all mean? She gave me no comfort. It meant simply that things were so in France. French families were like that. They clung together, and they did not admit divorce. If I tried to divorce Philibert I would fail and would in the attempt lose my child. Philibert, of course, was a rascal, but what would you, I ought to have known it from the beginning. American women thought too much of themselves. There was no modesty in the way I was behaving. Why should I suppose that the whole scheme of the social state should be upset because my husband liked another woman better than he did me? She liked me, of course she liked me—for that reason she had refused to take part in the family's councils of war. But she was disappointed in me, she had thought I had pluck. Here I was, behaving like a fish wife who has been knocked into the gutter, screaming for my rights, for vengeance. I had better go home and say my prayers. I went, and as if in answer to the dreadful old woman's bidding found a bishop in the drawing-room. My nerves by that time were in such a state that the suave and polished prelate soon had me in tears. He mistook them for tears of repentance. He talked a long time about the consolation of religion and the comfort of confession and rejoiced to find that I was less inimical to the benign influence of Rome, than he had thought. I scarcely heard what he said, but his fine ivory face and glowing eyes and thin set mouth, gave me a feeling of uncanny power. I remembered that I belonged to his Church, that I had been solemnly married at the High Altar of Rome, that there I had taken vows, had professed beliefs, and I felt a sudden superstitious terror. What if it were true, their truth? What could they do to me, these mysterious ministers of the Pope? What could they not do? In my fever, I saw myself tracked to St. Mary's Plains, followed up the steps of the Grey House by sallow figures in black cassocks, and suffering, labouring for the rest of my days, under the mysterious blight of an ecclesiastical curse.

When one lives in a country that is not one's own, among strange people whom one knows only superficially, surrounded by customs and conventions that one does not understand, one finds it difficult to decide moral issues. I felt bewildered and at a loss. It still seemed to me at moments inevitable and right to divorce Philibert. At other moments I felt less sure. The disapproval of the organized compact community was having its effect. The antagonism of the family acted on me with incessant pressure, however obstinately I repeated to myself the words "I don't care." I did care. I was alone. I could not even be certain that my Aunt Patience would approve. She might say in her terse way, "Quite right, Jane. He's forfeited your respect, get rid of him," or she might say, "You married him before God, you can't undo that," I did not know what she would say. And the problem of Geneviève tortured me. The fear of losing her if I divorced her father was no greater than the fear of seeing her gradually slipping from me as the years passed, if I remained his wife. No one knew better than I how charming he could be if he chose. I watched him in anticipation stealing her heart from me, turning her against her own mother. I saw her becoming more and more like him, becoming his pupil, his work of art. Philibert made things his own so easily. He had a genius for conquest. Everything that he touched became his. How different from me! There was nothing in Philibert's house that belonged to me, except the few sticks of furniture that I had hidden away in that room upstairs. The lovely things in the great rooms troubled me. They affected my nerves as if a chorus of small muffled voices were calling out to me in strange tongues that I could not understand. I realized their beauty, but was conscious of not appreciating them as they deserved. There was no sympathy between us. They affected me but I did not affect them. I could never make them look as if they were a part of my life. I was loath to handle them, but no amount of touching with my fingers would have given them a familiar look; the tables and chairs and tapestries remained there around me, enigmatic, permanent, unresponsive. My life spent itself, throbbing out among them, beating against their calm, smooth surfaces without reaching them. There was no trace in that house of the tumult of my own life. It continued cold, inexorable and strange.

It remained for your mother to seek me out in my loneliness and show me what I should do. I thought at the time that I recognized her words as words of truth. I do not know now whether I was right or wrong.

Claire never came. She sent her husband instead, not so much as a messenger, more as an object lesson, a mute reminder—I caught her idea—I was to look at him and realize what she was putting up with and draw from the spectacle of his awfulness the moral. Unexpectedly, his awfulness, appealed to me. There was something about this keen little stolid French bounder that was a relief. His oily head, his fat brown face, his monstrous nose and little bright beady eyes, these unattractive things made up a hard compact entity. He was solid and complete, round paunch, tight trousers, plump hands fingering a gold watch chain, smell of bayrum and soap, aura of success, of materialism, of industrial jubilance and all the rest of it. But he showed me for the first time that day something more, himself smarting under his thick skin with the innumerable de Joigny slights stinging him, controlled enough not to let on, determined to get out of them in exchange what they could give him, but not counting it much, a shrewd downright kind little rascal, with a good old middle-class self-respect strong in him, strong enough to make him feel himself their superior.

It didn't take him long to make his point. He talked quickly and neatly.

Claire was unwell, she had sent him to add his voice to the family howl. Claire never howled. When there was trouble, she withdrew. It wasn't her *genre*, to mix herself up in a fuss. Well—he wasn't at all sure that he had anything to say. Firstly because, after all, it was none of his business. He wasn't a member of the de Joigny family and never would be. They had made that perfectly clear, years ago. So why should he interfere?

I smiled. "Why indeed?" He smiled back, his hands crossed on his stomach; his smile took a cynically humorous curve.

"If on the other hand, Madame, my sister-in-law, you want an outsider's opinion, it is at your disposal."

"Two outsiders, confabing together," I ventured.

"No," he spoke abruptly, in a light sharp staccato, a nasal voice, not unpleasant, the voice of the phenomenally intelligent French bourgeoisie. "You are not as I am. You are a woman. They won't let you in—but they won't let you out. You belong to them. I don't—beside I am of their people. I am French—I have my own backing. They don't like what I represent but they are obliged to admit its importance. It is the backbone of France that I represent, the bread they eat, the stones they walk on, the nation they ground under their heels in the old days. They stamp on me now, but only in play, only to save their faces—not seriously—they can't. You, Madame, are different. You are a foreigner, and 'sans défense.' La famille de Joigny have a contempt for foreigners. Your protectors are in America. They snap their fingers at them. You are helpless—"

It was true. Well then?

He eyed me, humorously. "It depends on what you want out of them. I take it they can't give you much of anything. You didn't marry one of them, as I did, to ameliorate your situation in society. Putting aside the charm of the son and daughter, why did we do it? I did it as a bit of business. For me it was 'une affaire—' how it turned out is neither here nor there. I can look after myself. For you it is different, I repeat you are helpless. They are too many for you." He chuckled good-naturedly.

Again it was true; I assented meekly.

"Ah ha—Voilà, you see it. Then, my advice is—'Filez'—get out."

"And Geneviève?"

"Bribe them."

"You think—?"

He ruminated, his nose in the air—"Yes, I think—if you make it enough." He laughed again, rose briskly, took up his hat, his cream-coloured gloves, his gold-headed cane. For an instant his bright little eyes scrutinized me— he seemed about to speak, his thick lips formed, I saw them there, grave words, a confidence perhaps, a lament, a plea for sympathy, I know not what. He didn't speak them; he was very intelligent; he had a delicacy as fine as theirs, when he cared to show it. There was a nicer compliment to me in this clever little bounder's attempting no understanding with me, than any I had received in many a long day.

He left with me a pleasant feeling of my own independence, he left me invigorated and more sane than I had been, but your mother wiped out the impression he had made, with one wave of her hand.

I remember the sight of her in my doorway. I was so little expecting her that I had a chance to see her quite clearly during one instant, before I realized who she was. A small black figure in a stiff little ugly black hat and short cape, a dumpy forlorn little figure of no grace or elegance, and a worn nervous face, out of which stared a pair of very bright determined dark eyes. She might have been a very hard-driven gentle woman, determined to brave insults and apply for the post of housekeeper. This in the flash before all that I knew of her covered her like a veil, and before she spoke.

I did not want to see her. I knew in an instant why she had come. I remember wondering if I could get out of the other door before she spoke, before I really looked at her, and all the time I was looking and she was looking, we were staring at each other.

I had always had a deep regard for her. The fact that she did not like me, made no difference. That was where Claire's husband had fallen short in his putting of the case. He didn't know that I cared for Madame de Joigny; he didn't know that I wanted the family to love me, because I loved them. Now in your mother's presence, I felt the immense disadvantage of this. She cared nothing for me and I was bound to give in to her. I knew I would give in. I knew that I was about to make one last attempt to win her. I tried to rouse myself. I recalled and went over in my mind the opinion I knew she had of me. I knew that physically I was repulsive to her. Often when I approached her, I had seen her shudder. She thought me *outrée*. Once she had said, "Why is it Jane, that you can never look like other people? Everything you put on becomes gorgeous and exaggerated. It is most unfortunate." And she was afraid of my feelings, my violent enthusiasms and my deep longings. Oh, I knew, I knew quite well. Instinctively she felt my hot blood pounding in my veins—and recoiled from contact.

Most of all she hated me because of what I had done to Philibert. I had made him nouveau riche; I had made him ridiculous; I had made him unhappy, and worst of all, I had made him appear to her, cruel and vulgar. When he was unkind to me, she hated me for being the cause of his unkindness. You thought her love for Philibert a blind adoration but it was not blind. She understood him, she knew him to his bones, and she spent her life in shielding him from her own scrutiny. Her relief was in submitting herself to his charm. She delighted in him, but she hated his conduct. It seemed to her that he was a victim of what she most hated. She accused him in her own heart of being faithless to her faith, the faith of his ancestors. She saw on him the stains and distorting marks of the vulgar world that amused him, but she was continually falling in love with him and losing herself in his charm, seeking solace, suffering, being disappointed. I believe Philibert made your mother suffer more than he made me suffer, far, far more, for you see she couldn't stop loving him, she could never be free from him. He was her own, her first-born, the child of her passionate youth. He was her self that she had projected beyond herself, he was her great adventure, he was the gauge she had thrown down at the feet of fate, and it took all her courage to face calmly the travesty he made of her miracle.

My existence, you see, added immeasurably to the difficulty of her task. If he had married Bianca, Bianca, she believed, would have kept him in order and would have presented him to her soothed eyes in the light of a gallant gentleman. In marrying me he committed a serious error in taste to begin with, and having married me he behaved to me like a brute, and this was almost more than she could bear. The interesting thing to notice was that though she suffered horribly she made no attempt to remedy matters, did not try, I mean, to help us, and never gave me even as much as a hint as to how I should wisely have treated him, but limited her energy to just bearing her mortification without giving a sign of it. It did not seem to her worth while interfering to try and put things right when they were bound to go wrong, but it did seem necessary to keep up the make-believe that they were not going wrong. Almost everything in the world was going wrong. One couldn't face it. One must shut oneself up. One must ignore ugly facts.

Philibert's going off with Bianca in that spectacular fashion did, I know, very deeply hurt your mother. The horror of it to her must have been unspeakable. Here, at last, was an ugly fact of monstrous proportions that she could not ignore. She was bound at last to do something. She saw her son disgraced, her name dragged through the divorce court, she heard her world echoing with the clanging noise of scandal. She felt around her the brutal heaving of the foundation of her life. In her little tufted silken drawing-room that reminded me always of the inside of a jewel case, she had sat listening, shivering with apprehension. News came to her of the runaways. They were in Bianca's palace in Venice giving themselves up to curious orgies of pleasure. People told strange tales of their doings. They seemed to have gone mad. News came then from another quarter. I had consulted my solicitor. Claire was thoroughly frightened. Your mother did not hesitate then. She was old, she was tired, she was without hope or illusions. She saw her son as he was, and she saw Bianca at last as she was, and she believed that for her there was no happiness to be derived ever again from those two people. But she loved Philibert, she loved him with anger and contempt and a breaking heart, and she was determined to save him the last final ignominy, and so she put on her bonnet and came to me. And as I thought of these things I was drawn out of my chair toward her in spite of myself.

I begged her to be seated. I told her that I was touched and distressed by her coming to me, and that had she sent me word I would have gone to her. She smiled wanly with her old infinite sweetness. That smile was the most consummate bit of artistry I have ever beheld. It denied everything. It assumed everything. It fixed the pitch of our talk, it indicated a direction and a limit. It outlined before me the space in which I was to be allowed to move. It gave her the leading rôle in the little drama that was about to be played out between us, and it established her position once and for all as that of a great lady calling upon an awkward young woman. But I saw beyond her smile. I saw what she had been through, and was suffering. The combined play of her terrible reddened eyes and that lovely unreal smile impressed me profoundly.

For any other woman the beginning of such a conversation would have been difficult, but your mother, opened up the subject that lay before us with ease and delicacy. Her phrase was finely pointed. She used it as she might have used a silver knife to lift the edge of a box that contained something ugly.

"I do not know," she said, "whether or not you have ever loved my son, but I have felt that his sudden departure must have seemed to you very shocking, so I have come to reassure you."

I recoiled at this. It seemed to me that I was being attacked and that was the last thing I expected. I was startled and puzzled by those opening words. What difference did it make whether or not I had loved her son? For a moment I felt angry. After all it was he that had left me; why then, should I be accused? As for reassurance, I did not want any. This was no time for reassurance. An ugly spirit stirred in me. I was about to answer abruptly, when I saw that the purple-veined hand that lay across the table before me was trembling. It was animated by some painful agitation that shook it even resting as it did on that strong surface. The withered palm was rubbing and quivering against the polished wood, the worn finger tips were tapping spasmodically. My eyes smarted at the sight of it. I spoke gently.

"Yes, *belle-maman*, I thank you for coming."

"Ah, my poor child—and the family—I hear the family has been at you."

"They have been here."

"You must not mind them. They do not understand. In our world women, you know, take things differently, they do not expect what you expect."

There was a pause. What could I say? She seemed very reasonable and very kind. I had never felt her so near to me before.

When she spoke again it was even more simply. "I have had no news of Philibert," she said sadly. "Have you?" The tone of her voice was intimate and more natural than I had ever heard it when addressed to me. It implied that we were both unfortunate together. I responded to it with a flicker of hope.

"No," I replied, "I have no news, but I have reason to believe that he will not come back."

"Ah," she cried. "What makes you think that? But it is impossible."

"No," I continued, "it is not impossible. It is true. He gave me to understand that himself."

I felt her watching me closely.

"You mean?" she breathed.

"I mean that I must now take measures to live my own life. It is impossible for me to live in his house any longer."

It was then that she made one of her quick, characteristic mental turns.

"Yes," she said. "It's a monstrous house. I don't wonder you detest it."

I almost smiled, but I was determined to get to the point. "Dear *Belle-Mère*," I insisted, "that is neither here nor there. What I mean is that I must be legally free from Philibert." I hesitated, I saw her face whiten, but I pressed the point. "It is best for me to tell you that I have decided to divorce your son."

I don't know what effect I had expected and feared to produce. It may be that I thought she would break down or faint dead away, or something of that kind. She had seemed so frail that I had been really afraid of the effect of my words. But nothing of this sort happened. The blow I had dealt seemed to spend its force in the air. It glanced off and went shivering into the rich, cold atmosphere of the room.

"My dear," she said, enunciating her words very precisely, "*on ne divorce pas dans notre monde*." And she looked away from me, coolly taking in the room with its priceless objects as if summoning them to witness to the truth of her statement. She was right to look round that room. It was her room, not mine. It understood her, not me. She had called it a moment before a detestable house, but that made no difference. Its magnificence was to be made use of all the same. We were in the room that Philibert always referred to when he took people over the house as "*le salon de Madame de Joigny*," or "*le boudoir de ma femme*." It was the nicest room in the house. You remember it well, with its pearly grey boiseries fine as lace, its Frangonard panels, its green lacquer furniture, the three windows on the garden where a stone fountain lifted its fine sculptured figures from the lawn. The light in the room was silvery green and translucent as the light seen beneath the surface of clear water, and in that dim radiance the fine precious objects floated above the polished floor as if even the laws of gravitation had been circumvented in the fine enclosed space. The boiseries had been in the Trianon—you remember Philibert had procured them after much bargaining. They had been designed and executed for Madame de Montespan. Their perfect beauty constituted a document, a testimony to the marvellous taste and finished craftsmanship of an epoch. France, in all its delicate dignity, existed in that room. It is no wonder that your mother looked about her for moral support. The rest of the immense house might have belied her, here she could place her faith without hesitation. I opposed to it the profession of my own faith.

"In my country," I said dully, for I was beginning to feel baffled and confused, "we are not afraid to admit errors, to put away the past and begin something new."

"But this, my dear child, is your country," she said more gently. "You are a Frenchwoman now."

I smiled. "Do you really think so?" I asked her. She drew a sharp breath. "Ah, if you only were," she cried softly, "you would know how impossible it is to do what you want to do, and how useless."

My attention closed sullenly like a clamp on the words "impossible," "useless." I stared at the floor. Why impossible? Why useless? Why did I listen to this woman who did not love me, and who told me that my longing to live was useless? How was it she made me listen to her? Where was her advantage? She was certain and I was uncertain, that was it. I was not quite sure, but she was sure. Her definite idea was projected out at me and into me like a hook. It took hold of me. I felt myself wriggling on it, and I heard, through the confusion of my own ideas that seemed to buzz audibly in my head, your mother's voice talking.

"You are young," it said. "You come of a young people. You believe in miracles. You seek perfection on earth. Believe me, I am old and wise, ideals are all very well, but one must be practical about life. Philibert has behaved very badly. He has made a scandal, but you can remedy that and maintain your dignity by disregarding his escapade, or at any rate treating it as nothing more than an escapade. And such it is, nothing more, believe me. The acts of men are never anything more. *Mon Dieu*, if we took what they did seriously, where should we be, we women? We must take them for what they are. *Il le faut bien.* We must never count on them. We must count on ourselves."

But I seemed gradually to lose track of her words. It was strange, but the sound of her voice was conveying a meaning more profound and more direct than her spoken phrases. The sound of her voice rang in my ears like a light, mournful, warning bell, high metallic, hollow and sweet. It was old, an old sound much older than the lips through which it issued. It seemed to come from a far distance, from the distant past. Hollow and sweet and measured, its monotony insisted on the fine tried truths of the past, it called up proud, faded images of old resignations and compromises and lost illusions, and sounded constantly the note of the persistent obstinacy of pride. The words "we women" reached me. I was a woman, she was a woman. We were together. There were men in the world and women. When one reduced things to their last simplicity all women were bound together in the same bundle, dealing with the same problem. She, the older woman, was wise, I was foolish; but we were sisters in disappointment, we were weak, we must be proud. We had both loved Philibert, but even I had never loved him as she loved him. And he had broken her heart. The dignity of our life depended on our pride, to hide our hurt, to make no sound, no complaint, to arrange silently to make things bearable, to influence men without their knowing it. Our advantage lay in our clairvoyance. We could see through them when they could not see into us beyond our skins. We were weak if we treated them as they treated us, but we were strong if we remained mysterious, mute, proud. The children were ours. Everything we did was for our children. Philibert was her child. She must remember, she could not forget, he was her son. If we destroyed the family we destroyed our children. Even when the men destroyed it we must hold it together. We must pretend, for our children. When the man was gone we must pretend he was still there. Truth and beauty and dignity lay behind the pretence. We must pretend obstinately. If we pretended well enough it became true. We must not endanger our children's lives, anything but that.

Little Geneviève came dancing into my vision, her hair flying, her little skirts blowing, her toes dancing; a shadow fell on her, she stopped her gay jumping about. She was all at once pale. Her eyes gazed at me reproachfully, mournful eyes of a child, suffering. Something about her was wrong, twisted, maimed. I shuddered. Your mother's voice was still going on. The words she spoke were concise, delicate little pieces of sound strung together close like beads, they made a long, pale, shining chain that reached from the beginning of time out into the future. Over and over again I heard the same words. It seemed to me that she was endlessly repeating the same thing as if it were a bit of magic, of hoodoo. I wondered if she were hypnotizing me. Women must pretend—women, the protectors—the strong foundation—the family the basis of life. Women must keep the family intact. If we destroyed the family we destroyed our children—Philibert her child—Geneviève my child.

I looked up and saw your mother as I had never seen her before—she was bare—she was stark naked—she was fighting for her child, for her son, for what he was to her, for him as he must and should be to her and to the world, for his safety, and his dignity. There was nothing between us. We were together, two women. She was appealing to me as a woman like herself. Philibert was her child. Even if she were deceiving me, pretending to care for me, what did it matter? I understood her—she was there in the great simplicity of her pretence assuming me to be like herself, proud, gentle, sure, a woman like herself. Vulgar! I was vulgar; my struggling for freedom was coarse; I was making an ugly disgusting fuss; I was ashamed.

A sensation of warmth and delight crept over me—and I knew that I had decided to do what she wanted. It seemed to me that she became my own then, and that I belonged to her and she to me. It was impossible to wound her. The most important thing in the world was not to disappoint her. She expected something of me, renouncement. She expected me to spare her son. She asked for my life, my freedom, two little things I could give her, so that she would not be disappointed. I must give them to her. It would be beautiful to make her happy. That was wonderful. Whatever happened she would always know. There would be something fine between us. We would be together. I would belong to her and she to me: two women who had understood something together.

I touched her hand. I saw that her eyes were filled with tears. Her fingers clutched mine. "*Ma pauvre enfant, ayez pitié de moi,*" she quavered.

"There dear, don't think of it any more."

"Wait, at least, until I am dead," she whispered. I knelt beside her, just touching her hand. I was weeping, too, now, silently as she was, gently, mute tears.

"I will never do it," I said. It seemed to me wonderful to give her my freedom, gently, like that, in a whisper, kneeling close to her, not frightening her, asking nothing, putting things right, easily, at the cost of all my life.

IV

I did not go to America until the following year, and then I went alone, leaving Jinny with your mother. You remember about that, how after all they made me leave my child behind as a hostage. We won't dwell on it now. It was only significant in so far as it showed me that my new intimacy with your mother was not quite what I had believed it to be.

As for St. Mary's Plains, it gave me a different welcome from the one I had expected. It disapproved of me and showed it. My people went for me. They greeted me with the proprietary affection that claims the right to outspoken criticism. On the whole, I liked that. It was a relief. Although at first I was bewildered, amused and occasionally annoyed by their vigorous upbraiding, I was glad that they felt entitled to treat me as they did: their scolding gave me a feeling of their solidarity with me. And it was refreshing to find myself among a group of people who had no respect for my fortune but blamed me honestly for being so disgustingly rich and doing so little good with my money.

Paris gossip had reached St. Mary's Plains. I had thought it so far away, so safe. I was mistaken. Many acquaintances had been going back and forth across the Atlantic carrying information, more or less correct, of my doings. The fact that my husband was no longer living with me was variously interpreted. Had I come rushing home for refuge that first summer they would have been on my side, but I had not. I seemed to have cynically accepted his liaison with another woman and was brazenly continuing my worldly life.

My Aunt Patience, as I came gradually to realize, had been the person least affected by these tales. She lived the life of a hermit, wrapped up in her studies, and had refused to listen to gossip. "I guess Jane herself tells me what she wants me to know," she had said to more than one busybody, but of course I suspected nothing of all this on arrival. I had gone to America because of an unquenchable longing to be with my own people, but I was not without a certain feeling of pride. I was scarcely fatuous enough to consider myself as a martyr, but it did seem to me that I had suffered through no fault of my own and had taken my troubles with a respectable calm. Philibert was still wandering about Europe with Bianca. I had heard nothing from him directly. An occasional message reached me through his solicitors, that was all. I had continued to carry on. I was keeping my promise to your mother.

My Aunt Patty came to New York to meet my steamer. I saw her from the deck, before the ship was in dock, a powerful figure, something elemental about her, reducing others to insignificance; I waved. She looked at me but made no sign; she did not recognize me. As I came down the gangway I saw her peering about in the crowd still searching, and when I walked up to her and said "Aunt Patty, it's me, Jane," she dropped her large black handbag and gave a gasp. She of course was the same, only more so, bigger and grander, with her black mackintosh flapping, her bonnet askew and wisps of grey hair hanging down, a grand old scarecrow. How she hugged me, her long arms round me, people jostling us. That was a blissful moment. I was perfectly happy for that moment, a child at rest and comforted.

Then she said, "Where's your baby?"

"I didn't bring her, Aunt."

"Oh!" Her face fell.

"I couldn't, Aunt, such a long trip for such a short visit, and her father wouldn't let her come."

"I see." She shut her grim lips. It was clear that she was very disappointed.

We were to take the train that night for St. Mary's Plains. There was some confusion about my luggage and trouble about getting it across the city. I seemed to have a great deal. A great deal too much, my Aunt said. Celestine had a difference of opinion with the porters and scolded them in her high, voluble, native tongue. My Aunt did not know what to make of Celestine.

I was ridiculously excited when we arrived at St. Mary's Plains and drove up Desmoisnes Avenue, and then as our taxi stopped and I looked across the grass to that modest old house I had a feeling of immense relief. This was my home.

The Grey House welcomed me kindly. It had shrunk in size. It had grown shabby and ugly, but it had the charm of an old glove or shoe, much worn. I loved it with gratitude and pity and an ache of regret.

Standing in the front hall I knew that its spirit was unchanged. My mind reached out comfortably to its furthest corners, to the cupboards on the back stairs and the pantry sink that I knew as I knew my own hand. I remembered the smell of the carpet on the dark stairs and the way the Welsbach burner sizzled on the landing, spreading a round of light on the stained wall. My room was just as I had left it twelve years before. The white counterpane on the narrow bed, the flat pillow, the rag rug on the waxed floor that my Aunt Beth had made for me when I broke my arm falling off the stepladder.

Patience changed for dinner into a black silk blouse and serge skirt. Her high collar was fastened with an oval brooch of gold, the only ornament I ever saw her wear. There were two servants in the house, a cook and a housemaid. I suspected that one had been got in for my visit. It was clear to me that she was poor, even poorer than she had been. The house was not too clean and very shabby. Patience Forbes was no housekeeper. She never cared what she had to eat or poked into corners to find dust. The drawing-room looked forlorn in the pale gas light. I gathered that she never sat there but spent all her time in the museum among her precious specimens. The drawing-room made me feel dismal. In the days when my Aunt Beth kept house it had been a cosy room. Now the old mahogany sofas and chairs, covered in frayed black horsehair, were pushed back against the wall in ungainly attitudes. They seemed to watch me reproachfully. I loved their austere, proud forlornness, but I felt uncomfortable. The place did not disappoint me, but I felt that I disappointed it. The blurred and misty mirrors that held mysteriously behind their marred surfaces the invisible reflection of my little grandmother's sweet face and prim figure showed me myself, large, bright and vulgar, a great outlandish creature in an exaggerated dress, glittering, hard and horrible. I was profoundly disturbed. If I looked like that to myself, how must I look to my Aunt Patience? I soon found out. She was not a person to mince matters. She told me plainly that I looked wicked.

"Wicked, Aunt?"

"Yes, Jane, that's just about it."

"But, Aunt, this is terrible. What is it? What shall I do about it?"

She stared at me grimly. "I don't know. I guess it's everything—your clothes, that thick bang across your eyes, those ear-rings, that red stuff on your lips. It looks bad. It makes you look like an ungodly woman."

I rubbed off the lip salve and took off the ear-rings. "Is that better?"

"Humph. A little." Suddenly I saw her face quiver, her mouth twist. I crossed to her and knelt on the floor beside her, put my arms round her and looked into her working face.

"Aunt, tell me, what's the matter? Tell—"

"There, Jane, I'm an old fool." She tried to laugh but failed. Her voice cracked. "I can't help it. You're so different that I'm scared. Janey, Janey, you've no call to be so different." She put her large worn hands on my shoulders.

"I'm not changed in my heart, Aunt."

"Are you sure?"

"I am sure."

"There ain't nothing real wrong with you, Jane?"

"No, Aunt."

"You can tell me solemnly that your heart's not changed, that you've come to no harm?"

I looked into her eyes. Humbly, I knelt and looked into those honest eyes, not beautiful, with blistered, opaque irises, the whites yellow now with age. I knew what she meant, and I knew what would put things right between us. If I told her everything, all about Philibert and Bianca and my own loneliness she would give me the sympathy I wanted. Then all her criticism and disappointment would be swallowed up in pity. I hesitated. I did not believe that she knew anything of my troubles with Philibert. I had never written her one word about being unhappy. My happiness, I knew, was the most precious thing on earth to her. How, then, tell her now, and why? Break her old heart so that she might comfort me? Sadden the remaining years of her life that I might enjoy the luxury of being understood? And how explain? What could she ever understand of such things? She was an innocent woman.

So I lied. I chose my words in order to keep as near to truthfulness as I could.

"No, Aunt, I have come to no harm. I am just the same as the girl who left you twelve years ago. My looks, why should they matter to you, Aunt? They are not my own. All that is just dressmakers and hairdressers and the people round me. I have grown to look like them there, but I am more like you and yours than you think. I have been so home-sick, Aunt. I have longed so longingly for this, just this, Aunt, just to come home."

Her face had changed, her eyes searched mine wistfully now.

"You are unhappy, child."

"No, Aunt."

"Your husband?"

I felt myself turn pale as she held my head between her hands. What could I safely say? There was a look in her face that frightened me. Did she know after all? Had she heard?

"Aunt, he is a Frenchman, different from us."

"But is he a good man?"

"Yes."

"True to you as you are to him?"

"Yes."

For a moment longer she looked at me closely, then with a sigh of relief leaned back. "I believe you, Jane, I always said it wasn't true. I couldn't believe my girl wouldn't tell me."

I buried my head in her knees. I felt sick and guilty, and as I knelt there I saw that long ago I had thrown over my Aunt Patience for your mother, though I loved Patience Forbes better than any one in the world.

Presently she said humorously with her slow American twang—"Well, I guess I'll have to get used to your looks, Jane, and not be silly, but I reckon it would be easier if your voice weren't so French. You've got a queer sort of accent. I don't know what all your aunts and uncles will say when they see you. I expect if you explain it's just the effect of the world you've come from they'll think it's a pretty queer world."

But I had no intention of explaining myself to my relatives. Aunt Patty had the right to bring me to book, but no one else had. It seemed to me that night, lying awake in my cool, puritan bed, rather funny to think of the people of St. Mary's Plains holding me to account. What had I done, after all, to come in for a scolding? I had told my aunt I was unchanged. In a sense it was true. If I had not been the same I should not have wanted to come.

I could hear Celestine fussing about in the next room. Celestine was going to be a thorn in the side of the Grey House. She was out of place. There she was surrounded by my clothes. My clothes looked horribly gawdy littered all over that room. Presently her light was extinguished. I lay in the dark between the sheets that smelled of lavender, my eyes open in the kind familiar darkness, and told myself that it was true, that I was unchanged, the same—the very same person that had lain in that bed in that same homely safe obscurity years before—and for a time, the sounds and the unseen but palpable presences round me, seemed to agree, to reassure me.

I heard the tram rumbling by up the Avenue, I could see in my mind's eye, the arc light above the street shining on the high branches of the elm trees, the comfortable houses set back in their grass plots, shrouded in shadow, lighted windows showing here and there, and beyond them to the West, I knew was the river, filled with the dark hulls of ships, lumber schooners from the great lakes, pleasure boats, tugs, their red lights riding high above the black water. From the side of my bed my mind could move surely out through the night among known objects, along familiar and friendly streets, past houses and shops and churches, all acquainted with me as I was with them. And I felt the furniture of the room was kindly, sedate and prim, taking me for granted, assuming that all was well, that I belonged there—but did I? Was it true? The years seemed to have been rolled up, as if the intervening time were a parchment scroll, put away in a corner, but there was something else, something different that could not be put away. It was in me. It existed in my blood, in my body. It was restless and it gnawed me. No—no—it was not true. I was not the same. No miracle could undo what had been done to me. No relief could obliterate from my mind what I had learned. I was old—I was tired and corrupt—something irrevocable had happened to me—something final and fatal, that no longing and no prayers could ever exorcise.

St. Mary's Plains had "got a move on" during my absence, so my relatives told me. I saw as much. It had entered upon one of those sensational periods of industrial success that come to American towns so unexpectedly. Some one had invented a stove, some one else a motor car. Former modest citizens were making millions and building factories. Down town was encroaching on the pleasant shady districts of up town. The lots on either side of the Grey House had been bought by a syndicate who proposed to put there a hotel and an apartment building. The Grey House would be sandwiched in between them. It would become a little dark building at the bottom of a well, but Patience Forbes had refused to sell, though the price offered her would have left her more than comfortably off for the rest of her life. I asked leave to buy the Grey House from her for greater security, but she refused. "I'm safe enough, Jane, because I don't want money. No man alive can make me sell if I don't want to. You've no call to worry about me."

My Uncle Bradford was not in town but there were a great many other family connections who came to see us and asked us to come to them for large hospitable succulent meals. They greeted me with hearty kisses and handshakes. "Well, Jane, glad to see you home at last. Hope you left your husband well." And then we settled down into chairs.

"You certainly have changed. You're real French, aren't you? We've heard a lot about your doings. It sounds pretty funny to us, giving parties all the time to crowned heads, aren't you?" This from the men, or from the women more gently—

"Dear, couldn't you have brought your baby? We're so disappointed. Yes, you do seem different, but we hope you're happy. We can't imagine your life, you know. It seems so empty, so artificial. The papers give such strange accounts. All those gambling places, your cousin fighting a duel, it sounds so strange. France seems to be turning to atheism with terrible rapidity. The separation of Church and State might be good if it led to a spiritual revival, but they don't keep Sunday at all, do they? All the theatres are open Sundays they say."

The elders were gentle but positive in their disapproval, the younger generation frankly intolerant. They had been struck by various religious and emotional disturbances that had swept the country, evangelical revivals, a thing called the "Student Movement," and a university type of socialism. I felt myself being measured up to a certain high standard and found lamentably wanting. Had I forgotten their standards, I asked myself, or was this something new? When they asked me what I was doing with my life I said I didn't know, that it took me about all my time just to live it. Wasn't I interested in anything? Oh, yes, a great many things, music especially, and old enamels. They didn't mean that, they meant causes. I didn't understand. What causes, I asked, did they refer to? Women's suffrage, the negro question, sweated labour. No, I was obliged to admit that women's suffrage had not interested me and that there being no negro question in France I hadn't thought about the subject. As for sweated labour, I supposed it did exist in Paris, but that its evils had never been brought to my notice. All the young people were espousing causes. They quite took my breath away. They believed so hard in so many things, and they talked so much about the things they believed in. Really they were violent talkers. Their fresh young lips uttered with ease the most astounding phrases. They were fond of big words. Their talk was a curious mixture of undigested literature and startling slang. Some of the things they believed in were love, democracy, the greatness of the American people and the equality of the sexes. What they didn't believe in they condemned off-hand. There was for them no quiet region where interesting questions were left pleasantly unanswered. They abhorred an unanswered question as nature abhors a vacuum. Every topic was a bull to be taken by the horns. Everything concerned them. There was nothing that was not their business. They were crusaders, at war with idleness and cynicism, vowed to the regeneration of the world. They went for me, but how they went for me! I was a renegade, a back-slider, a poor, misguided victim of an effete and vicious foreign country. I had nothing to give them of any value. When I talked of the charm of Paris they yawned. When I mentioned my friends they called me a snob. When I spoke of my activities they laughed in gay derision. On the whole I didn't mind. I was too tired to mind. They were so young, so keen, so good to look at, so full of hope. I wouldn't have stopped their talking for the world, and I liked them for despising my money.

I envied them. They were happy, they were free. Deep in my heart I suspected that they were right to despise my life. In the evenings when they gathered on the shadowy verandahs of their comfortable countrified houses, the young men with mandolins, the girls in billowy muslin dresses, I listened to their laughter and their tinkling music, feeling so old, so very old. On those summer nights Aunt Patty and I would sometimes sit on the front steps of the Grey House as the custom was in the town, and all the street would seem to be charged with romance and joy and mystery. Through the trees one could see young forms flitting from house to house where lights streamed from hospitable windows down across the plots of grass, while on the shadowed verandahs young hearts whispered to young hearts, whispered of dreams that must come true, gallant, innocent dreams.

And there was the difficulty of religion. They couldn't swallow my having become a Catholic. On the first Sunday morning I asked my Aunt Patience if she would like me to go to church with her.

"Why, yes, Jane, but I thought you'd be going to the Catholic Church."

"I'd rather go with you, Aunt."

"Come, then." But I saw that she was troubled.

"You see, Aunt, I don't really care what church I go to; I'm only a Catholic for social convenience."

"That's too bad, isn't it?" She was putting on her bonnet.

"I don't know, I don't seem to have any feeling about it one way or another. I never could seem to learn much about God, Aunt, don't you remember?"

"But don't you believe in Him, Jane?"

"Honestly, Aunt, I don't know. Sometimes I wish I could, but that's when I'm in trouble and only because I want some one to help me out. That's not believing, is it? It's just cowardice."

My aunt grunted. "Religion mostly is, but there's something else, like what your grandmother had."

"Yes, I know."

She said no more, and I was grateful to her for taking it like that. We were companions in spite of everything.

But when my Aunt Beth came with her husband to visit us things became more difficult. She had taken my turning Roman Catholic as a dreadful personal problem of her own, and felt, dear little soul, that she must try to bring me back to the fold. The result was painful. She came armed with tracts and pamphlets, a whole bag full of appalling literature. I was greatly astonished, for I remembered her as a very gentle little creature. With age she had grown militant in the cause of evangelical truth. She took me to camp meetings and prayer meetings. She would come into my room at night in her pink flannel dressing gown, her little middle-aged face aglow with ecstatic resolve, and would press into my hand just one more message, a dreadful booklet, "The Murder of God's Word," or something of that kind. I was at last driven to appeal to my Aunt Patience for protection. She took up the cudgels for me.

"I guess Jane's all right, Beth, I wouldn't worry. God's the same, whatever your Church."

"But Patty, it's heathen idolatry, worshipping the Virgin Mary. The Virgin Mary was just a woman like you and me."

"Well, dear, what does it matter? Perhaps Jane doesn't worship her in a heathen spirit, do you, Jane?"

"No, Aunt, I'm afraid I don't worship her at all."

"But think of the Jesuits," wailed Aunt Beth.

"I don't," snapped Aunt Patty.

"Patty, I believe you're in danger of losing your faith."

"No, I'm not, Beth, don't you fret about me. I've a good conscience before my God and my Saviour. Now just you leave Jane in peace and trust her to God. That's what you're told to do in the Bible. Just you trust the Lord. He'll look after Jane."

And Beth would be momentarily silenced more by the sense of her elder sister's family authority than by any respect for her arguments.

Aunt Patty and I were happiest when we were left alone.

In July it became very hot. The back garden was ablaze with flowers. Rows of hollyhocks lined the wooden fences at either side. Butterflies fluttered in the sun. The bee-hives at the bottom of the garden were all a-murmur. We spent long hours on the back verandah, and Aunt Patty, her knitting needles moving swiftly (she knitted a good deal, but always had a book open on her lap), would question me about my life in Paris, and I would tell her as much of the truth as I could. Her conclusions were characteristic.

"Your set over there doesn't seem to have too much sense," she would say. "You sound a very giddy lot. You take no interest in science, do you? I don't suppose you've any of you an idea of what's being written and done."

"Oh, come, Aunt, some of us are awfully clever. Fan knows all about art and music. My sister-in-law paints and embroiders quite beautifully, and all our relatives are gifted."

"Humph, art is all very well, but do you keep up with the times?"

"How do you mean, 'keep up'?"

"I mean, child, with what's going on in the world of thought, intellectual progress. They're making great strides in medicine in Germany. France is doing most in mathematics. But I daresay you never heard of Professor Lautrand. He lives in Paris. Ever met him? Ever heard of him?"

"I'm afraid not, Aunt."

"Well, there you are, one of the great spirits of the age." And she rubbed her nose with her knitting needle. "A noble intellect. His books have opened up for me a new world. To think you could talk to him and don't even know he's there! Why, landsakes, Jane, if I were in your shoes I'd wait on his doorstep till my bones cracked under me." She laughed.

"Come and visit me, dear, do, and we'll have him to lunch every day," I urged. At which she laughed again her young, hearty laugh, but with a wistful look in her eyes as if the light of a lovely dream glowed a moment before her.

"No, Jane, no. I'm too old to go gallivanting about Europe, but I do wish you'd take my advice. You never did take any interest in science. If you did you'd not be so dependent upon mere human beings. If you'd only study geology and biology and the history of races, you'd see that human beings are no great shakes, anyhow, and don't count for much, save that they've the power of thought. Has it ever occurred to you to stop and consider how wonderful it is that you can think, and how little you avail yourself of the privilege? Go one day to the *Bibliothèque Nationale*, that's what it's called, they've got one of my books there, and just think for a moment that all that building is crammed full of the records of man's thought. Stupid, most of it, you'd say, too dull to read, all those books. Well, that may be their fault and it may be yours, but it's neither here nor there. The fact is that the recording of knowledge is a miracle."

Wonderful Patience Forbes, taking me to task for the frivolity of my world, sitting on the back verandah, her spectacles on the end of her nose, her knitting on her lap, her heelless slippers comfortably crossed, her little modest volume tucked away on a shelf in the *Bibliothèque Nationale*. She seemed to me very remarkable, and she seems even more so now. Time for most of us is just a process of disintegration, old age is often pitiful and ugly, but at the age of sixty-five Patience Forbes had the heart of a child and the robust enthusiasm of a student. She had been persuaded by the State Board of Education to write a series of text-books on birds, and in the evenings she would work in the room she called the museum, and I would sit watching her while she chewed her pen, rapped irritably with her hard old fingers on the desk, or went down on her knees before a shelf of books to look up some reference. Sometimes she would walk the floor and grumble—"Gracious, how difficult it is to write a decent sentence. English certainly isn't my strong point. I write like a clucking hen. Style never was in my line." And then she would laugh, her young, vigorous, chuckling laugh.

When I compared my life with hers, how could I not feel that there was justice in all that young American condemnation. Patience Forbes was old, she was poor, she went about in tram-cars, she worked for her living, and she was happy. There was no doubt that she was happy. She envied no man and no woman, and asked nothing of any one. She would not even let me help her. She said that she had everything she wanted and I was bound to believe her.

Early in August we went up to my Uncle Bradford's camp in the woods at the head of the lake. He had written urging us to come and saying that if we didn't he would come down to St. Mary's Plains as he wanted particularly to see me.

A white steam-boat, with side paddles churning peacefully through the water, carried us for a long day and night and part of another day west by north-west, past little white straggling towns, calling at long piers to deliver mails and provisions, moving on and on, farther and farther across the wide shining expanse of water, away from the world of men. Timber schooners passed us, square-rigged, coming down from the great forest lands. The skies were boundless and light and high above the water. We moved in marvellous translucent space. The air was new as if the world had been created yesterday.

Uncle Bradford and his sons with their wives and children had built themselves log houses on the shore of the lake. The forest stretched away behind them as far as the Canadian border, and a great tract of it belonged to them, with its rivers, its game and its timber. Some of them were in the lumber business, others came there merely for the summer holidays. I found my Aunt Minnie there, and an even greater crowd of youngsters than in St. Mary's Plains. Uncle Bradford, dressed in a red flannel shirt and a sombrero, ruled his camp like a Russian patriarch, and again I found every one interested in things that I had forgotten were interesting. There in that glorious pagan world surrounded by virgin forests they worshipped a stern and exacting God, read the Bible, and argued in the evening before the blazing log fire as to whether the mind were separate from the soul, or evolution incompatible with the principles of Christianity. And I wondered at them, for they were not afraid of their puritan God, nor weary of endless argument. Their consciences were clear. They could look God in the face, and their brains, if rather empty, were admirably keen.

I watched the women. They all seemed to have devoted husbands who assumed the sanctity of marriage to be the basis of life and took the beauty of their women for granted. Extravagant youngsters, how I envied them. Husbands who remained faithful lovers, wives who remained innocent girls, all contented and unafraid, and with their outspokenness, shy people keeping secret the sacred intimacy of love.

The children were splendid animals. They liked me and included me in their games. We used to go swimming before breakfast when the heavenly morning was crystal pale. I would slip from my cabin and join those little bronze figures, run through the clearing to the shore and down the wooden pier, stand an instant with them all about me breathing in the sweet air, then with a shout all together we would dive. I swam as well as any of those boys. It pleases me now to remember their respect for my prowess. And I could paddle a canoe and throw a ball like a man, and I caught the largest fish of all, a fine big salmon trout weighing fifteen pounds. My thought was—"I want a boy like one of these to become a man for Jinny. I want her to have a husband from my people."

It was a delicious life. The air was fine and dry and sharply scented with the scent of pine woods drenched in sunlight. Each morning was a miracle as clear as the first morning of creation. Swift rollicking streams tumbled over rocks, fat salmon jumped in deep pools. Mild-eyed Indians came travelling down from the depths of the vast forest, paddling their lovely canoes of birch bark, laden with grass baskets and soft moccasins embroidered in beads. The nights were cold. One was lifted up into sleep, one floated up and away into sleep under sparkling stars, hearing the waves lapping the shore and the wind murmuring through the branches of the innumerable pines of the forest that spread away, further and further away, endlessly, countless trees murmuring a strong chant under the wide sky, stretching beyond the edge of the mind's compass, as far as one could think, as far as one's soul could reach out, the forest, the sky, the water, calm, untroubled, eternal.

Then suddenly something crashed into that crystal space.

My Uncle Bradford took me one morning to his office.

"You are nearly thirty now, Jane."

"Yes, Uncle."

"I have a letter for you from your father. He left it with me to deliver to you when you were thirty years old."

I took the envelope he handed me. I was trembling. My uncle mopped his forehead and cleared his throat.

"You will be absolute owner of your property when you are thirty."

"Oh," I said blankly.

"Yes, you were not to know. It was your father's wish. Did your mother, before she died, tell you anything about him?"

"No, I don't think so."

"Well, I'm sorry. It was her place to tell you. Your father is buried out west, in Oregon."

"Yes, I know."

"He's not buried in a cemetery. He's buried on a hill. He bought the tract of land himself."

I waited. The noises of the camp came cheerily through the cabin windows. There was a strong smell of pine wood and resin and of bacon frying somewhere out of doors.

"Your father broke his neck falling down the elevator shaft in a New York hotel. The verdict was accidental death, but it was not an accident. Your mother knew, and I knew."

I stood up, staring at him stupidly, holding the letter in my fingers, then quickly turned and went out. I crossed the camp and struck off into the woods. In a quiet place I sat down and opened the letter. It began, "My dear daughter Jane." I know it by heart. This is the letter.

> *"My dear daughter Jane*: It is time for me to go. A man is free to choose his time. This I believe, not much else. I am sorry to leave you, but you are only five years old and you will be better off with your grandmother in St. Mary's Plains than you would be with me. Your grandmother and your aunts will take care of you. They are good women. It's not their fault that they don't like me. The truth is, Jane, that I'm not their kind. I'm nobody's kind and I'm awful tired of being alone in a crowd. This world is getting too full of people for me. I want space and I guess I'll find it where I'm going.

I wouldn't leave you so much money if I knew what to do with it. It never did me any good. It was only fun getting, not having. At first I worked with my hands—in the earth—then I found gold. I bought land and more land, built a railroad or two, and then Wall Street got me. That was like the poker table I'd known when I was a boy working on the Chippevale Ranch. That was just excitement, no good to any one, but fun for a spell.

When you are thirty years old you'll have as much sense as you're ever going to have. Perhaps you'll do better than I did. Perhaps you'll know how to spend. I didn't. I'd like you to enjoy what I've left you. It would console me some.

I'm not a believer in the Cross of Jesus and I don't want it on my grave, but I'm not sure there isn't something over yonder on the other side. I hailed from the far West. It's spoiling now, but a wide prairie and a high sky are the best things I know, that and working with your hands.

Good-bye, little girl Jane, you're the only thing I mind leaving behind. I'd kind of like to know what you'll be like when you get this.

Your Uncle Bradford's an honest man, there aren't many, you can trust him. He'll give you this and explain that there was no disgrace. Only I didn't feel like living any more. There are too many people hanging round. I want to get away. If I'm doing you a wrong by quitting I ask you to forgive me.

"Your loving father,
"Silas Carpenter."

I worked it out that night with maps and time-tables. I had just enough time to go to Redtown and get back to New York to catch my boat. I left the next morning. My aunt went with me. Uncle Bradford's steam launch took us down the lake. We caught a train at a place called Athens and joined the western express the middle of the next day. It took us three days and three nights to get to Oregon. We crossed the Mississippi river early one morning. The next day we thundered through the Rocky Mountains. The plains beyond were immense and stupefying.

I visited the grave alone. A block of granite, reminding me of a druid's stone, marked the spot on the hill where he was buried. It stood up stark and solid on the bare ground. It looked as if it had been left there endless ages before by some slow, gigantic movement of nature, some glacier travelling by inches from the north, or some heaving of the earth's surface. One side of it was polished and bore an inscription cut into the stones: —

"HERE LIES SILAS CARPENTER, WHO WAS BORN IN THIS PLACE BEFORE IT
WAS A TOWN AND WHO DIED IN NEW YORK ON JANUARY 5TH 1885."

From the hill-top one had a view of the city lying along the sea, a new, bright city, an unfriendly sea of a dazzling blue. I sat down on the grass by the great stone. Here, at last, was something that belonged to me and to no one else. No one would dispute with me the possession of my father's grave. I felt excited and uplifted as if I had come into a precious inheritance. And yet what had he left me? A message of failure, an unanswered question, a sense of not having counted for him enough myself to keep him on the earth. He had shuffled me off with the rest of it. My mother must have hated him. She must have had something to do with his giving it up like that. I would have loved him. I would have understood him. If he had waited for me we would have been good companions. If he had lived I would never have gone to Paris. I would have gone west with him to his wide prairie and high skies. Everything would have been different. I had missed something. What had I missed? I looked out across the dry grass, the rolling hills, the big, bare, blazing land, the glittering sea under the windy sun, and I recognized it as mine. I had missed my life. I had taken the wrong turn.

We boarded the train again next day and recrossed the continent of America. It took us seven days and nights to reach New York. We passed through Denver, Chicago, Cleveland, and countless other cities. We crossed deserts white as sand and overgrown with cactus. In the middle of the Mohawa desert we stopped at a place called Bagdad to give the engine a drink of water. Bagdad was a single wooden shed standing in a waste of sand. Bagdad, Bagdad. It was very hot in the train. My aunt and I sat most of the time on the open platform at the end of the observation car, watching the earth fly from under the train and drinking iced drinks that the coloured porters brought us. It is very exciting to be in a train like that, rushing across the earth at such speed, suspended in space as if on a giant bridge, and the vast, the immense, the overwhelming panorama flying endlessly past. Cities, rivers, prairies, mountains, lonely farms, the steel jaws of stations engulfing you, out again through the crowding buildings of a city you will never know, full of people you will never see, into the open, the horizon endlessly wheeling, the earth under the train flying backwards, but the far edge of the earth towards the horizon wheeling with you. Thundering along, the pounding of the engine, the grinding wheels exciting your brain to a special liveliness, the train is a miraculous thing, a steel comet cushioned inside imitating a dwelling, but a long comet whirring through space, a blaze of flying light by night, a streak and a noise by day, and from it you look out upon a thousand worlds flying past, and you have glimpses, instant, quick glimpses, of countless mysterious lives, a group of children hanging over a fence waving, a farmer in a wide straw hat sitting in a blue wagon at a railway crossing, a boundless golden field behind him of innumerable garnered sheaves all gold, a village like a collection of wooden boxes, saddled horses tethered to a rope in front of an unpainted post office. Cowboys driving cattle, rolling prairies, horses, wild, running, kicking up their heels, a lonely cabin against a hill, hens scratching outside, thin smoke coming from the wobbling iron smoke stack, lost in the boundless blue; families moving, all their household goods piled on wagons, the men walking beside the horses with long whips, a mail coach lurching along a mountain road, the driver has a Colt revolver in his pocket. You know that. You hope he'll get the highway robbers who will be waiting for him at dark. Bret Harte wrote about him. And now Walt Whitman's country—Leaves of Grass—a great poem, the greatest. He knew. He had found out. He understood the giant, the great urge of life, in this my country.

And I thought of my father, crossing and recrossing the continent, restless, lonely, powerful, dissatisfied, an isolated man moving up and down the land, handling money, gambling with money, not knowing what to do, growing tired of it all.

I said to my aunt—"It was twenty-five years ago, but it brings him close."

"Your father's death?"

"Yes, it makes a difference."

"How?"

"I'm with him. It clears the ground."

I did not quite know what I meant then, but I know now.

We reached New York. I was suddenly filled with foreboding. In the high window of our towering hotel I sat with Patience far into the night. We sat together like watchers in a tower, and a million lighted windows shone before us in the blue night.

"I am afraid, Aunt."

"Why, my child?"

"I am afraid to leave you."

"Yes, I know."

How much did she know, I wondered? What did she suspect? Philibert had not written to me, of course. She must have noticed. She must know a good deal.

"You have your little girl, Jane. Think of her."

"I do. She's a prim little thing, not a bit like me."

"Promise me to love your child, to love her enough."

"Enough for what, dear?"

"Just enough; you'll find out how much that is."

"I will try to love her as you have loved me, Aunt, always."

She gripped my hand. "Janey," she muttered, "my girl." We sat a long time silent. The desire to unburden all my heart was unbearable. But it was too late now.

"Europe is too full of people, Aunt. They have made the earth into a trivial thing. It is not good for people to subdue the earth. In Paris one is never out of doors. I don't feel at home there. I am sick for my own country, for a wide prairie and a high sky."

"You'll come back again, Jane."

"Yes," I answered, "I will come back."

I thought she was asking for a promise. I did not know that she was stating a prophecy.

And in the morning I went aboard my ship and my aunt left me and went down the gangway onto the pier, and the ship moved slowly away from the dock. There she was again, standing in the crowd in her queer black clothes, but this time the water between us was widening. She lifted both her arms to me in a last large gesture of full embrace, then her arms fell to her sides, and she stood there buffeted by the wind, jostled by the crowd, a strong old woman, looking after me bravely. I had a desperate moment. I wanted to jump, to swim back. I felt an agony of regret, of longing, of warning. I struggled. It was horrible, such pain. What did it mean? Why was I going? It was wrong, it was wrong.

I never saw her again.

V

I slipped back into Paris, its pleasant walls closed round me, and the voice I had heard over there, in my wide country was hushed. It was like coming out of a great open space into a room. There was all at once about me a multitude of nice pretty things, a shimmer of lights, a harmony of bright sounds, the smooth, soothing, flattering touch of luxury. No whisper of elemental forces could penetrate here. Men of incomparable taste and limited vision had made this place to suit themselves.

Jinny was waiting for me, a prim fairy with starry eyes, standing daintily on tip-toe to be kissed, smoothing her white frock carefully after my hug. She told me that she had seen her Papa. He had been on a visit to *Grand' mère*! He had given her a strawberry ice in the Bois and had taken her to see Punch and Judy. Then he had gone far away to a country where old kings were buried and one rode on camels across the sand. The *Guignol* had been very amusing, but she had agreed with her papa that she was rather old for Punch and Judy. Some day he would come back and take her to big parties. I looked at Jinny, little Jinny, who didn't like to be hugged, pirouetting on one toe and looking at herself in the glass, and I remembered my promise to Patience Forbes. It wasn't enough to dote on my child, to crave her sweetness, her caresses, her laughter. There would be a struggle. There would be endless things. I saw them coming, all the events of her poor little life, so spectacular in its setting. I was there to ward them off, to challenge fate and the future, to love her with enough wisdom and enough tenacity and enough self-abasement to—well, to see her through.

And I had an idea that she wouldn't help me much. She would perhaps always be content to curtsey to herself in the glass. I felt this, but I felt it with less keenness than I expected. There seemed something a little unreal about struggling desperately to ward off evil from my child. There were flowers in the room, orchids and violets and roses, sent to greet me. A sheaf of letters, invitations to lunch, to dine, to listen to music. The first night of the Russian Ballet was announced for the following week. Rodin asked me to his studio to see a new bronze. Beauty all about me, amusement, stimulus, within easy reach, treasures of pleasure like sugared fruit hanging from fantastic branches waiting to be plucked.

Your mother's kiss of greeting showed me that Philibert's visit had made a difference. It was a cold, gay little peck and was accompanied by nervous pats and hurried playful remarks on a high, forced note. Clearly she was nervous. Almost, it seemed, as if she were afraid of me. Poor little *belle-mère*. She had fallen in love with her son all over again, but why need that make her afraid of me? I was disappointed and annoyed by her renewed subterfuges. It seemed to me strange that she should think I would begrudge her the pleasure her son could still give her. I thought of explaining my feelings to Claire, but Claire was not in a receptive mood and there was after all nothing to be gained by it. I was a little tired of explaining. I was, I found, even a little tired of the de Joigny family. My obligations to them and theirs to me seemed less important since my return. It occurred to me that I had taken myself and my problems with a ridiculous seriousness. I was still very fond of your mother, but I no longer asked of her the impossible. All that I now wanted of the family was a sufficiently respectable show of approval and a mild give-and-take of friendliness. I felt equal to living a life of my own and I proposed doing so. When you suggested giving a dinner for me in your rooms I was delighted. You promised me Ludovic and half a dozen of the best brains in Paris. That seemed to me an excellent way to begin.

Aunt Clothilde sent for me one morning a few days later. I found her in bed under an immensely high canopy of crimson damask, sipping a cup of the richest chocolate, a coarse, white cambric cap, like a peasant woman's, tied under her double chin, her wig hung on the bed-post. The room was vast and stuffy and dark and hung with dingy tapestries. On one side of the bed sat her *dame de compagnie*, knitting, on the other a frightened priest with a sallow, perspiring face. Aunt Clo waved a plump hand as I came in. The duenna and the priest rose hurriedly.

"No, *mon Père*, I won't help you. You are no doubt a saintly man, but that's not enough for the business in hand. You've not got the brains. You couldn't preach to a lot of worldly women, you're too timid. Look at yourself now. You're trembling before a wicked old woman who may have some influence with the Archbishop but has none whatever with Saint Peter. Come, *mon Père*, brace up and go to the heathen. There's a nice post vacant in Madagascar. I'll put in a word for you there if you like."

The poor man's face worked painfully. He murmured something and scuttled away across the great room. The little companion held open the door for him and followed him out.

Aunt Clothilde turned to me. "Blaise," she began at once, motioning me to sit down, "has asked me to dine with him. Does he dine? Has he a cook? He says so, but how do I know? What will he give me to eat? He says the dinner is for you. Since when has he taken to giving his sister-in-law dinners? He wants me to put you in countenance, and to impress his disreputable bohemian friends. He says they are all geniuses. What is a genius? Your mother-in-law thinks they all died in the seventeenth century. She may be right. How can one be sure? And why should I dine with a genius? Is that a reason? He promises me, as if it were a favour, that man Ludovic, a monster with greasy grey curls who worships an Egyptian cat. Blaise says he is a very great scholar and that you deserve a little pleasure. Will you find pleasure in his old scholar? Why should you? I'd rather have a beautiful young fool myself. It appears the family is horrid to you. Is that so? Wouldn't let you take your child to America, eh? Well, I don't mind having a dig at the family. Tiresome people, always splitting hairs. And you're a good girl. You've got pluck, but I thought you were going to hurt Bianca that night." She chuckled. "Well, what do you think? Shall I come to this dinner to meet your crazy friends?"

"They're not mine, Aunt, I don't know them."

"You know Clémentine, she likes you. She's all right, a Bourbon and a S— — on her mother's side, but of course as mad as a March hare, and no morals. She doesn't need 'em. But don't take after her, you've got 'em and you need 'em. All Anglo-Saxons are like that. Take care. Of course it would be no more than Philibert deserves."

I laughed. "You talk, Aunt, as if Blaise's friends weren't proper."

"Proper, what's that? Aren't they just the most disreputable people on earth? Isn't that why they're amusing? Really clever people are never proper. It takes every drop of Clémentine's blue blood to keep her afloat, and that man Felix! these writers with their habits of sleeping all day, Blaise tells me he is writing a play without words. It must be witty. *En voilà une occasion pour faire de l'esprit.* And the Spaniard, the painter, it appears that he wants to do a fresco for my music room. Well, he won't. Only, if he doesn't for me, he will for François. Blaise says he's the greatest mural painter since Tiepolo. I detest that '*Trompe l'œil*' school, but I'd like to spite François. What do you think? I'm very poor this year. I sold a forest for half its value. Now then, what about Philibert—gone to Egypt with his little salamander, has he?"

"I believe so, Aunt."

"And you? You don't look very sad."

"I don't think I am, Aunt."

"Good, excellent; you console yourself, eh?"

"No, Aunt, I don't; not, that is, in the way you mean."

"Rubbish; don't look so virtuous, child. If you haven't already, you soon will. We all do. It's a law of nature. My husband was the dullest man on earth, I couldn't abide him. If he hadn't been the first Duke of France no one would ever have asked him to dinner. How do you think I put up with him for twenty years? You find me an ugly old woman, very fat, very fond of good cooking. My child, there are only two kinds of pleasure worth having in this world, and one of them has to do with the stomach. I've enjoyed both. I now only enjoy one. That's enough. What a face you make at me! If you go against the laws of nature you'll get into trouble."

"But, Aunt, seriously, these clever friends of Blaise—are they disreputable?"

"Child, child, how boring you are, you Americans have such literal minds. All I mean is that they've no moral sense. They've something else though in its place, something better, perhaps, or worse, anyhow more discriminating."

"I see."

"No, you don't, but it doesn't matter. You've a moral sense that bothers the life out of you. Now go along with you. I must get up. I'll come to your party. Your mother-in-law won't approve. She's a superior person. As for you, God knows what you'll be in ten years time with such a husband and such a conscience. I had better keep an eye on you. In the choice of a lover you can ask my advice. I know men. They're not worth much, but you don't take or refuse one for that reason. You've found that out for yourself by now."

She dismissed me, waving again her little fat hand from under the immense canopy of her bed.

I left her, amused and rather exhilarated. A wicked old woman and a very great lady. It didn't occur to me to take her seriously, but I liked her. All the same, the last thing I wanted was a lover. The mere thought filled me with disgust.

Your dinner was awfully nice, Blaise dear. I remember the evening well. A few snowflakes softly floated down in your little courtyard as old Albert, your manservant, in his ancient green coat, opened the door. He had cooked the dinner and arranged the table and made the fire in the living room and put the champagne on ice; I knew that, but his manner was of a fine, calm formality as he ushered Aunt Clo and myself into your presence. A group of men who somehow impressed one as not at all ordinary, and a bright little lady dressed like a parrot, in a tiny, shabby, candle-lit room, filling the place comfortably with their easy good-humour, that was my first impression, followed quickly by others, pleasant, special impressions, aspects sharp and neat in an atmosphere that gave one a feeling of tasting a fine subtle flavour. Each person in the room was an individual unlike any one else. With no beauty to speak of, several were old men in oddly cut clothes, they were more interesting to watch than any lovely creature. Their faces were worn and lined and gentle, thin masks through which one saw the fine play of intelligence. Some were already known to the great world of thought and public affairs, others have since become so, but all were simple, homely men that night, with a certain childlike gaiety that was very appealing.

Albert's food was excellent; succulent, substantial food that suggested the provinces. The wine was very old. For a moment as I watched your convives inhaling the bouquet from lifted glasses, I imagined myself far away in Balzac's country, a snowy street of silent houses stretching out between high poplars to a great river, a carriage at the door, with a postillion in a three-cornered hat, waiting to drive me to some romantic rendezvous. But the talk swept me along with its merry-go-round of the present.

I cannot, after all these years, recall what was said, impossible to recapture now the quick turns of wit, the dry little jokes, the swift touches of poetry, that followed each other with such rapid intellectual grace. It was all incredibly rapid. I could just manage to keep up with the sense of it. I didn't attempt to take part. Ideas were as thick in that room as confetti at a fête. Clémentine, in an apple-green dress, with a round red spot of rouge on either cheek, swayed this way and that in response to innumerable sallies, her face changing like lightning. She was a match for those men. Her wit played over the history of her country like a jolly little ferret nosing out and pouncing upon joke and anecdote from the vast field of the past. Cardinals, princes, and ruffians were held up to ridicule. International affairs were dealt with clearly and deftly by her cutting tongue. She played with the ideas round her as if they were a swarm of brilliant darting winged creatures. Her delight in this battle of wit was contagious. The talk grew faster and faster. Soon every one was talking at once. No one could finish a sentence.

Cambon was explaining to Aunt Clothilde why the Government would not tolerate an Ambassador to the Pope. Clémentine was defending the English, no one appeared to like the English. Felix was making fun of Diaghilev, the new Russian who had appeared with his Imperial Ballet a week before.

What delightful people! Certainly without reservation of any kind I find them now as I did then the most delightful people in the world. Ludovic wore a celluloid collar. His body was too heavy for his legs and his head too big for his body; no matter; his profound, quiet gaze and tired, brown face expressed a nobility that made one ashamed of noticing his ill-cut coat. Felix looked like a faun. With his exaggerated features thrust forward into the candle-light he said funny, penetrating things that kept Aunt Clo chuckling. I watched, fascinated. These were the people Aunt Clo called disreputable, utterly lacking in a moral sense. Were ever sinners so joyous, so light-hearted? Rebels against creeds, against the fixed order of society, against the didactic spoken word, they were kind to me, the Philistine, exerting at once and with unconscious ease the most disarming charm.

Vaguely I recalled the mentality of my American home. It was there behind me, like a cold and lifeless plaster cast behind a curtain. Here was something infinitely more interesting, something brilliantly living, something merry and subtle and fine that defied disapproval. The powers of evil? Chimeras! No room for them here, no room for anything dismal and boring. I felt an uplift, it was like an awakening. All that horror of soul searching, all the dreary puritan A. B. C. of right and wrong was a childish nightmare. These people understood the world. They made fun of evil. They loved each other and found no fault with their friends. Under their gaiety was a deep sympathy for poor humanity.

They said things that would have sent St. Mary's Plains reeling with horror into one large devastating revival meeting. If St. Mary's Plains could have dreamed of the character of their conversation it would call upon God to destroy them. I laughed. Albert filled my glass.

Some one was saying—

"Time is a circle."

"The sunrise, why the same sun? Who knows?"

"Truth? Why should one want truth? Truth is a thing we have invented. An accurate statement of facts? But there is no accuracy except in mathematics, and in mathematics there are no facts."

Were they joking? Or were they serious? Both. I felt like a schoolgirl, very ignorant, very crude, with a stiff blank mind like a piece of cardboard. They slowed down to listen to Ludovic. I remember Ludovic speaking to them all with his eyes smiling under their spiky grey eyebrows. I think I remember what he said. It was the first time I had heard him talk, as he talked to me so often afterwards.

"I sit in some old city of the past and look back upon the present and still further back into the future. Why not? Time is an endless circle, wheeling around one. Why trouble to imagine a beginning or an end? Why these unnatural conceptions? The old legends are more sensible. The ancient mystic symbol of matter, Ouroborro, the tail-devourer, a serpent coiled into a circle, symbol of evolution, of the evolution of matter. There is something there, something to think of. Let us all think of molecules, and remember the Philosopher's Stone. Have you ever laughed at the legend of the Philosopher's Stone that can transmute metals and give the elixir of life? What if it were discovered, this stone? Suppose radium were in the legend stone of long ago. Wouldn't that suggest to you that we have only just discovered out of the long labour of our known cycle of civilization something that was known before by another race of men? Who knows, perhaps that race conquered its earth with this stone, turned it from a savage planet like this of ours into a Garden of Eden, and then, surfeited with ease, died of inertia, lapsed into darkness, fell from the Heaven it had made. That is to say, Adam, the father of our race, may have been the last survivor of a race of fallen gods, supermen."

Clémentine took my arm as we went out of the dining-room.

"You find us a little mad?" she asked.

"Oh, no."

"Tell us how you find us. You are different, big and strong and young and strange. Your point of view about us would be something new."

"I find you extraordinarily happy."

"Oh yes, we are gay."

The men had followed us.

"We laugh."

"We find the world so funny."

"But we're serious too. There's Ludovic as solemn as a trout. He'd be dreary if we let him be."

"Only we don't. Why should one worry? One can't change anything. You must be one of us. It's so amusing with us. You will see how amusing it is."

So it was that they adopted me. And that night as I drove home through the moonlit streets I thought of St. Mary's Plains with distaste and impatience.

But what I remember best of all about that evening was the sweet funny way you beamed down the table when you saw that your friends liked me. You were, you know, just a little nervous about the impression I would make on them. They were so much more brilliant than any one else that I don't wonder. But it all went off well, bless your heart, thanks to the penetrating sweetness of your will that willed us to be pleased with one another.

There followed years of power and pleasure. Your friends made good their promise. They taught me to enjoy. Ludovic began to form my mind. Clémentine gave me the daring to use it. I learned how pleasant it was to follow one's caprices, to indulge one's tastes, to realize one's dreams. Do you remember the things we did? What indeed didn't we do, with our picture shows, our pantomimes, and our music? When we wanted to do a thing we did it. When we wanted to go to a place we went. What fun it was going off at a moment's notice to Seville, to Constantinople, to Moscow. Some one would say—"Have you seen the *Place Stanislas* at Nancy by moonlight? No? But you must." "Let's go tomorrow," and we went. Or—"I hear that at Grenoble there is a lady who owns a glove shop and who has in her back parlour a Manet, let us go and buy it, if it is true." Of course we went and found it was true and bought it. Felix it was who took us all the way to Strasbourg for one night and day, to eat a pâté de foie gras and hear mass in the Cathedral.

But we were happiest of all in Paris. Paris was inexhaustible. Not a nook or cranny of interest and charm escaped us. Sometimes early in the spring mornings we would walk through silvery streets or along the quais or take the penny steamer down the Seine. We sampled every restaurant known to our gourmet Felix. We sat in icy studios at the feet of shy ogres. Even Dégas thawed to us, while rare spirits from odd corners of the earth joined us in the evenings. And increasingly the beauty of Paris was revealed to me. I cared for it intimately now, and I loved its smooth pale historic stones with a delicate sensuousness.

I was happy. I was as happy as an opium eater. I lived in a continuous mood of enjoyment that had the quality of a dream. All this was mine to behold and delight in, and I was responsible for none of it. I was passive. I was calm. The play played itself out about me, and I was in no way involved. What people did and what they didn't do had no real significance. When Ludovic said: "A man has as much right to take life as to give it," I thought placidly, "Perhaps so, in this world." When he denounced property and capitalists and said we should all be poor, I thought, of course, that is so, and when he pointed out to me a woman who had killed her father because he was cross-eyed and got on her nerves, I merely looked at her with mild curiosity. He said that she was very sensitive and charming, and I believed him. It didn't seem to matter.

And if at times it occurred to me that I was becoming callous and selfish, at others I felt that I was becoming intelligent and charitable.

Jinny was my one responsibility, a little will-o'-the-wisp creature who danced into my room of a morning to drop a kiss on my nose and dance out again. Jinny, so entrancingly pretty, so ridiculously dainty, who never soiled her hands or tore her frock or spilled her food, who said her prayers night and morning to a silver crucifix that her father had sent her from Italy, and who confessed her minute sins every Friday to a priest but never confided in her mother.

My child baffled me. There was nothing in my own childhood's experience that threw any light on the little close mystery of her nature. She didn't like animals, she hated romping about, she was afraid of the cold. What she liked was to be curled up on cushions in front of the fire and listen to fairy stories. Her indolence was complete, her capacity for keeping still, extraordinary in one who moved so lightly when she did move. Sometimes when I looked up from the book I was reading aloud to her, I would find her great brown eyes fixed on me with a look of uncanny wisdom. She seemed to disapprove of me. I wondered if this had anything to do with the teaching of her priestly tutors that her father had prescribed for her, or whether it sprang from a natural precocious feeling of the difference between us. We were certainly a strange couple. Even in moments of my most anguished tenderness, I could not but feel the incongruity. The idea that she was much more her father's daughter than mine was one that I tried not to dwell on.

I had been going happily along, thinking that I could enjoy this adventurous life of my new friends without being involved in it, when I found out that I was much less free than I thought. Your mother did not approve, I knew, and I gathered that she blamed you for leading me astray, but it came nevertheless as a surprise when she gently interfered.

"Aren't you making yourself a little notorious, my child?" she asked one day.

"Notorious *belle-mère*?"

"Yes. Dining in restaurants in the company of such strange men."

"They are not very strange, dear, except in being so very intelligent, and I never, at least scarcely ever, dine alone with men. There is almost always Clémentine."

"I know, that's just it. For a chaperone, you couldn't have chosen worse."

"But surely, *Belle Mère*, I need no chaperone, I am old enough to go about alone?"

She closed her eyes wearily, opened them and spoke sharply.

"French women of good family never go about alone, and never dine in public places."

"But Clémentine—"

"Don't talk to me of Clémentine." I was startled by the sudden note of sharp personal grievance in her voice. "Her conduct is scandalous. Her mother was my first cousin and dearest friend. It is fortunate that she is dead. How could she be blamed for that marriage, yet Clémentine always blamed her and set to work deliberately to make her suffer."

"I know nothing of Clémentine's marriage."

"Well, her husband—but no matter, there is no excuse for her making herself an object of derision."

"I scarcely think she does that, dear, she is in great demand you know, in the very highest quarters."

"At foreign courts, perhaps, not in her own country. If it weren't for the obligations of kinship no one, but no one would speak to her."

"Just what is it that she has done that you so disapprove of?"

"She has made herself cheap. She has vulgarized her position, she plays at being a bohemian, she has bartered away her dignity for a little sordid amusement."

"And I?"

"You are in danger of doing the same, but in greater danger."

I was annoyed and rose and moved to the door.

"You are going?"

"I am afraid I must. I have an appointment."

"Ah, you resent my speaking to you?"

"No, dear, but—"

"But—?"

"I am afraid I cannot quite agree with you."

Her face hardened. I made an effort.

"*Belle-mère*, I am doing no wrong. Surely you believe that. These men are nothing to me, not one of them."

Her eyebrows lifted. "You love no one?" she asked.

"No."

"That too, is just as I thought."

"You wouldn't mind that, I suppose?"

"Mind it? How should I? How would it concern me?"

I was a little taken aback. "It only matters then what I seem to do, not what I really do?"

She smiled, rather sarcastically, I thought. "Put it that way if you like, my child."

"But, *belle-mère*, don't you really understand at all, that I am trying to be happy and keep my self-respect?"

She eyed me a moment strangely, then dropped her head.

"We will never understand each other," she said at last. "We won't discuss things any more. It leads to nothing."

But Claire felt that she, too, must make an attempt to bring me to reason. She attacked me on the subject of Geneviève. There she was clever. Was I not neglecting my child a little? No, I replied I was not. I was out so much, I seemed to take so little interest in her education. At this I flared up.

"Her education, my dear, is as you know, not in my hands. Her father has made clear his wishes on that subject. Her mind is confided to the keeping of Monseigneur de Grimont and you know what he is doing with it better than I do. What with her prayers, her masses and her confessions, her priestly tutors who instructed her in Latin and Greek, Italian and Spanish, and the good sisters who teach her to embroider altar pieces and to believe every ridiculous miracle in the lives of the saints, such healthy heathen interests as I can cultivate in her little ecstatic soul have small chance of flourishing."

"But Jane, surely she has her dancing, her riding, her music?"

"Yes, of course, she has everything, everything, but no time for her mother. Her days are as full as a time table. Try as I may, I can never get more than an hour a day with her. How then am I to make her my life's occupation? That's what you meant, wasn't it? You said I neglected her."

"What I meant was that you seem to have forgotten us all, Geneviève included, and to have forgotten what we and therefore what she must stand for in society."

"On the contrary."

"You mean—?"

"I mean that I constantly think of it, but perhaps not just as you do."

"Well, if you want your daughter to take Clémentine as a pattern."

"I don't," and then added with deliberate wickedness, "I wouldn't have poor little Jinny attempt anything so impossible."

"You admire her so much?"

"I do."

"But she's grotesque. She goes in for politicians and for journalists."

"I adore her."

"She's shameless—her affairs—"

I cut her short. "I know nothing about her affairs. What I know is that she has a generous soul, a warm heart and the most brilliant mind in Paris. No other woman in Paris can touch her for brains."

Claire lifted her eyebrows. I saw that she washed her hands of me. At the moment I was glad of it. As for Clémentine, she cared nothing for what Claire or any one else thought of her. She was a law unto herself. Her love affairs, of which I knew more than I admitted, were as necessary to her as her meals. She must have food, and she attached no great importance to it. An artistic find, an amusing trip or an exciting debate in the Chamber of Deputies, would make her forget with equal ease her lunch or a sentimental rendezvous. Her relations with men didn't seem to me to be any of my business. There was a certain recklessness there that I didn't understand. I left it at that. It was Fan who told me about Clémentine's marriage.

"My dear, her husband had unnatural tastes. He kicked her downstairs a month after the wedding. She can never have any children, and she hasn't spoken to him since. Also, she is said to have said that she would never again have anything to do with a man of her own world. If she did, well, she has kept her word. Her mother stopped her getting her marriage annulled. Clémentine never got over that. She's at war with the whole tribe of her relations, but of course she can't cut loose from them for she hasn't a son, and anyhow one doesn't in France. So her revenge is to do just those things that most irritate them. They wouldn't mind a bit how many lovers she had if she would choose them from her own class, and preserve the usual appearances. What they can't bear is her going about with men whose fathers made boots or sold pigs. And in justice to them you should remember that these men's grandfathers cut off their own grandfather's heads."

"They prefer, I suppose, a person like Bianca."

"Of course, a million times."

"It's nothing to Clémentine's credit then that she's a true friend and incapable of grabbing a man from another woman."

"No, as long as she dresses like a futurist picture, and carries paper bags through the streets and dines with Ludovic at Voisin's, she's a horrid thorn in their sides."

"Well, I'm sorry, because you know I don't propose to stop going about with her."

"Lord, no, why should you? You certainly deserve a bit of fun. Come to the Mouse Trap tomorrow night. We've a supper party after the Russian Ballet."

But I knew what that meant, a troup of theatrical people, and every one drunk by morning, so I declined. I saw a good deal of Fan these days, but she had certain friends I *couldn't* see. It didn't amuse me to watch women get tipsy. Those Montmartre parties depressed me horribly. And I felt sure of Clémentine and her band on this point. It was just one of the admirable things about them that they could be so daringly gay and never verge on the rowdy. I had seen her administer a snub to a hiccoughing youth. She could be terrible when she was displeased, and whatever one said of her, for that matter whatever she herself felt, no one could get away from the fact that she was as proud a lady as any in France, and perfectly conscious of her privilege of caste. It was just this consciousness of her lineage, I imagined, that gave her such a sense of security. She knew that she could do anything she chose and be none the less privileged for it, and actually none the worse. If she touched pitch she knew it wouldn't stick to her fingers. If she dipped into Bohemia, she did so knowing that she could never be said to belong there. There was always behind her a solid phalanx of relatives who would never disown her however much they disapproved. Always in her maddest escapades there were the towers of the family castle looming behind her. They cast an august shadow. She might dress like an artist's model, never would she be taken for one. She was safe, perfectly safe and she knew it, and so did every one else.

But with me, as Aunt Clothilde pointed out, it was different.

"There's nothing to prove what you are but the way you behave, my poor Jane. If Clem took it into her head to play at being a barmaid, the de Joignys and all the rest of them would wring their hands and call it a scandalous idiocy, but if you did the same thing they'd say, 'Of course, it's quite natural, she probably was a barmaid in her own country,' and they wouldn't wring their hands at all, they'd be mightily pleased."

"So they think my associating with Ludovic is proof of a low mind?"

"Well, what do you find in that old bourgeois?"

"I find a gold mine."

"A gold mine of what?"

"Information, ideas."

"Humph!"

"But it's true, Aunt, he is educating me. He gives me books, philosophy, history, all sorts of books, then we discuss them."

"Just like going to school, eh?"

"Very much like that."

"And it doesn't bore you?"

"On the contrary."

"Well, no one will ever believe you. If Philibert comes back, he certainly won't."

She broke off and looked at me closely.

"Ah ha, you still care for him, then?"

"No, no, how could I, I mean how could he? It's impossible that he should return now, surely."

A week later I found a note from him on my breakfast tray, announcing his return. He was installed in his own rooms in the west wing of the house, and he would "present his duties" at the hour I chose to name. And the post that same morning brought me a letter from Bianca. It said—

"If you blame me for taking away your husband, it is stupid of you. I did you a great service in doing so. Perhaps that was why I did it. I can think of no other reason. For myself I regret it, but not for you. I envy you. Bianca."

My fingers trembled as I read this strange epistle, and I felt cold. Actually—it seemed as if the room had gone cold as ice.

VI

It seemed at first as if Philibert's return were going to make very little difference to me. For some weeks I was scarcely aware of his presence in the house. There was plenty of room for us to live there without running into each other. When we did meet at the front door or on the stairs, his manner was marked by just that formal courtesy that was the usual sign of deference from a man of his world towards his wife. To the servants, there was always one or two present at such encounters; there could have been visible no flaw in his armour, nor in mine.

Our first meeting had been brief. Whatever his intention in seeking me out in my boudoir, it took him not more than five minutes to find out that there was nothing to be gained by a prolonged conversation, and on the whole, nothing to be feared from me, did he but leave me alone, but I imagined that I read upon his face more disappointment than relief. He had not been afraid, perhaps just a little uneasy, but he had been curious. He had expected something, and as he left me the expression of his back and the vague fumbling of his hand in the tail pocket of his coat, gave me the impression that whatever it was he had wanted, he was going away without it. This impression, however, was fleeting, a deeper and more painful one remained, and kept me a long time idle at my desk. He was changed in a way that for some subtle inexplicable reason had made me ashamed to look at him. There was in his pallid puffy face, in the sag of his shoulders and the crook of his knees, something that I did not want to understand, something that he had no right to show me. Inside his immaculate clothes he was shrivelled to half his size. His wonderful padded coat sat on him as if on a lifeless and flaccid dummy out of which had escaped a good deal of the sawdust stuffing. Bianca had done with him. She had worn him out. He looked old. His eccentric elegance no longer became him. It was as unsuccessful as a plastered make-up on the face of an old woman. That was the sharpest impression of all, he looked a failure. I wondered that he had the courage to show himself, not to me but to Paris, where he had always walked with such impudent assurance. His showing himself to me seemed to me not half so daring. It seemed to me to prove once more and finally his complete contempt for my opinion.

I went on with my life. If I found that the savour had gone out of it, I did not admit this all at once to myself. The situation didn't bear thinking about. If one thought about it one would be likely to find it quite extraordinary enough to upset one's mentality, and I proposed not to be upset by it, and Philibert, apparently, with a certain exercise of tact that reminded one of a burglar arranging the furniture and putting out the lights after ransacking a room, made things as easy for me as he could, by, as I say, keeping out of my sight. I soon found, however, that he wasn't keeping out of other people's. On the contrary, I began to be conscious of him moving about near me among his friends. It was really rather funny. Only at home under the roof that housed us both, was I quite free from him. In other people's houses I was constantly meeting his shadow. He had either been there, or was coming, occasionally I was certain, that he had but just taken his departure as I came in. Something of him remained in the room. I caught myself looking about for his hat, and the faces of my acquaintances betrayed varying shades of discomfiture or amusement. Mostly I gathered as time went on, was their feeling one of amusement. Paris had not been at all squeamish in welcoming Philibert, and it found our continued *chassé-croisé* rather ridiculous. But with its very special adaptibility and its extraordinary flair for situations, it continued to be tolerant of my evident absurd wish not to be coupled with my husband, and did not ask us out together.

Aunt Clothilde, sitting enthroned like some comic Juno above the social earth, put an end to this. As was her habit she sent for me and barged into the subject in hand.

"Now then, Jane, this sort of thing must stop."

"What sort of thing, Aunt?"

"You and Philibert playing hide and seek all over Paris like a couple of silly children. Don't pretend you don't understand. You chose your *'parti'* long ago when you didn't insist upon a separation, so now you must go through with it. Nothing is so stupid as doing things half way. You've ignored his behaviour. You've not bolted the door in his face, and to all appearances you're a reunited couple."

I tried to interrupt.

"Don't interrupt me. I don't care, and nobody cares what goes on between you and Philibert in your private apartments. Whether you're nasty or affectionate is nobody's business but your own, but as regards society, society expects people in it to behave in a certain way, and to make things easy and agreeable and smooth. That's its main object, its only *raison d'être*. We people who think ourselves something are nothing if we're not well bred, that is, if we don't know how to help other people to keep up the pretence that every one is happy, that life is harmonious and that there's nothing dreadful under the sun. Society, French society, is very intolerant of bad manners, not as you know of anything else. It is exclusive with this object and adamant on this point. It let you in, now it expects you to behave. You've enjoyed its favour, you owe it something in return. What a bore to lecture you like a school-mistress, but there you are. I'm going to give a dinner and you and Philibert are both to come, and that will be the end of this nonsense."

And of course I did as she said.

And again your mother's manner to me conveyed a sense of my action having made a difference, but this time an enormously happy difference. She beamed, she was more affectionate than she had ever been. She called me *"Ma chère petite" "Ma fille aimée."* Drawing me down to her with her delicate blue-veined hand, she would press her lips to one of my cheeks then the other, lingeringly, and with a pathetic trembling pressure, and look from me to Philibert with happy watery eyes in which was no scrutiny or questioning. She was growing old. Something of her fine discernment was gone. She was no longer curious to know what lay behind appearances. It was enough for her to have recovered her son and been spared the sight of his ruin. Like a child she clung to Philibert. I admit that his manner to her was very charming. He went to see her, I believe, every day.

Claire did not seem so pleased with our renewed family life that resembled so curiously the life we had lived round your mother five years before. Her smile was bitter, her tongue caustic, but she looked so ill, that I put her temper down to bad health. It was, strangely enough, Philibert who explained to me, driving home from his mother's one Sunday afternoon.

"You mustn't mind Claire," he began. "She is in trouble."

"I don't. I can see she is in wretched health."

"Her health is the result, not the cause, of her unhappiness."

"Oh?"

"Her husband has fallen into the hands of a scheming woman who wants to marry him. He has threatened Claire with a divorce."

I was taken aback. I stammered. For an instant I wanted to laugh, but Claire's haggard face was after all nothing to laugh at. I remarked mildly; "But I thought that in your world one didn't divorce?"

"He's not of our world, never was, never will be. Besides, it bores him, he's had enough of us."

"I see."

"He's had too many snubs. We've been stupid. That affair of the Jockey Club rankles."

"You mean that if you had taken him into the Jockey Club ten years ago he wouldn't want to divorce your sister now."

"Quite possibly. It would have involved him in other things, given him something to live up to. As it is, he has, as you know, gone in for politics."

"No, I didn't know. I never hear him mentioned. I'm very sorry if Claire is unhappy about it."

"She is, terribly."

"But she hates him."

"Not quite that. In any case the disgrace would kill her. She has always been a retiring protected creature. The publicity would be peculiarly awful for her."

I knew that what he said was true, but he had more to say, and he stammered over it.

"We thought that you, Jane, might do something."

I was startled. "Do something?"

"Yes, to help, to persuade the man not to."

"But I scarcely know him."

"He has a great respect for you."

"For me? What nonsense." I looked at him sharply. "What do you mean, Philibert?"

His pale blue eyes turned from mine to the Sunday pageant of the Champs Elysées.

"He wants a place in the Government. He would be greatly influenced by political considerations, a prospect of success. Your friend Ludovic could do something there."

"You mean that you want me to ask Ludovic to ask the Premier to give your brother-in-law a place in the Cabinet on condition he doesn't bring divorce proceedings?"

"It needn't be a big place, you know. An under-secretaryship would do." The car drew up, came to a stop. "You'd better talk to Blaise about it before you decide to leave Claire in the lurch."

But you showed a curious reluctance to discuss the question and referred me to Clémentine. I found her in the disused stables behind her house where she had fitted up a studio. She was in a linen overall, her arms smeared with clay, a patch of it on the tip of her tilted nose, her hair screwed untidily on top of her ugly attractive head. She pointed out a clean spot on a packing case and after lighting a cigarette I sat down there.

"I've come about Claire."

"I know." Her face twinkled. She gave a laugh and taking up a handful of wet clay slapped it on the side of the gargoylish head that she was modelling.

"Why won't Blaise talk to me about it?"

"He doesn't like their using you in the matter. He has delicacies of feeling."

"I don't quite see. He adores his sister."

"Of course."

"And is very unhappy about her, as they all are."

"Naturally."

I pondered. "After all, I belong to the family."

"Quite so, whether you like it or not." She ducked about scraping and smoothing with flexible thumb.

"But I'm fond of them."

"Of Claire?"

"Yes."

"People are."

"You sound very dry."

She gave a poke to her ugly old man's protruding eye.

"*Mon dieu*, I'm not too fond of your family, as you well know. They bore me. I was brought up with Claire. We know each other."

"You don't like her."

"She is uninteresting, no courage, no character."

"She has put up with a great deal."

"Has she? She liked her husband's money, you know, and he's not a bad sort, really, merely vulgar, quite good-natured."

"She loves her children," I said weakly. At that Clémentine looked round quickly.

"Do you call that a virtue?" she asked.

I stammered. "I don't know, I suppose so. It seems to me human."

"Well, my dear, when humanity has nothing more to recommend it than the fact that it cares for its young, I shall be ready to depart to another planet." She sat down on a high stool, one knee over the other, a foot hung down, dangling a shabby shoe. Her face was full of merriment. She chuckled. Her eyes danced. She gave me, as she always did, the impression of containing in herself an immense fund of interest and gladness and of finding life much to her taste.

"You mustn't destroy my belief in my love for my child," I said, half laughingly.

"Your belief in it?" She wondered.

"Yes, in its being—worth something."

"To which one?"

"To us both."

She puffed at her cigarette. "If I had had a child I should have loved it terribly, and stupidly," she said seriously. "I should probably have been worse than any of you. Maternity is a blinding, devouring passion, is it not? I don't know, but so I imagine. A mother's love for her child, what is there more admirable in that than in any other fact of nature? Only when it is strong, so terribly strong as to become wise and unselfish is it interesting. Even then, no, it is not interesting, it is only natural and necessary, and often, very often, it is a curse to the children." Her face had gone dark and intense. She jumped down from her stool, gave herself a shake, laughed, turned to her work—"No, your mother-women are dreadful. I prefer those who love men. Sexual passion is good for the feminine soul. It makes us intelligent. Tell me, is it true that in America sensuality is considered a bad thing?"

"Yes. We—they—admire chastity, purity."

"How do you mean—purity?"

"One man for one woman, love consecrated by marriage."

"All one's life?"

"Yes."

"How strange. Love, you say, consecrated by marriage. How very funny. You mean then seriously, not just social humbug? In their hearts do intelligent women, women like yourself, feel love, love as the interest and savour of life, coming unexpectedly, perhaps often, to be a bad thing?"

"Many do."

"And you—what do you think?"

"I? Oh, for me, I can't generalize about it. I have no ideas on the subject."

"I see."

She was silent a while. I watched her clever thumbs pressing and smoothing the soft clay. She was no sculptor, but the head she was modelling had a mischievous ugliness. Though badly done, it expressed something. Watching her I realized again her immense capability, her command of herself, her understanding of the elements of life. What was she thinking of now, her sensitive witty face blinking sleepily with half-closed eyes like a cat's? Inwardly I felt that she was faintly smiling at some pleasant memory or prospect. She was neither young nor beautiful. Her wiry little person suggested nothing voluptuous or alluring. She was dry and spare and untidy, yet her success with men was unequalled. Impossible to imagine her in an attitude of amorous tenderness, yet men adored her. And her lovers remained her friends. She puzzled me. There was something here that I would never understand. The high game of sex as a life occupation of absorbing interest and endless ramifications, a gallant and dangerous sport at which one became a recognized expert, in some such way I felt that she looked at it. As an Englishwoman gives herself up to hunting, I reflected, and exults in knowing herself to be a hard rider, just so Clémentine would go at the biggest jumps, keep in the first field. Riding to hounds or playing the daring game of love, the same sporting mentality, the same ecstatic sense of life, all our faculties sharpened by danger. Why not? Clémentine was sane, healthy, full of zest and delight. Impossible to think of her in terms of maudlin sentimentality or sordid secret pleasures. And yet for myself, I felt a loathing of men, a disgust at the vaguest image of the contacts of sex. It was very puzzling. There must be some deep racial difference between us, or some tenacious effect of my upbringing that held me in a vice, or was it only that Philibert had poisoned for me the sources of all emotion?

I moved about the dirty studio, brought back my mind to the subject I had come to discuss. "We have forgotten about Claire, haven't we?"

"Well, yes, what of Claire?" She yawned.

"Philibert says that Ludovic could arrange it."

"No doubt he could. The President of the Council is you know his greatest friend."

"Yes, I know, but surely giving away secretaryships—"

"Oh, la la! Why not? Don't worry about that. Madame de Joigny's son-in-law will make quite a respectable under-secretary as far as that goes. I only wonder he's not got what he wanted long ago."

"What shall I do then?"

She looked at me, her head on one side, screwing up her clever mischievous eyes.

"That, my dear, depends entirely on what you want to do."

"Do you think Ludovic would mind my approaching him on such a subject?"

She laughed. "Do you?"

"No, I don't. I should put it quite brutally, he would only have to say no."

"Quite so." She continued to watch me with her funny intelligent grin.

"And that wouldn't spoil our friendship, would it?" I asked again.

"No, I should say not, certainly not." She laughed again and somehow, frank as was that bubbling sound, I didn't like it coming in at that moment.

"Why do you laugh?" I asked, looking at her keenly.

Her face grew gradually grave, her eyes opened. We stared at each other and in hers I saw a light, a flash, something keen and swift and bright that made me warm to her, value her, exult in her friendship.

"*Vous êtes—vous êtes—*" she turned it off, waving a handful of clay. "*Vous êtes admirable.*" But I didn't understand then, only long after. I wonder what Claire would say if she knew that her fate hung on the thread of Clémentine's charity? For Clémentine saw it all, saw quite clearly her opportunity for revenge. She had only to suggest what they, unknown to me, were all thinking, namely that Ludovic, for the simplest of reasons, would never refuse me anything, and their whole little scheme would be undone. But she didn't suggest it. There was nothing spiteful in Clémentine.

So I went to him and told him the whole thing quite bluntly, and he, without any fuss or without giving me any feeling of doing me a favour, said that of course he would put in a word with the Premier. They, he and the Premier, were going to the country together for a few days. They were going to see Ludovic's mother in her little farm on the Loire. They would fish and sit in the garden. Perhaps over their fishing rods on the banks of the lazy, reedy river, something could be arranged. He then went on to tell me of his mother, who was very old, nearly eighty-five, and who would not come with him to Paris because of the noise. She was, he said, just a peasant woman, and had no interest in his career. But she sent him baskets of apples from her orchard and socks that she had knitted. She could not write. The *curé* kept him informed of her health. They had been very poor. As a child he had always been hungry and he and his mother had worked in the fields. Sometimes they had been so poor that they had had to beg for bread. His father, who had been of a different class, had done nothing for him. He had made his own way. The *curé* had taught him to read and write. His mother was content now. She had a cow and pigs and chickens, an apple orchard and a garden. But she could not accustom herself to having a servant in the house and did the cooking herself. He did not allude again to Claire's husband, neither then nor later. In time, as you know, the matter was arranged, and I like to think that it was settled in that *chaumière* where Ludovic's little old mother in her white cap and coarse blue apron sat knitting, while the hens scratched and cackled beyond the farm door. There is something humorous to me in the fact that Claire's luxurious home was secured to her in that place of poverty and courage and contentment.

In the meantime Philibert had recovered his health and his looks. His doctor and his masseur and his hairdresser and his tailor had in six months restored to him a very good substitute for youth. He had gone at the business methodically and with the utmost seriousness. Seeing as little of him as possible at home, I nevertheless was aware of what was going on. He lived by a strict régime. His rubber came every morning at eight o'clock, his fencing master at nine. At ten he dressed. At eleven he walked or rode in the *bois*. Faithfully he stuck to the diet his doctor had ordered for him. He drank only the lightest wine. He gave up smoking. His hand no longer shook. His face was smooth and rosy, he had put on weight, he walked with his old springy impudence. He looked almost the same, almost, but not quite. No beauty doctor on earth could wipe away from his face the mark Bianca had put there. The droop of the eye-lids, the sag of the lower lip, gave him away. To the crowd he might seem the same Philibert, the leader of fashion, the joyous comedian, the perennially young, but not to me, and not to himself. We both knew that he was an old man now, and this fact formed a sort of bond between us, a cold, grim, precise understanding that linked us inevitably together. And for a time I didn't quite hate this because I felt secure, I felt that I had the upper hand. He was afraid of me, and in a curious way depended on me. He depended on me, not to give him away, not to let on to any one that he was, or had been, in danger of breaking up. His vanity thus kept him at my mercy, while another part of his brain found relief in the fact that I saw him as he was. Sometimes I caught a look in his eyes that seemed to say—"I really wouldn't have the endurance to sustain this enormous bluff if I had to bluff you as well." I never answered his look.

I couldn't bring myself to reach out to him in even the most impersonal way. All I could do was to remain there beside him, in public sharing his life, in private withdrawn, impassive, stolid, non-committal, and do him no harm.

And so it might have gone on indefinitely, the atmosphere of our house coldly harmonious, calm as an icy lake, had not Jinny introduced an element of hot, surging, dangerous feeling.

He loved her, too. At first I wouldn't believe it, but I was bound at last to admit that it was so. When I first began to notice the increasing attention he gave her I had thought that he was "up to something." I suspected him to be playing the part of devoted father with motives that had to do with myself, and as I could not conceive of his wanting to make me like him, I imagined the reverse, that he wanted to make me jealous, and I set myself to conceal from him the fact that he had succeeded. I was terribly jealous, for whatever the meaning of his apparent feeling for her, there was no doubt of her affection for him. The child was obviously delighted to be with him. Repeatedly when I asked her if she would like to go with me for a drive, she would ask if "Papa" were coming too, and when I said no, her face would change from pleasure to a curious expression of boredom that was like an absurd imitation of his own. She would turn away quickly and put out her hands to the empty room in a funny, hurting gesture of exasperation, then suddenly, feeling my disappointment, would assume a polite cheerfulness and say, with a quick, tactful insincerity that reminded me all too vividly of her grandmother, "It is a pity Papa cannot come, but of course, Mamma, I like best being with you alone." And I would cry out in my heart, "My poor, precocious infant, where did you get such intuitions?" —but I knew where she got them.

There was between them a very striking resemblance. I looked sometimes with horrid fascination from one to the other. She would come in with him, swinging to his hand, twirling about, clasping it in both hers, and laughing up in his face. Her light, exaggerated grace was his, also the fineness of her little features. No one would ever at first sight take her for my child, no one seeing them together could mistake her for his. They disengaged the same brightness, the same chilly, sparkling charm. How was it that in one it displeased me and in the other so tormentingly appealed? Why, I asked myself, did I not hate her too, since she so resembled her father? But the muttered question was answered only by an inaudible groan. I had given him all my love, and had now transferred it all to her, a stupid, elemental woman, I felt that I was destined to be their victim. Strange thoughts, you will say, for a mother to have about her child. Why not? I was afraid of her, far more afraid than I had ever been of him. In the days of his power over me I had been young, ignorant, insensitive; now I knew what I was capable of suffering, knew only too well what little Geneviève could do to me, did she take it into her head to become as like him as she looked.

I tried to hide all this, but I felt that he saw. His manner changed. He was at once more attentive to me and more careless, less formal, more talkative, in a word more sure of himself. He took to dropping in on me in the evenings before dinner, bringing Geneviève with him and holding her beside him in the crook of his arm, while he unconcernedly chatted, and all the while her great shining brown eyes were fixed on me with their meaning lucidity. I was obliged to prevaricate, to seem pleased, to lay myself out in an elaborate assumption of happy intimacy.

One night she came running back alone after going with him to the door of his room, and threw her arms round my neck. I gathered her close. Her caresses were so rare that I held her, positively, in a breathless delight, with a sense of yearning tenderness so exquisite that it frightened me. "So sweet, so sweet," I murmured to myself, straining her to me. Then I heard her say intensely, "It's not true, it's not true, tell me it's not true."

I lifted my face from her curls.

"What is not true, my darling?"

"That you and Papa don't love each other." She kept her face buried. I felt her heart beating against me, a frail little gusty heart beating painfully. The room round us was very still, too still, no sound in it, only the felt sound of our heart beats, and the clock ticking on the mantelpiece. I must speak, I must lie to her, and as the words left my lips I knew that they were involving me in endless deceptions, in a long, long ghastly comedy, in countless humiliations.

"No, darling, it's not true."

Her little arms tightened round my neck.

"They said—" she whispered.

"Who said, my pet?"

"Some ladies. I heard them talking. They said, they said you would never forgive him." I felt her body trembling, and I too trembled, and as I realized that I had thought her incapable of intense feeling I felt deeply ashamed. "What did they mean, Mamma, tell me, what did they mean?"

"Nothing, nothing." I must have spoken harshly. "They were mistaken, they were speaking of some one else."

She lifted her face then and looked at me, her eyes were wide and accusing. "Oh, no, Mummy, they said your names, they said Jane and Philibert, your two names. It was at Aunt Claire's. Dicky and I were just behind the door, and I pulled him away so he wouldn't hear any more, but he only laughed at me and said, 'Every one knows your parents detest each other'—in French, you know, '*Tout le monde sait que tes parents se détestent*,' and then I kicked him."

"Jinny!"

"I only kicked him a little. It didn't hurt. I wanted it to hurt, dreadfully."

"My child, my child."

"I know, Mummy, that it was very wicked. I told Father Anthony all about it at confession, and he looked so sad, so beautifully sad. I wept and wept. He told me to pray very hard to the Virgin to save me from angry passions, and I did, but I enjoyed being angry. I felt big and strong when I was angry, quite, quite different from ordinary, and I thought you would understand. Were you never angry when you were a little girl?"

"Yes, darling, I was." Her question had startled me. I was profoundly disturbed by this sudden revelation of her character.

But again her little mobile face had changed.

"You aren't like that, are you, Mummy? You couldn't be?"

"Like what, my darling?"

"Unforgiving." Her eyes were on mine.

"I hope not, Geneviève." She flushed at my tone, but continued to look at me gravely and steadily.

"I thought you might have been angry with Papa for leaving us for so long," she said with an air of great wisdom. "I was, but I forgave him at once." I smiled.

"You see," she went on, "I couldn't bear him to be unhappy, for I love him."

"I know, darling."

"And you love him, too?"

"Of course."

She heaved an immense sigh.

"Then we are all happy."

"We are all happy," I echoed.

A minute later she was at the door, wafting me a gay little kiss. I had not been able to keep her. She was not more than ten years old at that time, but even then she was already the complete elusive creature of swift fleeting moods and superlatively lucid mind that she is today.

And still I suspected Philibert of playing the part of adoring father in order to make me do what he wished. So without alluding to Jinny, never, in fact, daring to allude to her, I tried to bribe him. He had hinted occasionally about wanting to resume our old habits of entertaining, and his hint had shocked me. Such a farce had seemed altogether unnecessary. Now I gave in to him and the same old extravagant theatrical life began. To me it was incredibly boring and at times quite ghastly. There were moments when it was as if over the old sepulchre of our married life he had built an enormous and hideous altar to some obscene heathen deity, some depraved Bacchus before whom he and I giddily danced, with vine leaves in our hair.

"But," I argued, "this is what he likes, and if I help him do it he will have got from me all that he wants, he will leave Jinny alone. He will have less time for her and will forget about her." Unfortunately all these social antics took up as much of my time as his. The result was that neither of us saw the child save in hurried snatches, and in that horrible house, now so constantly filled with people, with armies of servants, and streams of guests, I had a vision of her skipping about like a little white rabbit in a monstrous zoo. Poor Jinny, what a wretched mess we made of her childhood, Philibert and I, with our constant vigilant, yet inadequate, lying to each other in her presence, and our ridiculous absorption in the tawdry pageant of society. And yet we both loved her and were doing it, even he in his way, for her. He wanting her to have an incomparably brilliant position in the world, I wanting to keep him away from her, thinking in my jealous stupidity that she would belong more to me the more he belonged to the world.

It was when she fell ill that I was at last convinced of his caring for her. She had pneumonia, you remember, and was very near death for three days. I can see Philibert now, sitting through the night by her bed, he on one side, I on the other, I can see his face as he watched her painful breathing, a face clammy with sweat, contracting suddenly in a curious grimace when she struggled for breath. He never touched her. He left that to me and the nurses. But he never once took his eyes off her swollen little face. I was deeply impressed by the sight of that fidgety, nervous man sitting so still, hour after hour, and I remember his sobbing when the child's breathing grew easier and the doctors said the crisis was past. Poor Philibert, with his arms thrown across the foot of Jinny's bed and his head on them, sobbing like a child, I felt very sorry for him that night.

But it was too late for Jinny's illness to make any real difference in our relationship. We had gone too far, I knew him too well. All that I could do was add to my knowledge of him the fact that he loved his child and leave it at that.

VII

The years passed, crowded with incidents, colourful, varied, gay. I saw them going by, like gaudy pleasure boats, richly panoplied and filled with graceful merry-makers, floating down a sullen river. Sometimes I seemed to be alone, watching them go by, sometimes, beyond them, a long way off, I heard a sound that was like the sound of waves breaking on a distant beach.

You wince at what you feel to be my poor attempt at poetic imagery—I am not trying to be poetic, I am trying to express to you my experience, as precisely as possible. It was like that. In the middle of a crowded place, at the Opera where women in diamond tiaras nodded from padded cages, on the boulevards where a thousand motors like shining beetles buzzed in and out of rows of clanging trams, in a drawing-room ringing with staccato voices, I would find myself, suddenly, listening to a sound that seemed to come from an immense distance; a faint far rhythmic roar that was audible to my spirit, and that I translated to myself in terms of the sea because it affected me that way, like a booming murmur, regular as the booming of waves. I knew what it was.

I seemed at such times to see Patience Forbes, standing on the other side of the Atlantic, like some allegorical figure of faith, a gaunt weather-beaten old woman, her strong feet planted firmly on the shore, the wind whipping her black clothes about her, her brave old eyes looking out at me, under shielding hands, across that immense distance.

The distance between us was growing greater. I no longer wrote to her every week. There seemed so little to say. I found a difficulty in telling her of my occupations and amusements. When it came to describing to her the people I associated with, they appeared suddenly trivial and peculiar. There was no one about me, whom she could have understood. Clémentine with her genius for amorous-adventure, Ludovic with his nihilistic philosophy, Felix the intellectual mischief-maker; when I wrote to her of these people, I found that I misrepresented them, made up for them colourless characters that did not exist and would not distress her. Her innocence cut her off from us. The recital of my life was like telling a story and leaving out the point. I gave it up, disgusted by my feeble insincerity, and limited my letters to news of Jinny and comments on public events. And she understood, of course, that I was keeping everything back. She was no fool. I can see now, when it is too late, what a mistake I made, and what a pity it was. Now that she is dead, I think of her sitting alone in the Grey House, waiting for my letters, opening them with old trembling fingers, reading the meagre artificial sentences; her face growing tired and grim at the meaningless words, then putting away the disappointing sheets of paper in the secretary by the door. I found them there, all of them afterwards arranged in packets with laconic pencilled notes on their wrappers—"Jane doesn't tell me much. She's not happy." "A bad winter for Jane, she's taken to gambling; she says nothing of her husband." "Jane was coming but can't. I'm disappointed." That note was made the summer Fan died—I had determined to go to St. Mary's Plains. Fan's illness stopped me.

I had been seeing very little of Fan. She had established herself in a flat near the *Étoile* where she lived alone, but where her husband paid her an occasional visit. Ivanoff was pretty well done for in Paris. There had been a scene at the Travellers' Club, and afterwards his old victims had refused to play cards with him. So he had gone elsewhere. Men like Ivanoff can always pick up a living at Monte Carlo. He spent most of his time there, but when he came back, Fan always took him in. I never saw him on these occasions, nor apparently did any one else, but Fan would announce his arrival bluntly, and with a sort of defiant bravado, would put off her dinners and lunches to be with him.

She lived from hand to mouth. People who accused her of accepting his ill-gotten gains were wide of the mark. Ivanoff contributed nothing to Fan's keep. It was the other way round. He came back to her when he was on the rocks, came back to beg from her and to recuperate. Once she said to me, "Ivan's been asleep for thirty-six hours on the sofa in the drawing-room. I swear to you it's true. He has only waked up twice to eat a sandwich and have a drink."

But when I asked why she put up with him, she flung off with a laugh, and—"God only knows."

She lived from hand to mouth in a state of extravagant luxury. Her stepfather had died, leaving her four thousand dollars a year, that gave her twenty thousand francs before the war. One would have said that she spent at the least five times as much, but she didn't. She had resources, and little arrangements that made it unnecessary for her to pay for a good many things; and she earned a good deal. Her reputation as one of the smartest women in Paris, and her popularity, represented her capital, a very considerable sum. New and ambitious dressmaking houses clothed her for nothing, and in return she brought them the clientele they wanted. She had a standing account at certain fashionable restaurants, where she was allowed to lunch for five francs and dine for ten, and where to "pay back" she was the centre of many a cosmopolitan dinner party. For ready cash she wrote social notes in a fashion paper and occasionally launched a South American millionaire in society. Every one knew about all this; no one minded. She never gave any one away or presumed on her friendships and her frankness about her own affairs which was dry and desperate and funny disarmed criticism.

"My dear," she said one day to Claire over the tea table, "I've had a letter from Buenos Aires from a man who offers me forty thousand francs if I'll take his wife about next spring, and a five thousand franc tip extra, each time she dines at an embassy. Isn't it a perfect scream? I wrote back asking for a photo of the wife. It came yesterday. I've turned down the offer."

She borrowed from no one and accepted no gifts of money from her friends, men or women, and I take the last to be the more to her credit because half the people in her world assumed that she did and the other half wouldn't have blamed her if she had done so. Virtues, that you all held so lightly, have at least a relative value. Fan was incurably extravagant; she adored luxury, and I consider that her having married a poor man, and having refused to procure for herself in a manner so accepted by her world, the ease and comfort she craved, proves her to have been an interesting person. I see that you don't believe what I say, but I know that it is true. Men did not pay her dressmaker's bills. As for her little motor brougham that created so much comment, she bought that after an extremely lucky venture in rubber. She gambled on the "Bourse" of course. Old Beaudoin the banker gave her tips. Sometimes he invested her money for her. She would give him a few thousand francs and a month or two later he would perhaps sends her back twice the sum, but it is not exact to say that he always arranged to double her investment. And if he did take her wretched pennies and speculate with them and pretend that he had won when he lost, what harm did that do him with all his millions? It was all by way of repayment anyhow. Fan had got him and his fat wife asked to a lot of nice houses. He owed her far more than he ever paid. And when she crowned her services to him by making his daughter's marriage, surely she had earned the cheque he sent her or the block of shares, whichever it was.

To have a good time, to be happy, a more sentimental woman would have put it, that was her idea. Who of us all had a better, or a different one? Weren't we all looking for happiness, always?

Once I saw a street arab playing in the dirt with bits of mica, constantly threatened in his game by horses' hoofs, wagon wheels, policemen and hooligans. Fan reminds me of him. I remember his tiny eager hungry grimy face, intent on his game. Fan was like him, I watched her playing with bits of worthless brightness in the crowded muddy streets of life, jostled, buffeted, knocked about, a little rickety gutter snipe, fighting for the right to play, that is the way I see her. It had a beauty! you'll admit that, I suppose.

But we quarrelled. I bored her. She didn't like having any one about who couldn't keep up the farce of treating her as the happiest of women, and she made fun of my taking the intellectuals so seriously.

When I wanted to see her I had to go to her flat where luxury and poverty and dissipation and folly were mingled together in an unhealthy confusion. It was a curious place, very bare and new and totally lacking in the usual necessities of housekeeping, such as cupboards and carpets, table linen and blankets, but there were flaming silks thrown about, and a good many books and heaps of soft brilliant cushions. A grand piano stood in the empty drawing-room on a bare polished floor. The dining room table held always a tray of syphons and bottles. There might be no food, there were always cocktails and ragtime tunes to dance to. Sometimes the electric light was cut off because the bill wasn't paid, but there was a supply of candles for such emergencies, and if creditors were too pressing, Fan would take to her bed and lie under her cobwebby lace coverlet on a pile of white downy pillows all frills and ribbons, smoking endless cigarettes while weary tradesmen rang the door bell, and her friends sat about on the foot of the old lacquer bed telling each other questionable stories, and going off into muffled shrieks of laughter.

Her friends were many and various. Among them were people like Claire and Clémentine and the wife of the Italian Ambassador, but her own small particular set, the group that she went about with most, had its special stamp.

A cosmopolitan lot who had seen better days, and were keeping their heads up, by grit and bluff; they were I suppose the fastest set in Paris. The men didn't interest me, but the women did, rather. There was something hard and dependable about them that I liked. They bluffed the world but not each other. Their talk was terse and to the point, their language coarse and brutal. They made no gestures and seemed always to be looking very straight at some definite invisible thing that occupied their cold attention. It may have been the ugliness of life that they were looking at. If so, it didn't make them wince. It may have been the past, if so it didn't make them shudder or creep. They wasted no time in remorse or regret.

At times they reminded me of tight-rope walkers crossing a dizzy abyss. There was something tense and daring about their stillness, as if a chasm yawned under them. No doubt it did, but it was not their worldly position that was precarious, it was their actual hold on life. They would go on with their old titles and ruined fortunes leading the dance till they dropped, but they might drop any time. People in their entourage did, they were accustomed to violence. One had had a lover who called her up one morning and shot himself while she listened over the telephone. Another had tried twice to kill herself. Most of them drank and took drugs. Their hard glittering eyes gave out a glare of experience, but their faces were cold, calm, non-commital, and if they were worried by the caddishness of the men they loved, by debts and the torments of passion, they gave no sign and held together and helped each other. For damned souls, they made a good show, and I admired them.

They thought me a fool, however, and made a hedge around Fan, shutting her off from me.

One morning I rushed round to her flat on an impulse. I had had no message from her but a curious feeling of nervousness had bothered me in the night. Some one had mentioned Ivanoff at a dinner table. I had heard the words—"wife-beater"—"card-sharper."

I found things at the flat in an indescribable state of disorder.

The drawing-room was strewn with the remains of supper. The table had not been cleared. There were broken glasses on the floor, empty champagne bottles about; a puddle of wine, some one had spilled a bottle of Burgundy. The cook opened the door for me. The manservant and Fan's maid had decamped with the silver leaving word that they had taken it in payment of their two years' wages. A bailiff was sitting on the sofa. Fan was lying in her room in the dark with a wet towel round her head. She said "Oh, hell!" as I came in and turned her back on me. The room had a curious sickly odour, some drug she had been taking, I suppose. Her clothes lay in a heap in the middle of the floor. The dress was torn, the stockings soiled and stained. I felt sick at my stomach. Fan gave a groan.

"For God's sake, Jane, go away; I've got the most ghastly headache."

All I could do was settle with the bailiff and help the cook clear up the mess. Fan scarcely spoke all the morning. The telephone kept ringing.

"Tell them I'm ill. Tell them to go to the devil," she called out. She lay there in a dripping perspiration, the sheets clinging to her thin body. She looked like a corpse fished out of the Seine. Suddenly she sprang up. "Good heavens! what time is it? I'm lunching at the Ritz with the Maharajah's crowd at twelve thirty."

She sat with her feet dangling over the side of the bed holding her head in her hands. "My head's bursting—my head's bursting. Get me a blue bottle off the shelf in the bath room—six drops—no ten—I'll take ten. It's wonderful stuff—wonderful! I'll be alright. You're an angel." She talked in a kind of singing moan, a despairing half-crazy chant. "You're an angel, Jane—you're too good for this world. I'll never be able to pay you. How much did you give that man? Oh God! My head! I wish you hadn't—leave me alone now. I must get dressed. Those Indians won't know I'm half under. I'll be all right if I can find my things. Go along—no—no—I don't want any more help. Ivanoff was here last night; he went off at three this morning. I don't know where he's gone; they played chemmy. He won fifty thousand francs from that boy of Adela's—that baby. I made a scene; I made him give it back. He knocked me down afterwards. He won't come here again. Anyway he's gone for good this time. If you ever speak to me of this, I'll go mad. Leave me alone now. You won't tell me what you paid that man, but I hate you to pity me, and you're an angel—you'd no right to interfere. Do for heaven's sake leave me alone now. God! what a world!" She tottered to her bathroom, trailing her lace nightgown after her. It hung by a ribbon to her bruised shoulder. She shut the door. I heard her turn on her bath. I went away. She avoided me for weeks after that.

Bianca had come back to Paris; she had been, so gossip related it, travelling about Spain with a famous matador. Some people said she had joined his troupe disguised as a boy and had, more than once gone into the arena in a pink suit embroidered in silver and had planted once, the banderillas, in a bull that had five minutes later run his horns through her paramour. I neither believed nor disbelieved the story. José had seen her in the Stand at Seville looking marvellous in a lace mantilla, a black dress high throated and a string of pearls which she flung to the popular hero. She had been wild with excitement, had stood up in her box and called out, and had torn her pearls from her neck with twenty thousand delerious Spaniards shouting round her, and Bombazelta III the Matador on his knee before her, beside the carcase of his victim. Why shouldn't she have gone a bit further? She liked danger. She could look the part. Actually, I did see a picture of her; three cornered hat, slim tight jacket and breeches, embroidered cape. It suited her, of course; she had the body of a boy, and Bombazelta III was a peculiarly striking man. His photograph was in all the Spanish papers. I found them lying about the library in Paris. Philibert must have sent for them. His nervousness during those days betrayed his interest. Though he never mentioned Bianca's name, I knew that he was still in touch with her, that they wrote to each other, that he followed her movements. It did not surprise me, when during that summer he went for a week to Saint Sebastian, he called it Biarritz, but I knew where he was. It was Philibert's behaviour on his return that made me think the stories of Bianca's sensational caprice were true. Besides, it was just the kind of thing to amuse her for a time.

I wasn't interested. I didn't want to know anything about her. All that I wanted was never to see her again. But she had no intention of leaving me alone. Her bullfighter dead, she came back to Paris. Paris is a small place. The community in which we lived was crowded, cramped, intimate. Every one was constantly meeting every one else. Bianca stepped back into her place in it as if nothing had happened. Except for the fact that we were not asked to meet one another at lunch or dinner, one would have supposed that our acquaintances were unaware of our having any reason to dislike each other. The inevitable happened. A newly appointed ambassador gave one of his first dinner parties and found no better way of making it a success than having us both present. We sat on either side of a royal guest. Across his meagre chest we eyed each other. Bianca looked much as usual, younger if anything. She had simplified her make-up. Her fine eyelashes now unplastered with black, curled wide from her great blue eyes that looked as innocent as forget-me-nots. Her face was smooth and white. The smallest thinnest line of carmine marked the curve of her lips. Her dress was a piece of black velvet wound round her white body that was immaculate and lovely. She had the freshness of a water lily, and moved through the salons, cool and serene in an attitude of still dreamy detachment, and her curious magnetism emanated from her like a perfume. She drifted up to me after dinner.

"You must talk to me, Jane—" Her voice was cool and concise. "We have important things to say to each other."

"I have nothing to say."

She lifted her eyebrows. Her lips curved to a point. She gave a little sigh.

"Why do you lie? You are *très en beauté*, Jane—you are wonderful. Why do you lie?—You know you owe it all to me—"

I turned my back on her but I felt her standing behind me, watching me, her eyes shining, her delicate nose palpitating faintly, her eyes reading me. She had no intention of leaving me alone.

Our next meeting was at Madeleine's. Madeleine was the woman who looked after my face. Bianca went to her too. I was sitting in front of the dressing-table, my head tied up in a towel, my face plastered with grease, when Bianca came in. She chattered and gossiped and held up the photograph of herself in the costume of the Spanish bull-ring. "I was distracting myself—" she laughed. "I had been bothered by some very curious ideas. You remember our talk at the '*Château des trois Maries*.' Well, that sort of thing. I thought the excitement would help. It did. I was within a yard of the bull when he died. Some of the blood splashed me. I didn't like that."

I broke in saying that I didn't believe a word of it.

"Don't you, Jane? Well, it's no matter. It's unimportant. The important thing is that I'm sick to death of everything. Every one bores me. I find you are the only woman in Paris who is alive. I've been watching you—you are very extraordinary. You care for no one. You are self-sufficient. You have achieved the impossible."

All this time Madeleine was massaging my face and pretending not to be interested. I could say nothing. I boiled with rage, helpless, wrapped in sheets and towels, my face plastered with grease, and Bianca sat there, her little white face buried in her furs and laughed at me. When at last she had gone, Madeleine said the Princess had such a beautiful character.

I felt that I was being bated like one of her famous bulls. I resolved to make no move. I refused to be goaded to an attack. I was afraid of her.

Then one day Fan came to see me. Instead of rushing in with her usual shrill greeting, she walked up to me quietly, put her arm round me and laid her cheek against mine.

"I'm so happy, Jane dear; I'm so happy." Her voice was gentle. "I have found what I have been waiting for all my life." She went down on her knees and looked up into my face. Hers was calm and rested and had upon it an expression of sweetness that I had never seen there before. "I'm in love, Jane dear. I'm in love with the most wonderful man in the world. I wanted to tell you because I knew you'd be glad I was happy."

She stayed with me for an hour and told me all about it. It was the strangest thing, hard cynical Fan, suddenly become young and sentimental and timid. They had met at St. Moritz that Christmas. He was an Englishman, half Irish really, with a strong streak of Celt in him. His name was Mark. She called him Micky. He was very beautiful, as beautiful as a god. He had taught her to ski. They had been together high up on snowy peaks above the world. One day she had fallen and sprained her ankle. He had carried her down the mountain in his arms. He was strong and straight like a young tree. He wanted her to divorce Ivanoff and marry him. He said there was no other way for them to be happy. He wanted to meet me. Would I come to lunch now, right away? He was waiting for us. She had told him all about me.

I went, of course. That boy,—you remember him, and how handsome he was, with his golden head and fresh bronzed cheeks and the long curly eyelashes fringing his blue eyes, and his broad sunny smile. He was too beautiful I had felt until he gave me that very broad smile.

Our luncheon was a happy absurd affair. Those two were ridiculously in love—they behaved like children. They beamed, they blushed, they looked into each other's eyes, he very shy and sweet and attentive, calling her Fan, and in talking to me trying to be dreadfully solemn. "Please, Madame de Joigny, make her be serious. She must divorce that chap, you know. There's no alternative. It's got to be done and I want it done right away. Please back me up. I say, you mustn't smile, you know. It's dead serious."

How could I help smiling? He was very appealing. He rumpled his hair and his eyes grew dark, and little beads of moisture stood out on his high tanned forehead. I looked at Fan. Poor Fan! so much older, so worn, so stamped with the stamp of her harrowing racketing years, and yet a new Fan with a young light in her eyes; I was disturbed and anxious.

My fears seemed during the weeks that followed to be groundless. She held him. They continued their dream of bliss. He satisfied her utterly. It was of course his beauty that she loved. Always she had adored beauty in men—now she had it in its most charming aspect, fresh, clean, young. They had nothing in common, but their passion. He was stupid and rather a prude. He had grown up with horses and dogs and a family of sisters in an English country house, had joined the army and then had gone to South Africa with his regiment. He had ideas about womanliness and the honour of a gentleman and the duties of his class. He had never been in Paris before. Fan found no fault in him.

She began taking him about with her. Society was at first amused and indulgent, then again the inevitable happened. He became the rage. A number of women lost their heads over him. He was invited out without her. Soon he was everywhere in demand, and Fan rightly or wrongly persuaded him to go. This at first quite worried him. Women wanting him for themselves and finding him obstinately faithful, turned spiteful. He didn't understand, for he wasn't fatuous, but he must have heard a good many things about Fan that he didn't like.

I felt for him in a way. It seemed to me that he was holding his own pretty well and behaving on the whole very decently, but I wished that Fan's divorce could be hurried along. She had hesitated about divorcing Ivanoff. "Of course," she said, "he lives off women, but I've known that all along, and it doesn't seem quite fair to get rid of him now—" but she had given in, in the end.

The months dragged on. I began to wonder whether Micky would hold out. It had been difficult to find Ivanoff. A long time elapsed before the divorce papers could be served on him.

Micky still stuck to Fan, but he began talking about compromising her and, after a time, I had an impression that he stuck to her grimly, without enthusiasm. I imagined him to be cursing his own weak character. He was weak and he knew it, and so did we. He clung to Fan as a woman should cling to a man. This did not make her despise him, it gave her a feeling of strength and safety. She encouraged his dependence on her and adopted the rôle of guide and counsellor.

About this time I had a telephone message and a note from Bianca; both summoning me to her in her old peremptory style. The message was that the Princess wished to see me on urgent matters and would be at home all that afternoon. I did not go. The note, received next morning was as follows:

> "It is silly and dangerous to stand out against me. I am attacked by all the demons you know about and if you don't come, something unexpected and unpleasant will happen."

I paid no attention to it.

Fan's character and the quality of her life changed completely; she gave up going out and sank into the deep secretive isolation of a woman who lives for one man alone. Her other men friends melted away. Many of her women friends dropped her. Not those of her own little band, but Micky didn't like these. Claire who was fond of her, said — "*Elle se rend ridicule avec ce garçon*," and refused to have them to dinner together. Fan didn't seem to care; she stayed more and more at home. This created for her serious money difficulties. She had never had any meals at all to speak of in her own flat, and her butcher's bill had come to nothing, but now her boy had to be fed. He would come into dinner or lunch nearly every day, rosy and ravenous, and consume large beef steaks, fat cutlets, chickens, eggs, butter, sweets. Her bills became larger as her revenues dwindled. She could or would no longer avail herself of her old sources of wealth. Her vogue was vanishing, and with it the amiability of dressmakers and restaurant-keepers. She had a distaste now for gambling on the Bourse and asking Beaudoin for tips. Micky it seemed disapproved of women gambling. Her love affair was costing her her livelihood; and Micky himself gave her nothing, perhaps because he had nothing much to give; perhaps because of some idea of honour, perhaps because he didn't know how hard up she was. Fan was not the kind to let on. I know for a fact that she often went hungry to give him a good square meal, and I suspected that under her last year's dresses, she didn't have on enough to keep her warm.

It became increasingly evident as the winter wore on that there were influences at work, perhaps a special influence that was worrying them both, but I had no suspicion of the truth. Had I known I would have done something effective—I would have wasted no time with Bianca.

Fan had burned her bridges. There was no going back for her now, no slipping down into the old stupefying pleasures. He had changed her, he had purified and weakened her. There was for her a future with him or nothing. If she lost him, she would be done for. She knew this. She remained clear-headed and played her cards with desperate caution. And I watching her, saw just how frightened she was, but she told me nothing.

I did not know that Bianca knew Micky. She went out very little now. People spoke of her living shut up in her house as they might have spoken of some lurid figure of legend, some beautiful ogress, gnashing her hungry teeth in a cave, but I didn't listen when they talked of her. I wanted less than ever to hear about her. She still saw Philibert, I knew, but this no longer concerned me. And she seemed to have given up pursuing me. I ought to have known she was up to something. I am sorry now that I refused to think about her, for I might have reasoned it out and discovered by a process of logic, what she was up to—I might have known that she would inevitably choose Micky for her own, just because he was in love with another woman, just because he was the pet of Paris, just because finally, Fan's life depended on him and because I cared for Fan as if she were my own child.

In March Fan began to lose her nerve. She said to me one day—

"You know that I'm frightened but you don't know how frightened. Some day, any day, tomorrow perhaps, he'll see me as I am, a shrivelled-up hag who has played the devil with her life. Do you remember Jane, how your grandmother used to make us read the Bible on Sunday mornings in St. Mary's Plains? I remember a phrase—'Born again.' Well, I've been born again. My soul is beautiful, it's as beautiful as the morning, but I'm as tired and ugly as ever—and my mind is as old as hell. I'll lose him if I marry him, or if I don't, I feel it in my bones. I used to think—'I'm so much cleverer than he is that I'll be able to keep him.' My dear, don't talk to me about cleverness in holding a man. I'd give all the brains in the world for one year of beauty. If only I could be quite quite lovely for just one year. God! but it's tiring to be always trying to look nicer than you are."

On another day she broke down and sobbed and implored me to tell her that she was mistaken, and that he wouldn't get tired of her. "He's so sweet," she cried, "so sweet. He gets so cross with women who aren't nice about me. When they make love to him he doesn't seem to understand, he thinks them idiots, but each time that he comes back to me from one of them, I am afraid to look at him, afraid to see his eyes, veiled, shifting. It's awful—too awful! He couldn't hide anything from me, could he?"

The next time I saw her she was the colour of ashes.

"He hasn't been near me for a week. Some one has got hold of him. I know who it is." Her teeth chattered, she kept twisting her hands, but as I sat there miserably watching her, the telephone rang, and she was off like a crazy woman. "Yes, yes, I'm at home, of course. Oh, Micky darling, do—do—come quick, quick"—and when she came back to me she was laughing and crying and saying over and over, "I'm a fool! I'm a fool."

It was the end of March that they made up their minds to go away together to Italy. She was very lucid and calm about it. Paris had got on their nerves. The life they were leading was impossible. His family might cut him off without a penny, but that couldn't be helped. They would stay in Italy until the divorce decree was made absolute, and they could be married. Micky had a foolish idea about its being unwise for them to start together from Paris. They were to take the Simplon Express. She was to go ahead and board the train at La Roche Junction. As this was very near Ste. Clothilde, would I mind her going there and stopping the night?

As it happened I was going to Ste. Clothilde for Easter, a few days later, so I advanced the date of my journey and took her with me.

How much she knew or suspected of what had been going on between Micky and Bianca, I do not know. She never told me. All that she ever said was—"I know he didn't plan it deliberately, I know he didn't mean to—when I left him." But she must have known enough to be terribly anxious, and I imagine that her decision to go off with him to Italy was a last desperate move.

The Simplon Express left Paris at nine and stopped at La Roche at eleven o'clock at night. Micky was to take two tickets and the sleepers and get on the train at Paris, ready to lift her aboard.

"Once I am on the train," she kept saying, "I feel that I will be safe."

La Roche was a three hours' motor run across country from Ste. Clothilde, the roads were winding lanes, confusing and indistinctly marked; so we decided that she had better do the distance before dark. She might puncture a tire, the motor might break down, anything might happen, she was feverishly anxious to allow herself plenty of time. She started at three o'clock.

Her face was strained and seemed no bigger than a little wizened infant's face as she said good-bye. For a moment, on those immense stone steps in view of Philibert's great formal gardens with their fountains and statues and broad gravel walks, she clung to me. Then with a final nervous hug flung away and jumped into the car. Her last words were "I'll not come back till I'm married, Jane, so give me your blessing." And out of my heart I gave it, kissing both my hands to her as the motor swung down the drive, and through the great iron gates.

I felt singularly depressed. Fan and I in that formal and splendid panorama, were such minute creatures—were no bigger, no stronger than a couple of flies. Never had the Château de Ste. Clothilde seemed so cold, so inhuman, so foreign. I no longer disliked the place, I had grown used to it as I had grown used to other things. Its imposing architectural beauty, delicately majestic, serenely incongruous with nature, had made its effect on my mind. I understood to some extent the idea that had created it, the high peculiarity of taste that had chosen to mock at woods and fields, by building in their midst a palace smooth and fine as a thing of porcelain. Gradually I had come to appreciate the bland assurance of the achievement with all its bold frivolous contradictions of reason and common-sense. The moat that surrounded three sides of the château, was like a marble bath. It had no *raison d'être*. Never had any owner dreamed of defending this place from any invaders, but the moat was there, full of clear water, palest green in which were reflected the silvery walls and high shining windows. And on the fourth side of the house, a joke perhaps, or to contradict the chilling effect of the moat, the eighteenth century architect who adored Marie Antoinette in her shepherdess costume, built an immense flight of steps straight across the length of the south façade, lovely, smooth, shallow steps, made to welcome a crowd of courtiers in satins and trailing silks, and dainty high-heeled slippers. It had amused me at times to imagine them there in that theatrical setting, and to recreate for myself the spectacle of their *fêtes galantes*—but on the day that Fan left me to go to her boy lover, I took no pleasure in the ghostly place. The sky was grey, the faintly budding trees marshalled a far-off beyond the formal gardens, showed a haze of green that seemed to me sickly, and the suggestion of spring in the air gave me a feeling of "*malaise.*"

I remembered that Bianca and Philibert had gone off by the same Simplon Express five years before. They too must have stopped at the station of La Roche at eleven o'clock at night, or had they boarded the train farther down the line? I couldn't remember what they were supposed to have done. All that had nothing to do with me, yet I was waiting for Philibert to arrive with a dozen people who would be my guests, his and mine.

My chauffeur reported his return at nine o'clock that evening. They had reached La Roche at six as planned. He had left the Princess at the station. The Princess had not wished him to wait until the arrival of her train. He had insisted, *auprès de Madame la Princesse*, as I had told him to do, but she had been displeased and had sent him away.

It was a rainy night, loud with a gusty April wind. The big rooms of the château were peopled with moving shadows and filled with whisperings and sighs. The wind moaned down the chimneys and set the far branches of the trees in the park to tossing. I was alone in the house save for the servants. Jinny had gone to her grandmother for a few days.

I slept badly and woke early. My room was scarcely light. The sun was not yet up, or was obscured by a dismal sky. I listened apprehensively to the moaning restless morning. I listened intently for something—a sound, I didn't know what. Then I heard it. The telephone downstairs was ringing. I knew in an instant what that meant, and flew down the corridor, my heart pounding in my ribs. A clock somewhere was striking six, seven, I did not know which. A man's voice spoke over the phone,—"*La Gare de La Roche—La Princesse Ivanoff prie La Marquise de Joigny de venir la chercher en auto—La Princesse l'attendra à la Gare—La Princesse s'est trouvée malade dans la nuit et a manqué son train.*" I did not wait to hear any more. I was on my way in half an hour. The drive seemed terribly long, interminably long. Fan all night in the station of La Roche—what did it mean?

I found her sitting on a packing case on the station platform, her head against the wall. Her face was bluish, her lips were a pale mauve, her hands, wet, like lumps of ice.

"I've been sitting here all night," she said in a dull voice. "I'm cold." The station master helped me get her into the car. He seemed troubled and ashamed. He explained that they had not noticed her during the night. After the passing of the express he always went home to bed. The station was deserted during the middle of the night, and the waiting room locked. No passenger trains stopped between twelve and five in the morning. At five the Princess had been discovered by an employé but she had refused to move. They had tried to get her to drink some coffee from the buffet. She had asked him to telephone which he had done. The Princess had told him that she had felt faint during the evening while waiting and had thus missed the train.

On the way home she did not speak. Her body was as heavy against me as a corpse. Her head kept slipping from my arm. I held her across my knees and gave her a sip of brandy now and then. Half way home she began to shiver. Her body shook, her teeth chattered, grating against each other. By the time we reached home, she was in a burning fever.

That night Philibert entertained his guests alone. I sat with Fan in her room. About ten o'clock she stopped for a moment her terrible exhausting tossing from one side of the bed to the other and said—

"I heard her laugh. She put her head out of the car window and laughed."

"Who laughed, dear?"

"Bianca—she was with Micky in the train. They wouldn't let me get on. I had no ticket—"

She lay on her back now staring at the ceiling. Some one downstairs was playing a waltz on the piano. The wind had fallen. Out of doors the night was soft and still. Fan's voice came from her dried lips, distinct and harsh.

"I tried to get onto the steps of the train. The guard stopped me. Bianca must have fixed him beforehand. Micky was drunk. She had fixed him too, by making him drunk. He wouldn't have done it if he hadn't been drunk. The railway carriage was very high, but I could see into the lighted corridor. I saw Micky. His face was red and stupid. I called 'Micky—Micky, my ticket—quick; they won't let me on without it.' But he didn't seem to hear me. Some one was behind him in the compartment.

"The *wagons-lits* man asked me what I wanted. I screamed out—'That gentleman has my ticket.' He half believed me. I saw him go in and speak to Micky, and looking up—you know how high the carriages are—I saw Micky shake his head. The attendant came back then and told me that I was mistaken, the gentleman was expecting no one, there was no place, the car was full. A whistle blew. The train started to move, I grabbed the handle by the steps. The *wagons-lits* man slammed the door shut above me. The train moved faster, I ran along holding on. 'Micky' I called, 'Micky.' Some one pulled me back, wrenched my hand loose, I stumbled, then I heard Bianca laugh, I saw her. She put her head out of the window and laughed. I was on all fours, in the wet. It was raining. I scrambled to my feet and ran down the platform. The train was moving fast by this time. The last carriage passed me. I reached the end of the platform. I saw the red light at the back of the train. They were in the train together, Micky and Bianca. They were together, in the little hot lighted compartment. They were going away together. She had taken my place. I stood there. The red light disappeared. There seemed to be no one about, it was very windy and cold. I don't know what I did after that. I remember the steel rails stretching out under the arc light into the darkness. I wanted to run down the rails and catch the train, but the train was gone, and I was afraid."

They were dancing downstairs; I heard their feet scraping; the time was changed to a fox trot—but Fan did not notice. She lay in a deep dark empty place of her own, cut off from all the sights and sounds round her, watching something, following something, the red lantern perhaps at the end of a train going away in the dark.

I gave Philibert no explanation of Fan's presence or of her illness. The other people in the house thought that she had come for a visit and had caught cold during a walk in the rain. I had told my maid to suggest this explanation to the servants. She understood. They did not give me away. Philibert never knew what had happened to Fan, but he found out when he went back to Paris that Bianca had gone away with the English boy. I remember wondering afterwards, how he liked being the one who was left behind, but I wondered vaguely, without any feeling for him. He mattered less than he had ever done. Nothing mattered for the time being but Fan, very ill, with congestion of the lungs, who wanted so much to die and end quickly what was already ended. But she couldn't manage dying. Death eluded her. Life was unwilling to let her miserable body go. Like the remains of some sticky poisonous substance left in a battered dish, it stuck to her. Unwelcome, noisome, contaminated stuff of life, she couldn't get rid of it although the convulsing frame tried to eject it from her lips. The horror of her coughing! the shaking of her pointed shoulders, the sound of her wrenching stomach, the rattling of her breath in her poor bony chest, the great deep resounding noises of pain in the fragile box that held her wasted lungs! Her eyes would start out at me in terror. She would clutch at me wildly and gasp—"Hold me. Hold me, Jane, I'm shaking to pieces," and I would hold her through the long spasm, and then she would fall back exhausted and clammy with sweat. My heart ached and ached and ached. I wanted so, for her to die. If she had asked me to do it, I would have ended her life with an injection of morphine, but she said nothing.

Early in May she had a bad haemorrhage. All the scarlet blood of her veins seemed to me to be staining the cloths that I held to her mouth. And afterwards she lay at peace, and I thought "Thank God this is the end," but it wasn't. She rallied. Some strength came back to her. The doctors told me to take her to Switzerland. I did so, and did not remember until we were installed in our chalet near the sanatorium that we were within a few miles of the place where she had first met Micky, but she seemed not to mind at all being there, and would lie on the balcony in the sun looking across the valley at the mountains with a smile on her face, while I read aloud to her. Sometimes she talked of St. Mary's Plains, sometimes of Paris, a great many people wrote to her, women who had been unkind when she was happy, were sorry for her now; sometimes she was gay, laughing and childishly pleased with new chintzes and tea sets and cushions that I ordered from Paris but she never spoke of Micky.

Gradually she grew smaller and smaller. Her face was disappearing. There was nothing much left of it now, but a pointed nose with painfully wide distended nostrils, and two sunken eyes. I took the hand glass away from her dressing table one night when she was asleep—she didn't ask for it, but one day not long afterwards, she said suddenly "I would like something, Jane."

"What, my darling?"

"I would like some new clothes, especially hats. I would like six new hats from Caroline Reboux"; and then she looked at me suspiciously like a sharp little witch.

I said, of course, that I would write for them at once. She dictated the letter. Caroline was asked to send us the newest and smartest models she had. "She knows my style," said Fan from her pillow, "she'll send something amusing, won't she, Jane?"

"I'm sure they'll be ravishing, my dear."

"Do you think I'm silly, Jane? I've a feeling it will do me good to have those hats—when they come we'll try them on, we'll go for a drive. We'll pick out the most becoming and drive to—but how long will it be before they come?"

"Not more than ten days—I should think," I said avoiding her strange eager eyes.

The next day she was very tired, she asked if there were letters but only looked at the envelopes, saying—"They don't care a damn whether I live or die," and the next day and the next, she asked again for letters only to fling them aside.

In the evening she said, "I'm a beast, Jane—and a fool. Why did we write for those hats? I know I can't wear them, but I've always wanted to order hats like that, half a dozen at a time without thinking what they cost. You won't mind paying, I know—and I don't mind now. I've been a beast about you, Jane, I used to envy you so many things."

"What for instance—?"

"Well, your ermine coat with the hundreds of little black tails, the sable cape, and your jade necklace, and your pearls. I always adored pearls. I believe I could have sold my soul for pearls like yours at one time. Funny, isn't it? Lucky no one ever offered me any—no one ever did you know. I wasn't the kind to have ropes of pearls given me for the asking. If I had only been beautiful, Jane—I would have gone to the dogs sure as fate, but oh, I'd have had a good time. As it is, I don't seem to have had much fun, now that I think of it. My past is like a dingy deep pocket with a hole in it somewhere. I've been dropping trinkets into it all my life, and now I find it's empty, just an empty dark pocket—that's my past." She gave her old shrill laugh. "It's damn funny isn't it, Jane—life, I mean. We go on, hoping, hoping, looking forward, looking for something, thinking always there's something nice ahead for us, being cheated all the time, never admitting it, never giving in, always expecting—fooling ourselves, being fooled—up to the very end. What makes us like that? What keeps us going? Who invents the string of lies we believe in?"

She lay propped up on pillows, her head sunk between her pointed shoulders, her knees sharp as pegs pushing up the bed-clothes, and her skinny hands like birds' claws picked at the lace on her sleeve.

"Happiness—Jane? I was happy once, you know. It made me good, at least I thought so. I felt good. I tried to be good. Everything dropped away; it was like moulting. I came out a plucked chicken, no fine feathers left. What was the use? I was too far gone I suppose, when it came—" She stared up at me, her cheek bones flushed, her wide nostrils, great black holes in her small face, palpitating. "Love came—now death—and I'm not good enough for that either. What's death to me? Nothing. I can't rise to meet it. I want some new hats. That's all I can think about, all I can bear to think about. My death Jane, like my life, is empty. I fill up the emptiness with things, little things." She held her two hands against her side as if the emptiness were there, hurting her. "Jane," she said suddenly, "I wonder—" Her eyes widened, and in them I saw the shadow of the great terror that gets us all in the end. She stared, her dreadful gaping nostrils dilating, her mouth open, her hands out in front of her, pushing against the air. Then suddenly she laughed. "No, no, damn it all, let's be frivolous up to the end. It's as good a way as another of seeing the business through."

She died the end of July, with all her new hats strewn round the room and a piece of wonderful lace in her hands. "Lovely, lovely lace, isn't it, Jane?" she had said a minute before, and then there was a tearing sound in her chest and the scarlet blood flowing from her mouth, and one choking cry as I sprang to her side.

"Jane—Jane—I'm going now and I've not seen him. Jane, tell him, tell Micky I hoped—" Her eyes were agonized. The blood choked her. She couldn't speak, but I saw in her eyes what she meant—terribly I saw—how she had believed up to the end that Micky would come back to her.

It was Ivanoff who came and Ivanoff, great hulking shameful pitiable creature who wept over her poor lonely coffin. We brought her back to Paris, Ivanoff and I, and buried her in *Père-Lachaise* one rainy afternoon and then he disappeared again for the last time.

I went straight to Deauville. Philibert was there with his mother and Jinny, but I went to find Bianca. I had seen in the paper that she was at the Normandy.

I may have been out of my mind, I don't know. I remember that I thought I had Fan's disease, but that does not prove that I was off my head. The smell of it was in my breath, the dry sound of its hacking cough in my ears, and constantly I saw before me, Fan herself, pallid, shiny with sweat, two black holes in her face opening, panting for breath—and behind her, looking over her dank head I saw Bianca, her pointed lips smiling, cruel as only she in all heaven and earth could be cruel.

It is true that I took a revolver with me to the Casino that night. I remember putting it in my silk bag and pretending at dinner that I had a lot of gold pieces by me, for luck. I had. I was going to the Casino to gamble. I would find a place opposite Bianca and sit her out. You remember the scene. People talked of it enough Heaven knows. One would have supposed women never had played high before. A crowd gathered round us—half Paris was there. I remember the Tobacco King, a very fat man with a red face. It pleased him at first, he swelled with importance. By three in the morning he had lost five hundred thousand francs. His place was taken by the Brazilian millionaire—Chenal, the opera star, was opposite. A number of men accustomed to playing in the men's rooms, joined our table. They half realized there was more in it than just a game. Bianca opposite me, was white as a sheet. Her face was like a white moon among all those red bloated faces. I watched her. I watched her long carmine finger nails glinting as she handled her piles of folded notes. We played against each other. The luck was against me after the Tobacco King left. I was losing heavily. The fact made no impression on me. I wasn't playing with Bianca for money. The little wads of thousand franc notes were symbols. The game was a blind. I went *Banco* against her as a matter of course, automatically, but all the time I was playing another game. I was repeating silently to myself, words that were meant for her. Your psycho-therapists would say I was trying to hypnotize her, to subject her to my suggestion. Well, I was; I was attacking her brain with all the power of my will. I was concentrated on her to break her down. I was determined to frighten her, to fill her with dread, with frantic dread of my hatred, my loathing, my determination to make her pay for what she had done. I succeeded. At four o'clock she began to show signs; attendants kept bringing her whiskey, liqueurs, champagne; her face had turned blueish, she went on. She was still winning. But she knew now, that that wouldn't help her. At five I saw her waver. She started to scrape together her winnings. I did the same. She looked into my face; it was evident to her that if she left the table I would follow her. She went on playing. We sat there as you know till six o'clock. We left the Casino as the doors closed—we left together.

"I am going with you, Bianca—don't hurry, there is no hurry"—I kept her by my side. The sun was rising as we crossed towards the Normandy. "No—" I objected, "not there—come out on the beach." It was low tide. The sea was still. A light mist hung along the horizon. The little waves glinted in the first sun rays. We went out across the wet sand, Bianca's turquoise blue cape trailing behind her in the little pools where crabs scuttled out of the way of our high satin heels. The sunlight bathed us. It showed her pallid as a corpse. What I looked to her, I do not know. Our two long shadows moved ahead of us to the edge of the water. There was no one near. Behind us stretched the sands—in front of us the sea—afar out, was a ship, minute white sails, sea birds darted in the blue—space—sunlight—silence. We faced each other, and I told her very briefly what was in my mind. I told her that the earth must be rid of her, at any rate that part of the earth which held me, that I had a revolver in my bag and was quite prepared if necessary to put an end to her life, or give it to her, and leave her to do it herself. On the other hand I saw no particular point in suffering the consequences of her death, and would be content if she disappeared for ever from the world that I knew, from Paris, from France, from the civilized places where ordinary men and women like myself were in the habit of living. I told her that I would not allow her to live anywhere any longer where I was—that she could choose—either she would go—take herself off—disappear for ever— or shoot herself there in my presence—If she didn't, I would kill her the next time I came across her.

It sounds extraordinarily silly and puerile as I relate this but it did not sound silly to Bianca. You must remember that I knew Bianca and knew just how that sort of thing might affect her—and knew that physically she had always been afraid of me. I counted on her superstition, her morbidness, her lassitude. I counted on the stillness, the wide mysterious dawn, the still sea, the cold sky—and I counted on her lack of character—on her *"manque d'équilibre."* I was right. I told her that she was loathesome and that at bottom she loathed herself; I told her that she was sick of loving herself and in fact, couldn't go on much longer even pretending to herself that she wasn't vile. I told her that her vanity was strained to the breaking point, that any day it might snap and that she would collapse. When she could no longer keep up the fiction of her own interest to herself what could she do? Nothing. She would be a drivelling idiot—she would go insane as she had feared. Coldly I repeated it, over and over. She was diseased; she was a maniac— an egotistical maniac and she would one day become a raving lunatic. She could take her choice. End it now—or go off and develop her lunacy elsewhere in some far country where the curse of her presence would affect no one that mattered to me.

I can see her now—as she was that morning—standing in the sunlight in her evening dress, her feet wet, her cloak trailing on the sand, her face working. I had never seen her face twist before. That morning in the glaring sun, it twitched and jerked and pulled, until almost I thought that her mind had snapped and that she was already the idiot I had prophesied, but she pulled herself together to some extent and managed after a while to speak. What she said was trivial.

"It is your fault, Jane—you wouldn't do what I wanted so I had to hurt you again—you shouldn't blame me—you know that I am possessed of devils—Well, have it your own way—I'll go. Don't look at me like that— I'll go, I tell you. Stop looking, you frighten me—Yes, I'm afraid of you—I admit it. Your look is a curse in itself—Wasn't I cursed enough when I was born—what have I done after all—Fan's death—? Pooh! She'd have died any way."

But at that I gripped her. I must have twisted her arms. She gave a shriek, then a whimper as I let her go, and staggered away from me, back towards the shore. I followed her as far as the bathing boxes; all the way she made little noises like a wounded animal, whimpering, sniffing, almost growling. It was horrid. Her long swaying staggering figure, her head hanging forward, her hands twisting her clothes round her, clutching her sides—her shoulders twitching; she was, I suppose, on the verge of hysterics. I felt no pity for her. The sight of her was shocking and disgusting. She had gone to pieces as I thought she would do. She had no character.

I watched her go—From the wooden walk I watched her stumble towards the hotel, break into a run, turn to look back, disappear. It was seven o'clock. An attendant opened a cabin for me. I stripped and swam out—out—a mile, two miles, three, I don't know. When I got back to the villa Jinny was at breakfast. I felt hungry. We laughed over our honey and rolls. At twelve I was told that Bianca had left Deauville by motor.

That was in 1913, the year before the war.

VIII

Jinny liked to wear silks and velvets when she was quite a little girl. Her taste for pretty clothes was something more than childish vanity. I used often to find her in the room lined with cupboards where my dresses were kept, sitting on the floor amid a heap of soft shining garments, that she had dragged from their hooks, stroking the fabrics lovingly, and purring to herself like a blissful kitten. She couldn't bear the touch of wool or starched cambric, and screamed herself into hysterics when in obedience to the doctor's orders, I tried one winter to put her into woollen combinations. Her father humoured her in this. I think it rather pleased him that she should be so delicately fastidious. He found in it a proof of an exquisite sensibility and likened her to the fairy-tale princess of the crumpled rose leaf. Unfortunately he told Jinny the story and she immediately accepted it as illustrative of herself, acted it out literally in her nursery, obliging her nursemaid to make and remake her little bed, to smooth and stroke and smooth again until every imaginary wrinkle in the soft sheets was gone, before she would consent to get into it. This habit lasted for some weeks until she read one day in her *"histoire sainte"* of a saint who had acquired great spiritual blessing by sleeping on the floor of her cell, whereupon she took no more interest in the way her bed was made. The nurse was delighted until she discovered that as soon as she had turned down the light and left the room, Jinny hopped out of bed and lay down on the floor, choosing fortunately a spot near the radiator. The harassed women, governess, nurse and nursemaid said nothing to me the first time, nor the second that they found her asleep on the floor, but finally came to me explaining that Mademoiselle was very determined to die of pneumonia.

Jinny looked at me with grave shining eyes when I asked her what such naughtiness meant.

"It is not naughtiness at all, Mamma, you misunderstand, it is the saintly life, '*la sainte vie*.'"

Fortunately I was sufficiently aware of her romantic absorption in the lives of the saints, and of her habit of applying everything that she read or heard to herself, to guess what influence was working on her. The "saintly life" had come up before. She had already had periods of fasting that had given way before her great liking for bonbons, and periods of prayer, that had given way to sleepiness, and had even attempted at one time to beat her little shoulders with a strap off a trunk, all of which things had worried me considerably, but none of which had been immediately dangerous to her health, so I entered straight upon the subject in as sympathetic a tone, that is on as high a moral ground as I could find, using all my wits to adapt my conversation and my thought to her mind, as if, as indeed may have been the case, her idea was more lucid than my own.

"Darling," I said in a tone as grave as the one she had used to me, but with a certain timidity that she in her exaltation of the young devotee had certainly not felt at all, "the saintly life is a beautiful thing when rightly understood; it is too beautiful to be entered upon easily and capriciously. If you have a true wish to model your life on that of the saints who gave up every comfort for the salvation of their souls, then I will help you. I will do it with you. We will change everything. We will take away all the pretty things, and empty these rooms, yours and mine, of the pictures, and the rugs, keeping only the strict necessaries. We will sleep on hard beds, floor, we will eat bread and water every day, nothing more; we will wear no more nice clothes, we will each have a serge dress and very plain underwear, of some strong cotton stuff, we will—"

But poor Jinny had grown quite pale. "Oh, Mummy, Mummy, you are cruel. Don't you see I can't do all that? Don't you want me to want to be good."

That you see ended well. She cried a little in my arms, and listened quietly as I explained that being good was quite another thing to the saintly life as she had understood it, and that this latter was not vouchsafed to children, and we arranged between us that it would be much more truly good, to take a great many baskets of toys to the little poor crippled children in the big hospitals than to jump out of bed when no one was looking, but I was not immeasurably reassured by my victory. With Jinny it was always a case of its being all right till the next time, and the next time was never slow in coming.

I take it that my own feeling for Jinny needs no explanation. I am a simple woman, and I was her mother; she was all that I had. But Philibert loving her so much was curious, don't you think? It seemed so inconsistent of him! I don't even now understand it. Perhaps the most obvious explanation is the real one. Perhaps it was just because she was so very attractive. Had she been ugly I believe that he would have disliked her. She was never ugly, she had never had an awkward age. At fourteen she had already that look of costliness, of something luxurious, sumptuous and precious that she has today. She was slender and fragile and smooth. At times she suggested a child Venus by Botticelli. Her mouth had the delicate drooping curve of some of his Madonnas, her hands were full and soft and dimpled with delicate tapering fingers. Sensuous idle hands, they were to her instruments of pleasure. Touching things conveyed to her some special delight; with her finger tips she enjoyed. I know for I have watched those hands for years, moving softly and deftly over lovely surfaces, and following the contours of flowers, of porcelain vases, but she never did anything practical with them. Even embroidery, she disliked. But jigsaw puzzles amused her—she and Philibert always had one somewhere spread out on a table. They spent hours together fitting in the innumerable tiny bits, their heads close together, excitedly comparing, fitting, exclaiming. Philibert liked the idea of his daughter's distaste for doing anything useful. He encouraged her laziness and her absurd little air of languid hauteur. When she dropped a glove or handkerchief and waited for a servant to pick it up for her, he laughed.

Sometimes I tried to reason with him.

"You are spoiling her," I said on more than one occasion, but he only shrugged his shoulders.

"Don't you see, Philibert?" I would insist, "that it is bad for her to live in this atmosphere?"

"What atmosphere?"

"The atmosphere of this house, of Paris, of the world we live in."

"Well, my dear, it is her house, her Paris, her world—she's born to it, and belongs to it, so she may as well grow up in it. What would you have for her—something more like your own home over there, eh?—the place that turned you out, so admirably fitted for our European life—you want her to be as you were, is that it?"

"God forbid."

"Well then—"

I couldn't argue with him. I couldn't tell him what I really felt and feared, or explain to him how I hated for Jinny, all the things that I now accepted for myself, for he was one of those things, the principle one; I had accepted him. I had even grown to understand him, and if it hadn't been for Jinny, I felt that we might become friends. His extravagances, his cynicism, his fondness for women were things that I now took for granted. They no longer bothered me. For me, he would do now, I no longer asked anything of him, but for Jinny he wasn't half good enough. As a father to my child, I found him impossible.

One often hears of estranged couples being brought together by their love for a child. With Philibert and myself, it was the contrary. We were both jealous of Jinny. We were afraid, each one, that she loved the other best, and our nervousness on this point acted to keep us in each other's company while it made friendship impossible. Neither of us liked to leave the other alone with her for any length of time. I had stayed with Fan for three months and had come back to find Jinny hanging on her father's every word, and to find what I imagined was a coldness between her and myself. This may have been my imagination, or it may have been true; I don't know, but I suspected Philibert of working to alienate her from me, and he suspected me of the same thing. If I suggested taking Jinny to Ste. Clothilde for a fortnight, he either found a way of keeping us in Paris or accompanied us, and if Philibert wanted for some reason to go away, to London or Berlin or Biarritz, he was haunted by the idea that in his absence I might steal a march on him with Jinny, so really bothered I mean, that nine times out of ten, he would give up going unless I went with him. The result was that we were more constantly together than we had been since the first year of our marriage.

Looking back now to that winter of 1913-14 I see it as a season of delirium, of fever, of madness. Paris glows there, at the eve of war, in a lurid blaze of brilliance, its people giddy, intoxicated, dancing over the quaking surface of a civilization that was cracking under them. A period in the history of the human race was drawing to a close. The old earth was rushing towards the greatest calamity of our time, carrying with it swarming continents that in a few months were to seethe and smoke like beds of boiling lava—and the people of the earth as if aware that the days of pleasure were numbered, were possessed by a frenzy. I say the people of the earth, but I mean of course, the rich, the idle, the foolish, the so-called fortunate who make up society and of whom Philibert and I were the most idle, the most foolish, as we were perhaps the richest.

That winter marked the height of our folly and of our worldly brilliance, and for me it marked at the same time the deepest depth of futility and cowardice.

Philibert and I were like two runaway horses harnessed together, and running blindly, with the smart showy vehicle of our empty life rattling and lurching behind us, and poor little Jinny inside it.

His extravagance that winter was colossal. I did not try to restrain it. He felt the inertia of old age coming on him, and was having a last desperate fling: I felt sorry for him. His parties were fantastic. He bought the servants' under-linen at Doucet's; I only laughed when he told me. Money? Why not spend it! The more he spent, the less would be left for Jinny, and that, I argued, was all to the good. If only he could manage to run through the whole lot, then Jinny and I would be free. Dinner succeeded dinner, dance followed dance. We received half Europe and were entertained in a dozen capitals. London, Brussels, Rome, Madrid, we took them all in. It was very different from my picnic trips with you and Clémentine when we travelled second-class, carried paper bags of sandwiches and had literary adventures in old book shops with ancient scholars in skull-caps and spectacles. Philibert and I travelled in Rolls Royces or in private trains. We had maids and valets and couriers to smooth away every discomfort and every bit of unexpectedness. Philibert never missed his morning bath and massage, his Swede, too, travelled with us.

It was not very interesting. One glass of champagne is like another. Royal palaces are as alike as cabbages. Everywhere we met the same people and did the same things. We danced, we gambled, we gossiped, we ate and drank and changed our clothes, and I was often bored, and often gloomy. Too much brilliance has the effect of darkness.

In my dismal moods I told myself that I hated it, but probably I didn't. No doubt it had become necessary to me to be surrounded by a crowd of flatterers. We are all fools—And I had no precise idea of myself. Even at night, when I was alone, and when I should have been stripped naked to my soul in the dark, I was still wrapped about to my own eyes, in the flattering disguises of the world's adulation.

In Jinny's eyes alone did I seem to see myself as I really was. I trembled as I looked into them.

I wonder if all women are afraid of their children? Perhaps not, the woman who has the love of her husband and a clear conscience and a sure hope of heaven. I had none of these things, and I was afraid. I had staked everything on Jinny, but my conscience was not clear about her. Instead of a hope of heaven, I had the hope of her happiness and yet I knew that I was not doing what was necessary to realize it. What I was doing was, when one thought it out, futile and ridiculous. I was wasting my life to save hers; because of her, I had been involved in this endless round of futility and I was behaving as if I believed that if I were wretched enough, she would be happy.

What I wanted most of all was to save her from an experience like my own. For her, there were to be no wretched sordid compromises with life, no unclean pleasures, no subterfuges, no lying, no fear. She was to remain good and brave and lovely and I was to find a true man for her who would love her as I longed to have her loved, reverently.

And in the meantime, she was growing up surrounded by slavish servants, by doting relatives, by luxury and dissipation and all that I did to protect her, was to shut her up as much as possible in the schoolroom.

I had always been in the habit of talking to her of Patience Forbes, her great aunt in America. It had seemed to me important for Jinny to understand and value my people. I wanted her to love the woman who had so loved me. To secure for that distant lonely admirable character the respect and affection of my child was, it seemed to me, my duty. And as a little girl Jinny had been interested in hearing about the Grey House in St. Mary's Plains, the waggon slide down the cellar door, the attic full of old trunks, crammed with faded panniered dresses and poke-bonnets, and the back garden full of hollyhocks and bachelor buttons, and larkspur. She liked to hear of the great river that one glimpsed between the houses at the bottom of the street behind the garden, and of the ships that came smiling down laden with lumber from the great forests, and she would climb into my lap and say—"Now tell me more about when you were a little girl"—but as she grew older she lost interest in these stories, and was more and more unwilling to write to her great aunt and one day, when I finished reading to her a letter from Patience, she gave a sigh and said petulantly,

"What a boring life—'Quelle vie ennuyeuse.'"

"Jinny!" I exclaimed sharply.

"But it is, Mummy. It must be. I see her there. Ah, Mon Dieu, so dismal. 'Une vieille—vieille.' An old old one—in dusty black clothes, in a horrid little room. All her stuffed birds round her in glass cases—so funny! But the atmosphere is cold. It sets the teeth on edge, and she is ugly, like a man, with big feet and hands. There—look!" She took up poor Aunt Patty's photograph from the table. "Look—what has that old woman to do with me? Why does she write to me 'My darling little Geneviève'—I'm not her darling, I don't love her at all. I don't want to think of her."

I was very angry. "Jinny, you make me ashamed."

"I can't help it," she almost screamed at me. "I can't help it. C'est plus fort que moi—she's strange—she's ugly." And she flung the photograph on the floor and stamped her feet—her face was white, her eyes blazing—"I don't want to think she belongs to us. I don't want you to love her," and she flung herself into a chair in a paroxysm of angry tears.

I sent her to bed; it was five o'clock in the afternoon, and gave orders that she was to have bread and milk for her supper but when I went to her later in the evening, though she was quiet, she stuck to her idea.

"What did you mean by your terrible behaviour, Jinny?"

She eyed me gravely from her pillow.

"I don't know, except that it is all dismal and strange in America, and I can't like Great Aunt, and if I can't—why then I can't—*Cela ne se commande pas.*"

I sat beside her, strangely depressed. Her little white bed with its rosy hangings, her curly blond head on the lace pillow, the white fur rug, the shaded lamp, the flickering fire, swam before me, blurred; I half closed my eyes, and saw another child, an ugly child with a long pigtail, in a cotton nightgown and flannel wrapper, kneeling by an old wooden bed in a bare little room, and a tall grizzled woman standing with a candle while the child said her prayers. "God bless my mother in Paris and take me to her soon, and make me keep my temper and be like my Aunt Patty—"

I had failed—I had failed.

But Jinny's voice roused me. "Papa says it is an ugly country, America— miles and miles of empty fields, just grass and grass stretching all round."

"Your father has never been there."

"I know, but he knows about it. He says he would never go there, not for anything, and that I needn't—so if I'm never to see Great Aunt—why bother?"

Why indeed? They were too much for me, those two, my husband and my child.

In my depressed moods I used to go to see Clémentine. She listened patiently, lying on a couch in purple pyjamas, smoking a cigarette through a holder a foot long, and watching me intently while I explained that I was no longer in control of my own life, that I was as impotent as a paralytic, and that I hadn't even the feeling of being a part of anything that made up existence.

"It is all unreal—I have lost touch. I can't grasp anything. There's a space,—'*infranchissable*,' between me and it. At times I feel that the only reality is the past, the remote past. My childhood is real to me, nothing much else. I remember my home in America, now this minute sitting in your room, more vividly than the house I left half an hour ago. Pleasure is a narcotic—I drug myself with it, but I don't really understand joy—I understand sorrow. Joy is a perfume that evaporates—suffering is a poison that remains."

Clémentine broke in abruptly.

"*Ma chère amie*—take my advice, I know what you need—take a lover."

I burst out laughing, but she eyed me gravely.

"You laugh, but I know what I am saying. Your life is abnormal, don't go against nature." She rolled over on an elbow and laid a hand on my knee. "You must love—it will wash away all your sick fancies. You'll see. Any one you've a liking for will do; surely you like some one? Don't be romantic, be practical. Face facts. Take things as they are, and you will find beauty, mystery, rapture and sanity. Beyond the little prosaic door of compromise you will find the world of dreams. Believe me, materialism is the only road to happy illusion, and to remain sane, we must have illusions."

Well, that was her point of view, and she may have been right. I never found out. I didn't take her advice. Perhaps had I done so, I would be in Paris now content with the illusion she promised me. Who knows?

That sort of thing is the solution of most lives. A growing lassitude, a growing fear, the feeling that one has missed life, that it will soon be too late, and at last we give in and take in the place of what we wanted, what we can get.

I couldn't. There was no one about who in the slightest degree resembled a lover—my lover. And I was sick of the subject of love. For years and years and years it had been served up to me, for breakfast, for lunch, for dinner. Every theatre, every music hall, every novel one opened, every comic paper was full of it. Travestied, caricatured, perverted or idealized, but always the same old thing—sex—sex—sex in all its ramifications—always monotonously the same; it bored me to extinction.

Philibert, fastening on this woman then that one, all my friends falling in and out of love, like ducks round a muddy pond; it put me in a rage with the world.

The War came—and with it the end of a world.

I sometimes think that God's final day of judgment will not be so very different. The Edict will go out from Heaven. Life will stop. Humanity suddenly arrested on the edge of time will look over the precipice of Eternity—will pause—will shudder—then, why should it not act? Why not revolt as it did in 1914 against the menace of universal destruction? Was it not just like that?

Death was let loose on the earth. And men refusing to die, gave their lives so that man might live.

The obliteration of life! Something else took its place. All the usual things of life disappeared, human relationships, amusements, ambitions, business, hope, comfort. The people vanished. No familiar faces anywhere. Armies took their place. Men were changed into soldiers, all alike. Women were turned into nurses. Their personalities fell from them, they appeared again, a mass of workers, colourless, uniform, with white set faces in professional clothes.

Our world, Philibert's and mine suddenly fell to pieces; all the men servants left, most of the women, called to their houses to send their men to the war. Philibert found himself one morning a private in an auxiliary service of the army; he too disappeared. The enemy was marching on Paris; Ludovic telephoned me to say that I had best leave for Bordeaux. I packed off Jinny to Nice with her grandmother. A woman whose work in the slums I had been interested in for some years, was taking an *équipe* of nurses to the front. I went with her. Philibert's secretary had orders to pack up all the valuables in the house. I forgot them. I forgot everything.

We went as you know to Alsace—were taken prisoners—sent back again.

On regaining Paris, I turned the house that I had hated into a hospital. Most of its treasures had already been packed up and sent away to a place of safety. The empty salons were turned into wards, my boudoir into an operating room. I enjoyed filling the place with rows of white iron beds and glass topped tables and basins and pails and bottles and bandages. It had been a hateful house, it made a good hospital. When it was in running order, I left again for the front.

I enjoyed the War. It set me free. I reverted to type, became a savage, enjoyed myself. In a wooden hut, on a sea of quaking mud under a cracking sky, I lived an immense life. I was a giant—I was colossal—I dwelt in chaos and was calm. With death let loose on the earth, I felt life pouring through me, beating in me; I exulted. Danger, a roaring noise, cold, fatigue, hunger, these my rations, agreed with me. I was a giantess with chilblains, and a chronic backache; I was a link in an immense machine, an atom, a speck in an innumerable host of atoms like myself, automatons, humble ugly minute things doomed to die, immortal spirits, human beings, my brothers.

I observed that my little tin trunk contained everything needful for life; soap, warm clothes, rubber boots, a brush and comb. I wanted nothing; I was content to go for days without a bath. The beef and white beans of the soldier was sufficient. I ate it ravenously.

I worked and was happy. I lifted battered men in my arms, soothed their pain, washed their bodies, scrubbed their feet; poor ugly swollen feet tramping to death in grotesque boots, socks rotting away in them. I enjoyed scrubbing them. I had, for the business, pails of hot water, scrubbing brushes, the kind one uses for floors, and slabs of yellow soap. For some months, it was my job to wash the wounded who came in from the trenches. Many of them were peasants, old bearded men who talked patois, in soft guttural voices and called me sister. Their great coats were covered with mud and blood, they crawled with vermin. I loved them. They had given their lives, they had given up their homes, their deep ploughed fields, their children, their cattle. They did not complain. Their stubborn souls looked out at me kindly from weary eyes, sunk under shaggy brows, and loving them, my brothers, I loved France, the France I had not, before, known.

We were sent from one part of the front to another. Our *équipe* had a good reputation. Passing through Paris from time to time, I found opportunities for using money. I gave, gratefully. Supply depots were organized. Every one was in need, every one was doing something. The de Joigny family were pleased with me. They made a great fuss over me when I came to Paris. They spoke of my generosity, my devotion, my courage. I loved them too, bulking them together with my comrades, my *poilus*, the men of France.

I had lost track of Philibert during the first months of the war. Then I heard that he had been put to guard one of the Paris gates. He stayed there for three months, standing in the road, with a gun, stopping the motors of officers, looking at passes. Poor Philibert! And there was no one to take any interest now in what became of him. His world was finished, his friends could do nothing for him. The France that was at war with Germany did not know him. The men who were leading the nation had never heard of him, or if they had, remembered him with a sneer.

Ludovic had entered one of the ministries. I went to him. Philibert, I pointed out, was being wasted. He was a linguist. A month later he was given the rank of interpreter and attached to the General Staff. Occasionally he accompanied Ludovic to London, or Rome, or Boulogne. Poor Philibert! He would have gone to the trenches if he could. He was too old. I scarcely saw him, for four years.

When I had leave I spent it with Jinny. He did the same, but our leave didn't often coincide.

Jinny came back to Paris and lived with her grandmother. There was a room kept ready for me in the flat.

Sometimes I motored down from the front, along the thundering roads where armies moved in the dark, and with the gigantic rumble of motor convoys, and the pounding of the guns in my ears, I would step into the little still bright sitting room with its glinting miniatures and silk hangings to find the two of them rolling bandages or knitting socks.

Jinny seemed to me quite safe there.

And in a way I was glad that the years of her girlhood should be passed in a seclusion and quiet that would have been impossible in peace time. There was no one left to spoil her now, no army of servants for her to order about, no pageant of pleasure to dazzle her eyes. The problem of her life seemed like everything else to be simplified out of recognition.

I did not know that Bianca had come back to Paris. I had forgotten her. Jinny was very sweet to me when I came. She would turn on my bath and help me take off my things, and wail over my dreadful hands, stained with disinfectants and swollen with chilblains.

"Oh, darling," she would say, "how brave you are to do it," and then she would shudder and add—"I couldn't—the sight of blood makes me sick. How you can bear the ugliness—"

And I would assure her that she was much too young to do nursing.

Your mother was very kind to me. The war had aroused her from the lassitude of old age. She had risen to meet it. Lifting her gentle head proudly, she had seemed to look out beyond the confines of her narrow seclusion, across the years, and to see her country rise before her in its old beauty, its one-time grandeur.

"France will have her revenge now," she had said, with a flash lighting her weary eyes.

And her mind appeared more vigorous. She read all the newspapers or asked Jinny to read them aloud to her. She took a great interest in my work, and seemed to regard me as some admirable but inexplicable puzzle.

"You are too brave, *mon enfant*, and too exalted. When the war is over and you come back to your old habits, to take up your old life—you will see—"

"Maybe I shall never come back to it, dear—never take up again the old life as you say."

And again she smiled, thinking that I was joking, but I was not joking, my brain was clear, I believe I knew even then, that I would never run Philibert's house again.

"You look happy, my child," she said to me one day.

"I am, *belle-mère*."

"Ah—but how curious!"

"But dear—it is not as if any one very near or dear were in danger. Philibert is safe, Blaise too, driving his ambulances."

"But the horror, the pain, the suffering all round one—look—already in our family five young men killed—your Aunt Marianne bereft of her sons—your Uncle Jacques crippled—"

"I know—I know—I do feel for them, and I do feel for France. When I say that I am happy, I only mean, that for me the equation of life is so simple, that I am content as never before."

"I see—you are happy because of the sacrifice you have made—because of all you have given up in the cause for our country. *Cela est très beau*."

"No, dear." I felt bound to try and explain. "It is not that. It is not fine at all. I haven't given up anything that I cared about. I have only got what I wanted. I have found my place, my right place—the place of a worker."

She looked puzzled, then turned it off with a smile.

Jinny was growing up and the war was slipping by over her little blond head like a monstrous shadow. She seemed in that greyness, to become unreal. I did not know what was going on in her mind.

One night in March 1918 I staggered in on her. I must have been more tired than I realized. My head was burning. The little soft still room, your mother with her hair in stiff regular waves, a lace shawl round her shoulders, and Jinny, smiling over a story book; it was like a dream.

And Jinny was like a little creature in a dream. Her idle delicate hands, her plaintive voice were strange. She had on a rose coloured frock, and was eating sweets. Some one had sent her a box of chocolates.

"Look, Mummy, chocolates—we never have them any more, do we, *petite mère*?"

I had seen the world rushing to destruction; the powers of darkness triumphant. Just beyond those walls, along the road, one came to the edge of the abyss.

"Mummy, I hate the war, *c'est si bête*—when will it end?" she pouted.

Suddenly I was angry; I felt that it was wrong for my daughter to be like that, wrong and stupid.

"Jinny," I cried—"are you asleep? Don't you understand that the world is coming to an end?"

But she looked at me with curious defiant eyes and asked, "What do you mean?"

"I mean what I say. Come with me tomorrow. Come and see. Come and help—you're no longer a child. Come!" But she drew away from me with a shiver.

"I couldn't," she said in a fine hard little voice.

And your mother broke in,

"Jane, you must be mad to suggest such a thing."

"But I want her to know—to understand—to share—"

"That is wrong. What is there for her to understand? She is a child. Her life is not involved in the war. It lies beyond. She should be protected from this nightmare."

"I want her with me."

Your mother shook her head sadly. "If you want her with you, you should stay at home and look after her. You have been admirable, you have devoted yourself, but when the war is over, you will perhaps find that you have made a mistake."

"Mistake! Would you have me stay at home while men are dying by thousands!"

She sighed gently. "Ah—well—dear—you know best, but I wonder sometimes, if you are not deluded—"

Jinny had disappeared. I found her in her bedroom, her head buried in her pillow.

"I'm a coward," she sobbed, "a coward. I would be afraid to go."

I took her in my arms. "My poor little lonely Jinny." I held her a long time—a long time—comforting her, conscience-smitten, troubled, but the next day I left again for the front, following my monstrous illusion, answering the terrible call of the greatest imposture in creation. For I was wrong and your mother was right. The war was not a fine thing. It did not save the world or renew it. It left nothing fine or noble behind. It was an obscene monster. It called up from the soil of a dozen continents all the fine strong men, and devoured them, it summoned out of the heart of humanity, heroism, and it devoured that. Courage, faith, hope, self-sacrifice, all the dreams of men were poured into its jaws and disappeared. Nothing was left but broken men, and a ruined earth.

I ought to have stayed with Jinny. That was my job.

Her nineteenth birthday was a week after the armistice. She had changed from a child to a woman while I was away, helping men to die uselessly and suddenly I saw that she was wise as I had hoped never to see her. She said to me that day,

"I know Mummy about you and Papa—you needn't pretend any more."

It was time, the family said, that she should be married.

IX

We lived at the Ritz, Philibert and Jinny and I, and we were all at sixes and sevens. Philibert's world was in pieces. He would sit by the window of our hotel salon that gave out on the Place de la Concorde, twirling his thumbs and looking at the floor as if he saw the big bright brittle thing that had been his world, lying about him in fragments.

My world! I had glimpsed it during those four years in the open; it had nothing to do with this profane ostentation of luxury, this coming and going of discreet servants, this ordering of meals and of clothes. The war had caught me up like a hurricane, had kept me suspended above the earth in a region of thunder and lightning, had carried me a long distance. Now that I had dropped to earth again, I could not get my bearings. The objects about me, the shining motors, the ermine coats, the jewelled clocks, the rich dandies, the smirkings and grimaces looked silly, detestable. I had never liked them so very much, now I hated them. I remembered the *poilus* of France who had been my comrades, dogged humble grimy heroes, who plodded to death across fields of mud in clumsy coats of faded blue that were too big for them; I thought of France, their France, a nation of men who had humbled me to the dust and had left me weeping as a sister weeps who is bereft. I belonged somehow with them, with those who had died, asking me to send their pitiful treasures to their obscure homes, and with those who still lived, who would have to begin again now the struggle for their daily bread. And I felt akin to them in their toil, on the broad brown life-giving earth under the open sky. I suffocated in Paris.

And the peace they had fought for became in the hands of diplomats and politicians a tawdry thing. Their glib trivial lips talked of it as if it were an annoying and exasperating, but still a rather amusing puzzle; the peace a million men had died for had become the sport of bureaucrats.

One asked oneself—what was the use?—No use—they had given their lives in vain. But these were the men who had sent the nations to war. Had this group of well-fed clerks and shopkeepers the right to condemn a million innocent men to death? Would they, the men of France, have gone, had they known, had they understood? Ah, the pity of it,—all the young, all the strong, all the simple folk were gone. I heard talk of Alsace-Lorraine, of the Rhine Provinces, of indemnities. Very difficult it seemed to fix the boundaries of all the new nations that had come into existence. Impossible to get enough money out of Germany to pay for the war.

Reparation! Every one was talking of reparation! But how could they hope to repair the irreparable. The war had been a gigantic crime against the "people." Who was responsible? I wanted to get out of this crowd of jabbering diplomats. I wanted to get away and think things out, but I couldn't. Jinny kept me.

Jinny's world, where was it? What was it to be? That was the immediate question, the pressing problem. She had told me that she knew all about Philibert and me. What did that mean? How much did she know? I could not tell. Her mind was closed to me.

She eyed us, her parents, strangely. "What," her eyes seemed to ask, "are you going to do about me? You must do something. You may be done for, both of you; you may have ruined your lives; I've a right to live."

It was true. We both felt it. Our nerves on edge, we saw and with exasperating clearness that we ought to join together, try to understand each other for her sake, and set about the solution of her future.

But we were strangers. The war had driven us in opposite directions. We looked at each other across an immense distance. And the fact that Jinny knew we were strangers to each other made us feel more strange. It was as if the pretence we had made for her sake had really almost become a reality; now that we need no longer keep it up, we felt uncomfortable without it. And we knew further that there was going to be a struggle between us about Jinny and we were both afraid to open the subject of her future. And we were both afraid, a little, of her. She stood there between us, lovely, aloof, mysterious, reading us, divining our thoughts, judging us. Obscurely we felt this through the lethargy that enveloped us.

Philibert was peevish. He kept asking me how much longer the Government would want to keep our house as a hospital. When I said I didn't know, he snarled, scuffled his feet and said: "Well, can't you tell them to take their wounded away? I want to get back there. I want to reorganize my existence. This, living like this makes me sick. Who knows what state the pictures are in? Some may have been stolen. The Alfred Stevens I've reason to believe were not properly packed. Everything will be damaged. I feel it. I feel it. The Aubusson tapestries from the blue salon—Janson you say, saw to them—a good firm, but I'm worried, and any way, it will take months to get everything back. What a world, what disorder! I detest disorder. Look out there at those American soldiers on their motor bicycles—riding like mad men—Paris isn't fit to live in. It's too bad—too bad—what is one to do? All these foreign troops swarming about. One can't call one's soul one's own."

"They helped to win the war."

He flung off with a growl. He suspected me of not doing what I could to help him get back to his house. He knew that had I wanted to I could have got the wounded transferred at once, but he didn't want to make the move himself at the *"Service de Santé"*—for fear that his action might seem unbecoming, and he was afraid to ask me point blank what my idea was. I had no idea—I was waiting for something to happen.

I didn't have to wait long. It is all so curious, the way it worked in together. Bianca's coming back. Why should she have come back? She was a woman of no character. I had frightened her and she had crumpled up and run away. But she hated me for humiliating her. She could never forgive me for having broken up her surface of perfection. So under the monstrous cloak of the war she had crawled back to get in my way, to trip me up, to do me in, somehow, and she had stumbled on the way to do it. She had come across Jinny.

And to a woman like Bianca, Jinny must have been like a spring in a desert, a thing of a ravishing purity and freshness. Like a woman dying of thirst, she flung herself at the child's feet. I see it all now in retrospect. Poisoned, diseased, tired to death, addled and excited by drugs, sick of men, unutterably bored with herself, here was the one thing to appeal to Bianca, the one charm capable of distracting her from the nightmare that possessed her. It is the usual tale of such women. The cycle is completed. They all end that way. And add to her corrupt affection for the child the impetus of doing me a final and deadly hurt and you have the situation before you.

By the time I came back from the front, she was sufficiently intimate with Jinny to prevail upon the child, never to mention her name to me. I knew nothing. I was unaware that they had ever spoken to each other.

It would have been better if the family had been frank with me about their plans for marrying Jinny. It would have been better because it would have been kinder, and when you want to get round a person it is as well to try kindness. Also, it would have been more intelligent. Surely they might have understood me, by this time. How is it that they did not foresee what would happen? How is it that they did not know that if they tried to force my hand I would see red? You can persuade a savage to do almost anything, but if you frighten him, he smashes things. I was the savage. They should have known better how to deal with me.

It was foolish to plot and scheme behind my back and plan to put me in the presence of a *"fait accompli."*

I can see, nevertheless, why they did it. They were afraid of me. They distrusted me. After twenty years among them, I remained for them the "foreigner." It is painful to me now to realize this, but it was so; I had not succeeded in becoming one of them. True that during the war they had admired my work, but alas, even that service now assumed a strange aspect, for the war, it appeared, had left me very queer. I had come back with very strange ideas. Once when they were all talking of the Russian Revolution and the danger of Bolshevism spreading through Europe, I had said,

"Well, what of it?" They had looked at me aghast. "But Jane," some one had cried, "it would be the end of civilization"; and I had, perhaps a little abruptly, brought out,

"Surely our civilization hasn't so much to recommend it."

They tried to laugh it off, but they were really very much worried. Aunt Clo again sent for me. "I hear you have turned socialist and are consorting with strange violent men in red ties—"

"That, dear Aunt, is nonsense. I still see Ludovic if you call him violent, and he has, at my request, presented to me some socialists. Clémentine and I are interested you know in the strange ferment of ideas that is the aftermath of the war. Frankly I find these people more alive than those of my own class, but the socialist deputies don't really appeal to me," and I added maliciously, "they don't go far enough. Lenin, now, he is consistent, he has an idea—"

Your Aunt Clo chuckled—"No wonder the family is in a fever about you."

I was annoyed. "You must tranquillize them. Clem and I go to the meetings of the third International, but I'm not going to do anything you know. It's only that I find it such a bore to go on talking as if the world were or ever could be as it was before the war. Let me have any little distractions. They'll do no one any harm. As long as Jinny exists, they can feel quite safe. I shan't throw a bomb or take the vow of poverty. Communism doesn't appeal to me when I think of my child. I want her to be safe."

At the mention of Jinny your aunt's face had grown serious, as serious as such a round expanse of placid flesh could grow.

"Well, what are your ideas for Jinny," she snapped.

I was startled. I stammered. "My ideas—?"

"Yes—you know don't you, that she's got to be married?"

"Ah—but in time. In my country—girls don't—"

"This isn't your country. Jinny is nineteen, she's very conspicuous. There are already several *prétendants*—"

"*Prétendants?*"

"Yes. Hasn't Philibert consulted you?"

"No."

"It is as I thought."

"What do you mean, Aunt?"

She pounded on the floor with her cane. She was almost impotent now and spent her days in an armchair, from which she had to be lifted to bed by two servants. And her temper was short.

"Don't be a fool! I am warning you. You'd better ask Philibert. Don't tell him I told you. Oh well—do if you like, what is it to me, to have him angry?"

I was very much disturbed but didn't go to Philibert and ask him what he was up to, because I wanted to gain time, and it didn't occur to me as possible that he would really commit himself without consulting me. I wanted to gain time for Jinny herself. I had hopes for her of what seemed to me the happiest of all solutions.

Philibert thinks to this day that the poor little abortive romance of Jinny and Sam Chilbrook was my doing. Poor sweet babies. I had had no hand in their falling in love. It had seemed to me to be the work of God and I had kept out of it.

Sam had come to Paris from the army for the peace conference. He was attached to the President's suite. I had known his father and his mother and his grandfather and grandmother. Every one knew the Chilbrooks. They lived in Washington and Philadelphia, and the men of the family had a taste for the diplomatic service. The grandfather you remember was the American Ambassador in London, years ago. They were very well off.

Sam was a romantic, with a humorous grin and the nicest voice in the world. He had nice young eyes, and freckles on his nose. He liked to do things in a hurry. He met Jinny at luncheon at the American Embassy and fell in love with her at first sight.

"Please ask me to tea alone," he said to me after lunch. "I want to talk to you. I want to marry your daughter"—and he cocked an eyebrow like a puppy.

I laughed and said, "But I don't think you can."

"Please ask me to tea anyway and please Madame de Joigny don't laugh at me. Love at first sight is sometimes true love, you know."

I asked him to tea, and he put us into our car.

Jinny wrapped in grey furs, her face flushed palest pink, her eyes shining, snuggled up to me and took my hand.

"What a nice lunch party, Mummy."

"Did you enjoy it, darling?"

"Yes. I talked to the American with red hair. He has a face like a sky terrier—he was very amusing." Then with a little sigh, "Darling Mummy, I do love you so."

When Sam came to tea—he had seen Jinny twice in the meantime—he wasted no time.

"I do seriously and truly want to marry your daughter, Madame de Joigny."

"But you can't, she's a Roman Catholic."

"That's easy. I'll become one."

I laughed again. I was beginning to adore him. "I will take care of her," he said, "as you would want me to take care of her. She would be safe with me. She would be worshipped. I would kneel to her, and I would make her happy. She would be happy, I vow to you, she would be happy."

"I am afraid it is impossible."

"Why—?"

"Her father has other ideas."

"Let me go to him."

"You may of course, but he will send you packing."

He flushed painfully and I saw in his eyes a deep shy hurt look, the look of modesty and innocence—and faith.

"But if she loved me, surely he wouldn't refuse then—"

"Perhaps not. I don't know. He might all the same. It would depend on how much she cared."

"I will make her care."

"But," I broke off, I hesitated. Why should I have been so scrupulous? What obligation had I to warn Philibert that his daughter might fall in love with this eligible American? Still I did have a scruple.

"It is not considered fitting, you know, in our French world, for a young man to pay court to a *jeune fille* without her parents' approval."

"Then what am I to do?"

"I don't know."

We sat in silence a moment.

Suddenly he got up. He stood there before me, tall, clean, honest.

"You're not against me, Madame de Joigny?"

"No, I'm not against you."

"Well then, I guess I know what to do. I guess I can wait. You can trust me, you know. I won't bother your daughter. All the same, we are all in Paris together, and I can't help seeing her sometimes, can I?" His eyes smiled, but he was very serious. I realized how serious he was when Philibert remarked a few days later that he had met quite a nice young American lunching at the Jockey Club, quite a man of the world, a national polo player, a Monsieur Chilbrook. Did I know him? Yes, I said I knew him, and had known his family always. Philibert thought I might ask him to dinner with Colonel and Mrs. House, the following week. I did so, but Sam made me no sign. He was perfectly correct. The only thing that was noticeable was his successful effort to interest Philibert. I myself was surprised. Poor Sam—little good it did him.

Jinny seemed happy. She enjoyed being grown up and going to parties. In June we gave her a coming out ball, for in spite of all my premonitions we had again taken possession of our house. After that I took her to a number of dances. She was surrounded by young men of course. Sam was only one of a dozen; she treated them all with the same radiant aloofness. She made me no confidences. Her intimacy with her father was greater than ever. Together they had supervised the unpacking and rearrangement of the household treasures. Philibert was educating her. I observed that she had his flair for bibelots. She had already all the patter of the amateur collector. They went shopping together a good deal. More often than not, coming in from some luncheon I would find that they had gone out together for the afternoon.

On one such day, when I was sitting alone, Sam Chilbrook was announced. He was troubled. His eyes were dark, his young face tired.

"Jinny loves me, I know she does, Madame de Joigny, but she is unhappy. It is time I went to her father. You see I'm afraid," he stammered, "afraid that she won't have the courage—if I don't—"

"But have you spoken to her—I thought you promised."

"I've not spoken—I've kept my promise, but I wish you hadn't exacted it. I know your daughter now. I know her character, and I love her. She spoke yesterday in a way that frightened me—"

"What did she say?"

"She said that she loved her father better than any one in the world."

"That was all?"

"Yes, no—not quite."

"What else did she say?"

"She said that if it came to a struggle between them, or between you and him about her—she was sure she would do what he wanted."

"Well, then go to him!" He left me at five; it was that same afternoon only a few minutes after he had gone, that you, Blaise, were announced.

I understand now what it cost you to do what you did. *Tout simplement* it cost you the affection of your family. You ranged yourself on my side, against them. That was what it amounted to. That anyway was the way they took it.

I remember your face when you told me that I had best go round to your mother's flat at once, that Philibert and Jinny were there and some other persons whom I ought to see. I didn't at first grasp what you meant. What other persons? The little Prince Damas de Barbagne of the family des Deux Ponts and his uncle.

"In your mother's drawing-room?"

"Yes."

"With Jinny?"

"Yes."

"But I refused to present him to her only a few months ago."

"I know."

"What then—?" Suddenly it dawned on me.

"Philibert!" I almost shouted, "Philibert has done this without consulting me. That miserable little creature."

You nodded.

I knew the Damas boy. Philibert and I had stayed with his uncle in their dreadful old prison of a place.

The young man had made on me a very disagreeable impression. His reputation was of the worst, and his appearance did not belie it. He was small and weak legged and had no chin. His skin was bad and his eyes yellow. He professed in those days a great admiration for the Crown Prince of Germany, and I fancy had taken the latter as his model. One of the things that amused him was, I found out, the torturing of animals. Fan had told me a tale about him that I had never forgotten.

One day he was terribly bored. Not knowing what to do with himself he brought all his dogs into the house. He had twelve, all kinds, greyhounds, setters, great danes. He told his man to keep them in one of the salons, while he went into the next one, and loaded his revolver. Disgusted with life, he had become disgusted with his dogs. He called them one by one. Then as they came through the door, shot them dead. He didn't miss one. He got each one between the eyes.

"Pour parlers" of marriage were going on you told me, between Philibert and the august uncle of this heir to a bankrupt principality. I saw it all. The house of the Deux Ponts was royal. It was a branch of the Nettleburgs but had maintained a strict neutrality during the war. With nearly every throne in Europe crumbling into dust, Philibert still wanted a crown for his daughter's head. In the midst of the savage passion of anger that had seized me, I could have yelled with laughter. Philibert still believed in his ridiculous baubles. He wanted to put his little girl on a throne. Well, I would stop him.

She was mine. She was mine.

I had borne her out of my body. She belonged to me. I remembered the months before she was born, I remembered the child in my womb, stirring — the obscure passionate tenderness welling up in me—the mysterious sense of union. I remembered Philibert's disgust with my deformity, his constant absence. He had left me to myself during those months. He had left me, of course, to go to other women. I had brought Jinny into the world alone. The pain had been mine, and mine the ecstasy. What had Philibert to do with my child?

Now they proposed to dispose of her without my consent. They proposed to hand her over to a degenerate. Well, they wouldn't, I wouldn't stop them.

My entrance created something of a sensation in your mother's drawing-room. They were all there. I had time to take them all in, while they stared at me. The august uncle who looked like the Emperor Francis Joseph was standing in the window with Philibert. Your mother had Jinny on one side of her, at the tea table, the Princeling on the other. Her face blanched when she saw me. There was terror in her eyes, physical terror, what did she think I was going to do?

Philibert was of course the first to recover himself. He came forward in his most perfect manner.

"*Chère amie*, I am so glad that after all you were able to come. I had explained to his Royal Highness about your terrible migraine—"

I took his cue. The pompous uncle and the pimple-faced Damas kissed my hand, first one then the other. I asked your mother for a cup of tea, and drank it slowly, conscious of Jinny's eyes on my face. What did they mean, those great brown starry eyes? What was going on in her mind? I hadn't any idea.

"I have interrupted you," I said putting down my teacup. "Pray continue your talk."

No one spoke.

"You were perhaps gathered together for a purpose that concerns my daughter? No?"

Philibert went crimson; the uncle coughed; I waited; your mother rattled the tea things; she looked at Philibert, he looked at her. "*Mon enfant,*" she quavered, at last, "His Royal Highness has honoured you with a demand for your daughter's hand in marriage, and as you no doubt are aware, your husband," her voice almost failed her, but she controlled it, "your husband, my son, is disposed to think that possibly these two young people would be very happy together."

"Is it to ask their opinion that they have been brought here?" I asked quickly.

The uncle coughed again. The little shrimp at the table stammered— "Not at all, not at all. My opinion is very well known to Monsieur de Joigny. I should be honoured."

I rose to my feet. I knew now just how far matters had gone. They had gone very far indeed! I had no choice. It was necessary to be quite definite. I faced the older man.

"There has been a mistake, your Highness, I do not approve of this marriage."

Philibert made a jump towards me—an exclamation. I waved him off.

"I have other ideas for my daughter. You must excuse me from explaining what they are. And now I must beg you to let me take this child home. Come Geneviève." For a moment she hesitated, her poor little face crimson, her eyes filled with tears. I took her hand and drew her with me out of the door.

That night Philibert and I had a terrible scene. I need not go into it in detail. I cannot bear to recall it. It seems incredible now that we should have behaved as we did. Things were said that will rankle for ever, things that would have made it impossible, even if it hadn't been for the last ghastly episode of Bianca, for us to go on living side by side. I look back with shame to that hour, I must have been beside myself. What was goading me on more than anything else, was the realization that Jinny was against me. She had been shocked by my behaviour. That was how it had struck her. She had been horrified and humiliated. That was all. I saw it in her eyes. She didn't care to know why I had done what I did. She only hated my having done it. She looked at me with fear and almost, I thought, with a shiver of repulsion.

I refused to give Jinny a penny if he married her off without my approval. He informed me that I could not, by French law, disinherit her and that he would find a way of bringing me to my senses. As for Sam Chilbrook—Philibert dealt with him the next morning, I don't know what he said to him, but the boy never came back. I never saw him again. It must have been something pretty horrible.

X

There is little more to tell you. You know about Jinny's subsequent marriage and how after all Philibert, if he did not secure Prince Damas, his heart's desire, is still well enough satisfied with the young Duke, his son-in-law. Philibert wanted the Duke, so I let him have him. Jinny wanted the house in Paris so I gave it to her. The three live there together, quite harmoniously I am told. And I? I do not pretend that Jinny's husband is a cad. He is no doubt, as nice as most young men about town. I merely regret that he does not love her nor she him. Doubtless they will get on very well once that fact is established between them.

You see Jinny's marriage was my supreme failure. I have lost her, I can never do anything more for her. She will never turn to me in joy—or in trouble.

She hates me. It was because she came to hate me that I gave way. She believed that I killed Bianca. I didn't, but then I might have, I have no way of knowing whether or not I would have killed her.

I am trying to explain to you why I have come back to St. Mary's Plains. You remember Patience Forbes' will. It read—"To my beloved niece Jane Carpenter, now called the Marquise de Joigny, I leave the Grey House and all that is in it, because some day, she may want some place to go." Well, she was right—I came back because I had no other place to go to. I came back but I came too late. The people who lived here and who loved me are all dead and I cannot, somehow, communicate with them as I had hoped to. I do not know what Patience Forbes would say of my life, and I shall never know. Her ghost does not comfort me because I failed her too. I let her die, here alone.

They found her, you know on the floor by her bed, in her dressing gown, the candle on the table burned down to its socket; she must have been saying her prayers. Her Bible was open on the patchwork quilt; her spectacles were beside it and three of my letters, some weeks old, also, strangely enough, a facsimile (reduced) of the Declaration of Independence, with a pencil note "To send to Jane." You know how it reads: "When in the course of human events, it becomes necessary for one people to dissolve the political bonds which have connected them with another and to assume among the powers of the earth, the separate and equal station to which the Laws of Nature and of Nature's God entitle them…. We hold these truths to be self-evident, that all men are created equal, that they are endowed by their Creator with certain unalienable rights that among these are Life, Liberty and the pursuit of Happiness—"

The last lines I have quoted were underlined. What did she mean by them? What did she want them to mean for me, lying there, dying, going out on the great journey alone from the empty Grey House—dead, alone in the house through that long night with the Bible and the Declaration of Independence beside her?

I do not know what she meant—I only know that I left her alone to die.

And I do not know whether I have come back defeated or victorious. In the conduct of life I was defeated. Whenever I tried to do right, I did wrong. To the people I loved I was a curse. I had a few friends. You remain, and Clémentine and Ludovic. But I must lose you too, now. I feel it my destiny to be alone. I did not understand how to live among men. But there are hours when sitting here in this shabby room, I am conscious of a feeling of high stark bitter triumph. At such times I think of my father's grave over there beyond the horizon, on a wide prairie under a high sky. A stone. That stone and I are linked together. I loved Philibert once, I love Jinny. I am alone now, but I shall hold out. I shall not give in. My life has been wasted, but I shan't end it. I shall see it through. It stretches behind me, a confused series of blunders. I try to understand. It is finished, but I go on living. There is nothing left for me to do but wait. Maybe if I wait long enough I shall understand what it is all for.

I love France, but I had to come back here, and I know that I will stay. It is right for me to be here. It is fitting and just. In some way that I cannot explain the equation of my life is satisfied by my coming, and the problem—I see it as clear, precise and cold as a problem in algebra—is solved.

Here, in St. Mary's Plains there is nothing for me. The big bustling awkward town is full of strangers who have no time to interest themselves in a derelict woman who has drifted back to them from "foreign parts." My return seems to those who remember me to be a confession of failure. They are not interested in failure, so they leave me alone. It is as well. I did not come back to talk but to think. I did not come back to begin something new, but to understand something old and finished. I do not need these bright brave ignorant young people. To do what I am doing it is necessary to be alone.

But to go back to my story. Jinny had a shivering fit that night, after the scene in your mother's flat. Her maid called me. She lay on her back in bed her teeth chattering, her knees drawn up and knocking together. We put hot water bottles to her feet and her sides. It was a warm night late in June, but she kept whispering that she was cold. The doctor when he came said that it was nerves. He prescribed bromide and perfect quiet for some time, afterwards a change. He told me that she had a hypersensitive nervous organism, and should be protected always as much as possible from excitement or emotional strain.

She slept quietly towards morning. Her hair clung to her forehead in little damp curls, soft pale golden hair like a child's. Her closed eyelids were swollen above the long brown eyelashes. She lay on her side with both hands together under her cheek, her lovely young body at rest. Beautiful Jinny.

I sat watching her. The sound of her father's voice and of mine, saying hideous things rang in my ears.

Beyond the open window, the darkness was turning to light. All about were still shuttered houses filled with sleeping people, a million sleeping men and women. Their dreams and their weariness, and their disappointments seemed to be rising like a mist above the hot close houses.

I had promised Patience Forbes to love Jinny enough—enough for what? Enough—for this—to save her this.

I had failed, and I felt old, so very old, and at the same time my heart was full of childish longings and weakness. If only some one would come and comfort me. If only some one would take my responsibilities from me. I wanted help and relief. I thought of you. I knew that you, Blaise, would have helped me, but Philibert had shut the door in your face that evening and had snarled at me horrible things, saying he would never have you in the house again. He had accused you and me of a criminal affection for each other. I remembered his livid face and twitching lips. A feeling of sickness pervaded my body and soul. Jinny, asleep, was fragrant as a flower. I was contaminated, unclean.

Suddenly she was there,—Patience Forbes, my Aunt Patience, standing on the other side of Jinny's bed. She had on her black mackintosh and her bonnet with the strings tied in a knot under her chin. But she was not quite as I had last seen her. The wisps of hair that straggled down under her bonnet were white. There was something terrible and grand about her. She was old, very old. Her face was brown and withered. She looked thin, emaciated, her eyes sunken. She looked starved. Her clothes were very shabby, the clothes of a poor woman. She was grand and terrible. Her sunken eyes shone with a splendour I had never seen before. She was looking down at Jinny—I saw her smile an ineffable smile of unutterable beauty, then I waited breathlessly, with such longing, with an anguish of longing. Surely in a moment she would turn to me, gather me into her arms—now—now she was turning—

"Mummy—what time is it?" Jinny was sitting up in her bed rubbing her eyes, yawning. Sunlight shone through the parted curtains. I looked at my watch.

"Seven o'clock, darling."

"I would like some coffee. Is any one about? I'm so hungry. Oh dear—" She sank back onto her pillow. "I remember now, I remember—why did I wake up?"

The next day, I received a cable announcing my Aunt Patience's death. Jinny was lying on her "chaise longue" eating chocolates. She said—"Poor thing, but she was very old, wasn't she?"

"Yes, seventy-five years old."

"Older than *grandmère*!"

"Yes, several years older—" Jinny was not interested. There was no one in Paris who had ever seen Patience Forbes.

Jinny seemed quite well again; only a little languid and silent. She spent most of the day on her chaise longue, reading, having her nails manicured, having her hair brushed, eating sweets, dozing; she was quite affectionate.

One evening she said, "I think, Mummy, that I would like to go into a convent." She had on, I remember, a white satin négligé trimmed with white fox, and emerald green brocade slippers. I must have smiled.

"Don't smile, Mummy. I'm not joking, I have thought it all out. '*Il faut se connaître.*' I am weak, I have a weak character. I liked Sam Chilbrook, but I didn't dare say so. I disliked the Prince very much, I didn't dare say so. If you and Papa could agree, I would be content to do what you decided for me—but you can't agree. No, no, don't be tragic. Don't be so sorry. Let us be reasonable. If you never agree on a husband for me, I must either choose one for myself and run off with him and be married, or become an old maid. Neither seems a very nice idea, does it—but to be a nun—that is beautiful. You remember when I was little and tried to lead the saintly life—you thought it ridiculous. You did not understand. There is something in me that you do not take seriously because I am lazy and like pretty things and marrons glacés. But it is there all the same. If you were a true Catholic I could explain. To be a nun is beautiful—beautiful, and I would be safe there, and out of the way. For you and Papa there would be no more problem, you would not have to live together any more. And the sisters love me;

they would be glad to receive me. They are so gentle, so sweet—you have no idea, and quite happy you know. Sometimes they laugh and make little jokes, like children. It is much happier in the convent than here."

It was I that broke down then, and cried. I cried miserably, ugly tears, sobbing against Jinny's languid knees. I, a middle-aged woman, disfigured, with a swollen face, a great, strong, tired, drab creature, in whose tough body life had gone stale, was humbled before my beautiful child.

I asked her forgiveness. Brokenly I begged her to be kind. And I apologized to her. Kneeling beside her I tried to explain my inability to believe in any creed, any dogma of the Church, I spoke of truth, I proclaimed as if before a high spiritual judge, my honest search for truth. Pitiful? Yes— but do you not believe that it is often so—mothers kneeling to their children, avowing their mistakes, their failures, begging for love?

I was desperate to destroy the thing that separated us—I was so lonely so alone—it seemed to me that this moment held my one chance, my one hope of drawing my child close to me. I looked up at her. Cool, lovely youth holding aloof, if only she would come, if only she would respond and take me in her slim fresh innocent arms. Ah, the relief it would be—the comfort!

"Jinny—Jinny—love me—I need your love, I am your mother. I am growing old. There is no one left for me to turn to—no one to advise me, no one to care for me, except you. Do you realize what I mean? My life is finished, it goes on only in you, only for you. Jinny, Jinny, don't you understand, I need you."

She stroked my hair lightly with delicate fingers, but looking up, I saw that her face was contracted in a nervous spasm—of distaste. A moment longer I waited staring up at her face with a longing that must have communicated itself to her, a longing so intense that I felt it going out of me in waves but she made no sign.

"I do love you, Mummy—you know I do," she said in a dull little voice.

I stumbled to my feet and left the room.

Philibert had gone away, so when the doctor said a few days later that Jinny should go to Biarritz it was I who took her, though I knew she would rather have gone with some one else. I should have sent her with a companion. Had I left her alone then things might have been mended, but I was too jealous, and though I knew the truth in my heart I couldn't bear to admit that my child didn't like being with me. I kept on thinking of ways to win back her love, silly feeble ways. I was like a despairing and foolish lover who cannot bring himself to leave the object of his passion though he knows that everything he does exasperates her. I had no pride. I gave her presents.

I did errands for her that the servants should have done. With a great lump of burning pain in my heart I went on smiling and busy, avoiding her eyes and fussing about her, and she was exquisitely patient and polite.

I do not know to this day whether Bianca followed us to Biarritz knowingly and with intent, or not. Clémentine told me afterwards that she had seen Bianca with Philibert at Fontainebleau at the Hôtel de France on the Sunday, the day he left Jinny and me, after our scene, but whether she learned from Philibert during the week they spent together of Jinny's whereabouts and tracked her down, I cannot tell. Probably not. Yet it may be.... It is all so strange that one can believe anything. Philibert and Bianca together—after all those years—that in itself is extraordinary. What sort of relationship could have existed between them at the end? I don't know. I do not attempt to understand. They were people beyond my comprehension, but some thing that they possessed in common, some bond, some feeling profound and complex, had evidently survived.

It is useless dwelling upon their problem. Revolting? Evil? I suppose so, and yet their infernal passion has somehow imposed upon me a dread respect. Philibert after Bianca's death crumpled up as if by magic into a silly little old man. I saw it happen to him, there in that hotel where he came rushing on receipt of the news. He stood in my room shaking and disintegrating visibly before my eyes, profoundly unpleasant, pitiful. It was as if Bianca had held in her hand the vital stuff of his life, and as if with her death he was emptied of all energy and power.

All this happened you see at Biarritz where Bianca came and found us.

I am almost sure that I did not think of killing Bianca, even at the very end, when I found myself in her room, standing over her. And yet, if she hadn't taken that overdose of morphine herself, that very night, what would have happened I don't know.

It is very curious, her dying like that, whether by accident or intent, no one will ever know, on just that night, and in just that place, involving me in Jinny's eyes, for ever. God knows there were plenty of other places on the earth where she might more logically have chosen to breathe her last. Why not in Venice in that great dark vaulted palace of hers with the black water lapping under her balcony? Or in her castle in Provence, where she lived with her demons, or in Paris in the red lacquer den with its golden cushions? Any one of those settings would have been more in keeping—but in the Plage Hôtel—above the sea, no, there was no poetic justice in her choosing that spot. And if it was an accident, then the freakish spirit who planned it did it with his diabolical eye on Jinny and me.

We had been a week in Biarritz. Jinny had found some young people with whom she played tennis in the afternoon. Occasionally I left her for a game of golf. One day coming back I saw her sitting on the terrace with a woman whose eccentric elegance was familiar, but whom I did not at first recognize. I saw her back, long and narrow, a fur wrap slipping from the shoulders, an attenuated arm hanging across the back of her chair. Jinny, all in white, her hair a golden halo in the light of the sun that was setting behind her, was facing her. Their faces were close together. The older woman was leaning forward. She had Jinny's hand in both of hers. There was about this pose something intimate and intense. Jinny started up at the sight of me, and the woman turned her small dark head round and gave me a little nod. It was Bianca.

She was very much changed. I remember every detail of her appearance, her red turban, her soiled white gown, her fur coat that looked somehow rather shabby. She was carelessly dressed, she had an air both tawdry and neglected. Actually she didn't look clean. Her face was startling. The makeup was badly done. Once it had been a smooth even white, now the eyelids were yellow and on the thin cheek-bones were spots of red. The finger nails of the beautiful hand that hung limp over the back of her chair were enamelled pink but dirty. She had obviously been going down hill at a rapid pace, and for one instant this realization in the midst of my panic at finding her with Jinny, gave me pleasure. For Bianca to turn into an untidy hag; that was something to make me wickedly exultant.

She looked at me calmly out of her monstrous eyes. "It is centuries since we met," she said. I did not reply. I was trembling and I saw that she saw my trembling. Her discoloured eyelids lifted, and sent out their old fiery blue light. Her eyes grew more enormous. She stared into mine and her thin pointed lips curved into a smile. "Not since Deauville, after the death of poor Fan Ivanoff—four, five, six years—is it not? Before the war. I have been so little in Paris." Her eyelids fluttered, her eyes deadened, a curious lassitude spread over her suddenly. She drooped in her chair, she was like a bruised soiled faded plant, almost to me she seemed to exhale the odour of decay. "I have travelled—I have wandered—Spain—Portugal—America—Buenos Aires—I am so restless, I go anywhere—" her voice trailed off. She gave herself a little jerk. Her eyes slid to Jinny, dwelt upon her. "Your daughter and I have been talking. '*Quel amour d'enfant*' —so *exaltée*, so sensitive."

Jinny, it seemed to me, was rather pale. She stood nervously clasping her hands, her eyes moving from one of us to the other.

"The Princess brought me a message from Papa," she said in a shrill defiant note.

"Ah yes, I saw him just the other day—where was it? I cannot remember, I have no memory, but he told me you were here."

The long unclean hand again went out to Jinny. It caressed her arm. I shivered. "Don't," I muttered in spite of myself.

Bianca jerked, a nervous twitch, and gave a little laugh.

"Ah, you see, my child, your mother doesn't like—" She broke off. Jinny's face was crimson now. "Never mind—she is perhaps right. I will leave you now. I go to the Casino. It is all so boring. Perhaps later—"

She did not look back at us as she trailed away. I thought to see toads jumping up from the imprint of her feet.

Upstairs, I said as quietly as I could:

"How is it that you know the Princess?"

"Papa introduced me to her long ago—when I was quite a little girl."

"You have seen her since?"

"Yes."

"Often?"

"Several times."

"You admire her?"

"Yes—she is strange. I like strange things."

"I do not like her at all," I said curtly.

Jinny sat on the edge of a table, poking into a box of chocolates.

"Why don't you like her, Mummy?"

"Because she is a bad woman."

"Oh no, surely you are wrong. She is Papa's oldest friend." She popped a sweet into her mouth.

"Who told you that?"

"She did herself—and besides, I know—I have known a long time. She was his first romance, his—what do you call it,—his calf love."

I burst into harsh laughter. My laugh sounded to me ugly and terrible. Jinny's face went pale; I crossed to the window.

"What else did she tell you?" I asked with my back to her.

"She has told me about life in convents, she is very devout. She has often been in convents to '*faire une retraite.*' She says it is very soothing there, but that I should not be in a hurry about making a decision."

"Ah!"

"Yes—she seems to understand me—she conveys much sympathy. She has a magnetism—it draws one."

"I know."

"What is the matter, Mummy? You are angry. I feel sorry for the Princess, she is so alone in the world, and she says she loves me, that she is wonderfully attracted to me, that I would do her good. She called herself laughing you know, but with a sadness—she called herself '*une damnée*.'"

I could contain myself no longer. "*Une damnée*—well, that's just what she is—" I wheeled about. I felt my voice rising in spite of me. "I forbid you ever to speak to her again. Do you understand? You must never speak to her again." My child's face hardened. The eyes widened, the nostrils dilated. She was very pale. Something sinister seemed to rise between us. She receded from me.

"Don't—don't!" she whispered backing away.

"Don't—don't what?" I cried back. "You don't want me to stand between you and this horrible woman who has ruined my life—ruined your father—ruined us all—and who wants now to ruin you."

"No, no, no—don't say such things." She was screaming too now. "It is wicked of you to say such things. I don't believe it. I don't believe you. I won't believe it. I love Papa, I love Papa better than you, better than you. You have done it. You have ruined his life. I know it, I have seen it. I have seen you look at him with hatred. How do you think it feels to see one's parents hating each other? Ruined? Yes, you have ruined my life. You—you—you ought never to have brought me into the world. I wish I were dead—I wish I were dead—" She rushed into her room and banged the door.

I told myself looking out over that horrible sea, immense, restless and cold, that nothing irretrievable had happened, that Jinny would come back to me, that she would forgive, that things would be the same. But I had no faith, and what did that mean, if things were the same. Was that sufficient as a basis for the future? What if we went on and on having scenes—screaming at each other. I was ashamed, and shaken, and I was afraid. Bianca had come back—Bianca was there, down the corridor—close to us, close to Jinny. "Une damnée"? she called herself.

I must take Jinny away in the morning, but what good would that do in the end? Bianca would follow us sooner or later to Paris. Jinny would be sure to see her. I had a ridiculous picture of Bianca pursuing us from place to place, lying in wait for Jinny—laying infernal schemes. I remembered what

I had recently heard of her strange habits, her vicious tastes, of the effect she had had on certain women. I saw her, a restless, haunted damned soul, the slave of infernal passions, a prowl in the world, hunting for victims, growing more implacable as she grew old.

I dressed for dinner. Jinny sent word she would dine in bed. On the way to the lift, I saw Bianca go into her room. She looked back at me over her shoulder, half smiling but with a curious look in her eyes. Was it fear? Was it regret? I thought for a long time of that look, I thought of it all evening sitting in my high window, listening to the interminable boom of the waves. Her presence, near, under the same roof was intolerable, like a dreadful smell, or an excruciating nagging sound. I was feeling again, even now, through my terror for Jinny, and in spite of my sickened sense of the woman's decay, the impact of her personality. She existed there beyond my door, special, vivid, intense, and I began to feel her decrepitude as a reproach, her ruin as a responsibility. Moment by moment I felt her, exerting on me a horrible pressure. There had been in her dreary face, an appeal, a claim, a despair that laid on me a weight. In her eyes, there had been, memory. It was that that haunted me. Somehow, actually, her eyes had reflected the past and had dragged my mind back, afar back to the days when we had been friends. I remembered everything. In their deep burning blue light that was like a lamp lighted inside a corpse, I saw her youth and my youth glowing, and I remembered how we had been together, two strong young things, curiously linked, responding to each other, with a sympathy that should have been a good thing to us. She had said once, "Jane, I love you—you are the only friend I have ever had." And I remembered the day she had talked to me of herself in that old castle in Provence, above the white road and dusty vineyard.

I felt sick and was aware of an intolerable physical pain in my side. Bianca, who had been so beautiful, and whom I had loved divinely once, was a rotten rag now, soiled, dingy, bad smelling—and I hated her. We hated each other. Our youth was gone—and all its beauty. There was nothing under the sun but ugliness and hatred and the principle of life was decay.

I walked the room. Jinny was asleep—lovely youth—fresh and sweet. What would become of her? Bianca and I were two old women, done for.

To protect Jinny from her, Jinny who hated me, that was all I could do now. I must go to Bianca. Either she would respond to me and give in to me because of the memory that had stared out of her face, or I would make her; I would force her to do what I wanted as I had done before, but this was to be the last time—this must be the end.

I looked in at Jinny. She seemed to be asleep. Out in the corridor some one had turned the light low. The long red carpet of the corridor led straight to Bianca's room. I went out quickly closing the door after me. It took an instant to reach the door of Bianca's sitting room. I knocked. There was no answer. I opened it and went in. To the right another door was open, a light shone through. Bianca was in bed. I could see her. Her eyes were closed. The lamp beside her bed shone on her face, a peculiar odour pervaded the room. "I will wake her and have it out with her," I thought to myself.

I went into the bedroom. A number of bottles, a small aluminum saucepan and a hypodermic syringe were on the night table beside her. She was breathing heavily and noisily, drawing quick, regular, snoring breaths. It was obvious that she was drugged; the noise of her breathing was very ugly. Her face was sharp and pinched and evil. An extraordinary disorder prevailed in the room. I remember now being astonished by it. Untidy heaps of underwear about, not very clean, dragged lacey things on the floor, a high-heeled slipper on the centre table, a litter on the toilet table that reminded one of an actress's dressing room, a tray with a champagne bottle and a plate of oyster shells on the end of the chaise longue. And pervading every thing that horrid odour of drugs and the sound of snoring.

I stood for a moment looking down at the woman in the bed. The sight of her filled me with loathing. How unclean she was! She was like a corpse. Already she was half dead. She was something no longer human, scarcely alive. Her sleep had the quality of a disease, her breath was poisonous.

Suddenly I felt some one beside me. It was Jinny, wrapped in her dressing gown. White as a sheet, she stood staring down at that dreadful face. "I heard you open the door," she whispered, "I followed you. What is it? What is the matter?"

"Nothing," I murmured. "She is drugged, that is all." I pointed to the bottle of ether, the syringe in its little box. "Come," I repeated nervously, "come away." It was horrible to have Jinny in that room.

"But, Mummy, can't we do something, oughtn't we to do something?"

"No—come—it's nothing—I mean she's used to it." I dragged Jinny away.

The next morning, the people in the hotel were informed that the Princess was dead. She had died in the night of an overdose of morphine.

It was Marie, Jinny's maid, who burst in on her with the news, while she was having her café au lait in bed. I heard Jinny give a shriek and ran in to her—she had fainted.

Isn't it strange the way it all happened? One would think that God had a hand in it, but if there is a God, why should He want my child to believe that I had committed a murder? It is that that I do not understand.

Jane's narrative was ended with those words. She had talked that last night of my visit to her in St. Mary's Plains, until nearly morning. Her forehead grew damp as she talked and her lips dry and her words carried along the sustained note of her voice like little frightened sounds.

And during all those hours that she talked, I remember hearing no other sound. I heard no voice in the street, nor the sound of trams going by nor of dogs barking. In our concentration we were as cut off from contact with the living world as if the whole city of St. Mary's Plains had been turned to stone.

That was just a year ago today. I suppose she is still there in that meagre faded room, I can see her there, sitting in the high wooden chair that belonged once upon a time to Patience Forbes. The wind is hurrying across the immense prairies of her awful wide empty country. It rattles the windows of that frail wooden house. She is alone there.

Last night we talked of Jane in Ludovic's rooms. Clémentine was there and Felix, we had been to Cocteau's ballet. Jane would have enjoyed it, they said; she would have understood the joke, and perceived the beauty.

Clémentine moved restlessly about. "What is she doing now, I wonder? Surely she is doing something—"

"She is thinking things out."

"Good God!" groaned Felix. "Our Jane—our great haughty creature— she wasn't meant to think. She was meant to be looked at—she ought never to have had an idea in her head. What a waste—what a wicked waste."

Clémentine on a footstool by the fire nursed her knees. "She did really think we were immoral. We took life as a joke. She couldn't understand. She believed in the Bible—all the part about being wicked. She didn't know it, but her creed was the ten commandments. She is a victim of the ten commandments."

Ludovic shook his head. "She was right," he said, "all her life she wanted to do right—now she has done it. She has gone back to her people. She should never have come here. There was nothing for her here, but ourselves."

"And were we nothing?" cried Clémentine, "didn't we love her well? Didn't we understand?"

"No, we didn't understand. And we didn't count. We didn't count for her."

Ah, Jane, Jane, it was true. We didn't count. In all your story, you scarcely alluded to us. We were just your friends who loved you, and we didn't count. If only you could know what we know about yourself; if only you knew how we cared for you beyond all the differences of conduct; if only you could have realized that life is not a thing to fear, that it is a little trivial thing, or again, just a thing like food, an element like air, to be eaten, or breathed or enjoyed. But you thought it a mysterious gift, a terrible responsibility, a high and serious obligation, with a claim on your soul. You thought it a thing you could sin against. You confounded life with God.

This little street is so quiet tonight, so quiet and small. It shuts me in. It shuts me comfortably in, but beyond it there is a great distance—a great land—a great sea—a high and terrible sky.